THE
SHADOWS
CALL

By
MATT HILTON

THE SHADOWS CALL

First published by Sempre Vigile Press 2014
Copyright © 2014 Matt Hilton

1

Cover image © 2014 Matt Hilton
Cover design © 2014 Matt Hilton/Nicola Birrell-
Smith
Back cover image © 2014 Matt Hilton
/David Foster

This book is dedicated to Mike Kirkpatrick.
"Seek and you shall find."

THE SHADOWS CALL

CONTENTS

"Everything that we see is a shadow
cast by that which we do not see."
- Martin Luther King, Jr.

"What is right is not always popular
and what is popular is not always right"
- Albert Einstein

THE SHADOWS CALL

Prologue

From the Cayton

I was never a man who believed in ghosts, even when I first stood face to face with one of them. I put the weird sighting down to fatigue, hallucination, possibly a side effect of the medication I was taking. To me, ghosts were the product of over-active imaginations, wishful thinking, and Hollywood scriptwriters. I mean, to believe in ghosts you had to believe in an afterlife, right? Well, I didn't. Dead meant dead. The end.

Back then I viewed the subject with a closed mind and lack of understanding. I thought ghosts were supposed to be the restless spirits of dead people. Well, apparently that's only part of the story. I've come to learn that "ghost" is a catchall term for a number of supernatural and paranormal phenomena. It seems I'd always grasped at the wrong end of the stick.

There's nothing wrong with having a hefty dose of scepticism. Even after what I've come to experience, I also know that most of what is presented as proof of ghosts is nonsense, misidentification and, yes, wishful thinking. Surf the internet and you'll find a plethora of alleged ghost sightings. Most of them are outright hoaxes or pranks; the large remainder of them misidentified natural phenomena. Very few of those videos and photographs purporting to contain the image of a ghost really do. But then there is the minority that contain something otherworldly, that defies scientific explanation, and that I now know are the real deal.

Real, yes.

But I don't say these particular ghosts are the spirits of deceased people.

No. What I came to believe in is something else entirely.

Ever heard of the shadow people?

Yes? Then I still doubt you have a clue as to what they really are.

If you have an open mind, I'll show you.

1

The House

'It isn't exactly fit for purpose, Jack.' My work colleague, Sarah King, hadn't even got out of the car yet and was already being dismissive of the house.

'It's a bit big,' I had to agree, 'but I'd still like to take a look around.'

'Your choice,' Sarah said, wiping condensation off the window for a better view of the tall Victorian dwelling. 'You're the one who'll be living there. If you ask me, though, it's a bit of a dump.'

I shrugged, turning off the engine. 'That's probably why it's in my price range.'

In the last decade there had been some gentrification of Carlisle city centre, and rental prices had gone up to reflect the kind of clientele moving into the centrally located dwellings. The less than salubrious tenants had been pushed out to the fringes, and where this street had once been a desired location it was now turning into bedsit land for those on a budget, or on benefits. To be fair, I'd have found a nicer home nearer to the bars and cafes, but with it the noise when the nightclubs spilled out. I preferred a quiet life. Sarah didn't.

'Have you checked that you get the full building?'

'I get sole tenancy. All four floors.'

'I still think it's a bit much for one man.'

'I need the extra space for when my kids come over, or if any friends stay the night.'

She didn't immediately answer, and for a second I feared I'd overstepped the mark. I wasn't suggesting that she could stay over...not *exactly*. Except she hadn't caught the hint, or if she had she chose to ignore it, because she screwed up her nose and said, 'You'd really let your children stay here?'

'We don't know what it's like inside,' I said, eyeing the grubby exterior walls and flaking window frames, 'maybe it won't be too bad.'

'Fiver says your wrong.' Sarah stuck out her hand.

'Tenner,' I said. 'Let's make a bet worthwhile.'

'A tenner it is,' she agreed, and I clutched her hand and gave it a shake. I was a tad slow in releasing it and our eyes met briefly. Hers were the colour of toffee. Sarah's mouth slowly turned up at one corner. 'Remember: I don't take cheques, you loser.'

We got out of my car. It was a three-year-old Volvo V70 estate. Not exactly a stylish car, being on the conservative side of bland, but it suited me the way I thought the house would. It was spacious. Some of my belongings were already in boxes in the back, but there was room for another three passengers and more. I enjoyed my personal space:

one of the problems that had finished my nine years marriage to Catriona.

We stood together on the pavement, craning up at the three visible floors and peaked roof of the house. It stood on the corner of a junction, the end house in a terrace. Next door the building had been converted to office space, a well-known insurance brokerage firm having a shop front on the ground floor. The stonework was black with exhaust fumes, the sash window frames peeling paint, the front door scuffed. But the house still stood strong and sturdy, and had done for more than a hundred and fifty years.

'Welcome to the Bates Motel,' Sarah said.

'Give it a chance. Things always look worse when it's raining.'

It wasn't fully raining, just a dull drizzle that was a regular feature of northern England. Grey clouds crowned the roof of the house, setting everything in shadow. The windows were blind, slate grey with no colour to reflect.

'Is that your landlord?' Sarah's voice was a stage whisper. But her elbow to my ribs and grandiose leer towards the unkempt man was none too subtle.

I watched the man struggle out of a Nissan Micra parked further up the street. He'd parked in a disabled bay, one of the only free spots at roadside. The car was far too small for him. He held an old-fashioned clipboard over his head as he locked the car, then turned to us. If he was trying to keep his hair dry it was a waste of effort. He barely had a few tufts over each ear. The top of his head was completely bald, mottled brown in places. He wore thick-framed spectacles that were too dark for his pale complexion and bushy white moustache. Over grey trousers, cream shirt, and navy blue tie, he wore a rumpled raincoat *à la* Columbo from that old TV show. He'd too much girth for the coat and it strained at his shoulders as he held up the clipboard. He rushed towards us as if the rain was acid. Then again, in this grim part of town, the atmosphere was probably polluted. I unconsciously batted raindrops off my forehead, wiped drips from my nose.

'Mr Newman?' The man offered a smile as he extended his free hand. He did so without halting his forward momentum. I took his hand in a short greeting, and was hauled along with him as he steered me for the front steps. 'Should we get out of this bloody rain?'

We were up the short path and under the pillared porch before I could confirm my identity. 'John Newman. But everyone calls me Jack. This is my friend Sarah. You don't mind if she takes a look around with me?'

Peter Muir, my prospective landlord barely glanced at Sarah. Sarah's granddad was Jamaican. Her skin tone was on the darker side of cream, and she had a natural kink to her hair that she loathed. I thought she was very pretty, but Muir was unimpressed. 'Always pays to hear a woman's opinion on these kind of things,' he said, sounding as if he meant the absolute opposite.

'Charming,' Sarah said under her breath.

Muir unlocked the front door. It was an old door, probably pre-war. It was maroon now, but had been painted dozens of times over the years, and I could see a veritable rainbow where the door was chipped around the latches and kickboard. It still had an ancient cast iron knocker and letterbox. Two small arched windows at the top were designed to let in light, but they were opaque with grime. When he opened the door and we stepped into a short vestibule it was no less gloomy than I expected.

Sarah grunted under her breath, but a glance showed a gleam burning in her gaze. She was confident that she was going to be a full ten pounds richer by the time we left.

Kicking to one side a drift of junk mail, Muir reached for a light switch. It was almost as if he was crossing his fingers as he flicked the switch. A light blazed, chasing back the gloom. The cheerful glow could do little for the smell of mould and damp paper. Muir appeared pleasantly surprised that we had power.

'How long ago did your cleaner die?' Sarah was shameless.

Muir looked at her fully for the first time. From the rapid blinking behind his spectacles he didn't know how to take her brand of humour. He chose to ignore it. He beckoned us further inside and closed the door. 'Right,' he said, and his voice was more Geordie than it had sounded on the phone when first we spoke. 'I'll give you the grand tour, shall I?'

'Please,' I said, giving him the lead.

Sarah grasped my elbow. 'Remember to wipe your feet, Jack…on the way out.'

If Muir heard her, he didn't let on. I just shook my head. She teased me, poking out the tip of her tongue. It took an effort to look away. When I did, Muir was already disappearing into a room to my right. He turned on lights as he went.

The first room was what was once called a "parlour", except that was a bit pretentious now. Back in the nineteenth century when the house was built, it was seen as a status symbol to have a parlour – literally an audience or entertainment chamber – but they had declined in usage through the latter decades of the twentieth century. In keeping with this decline, the parlour had become an office space, sometime in the late 1980s, judging by the décor. The carpets had been lifted, displaying bare floorboards, and a stone hearth extending out a metre from the fireplace. A gas fire had replaced the original coal fire, but it would need servicing before

I ever struck a match to it. Some Formica tables were pushed up against one wall, as well as a small stack of generic plastic office chairs. They all carried a layer of dust. An ancient Apple Macintosh Classic computer was deposited in one corner, and a printer that looked as if it had been salvaged from Noah's Ark. They were museum pieces, or junk, dependent on your outlook. Dusty venetian blinds covered the windows.

'As you can see, it's a good sized room…' Muir was giving the full spiel, but I ignored his patter.

The place was a dump, but I could see the potential, and I was currently arguing the pros and cons. Muir led us to the living room. It was similar in size and dimensions as the parlour. Here the fire had been more recently replaced though: this gas burner didn't look as much of a death trap as the first, but you never could tell. I made semi-pleasantries with Muir as he led us to the kitchen.

Sarah remained quiet as she scuffed along behind us. Her silence said it all.

The kitchen was small and the décor in keeping with everything else I'd seen. Dour. But it would do.

'This isn't the original kitchen,' Muir announced. He motioned down. 'Back in the old days all the cooking was done downstairs. You get to use the cellar if you want, but the previous tenants boarded it up. Won't take much work to open it up again.'

A rear door opened onto a cobbled yard. Tall brick walls hemmed it in. A gate allowed access to a lane where Muir had mentioned there was a garage where I could keep my car. Someone had planted shrubs in terracotta pots, but several seasons had since passed since they'd had any care and the plants were now shrivelled wispy stalks.

Muir indicated the yard. 'It might not look that inviting during the winter, but it's a lovely sun trap in the summer.'

What he didn't mention was that the north-facing house rarely got any sun at the front. Such features didn't matter to me though. I just nodded eagerly. 'Can you show me the bedrooms?'

'Aye,' Muir said. Then he shrugged. 'Unless you want to have a look around yourself?'

I agreed to the offer.

'Bathroom is on the first landing before you reach the next floor,' Muir said, 'all the other rooms are bedrooms, or spare rooms, whatever you choose to use them for.'

He was couching his phrases in a way that said the house was already mine. To be fair, I was thinking the same thing.

'Want to take a look around with me?'

Sarah gave me a dour look. 'I've seen all I need to.' She slipped on a fake smile for Muir. 'Lovely old place, isn't it?'

'I think it has...' Muir offered an equally fake grin. 'What is it they say: it has character?'

'So has Mickey Mouse,' Sarah whispered for my ears alone. 'Just like the character who's supposed to maintain the dump.'

'I won't be long,' I told her. 'I just want to take a quick look around.'

'Uh-oh,' she frowned. 'You've already made up your bloody mind.'

'I like the place,' I said.

'You just don't want to honour our bet. Whether you take the house or not, I still win. You owe me a tenner, Jacko.'

I gave her a noncommittal wink, turned my back on her and headed for the stairs. Years earlier during a rugby match I tore my ACL – my anterior cruciate ligament – in my right knee. Stupidly I hadn't had it looked at by a surgeon, so it still troubled me now. Naproxen kept the pain at bay, but gave my stomach jip, to a point I had to take a second medicine called Lansoprazole to stave off the sharp pains in my gut. There were also some other pills I'd to take, the names of which were unpronounceable, but I'd given up on them when they proved ineffective. I went up the stairs feeling the strain in my weakened knee, thinking that the exercise could only do me good over time.

I found the bathroom on the first landing as Muir said. It wasn't an original feature from the

Victorian era when the building was erected. When we'd looked out on the backyard, I was aware without taking much notice of an overhang and I could now see that it was where a suspended bathroom had been tacked on the back of the house. It was a narrow structure, with room for a bath and separate washbasin pedestal. At the far end a second door opened into a small cubicle where I discovered a toilet. I made a mental note to purchase bleach to clean the stained bowl, and a new seat to replace the faded wooden one that looked hand carved by a less than skillful carpenter.

Moving from the bathroom I noticed for the first time a stained glass window above the door. It was unlike those seen in churches, more like a mosaic of opaque red glass, but was a nice original feature all the same. Roseate light made the next landing cheerier than downstairs. When Muir had described the bathroom's location he'd only been partly correct. It was actually situated a few feet lower than the first upper floor on a half-landing, and I had to negotiate a few more steps before I reached the landing proper. Here I found two more rooms – bedrooms or living rooms I couldn't decide – and another smaller room at the front right corner that I earmarked for a storage closet. A door to the right of it opened to a narrow stairwell that led up to the final floor. As I went up I could feel my shoulders touch the walls on both sides. Each step creaked. At the top I found a small vestibule and was greeted by three blind doors. If I'd closed the stairwell door behind me, closed my eyes and done a pirouette, I would have had no sense of direction and no idea which route led back down. I left the stairwell door open.

The door to my immediate left opened into what could only be described as a cubbyhole. Not large enough for anything but a small storage space. I was about to turn away when I noticed that what I was looking at was actually an archaic lift mechanism, one of those old-fashioned dumbwaiters. I could imagine servants down in the basement scullery loading food into the dumbwaiter, then hauling the food up to the top floor by pulling on the ancient cords hanging alongside the lift. I leaned in for a closer look. I caught a draft on my face, gritty, tickly, as if I'd poked my head through a cobweb. I reared back, wiping at imagined creepy crawlies skittering across my flesh. I shut the door. Checked the facing door. It let into a dormer-style bedroom. It was bare of furniture and the wallpaper had been stripped back to the plaster. Somebody had scrawled graffiti on the walls.

I backed out of the room and opened the door to the final room. My bedroom, I'd already decided. It was more spacious than the other uppermost rooms. Like the other bedroom it had been situated beneath the peaked roof, and had two old sash-style bay windows in recesses that overlooked the front street. The ceilings angled down to meet the tops of each window. In the wall to the side of the leftmost window was a tiny door that let into a crawl space under the slope of the roof. To my immediate right was another set of doors, which, when opened allowed entrance to a walk-in wardrobe built into the very walls of the house. The house was laid out in a strange fashion, but I enjoyed its quirky nature. As Muir noted earlier, it had character.

My mind made up I turned.

A shadow darkened the small hallway. Undeniably it was a male figure.

I halted mid-stride.

The floorboards creaked underfoot, as I recalled the ones on the stairs did. Yet I hadn't heard Muir climbing the stairs. He was bigger built than I, heavier, I should have heard the groaning of the stairs and the scuff of his raincoat on the walls. I opened my mouth to speak, took a step and in correspondence, so did the shadow. It zipped left and out of my line of sight. Frowning, I poked my head out of the door, looking immediately left to the narrow stairwell. There was nobody there, no sound of anyone going down the stairs. Surprised for the second time in as many seconds, I went to the head of the stairs and peered down.

Nobody. No sound. Nothing.

It was impossible for anyone to descend the stairs in such a short time, not without raising a racket. I quickly turned and checked the other rooms. Nobody was in any of them.

A cold prickle shivered up my body, and my guts clenched. There was something decidedly unnatural about that shadow.

Back in the vestibule I checked around myself. I could see my own shadow; it was in triplicate, cast on two different doors and up a short strip of wall adjacent to the stairwell. The odd configuration of the bedrooms, sources of dim light leaking in from each angle, all conspired to form shadows where you wouldn't expect them. That was it, I told myself. Mystery solved. Natural after all.

Except it wasn't.

I conveniently disregarded the fact that my shadows were pale, grey, insubstantial, whereas the one I'd just witnessed was deep black, darker than night, two dimensional and freestanding.

Now you're just adding to it, I warned. You're tired, in an unfamiliar place, and you know that your meds have had a few odd side effects.

It was nothing.

So why was I trembling?

I shook off the uncanny sensation and went downstairs to get the legal paperwork started.

Peter Muir was pleased. Sarah wasn't. Later we agreed to disagree and split the difference. I gave her five pounds, but it cost her a promise she'd help me to move in to my new home.

2

The Door

I moved into the house within a week.

Muir eagerly accepted my signing of a year's lease. Apparently the house was still registered as a commercial premises, but could be sub-let for occupation, and paying the lease fees was a legal necessity, but he gave me a discount on the first three months' rental with the coda that I paid the council tax, utility bills, and made the place habitable at my own expense. It wasn't as if I'd have to renovate the house, just throw around some paint, maybe fork out for some new carpets, and a few hours work with a mop and bucket would do for most of the rooms. It was still a lot of money to sign over in one go, but I didn't mind paying up front: where else was I going to live for the low price I'd got it for? Muir delivered the keys into my hand by Thursday. My miserable boss at BathCo, Daniel Graham, wouldn't give me any time off work, so I'd to wait until Friday evening to move in. I had an electric kettle, coffee and milk and a sleeping bag with me, but that sufficed. Saturday morning I began hauling my belongings from a rented storage unit in the back of my Volvo. Sarah had promised to help, but was notorious for finding it hard to get up in the morning, especially after a night out with our work colleagues. I wasn't disappointed; I'd kind of expected it. But I was sure she'd turn up later.

It suited me to be honest, because I wasn't at my best. I hadn't got much sleep, and it had nothing to do with camping out in the parlour, surrounded by cobwebs and the stink of must. Dreams had disturbed my rest; horrible nightmares that forced me awake, sweating rivers, my guts clenching in dread but with little memory of what had terrified me so much. All I could recall was clutching hands, a bloody face, and a red dress. I was so fatigued that I'd fall back asleep almost instantly, only to be wakened again by the recurring nightmare. I announced the dawn as I sat up with a shriek. The scream still echoed around the hollow room as I'd struggled out of my drenched sleeping bag, tremors stealing about the walls like furtive devils.

It took three coffees and a quick wash in the kitchen sink to get me going, and I hoped that by the time Sarah did show up my bloodshot eyes would've cleared a bit.

Because it was Saturday morning, there was no school run. The road was quiet and I was able to park outside the house. I'd placed a handwritten note in the windscreen to stave off any ticket-happy traffic wardens, explaining I was moving in and hadn't yet arranged for a resident's parking permit. I propped open the front door and carried boxes inside, depositing them in the defunct parlour room. I could distribute them to their proper locations later, once I'd cleaned out the junk and dust.

I didn't have many belongings. When I split from Catriona, I'd basically cleaned out my man cave, grabbed my clothing and toiletries and left the rest to her. She was still in our marital home in one of the upscale housing estates to the north of town with our children, Jake and Gemma, and they needed the furniture more than I did. I'd ordered a new bed and a settee and easy chair, to be delivered in the next few days, and had made a mental note to go shopping for kitchen appliances. First trip in the Volvo I'd brought my TV and DVD player, clothing, and other odds and ends. Another couple of trips to the storage unit would probably do it.

My knee was playing up. I'd a deep-seated pain in the muscles above the patella. All the toing and froing, bending and twisting was playing havoc on the fragile make up of the joint. I popped some Naproxen, and tried to dry swallow them. They were the size of jellybeans, dry as chalk, and didn't go down easily. The Lansoprazole capsules I also took inhibited the production of stomach acid, to protect me from being eaten alive from the inside out, because the first meds had the habit of stripping my stomach lining. Wonderful stuff.

In the parlour I found a clear spot between some stacked boxes and sat on the floorboards, my back to the wall. I'd moved the abandoned office clutter into the back yard, except for the computer monitor. I'd heard some people collected old monitors and stuff and wondered if it would fetch a few quid on EBay or some other on-line market place. I doubted the Classic worked, but someone might buy it to convert to a fish tank or something: they do that these days, apparently.

Rubbing my knee, I took a look around my new home. Sarah had been correct in her summation, but only at face value. The place was a dump, and would take hard work to bring it up to a liveable standard, at least one where I could have my son and daughter over, but on deeper scrutiny I spotted original features everywhere. Some people would die for those deep skirting boards, the picture rail, and the tiled fireplace partly concealed behind the ugly gas fire. The window frames were original, as were most of the windows. The glass was very old, warped in places, flawed, but that added to the charm. One window had been replaced at some time in the near past. The clear glass was at odds with its slightly smoky neighbours. Even the door that led into the reception vestibule was aged. It wasn't like the cheap crap you could buy these days from DIY superstores; this door was heavy, with four recessed panels and a circular brass handle. It had a snib, so that once the door was closed you could lock it in place. Maybe back in the day the sort of entertainment that happened in this room demanded a degree of privacy. Those enlightened Victorians were up to all sorts of kinky stuff, I'd heard.

I was studying the door from my seated position when it slammed shut. I watched its abrupt swing, heard the gunshot crack, but still jumped in fright, swearing out loud.

Remembering I'd left the front door propped open for easy access, logic told me that a sudden breeze had caused a shift in the atmosphere within the house, and the door had slammed as a result. Made sense to me. I pushed up, using the wall to steady myself, and limped across the room. Best I closed the front door while I took a break. While I was in the parlour with the door closed anyone could walk in uninvited and have a stroll around the house. They'd be disappointed by what they found, but it was still mine. Private.

I turned the handle and pulled.

The door didn't move.

'What the…?'

I twisted the knob again, pulled harder. The door resisted me.

I checked the snib mechanism but it was in the open position. I could see where the latch was seated in the equally old brass retainer, and when I twisted the handle watched it pop in and out. Nothing was inhibiting the lock, or the hinges that were visible.

I twisted the knob and yanked at the door. It didn't budge.

'Bastard!'

OK. Calm down, I told myself. The house is old and has been sealed for a long time. You can smell the damp; the door's probably swollen and has jammed in the frame when it slammed shut. All it would take was a little more energy and the door would pop open.

I set my feet, got one hand on the knob and the other on the frame. I pulled.

The door opened.

An inch.

Then it was yanked out of my grasp and slammed shut with equal ferocity.

'Jesus, that's some draught.'

It was my fault for leaving the bloody outer door open.

I yanked again.

Nothing.

I tried to jostle the door out of the frame. My knee twinged.

I swore again, which did nothing to move the door or soothe my anger.

'This is ridiculous,' I said. But then so was talking to an inanimate object. I put my back into it this time, but the door remained resolutely jammed. I could feel the knob working loose and let go. All I needed was to pull the bloody knob off and I would be well and truly trapped. I swore again, backed away, giving the door sour glances as I thought the problem through.

The hinges were set on my side of the frame, the door opened into the room. It was jammed in the frame, and the requisite pressure to haul it open would probably be more than the knob could handle, and it would pull off in my hand. But from the other side, it would take little effort to push open the door.

Dipping my hand in my pocket I pulled out my mobile phone.

Phone Sarah, I thought. She was due to arrive any way. Tell her to come in and give the door a nudge from the other side.

Yeah, right! That would give Sarah a good old laugh. I wouldn't hear the last of it. She'd tell everyone at work how she had to rescue my sorry arse. I shoved away my phone.

While the side windows overlooked the alley that led round to the backyard and parking garage, the front windows looked out onto the street. Maybe there was somebody out there who I could ask to come inside and give the door a push. I strode to the front windows, had to clamber over a stack of boxes and peered out. Traffic was building up, but I couldn't see one pedestrian. Bloody hell, didn't anyone walk anywhere these days? Then again someone could be just out of my line of sight. I reached for the hasp, threw it open and then applied pressure to the rope that would raise the window. The rope was rotten. It snapped off, frayed and brittle.

'Bloody hell,' I groaned, looking at the length of rope in my hand. I wadded it up and stuffed it on the windowsill. More traffic went by but nobody on foot.

Backing from the window I pulled out my mobile. There was nothing for it. Sarah could laugh all she wanted.

No. I was determined I'd try one last time.

I put away my phone and approached the door with as determined a stride as my gimpy knee would allow.

'OK, you stubborn git. You're going to open this time or I'll kick you off your bloody hinges!'

Grasping the handle and pushing my left shoulder to the frame, I took in a deep breath. I twisted the knob and yanked.

The door swung inward effortlessly.

Too effortlessly. I'd put so much in to the act that I staggered backwards, and went down on my backside on the floorboards. Dust wafted up around me.

I could hear laughter.

Faint mocking laughter.

I struggled up, gave the door a quick look and saw it standing open as it had earlier. I jammed my foot against it, holding it wide as I bent and peeked out into the vestibule.

Nobody was there.

The laughter must have filtered in from outside, maybe from the neighbouring insurance brokers' office. More likely it was in my head. I pictured Sarah having a great laugh at my expense, and was pleased she hadn't arrived on time to witness my prat fall.

Stepping into the hall, I closed the door behind me. I opened it again. No problem whatsoever. I checked the edge of the door, then the frame, looking for marks where the wood had swollen and stuck in the frame. There was nothing evident. I closed the door. Pulled it to me, thinking to replicate the slam. When I turned the handle again the door swung open with no hindrance. If anything, when shut, the door didn't even fit snug in the frame; I could see light around the edges and the latch jiggled freely.

I shook my head.

If I didn't know otherwise I'd say that someone had been standing at this side of the door holding it shut.

That was a crazy notion, and I immediately discarded the idea. Still, I closed the front door, and made a quick search of the house for trespassers. I found neither hide nor hair of anyone, as I suspected I wouldn't. On my travels I found a wedge of wood, and I returned to the parlour intending to prop open the door so I didn't suffer a repeat performance. I opened the door wide and pushed the wedge under, then kicked it in tight. I stood wiping dust off my palms, inspecting my handiwork.

Giving a satisfied nod, I turned.

It was there again.

The shadow.

Man shaped.

Full black.

It stood no more than two yards from me, and malevolence radiated from it in waves. Full of hatred and rage, it was seeking a target.

It lunged, fingers coming for my throat.

I cried out, stumbling backwards, and the shadow's hands became claws before my face.

Then it was gone.

Quicker than the sob of relief that rose from my chest it had disappeared, but the atmosphere was redolent with its uncanny passing. In my head I heard the mocking laughter once more. But was it in my head?

3

The Phone

'You saw a ghost?'

Sarah's eyes twinkled, but I was pleased to note it wasn't with humour, more excitement at the prospect I was sharing my home with a supernatural entity. I'd forgotten she was into all that woo-woo stuff, watching all those paranormal TV programmes on the alternative TV channels, and even attending a few sessions at a local spiritualist church whenever another hokey medium was in town. One lunchtime at work, she'd tried telling me all about those sessions, how the medium had known things they possibly couldn't have known, until she got the message that I thought the entire subject was bollocks. Having mentioned my sighting of this shadow figure, she was over the moon: it gave validity to her beliefs and made me look the one with egg on my chin.

'I didn't say I saw a ghost,' I corrected her. 'I said I saw a shadow.'

She leaned towards me, her face serious. 'And you're happy to stay at the house after that?'

'Yeah. I'm not scared. Any way, I've paid a year's lease and I forfeit it if I move out before the end of the term.'

'Nutter,' she said.

We were sitting outside a Starbucks in the centre of town. Sarah was smoking. I was trying hard not to. It was cold, breezy. We were seated at a metal table on uncomfortable chairs: kind of *de rigueur* treatment of smokers these days, being banished from the comfy loungers and low tables inside. But it suited me fine. There were few other customers sitting out in the wind and the threat of rain. Beads of moisture still stood on the table between our coffee cups, evidence of an earlier shower, and there was more to come. It meant that our loony conversation wouldn't be overheard.

Sarah sparked up her lighter and touched it to her second cigarette since sitting down. She exhaled blue smoke. 'You said it was shaped like a person?'

'So what? It doesn't make it a ghost. It was probably *my* shadow.' I hadn't told her about the similar experience I'd had on my first visit to the house, or that this latest shadow had gone for my throat, and had no intention of mentioning it either. 'There are windows on two sides, so the light comes in at odd angles. Maybe there was a brief break in the clouds and my shadow was cast from a different angle. Then the clouds closed in and that explains why it disappeared again.'

'Maybe.' Sarah wasn't convinced. She eyed me expectantly. 'Is that why you did a runner from the house: because you saw your own shadow?'

'I didn't do a runner. I finished what I was doing. Needed a coffee. Thought you might appreciate one too.'

'I do. My head's still banging after last night.'

I held open my palms. 'Never again, eh?'

'Never again,' she agreed.

'Until next weekend,' we both quipped in unison. Then we laughed without any real vigour. It was a clichéd joke between drinkers, done to death.

'You should come with me next time,' Sarah said.

'I'd cramp your style,' I said.

'You could watch my handbag while I go outside for a ciggie,' she said.

'That's about my lot. You know I don't drink any more.'

'Yeah.' Sarah hung her head, sorry for suggesting a night on the town. But I was secretly thrilled. It was the first time she'd mentioned personally socialising with me; it gave me hope that the attraction I felt towards her might actually be reciprocated.

'I didn't think that you "management types" liked fraternizing with the plebs off the front line.' I grinned to make sure she knew I was teasing. 'Aren't we below you?'

'Don't be stupid, Jack.' She leaned forward jabbing her cigarette to emphasize her point. 'I'm store operations manager, but just because I earn a higher wage, it doesn't make me any better than you. Any way, you should aim higher. You used to be an English teacher, right?'

'I used to teach English as a second language,' I corrected. 'Not quite the same thing, is it?'

'You're just being finicky now. My point is you're an intelligent guy. You could do much better than sales if you applied yourself.'

I wondered if that was some kind of code; that she was offering me an opening to make a move on her. I overthought my response, and never got the opportunity to reply.

'You probably wouldn't enjoy yourself any way,' she said. 'It tends to be all us young ones from work. You'd feel out of place.'

Maybe she didn't mean to, but she'd just metaphorically dashed cold water on my rising ardour.

'Are you calling me *old*?' I mock scolded.

'*Older*. What are you? Forty-four, forty-five?'

'I'm only thirty-four,' I said, as if the disparity was massive.

'Oh, I thought…'

I knew what she thought. I'd been married for nine years, had two kids and an estranged wife behind me, and that was only one of my two long-term relationships she knew about.

'I was young when I first met Naomi,' I said. 'My first serious girlfriend and I was only sixteen. I met

Catriona when I was twenty-three, and got married a couple years later. We did that kind of stuff back in the old days.' I meant my last as a joke, but it sounded more like criticism.

'You speak and act like someone much older,' Sarah pointed out. 'Probably comes from teaching all those immigrants how to speak proper.'

'I'm mature for my age,' I said.

She mimed patting a hand over a yawn.

'So that makes me boring does it?'

She only looked at me steadily, and then without comment she looked off across the street, watching shoppers hurrying between stores. Around us, pigeons with deformed feet pecked for crumbs between the cracks in the pavement. I took a long gulp of coffee. It was bitter, going cold. Much like our conversation. I cleared my throat, brought Sarah's attention back.

'This shadow,' she said, 'tell me about it.'

'What's to tell? It was my shadow.'

She took a drag on her cigarette, watching me over its glowing tip. She pouted her bottom lip and blue curls wafted around her darker curls. She waited.

'It was shaped like a person,' I said.

'Like a man?'

'Well it would be, seeing as it was *my* shadow.'

She rocked her head, noncommittal. 'Debatable.'

'What, that it was my shadow or that I'm a man?'

She continued watching me over her cigarette. Now it was her eyes that were smoky. I caught myself looking too long and quickly averted my gaze.

'It was black,' I said, trying to get back on track.

'As opposed to what?'

'To grey. Most shadows are light grey when there isn't a bright source of light to cast them.'

'You said there was a break in the clouds.'

'It was only a theory.'

'How black?'

'What do you mean "how black"? Black's black, isn't it?'

She shook her head, used the cigarette as a pointer. 'Your jacket looks black at first glance, but it isn't really. It has a blue sheen to it. Nearer navy.'

She had a point. But what was the point? 'It was *black*-black,' I emphasised.

'Which,' she pointed out with a note of glee, 'proves that it wasn't an ordinary shadow. You said it yourself, the shadow should've been light grey.'

'Maybe I was mistaken. Maybe it was just dark grey or something. I only saw it for a second at most. Then it was gone.' I clicked my fingers, shoving my argument home. 'There was traffic passing on the street. Maybe the sunlight reflected off a truck or something and cast a pedestrian's shadow inside the room. The truck sped on, and the shadow was gone. It's simple when you think about it.'

It was a fair explanation. But I knew I was lying to myself, let alone Sarah. There had been no pedestrians outside. The shadow was in my room, free standing, and full black. Not part of an insignificant shadow cast from many yards away by the momentary play of reflection, but a solid-looking figure I could have reached out and touched. In that briefest glimpse before it lunged at me I knew it was staring at me, planning on tearing off my face.

I shuddered.

Sarah caught my unease. But she was on a roll now.

'Describe it to me.'

'I just did.'

'No, I mean in detail. Was it like a mist, were the edges blurry or defined?'

'How would I know? It was *just* my shadow, Sarah. It was nothing.'

'For being nothing it's sure got you spooked.'

'I don't believe in ghosts or spirits or anything else like that. It's all bullshit. People die, they're gone.' My last word came out hard, and louder than I expected. The nearest customer sat twenty feet away near the entrance to the coffee shop, but the man looked up from his damp newspaper to give me a sharp glance. He was annoyed at the intrusion into his day. I studiously ignored him, as if our gazes hadn't crossed. I folded my hands around my lukewarm cup. 'Sorry, Sarah, I didn't mean to sound so sharp.'

She shrugged. 'I'm not easily frightened.'

'Neither am I. It was nothing. Probably my body telling me I needed caffeine.'

'*Hallelujah* to that,' she said picking up her latte and downing half the contents.

'Want another?' I offered. 'Extra espresso?'

'I could be tempted.' She gulped the remainder and then pushed her cup towards me. I stood, scattering the pigeons. They didn't fly far before alighting and continuing their search for a meagre meal.

I went inside and joined the queue, wondering when this old working class town had become the domain of university students and immigrants. I didn't recognise a single face, or even pick out a word spoken in English. Two locals did join the queue behind me, and the only reason I knew that was because the bloke was wearing the blue, white and red Carlisle United home shirt – though it was out of date by about a decade. His girlfriend was overweight, wore too much make up, and her black leggings stretched so tightly I could see the colour of her underwear through them. They looked anachronistic, a throw back to those earlier days, when compared to the clean-cut students with their designer clothing and coiffed hairstyles. They swore unashamedly at each other like rejects from the Jeremy Kyle Show and it was horrible to listen too – hell, when I was a ESL teacher, I met foreigners with a better grasp of English than those two. Maybe the influx of more cultured people to the city weren't a bad thing after all. I made my order to the bright young thing at the counter, paid then joined the second queue where the baristas doled out the finished product. I was waiting for a fresh Americano and skinny latte both with an extra shot when my mobile phone bleeped in my pocket.

Taking out the phone I saw the "message" icon was starred. I pressed the screen, bringing up the message.

I WANT YOU

I'm not sure why, but my gaze immediately zoned in on Sarah sitting outside at the table. She was just visible through the window, at the far right, and she was looking back at me. Discretely she fed something into her handbag. Her phone? Then she nodded once to herself and looked down, searching for a fresh cigarette.

A thrill went through me. But I couldn't be sure that my playful workmate had just sent me the text. I checked, but there was no number registered from the sender. I had Sarah's saved in my contact list. But, hell, a lot of people carried more than one phone. Maybe she had sent the message from a different phone knowing full well I couldn't be sure whom it was from.

'You little tease,' I said under my breath, experiencing a shiver of titillation.

Yet at the same time I felt a strange qualm of unease worm through my bowels and it placed a dampener on the moment.

Sarah was forever checking her phone. Maybe she'd taken my trip inside the shop as a good opportunity to check in with the rest of the world, and she hadn't sent the text at all. It was wishful thinking that the text had come from her.

When I returned to her, I made no mention of the text message.

For that matter, neither did she.

By the time we got up to return to the house, I'd pushed it to the back of my mind. But the memory of the shadow figure still troubled me.

4

Sarah's Phone

Sarah appeared in the doorway of my kitchen, wearing a frown and a layer of dust on her forehead. She'd been brushing the floor in the sitting room next to the parlour while I tried to scrub some of the rust stains out of the kitchen sink. I was coated in soapsuds up to the elbows.

'Have you seen my iPhone?' she asked.

'Eh?' I replied in my most eloquent way.

'My iPhone? I was going to put some music on while we worked.'

'The TV's wired up now,' I said. 'You'll get one of the radio channels on it. Put it on if you want.'

She nodded at my wisdom, but remained troubled. 'Still doesn't explain where my phone is. I'm sure it was in my handbag.'

'You've checked?'

She showed me her palms, went "D'uh!". 'I hadn't thought of that, Jack. Of course I checked, how else would I know my phone was missing?'

'I meant taken a second look. If you're like me I sometimes can't see what I'm looking for and it's right under my nose.'

'That's a man thing,' Sarah said. 'I've checked. Double-checked and it's not there.'

I found a dry cloth and rubbed the suds from my hands. My question was loaded. 'When did you last use it?'

'When we were at Starbucks earlier.'

I watched her expectantly, waiting for her to elucidate.

'I updated my Facebook status. Told the world I was "having coffee with the ugliest man on earth".' She gave me a quirky shrug of one shoulder. I tried not to look offended.

'And you remember putting it back in your bag?' I didn't need to ask, I'd watched her put away her phone.

'Yes, Mother, I put it away safely. Now it isn't there.'

For some reason I felt guilty. Earlier I'd seen her handbag sitting on the floor in the parlour where she'd set it down out of harm's way. I'd seen her iPhone sitting in the bag, on top of the rest of the stuff women seem to cart around with them everywhere. I'd briefly considered taking a sneaky glance through her sent messages to check if she had been behind the teasing text earlier. Simply the thought of invading her personal space had been enough to make me flush and I'd hurried into the kitchen and got jiggy with the Mr Muscle. I didn't confirm that I'd seen her phone, for fear my guilty streak might show and be misconstrued.

'I'll ring it,' I offered and went to fetch my mobile from my jacket pocket. 'You're still using the same phone, right?'

Again she didn't pick up on my loaded question. I took her silence as confirmation that she was using the original number I'd saved in my contact list.

I found her number and hit the call button.

From somewhere in the house jangled the strains of her ringtone: It was the Darth Vader theme from Star Wars.

'Do you use that ringtone for every call, or just those from me?' I asked.

Sarah smiled mischievously, but she chose to ignore my question, heading out into the hall, listening hard. 'Where's it coming from?'

I joined her in the vestibule, staring towards the back door into the yard. Neither of us had been outside today. I pointed up the stairs. 'Have you been to the bathroom since we got here?'

'Yeah, I needed to go after all that coffee.'

I nodded. 'That's where your phone is.'

'How'd it get up there?'

'You must have taken your bag with you. Maybe you updated your Facebook status while you were on the loo.'

From the look on her face, she was positive she hadn't. But the act of checking phones had grown to be second nature these days, almost a ritual performed by rote, often unconsciously.

'I left it in my bag,' she said. But a flicker of uncertainty darted across her face. 'I'm positive I did.'

'Who else would have taken it?' I said, and had to try hard to keep my face deadpan. 'Mr Nobody?'

The ringtone still sounded. It was tinny from behind the closed bathroom door. I left my phone on call while we walked up the short flight of stairs to the split-level landing. The theme tune was ideal for our slow trudge upwards. I wished I hadn't posed the question. Giving the shadow man a name, even a jokey one, was almost akin to inviting him in. 'You must've taken it with you. You just don't remember that's all. I do stuff like that all the time. Can't find a bloody thing if I don't make a mental note of where I left it last.'

I was blathering, and Sarah knew it. I'd seeded her with the idea that something weird was going on in my new home, and I wasn't helping to dispel the notion.

We reached the landing. Above us the stained glass window glowed in the late afternoon sun. While we'd been cleaning, the earlier rain clouds had apparently pushed further inland, heralding in a calm and pleasant evening. We stood there for a second or two, absorbing the unexpected warmth of the winter sun. It didn't feel as uncomfortable listening to the ominous music when the sun kissed our upturned faces.

Seconds passed before it hit us why we were hanging there like a couple of plums. The door was shut, and looked insurmountable.

'You go in first,' Sarah whispered.

'It's only the bathroom,' I said. But I didn't step forward. Part of me feared the door would resist my entry; the way the other door had earlier prevented me leaving the parlour. I ended my call and the Darth Vader theme tune cut off mid-chime. Suddenly the silence was all consuming.

'Go in then,' Sarah commanded, breaking the wall of quietude.

I mentally hitched up my trousers. Took a step forward and pressed open the door. Without entering the bathroom I could immediately see Sarah's iPhone sitting on the edge of the old cast iron tub. 'There you are,' I said.

'Fetch it for me.' Sarah's voice was hushed.

Being the big brave hero, I gave an unconcerned shrug and stepped into the bathroom. I reached for the phone.

It jumped off the lip and clattered into the tub.

Sarah emitted a short yelp. Maybe I did too, but have purposefully elected to wipe it from my memory. The way I hoped Sarah had when she'd fetched her phone to the loo with her. Though why she'd have placed it precariously on the edge of the tub I couldn't work out.

I leaned over the tub. Thankfully there was no water in it. I picked up the phone and presented it to Sarah who was now in the doorway. The iPhone was ice cold, but undamaged. 'It looks OK,' I announced.

'What made it jump like that?' Sarah still hadn't taken possession of her phone; too busy glancing around searching for the otherworldly.

I experimented. Found that the floorboard underfoot was loose. I pressed it up and down. 'When I stepped on the loose floorboard, it made the bath vibrate and the phone slipped in.'

'It didn't slip…it jumped.'

'I'm heavy footed. This damn knee of mine.'

Sarah wasn't buying my explanation. If I was honest, neither was I: the loose board didn't as much as cause the bath to shake, let alone launch an object from its lip several inches through space.

Sarah took the phone from me, holding it between both palms. 'It's freezing,' she said, and her eyes glittered with barely subdued excitement.

5

Antigonish

"Yesterday upon the stair
I met a man who wasn't there
He wasn't there again today
Oh, how I wish he'd go away."

I couldn't shake the words of that damn poem from my head. I wasn't even sure where I'd heard them, or how they'd become ingrained in my psyche. But they spun around and around, repeating over and over, and finally lulled me into a fitful sleep.

Twice I awoke in the night, blinking furiously around the room, expecting to see a man who wasn't there peering back at me from the darkness. But he wasn't there.

Finally, about three a.m. on the Sunday morning, I kicked free from my sleeping bag, and immediately felt the slick of night sweat cooling on my body. I shrugged into a T-shirt and jogging bottoms. I was right at the top of the house, in the room I'd earmarked for my master bedroom, despite the fact it was still a relatively empty space. My sleeping bag was where my soon-to-arrive bed would be situated and I'd also brought up a lamp, so I could read.

There was a dog-eared thriller novel I'd been making my way through unopened against the wall. I'd also plugged my mobile into a socket, recharging the battery. I switched on the lamp and picked up my phone. Piggy-backing a nearby BT Wi-Fi Open Zone, I could get the internet on it. Opening a browser I typed in "I MET A MAN WHO WASN'T THERE" and was offered various links to pages describing an old rhyme by William Hughes Mearns.

Following the link to a Wikipedia page, I discovered that I'd been repeating lines from a poem written in 1899 but first published in 1922 under the title "Antigonish". I'd only been repeating the first few lines of the rhyme, and those following that I read didn't help my unease. Especially when I glanced at the time display and saw the correlation.

"When I came home last night at three
The man was waiting there for me
But when I looked around the hall
I couldn't see him there at all."

I quickly swiped the webpage shut and put down my phone.

'This is frigging nuts,' I told myself out loud. 'Stop now. You're letting your imagination get away from you.'

I *was* allowing my imagination to run wild. I didn't believe in all of that hocus pocus, mumbo-jumbo bullshit. Sure there had been a few unusual occurrences in my new house, but that was to be expected. "New house" was a misnomer. It had stood on this ground for more than a century and a half, a long time before the roads were ever expected to carry the volume and weight of traffic they did these days. There would be an element of subsidence; there'd be vibration; settling of the building on its foundations. I also knew that the house had stood empty for a long period. Simply by opening the doors, allowing the ambient atmosphere to shift was enough to cause a chain reaction as floor boards, doorframes and support joists all shrunk and contracted, or indeed swelled and expanded, dependent on the ambient temperature. Such movement would have an unexpected effect on the structure, causing doors to seemingly jam in their frames one second, spring free the next. It could even explain why a phone sitting on a bathtub would appear to jump in the air. All it would take was for a large vehicle to pass on the street outside, the vibration to pass through the building, and cause the metal tub to rattle and throw off the phone.

Yeah, I decided. That was it.

It didn't however explain how Sarah's iPhone had made it all the way from her handbag, up one flight and into the bathroom. I sure as hell hadn't taken it there, so Sarah *must* have. Sometimes, as I've already suggested, you can perform tasks on almost remote control, trance-like. You have no recollection of having carried out the task, the way I believed that Sarah had. She'd visited the loo, taking her phone with her. Had perhaps placed it down on the edge of the bathtub while she washed her hands at the pedestal sink, then neglected to retrieve her phone when returning to her chores in the living room. I'd experienced similar events, many times at the wheel of my car. There were examples where I'd driven miles, negotiating roundabouts and busy junctions, only to later realise I was further along my journey than expected, with no clear memory of having got there. Maybe our brains have a capacity for blocking out the mundane. That had to be the explanation. It was logical. Sound. Made sense.

But that went no way towards explaining the shadow I'd witnessed. Not once but twice.

The man who wasn't there.

'Aw, for God's sake! Come on, Jack. Get a bloody grip, will you?'

I didn't believe in ghosts.

I've said it before, but I reiterated it to myself once more.

'You asked for proof, demanded it, but got none. Why would it be any different this time?'

I suddenly realised I was standing at one of the bedroom windows, peering down at the street outside. It was late, or very early depending on how you marked the progress of your day. A young couple wandered by, looking a little worse for wear from the way they staggered, arm in arm along the street. Their voices were loud as they cajoled each other on, but muted by distance and the almost tangible weight of the night. To them it would be late: an end to their Saturday evening on the town. To me, who usually rose quite early for work, it was already Sunday morning. I'd no need to be up at this ungodly hour. Normally I slept in to around mid-morning on a Sunday – my only real day of rest. But this Sunday was different. As part of the cheap deal on my rent, I'd agreed with Muir that I'd see to the necessary work to get the place up to a habitable standard. I had much to do and the weekend would soon be over.

'I'm awake now.' I stated the obvious, and to no idea who. 'May as well make the most of it.'

I found my trainers and pulled them on. Neglecting to tie them, I shoved the laces under the tongues of each shoe. Had the house come with carpets I wouldn't have bothered with footwear, except here I'd come across a few floorboards where the heads of nails protruded, or where the wood itself had cracked and laid a trap of jagged splinters for the barefooted. Now, I supposed, would be a good time to solve those minor problems.

My only neighbours were those employed at the insurance brokerage. But they'd shut up shop at 6 p.m. and I doubted there'd be anyone in the building at this hour on a Sunday morning, not even a night watchman. Hammering in nails I'd make a racket, and it would be more of an inconvenience to the office workers if I chose to do it during a weekday. My tools were downstairs. I went to find them, switching on lights before I progressed.

I found my tools in their plastic carrying box in the parlour, and dug out a claw hammer, a chisel and some sandpaper. The door was still propped open on its wedge of wood. Tools clenched ready for action, I wandered out into the hall, trying to decide where best to start. The front door was as good a place as any: concentrate on the well-trodden paths first, I thought, and work into the other rooms as you go. There were some black plastic sacks piled in the vestibule, filled with trash Sarah and I had collected earlier. I moved them, checking the floorboards for rogue nails and splinters. Here in the hall the boards were largely free of protrusions, but I did sand down a couple of boards, mainly to get into the swing of things. Next I went into the living room alongside the parlour. Sarah had swept it clean. I'd put a bulb in the ceiling rose and the light was stark. The wallpaper was stained. In the less than enlightened eighties when this had last been a dwelling, its occupants had been heavy smokers. The ceiling and upper corners of the room were caramel in colour, and the nicotine stains extended half way down the walls. It was ingrained in the wallpaper, the paint on the window frames, but old enough that there was no hint of the tarry smell. Some people would be disgusted, not me. I'd had a thirty a day habit until very recently so who was I to criticise?

Crabbing around the floor, I knocked in nails and then chiselled out a large splinter of wood, smoothing the edges with the sandpaper. It took minutes at best before I moved on. I'd barely visited the rooms on the first floor yet, and now would be no different. The bathroom on the lower split-level had a floor covering – "oil cloth" I think it was called – so I continued up the stairs, knocking and banging as I progressed, and onto the first landing proper. The stained glass window was directly behind, and slightly above me, and I paused to look at it over my hunched shoulder. No late evening sunshine spilled in now. The window reflected the interior light, looking more like a mosaic than ever.

I've heard of the term "matrixing". It's the capacity of the human brain to recognise familiar images in random patterns, like seeing the man in the moon, faces in the clouds. Apparently it's an inherited trait, the ability that allows a newborn baby to recognise the face of its mother. When I peered up at that window I too thought I saw a face, one that was familiar. But the second I blinked, the pattern was gone, and the jumble of coloured glass wouldn't give up its secret a second time. Nevertheless I had seen that face and a sense of unease wormed its way through my guts. A prickling sensation ran from my neck to the crown of my head, as if a faint electrical charge danced in my hair. I scrubbed the sensation away, forced the face from my memory and bent to my task again.

My injured knee was killing me. But it would be no less painful if I gave up on the job and had to return to it at a later stage. I gritted my teeth, continued my way along the hall, hammering away. I bypassed the two rooms and was then faced with the room at the front right I'd earmarked for a junk closet. The door was open, and I paused. I didn't recall opening it. Then again, I didn't remember closing it either, or even noted its position while working. I grunted as I stood, using the near wall for support. I lifted my right heel, manipulated my foot side-to-side, and could feel the angry remonstration of the muscles above my kneecap. Placing down my foot, I tested the leg for stability. Sore but firm enough. I limped into the junk closet and stood looking around. I hadn't got around to fixing a bulb in the light fixture yet, but there was enough of a glow from the streetlights outside.

There wasn't much to see. A square box about twelve by twelve feet. Bare plaster. In one corner some of the plaster had blown from the brickwork and fallen chunks lay piled on the floorboards. There was only one small window, and if viewed from the street outside it was situated directly over the front door. I peeked through it. By now it had to be nearing five o'clock and even the last stragglers from the nightclubs had made it home. The street outside was still and quiet. All I could hear was my own breath – in and out.

Not true.

Beyond my internal noises I could hear a soft murmur, so indistinct it was barely recognisable as a human voice. I craned nearer the window, checking for anyone on the street, but there was no sign. On other mornings people would be out by now, heading for the early shifts at the factories, but I doubted that was the case on a Sunday morning. I held my breath, listening hard. I could make out a cadence to the mumbling, high then low, as if a radio volume button was being turned up and down, but never to a point where the voice was loud enough to make out individual words. Turning from the window, I stood again. The voice didn't originate from outside but from somewhere within the house.

An illogical fear crept through me, like a dull weight that crept from my gut and formed a hand to squeeze round my heart. I sucked in air. Took a firmer grip on my hammer.

As I moved for the hallway, I realised that the sound grew louder – not much, but I could now make out that that rise and fall in tone was because there were two different voices. Male and female. For the life of me I still couldn't make out what was being said: the language was English, I was certain, but the capacity of my hearing wasn't enough to make out the mumbled words. Out of the door, I paused again. The hall was lighted, and I could see the stained glass window and top half of the bathroom door at the far end. The doors were shut to the two living spaces to the right. The sound of voices didn't filter from that direction, but from my left. A shudder went through me as I realised that the conversation was emanating from somewhere above me, from up near or in my bedroom.

Was I afraid?

Maybe, but I was more intrigued at that point. I was confident that no trespassers had found a way inside, and they certainly hadn't had an opportunity to get by me while working in the halls and up the stairs. But there were undeniably voices and I wanted to find out their source. There had to be a logical reason. And I thought I knew what it might be.

Earlier I'd used my phone when browsing the Antigonish poem, and I convinced myself that when I'd put down the phone then I'd accidentally hit a button and set my voice messages playing. Perhaps the programme was stuck in a loop and had been playing the saved messages for the last couple of hours, and I'd been unaware of the faint voices while hard at work.

I went up the narrow stairs, shoulders brushing the warped plaster walls. Though I was positive I'd figured out the source of the voices – what else could they be? – I clutched the hammer in one hand and the chisel the other, rudimentary weapons of defence. I'd not stopped listening to the conversation, still trying to make out if the voices were familiar, but the shwish-shwush of my shoulders on the wall, the steady creak of my feet on the stairs, covered it. As I reached the short hall, I found I was crouching, with my weapons held before me, and it was a strain to straighten up and relax my aching spine.

A whisper.

That's all the voice was.

I turned immediately right for my bedroom, then looked where I'd left my mobile plugged in to recharge. The screen was dimmed, but that meant nothing. Placing down the chisel, I moved the hammer to my left hand, and picked up my phone. I placed it to my ear even though I needn't. I could already tell that the faint murmur was from behind me. The static sensation in my hair was back, but this time it extended the length of my spine. I felt the sudden need to visit the loo. Along with the movements in my bowel, I felt a tightening of my scrotum as I prepared for fight or flight: now I was *genuinely* frightened. Someone had gained entry to the house.

I knew I wasn't much of a scrapper, but faced by the prospect of tracking down a house invader, I experienced a sudden charge of atavistic fury and a large spurt of adrenalin. I nigh on leapt into the next bedroom, swinging around my weapons like a barbarian swordsman, and hollering a challenge.

The room stood bare, but for the graffiti on the walls and the scabby curtains.

One tatty curtain stirred, fluttering gently.

I stepped back as if expecting the thing to throw itself over my face like a dead man's shroud.

Fuck me, Jack! It's only a bloody breeze! Likely some of the putty had come loose from around the windowpane, letting the wind and outside noise in.

Exhaling deeply, I made for the window, pushed aside the curtain. It was greasy with mould. I wiped my hand on my pants and peered down on the back yard. No streetlights aided my vision, but there was enough light in the moonlit sky to see that the narrow yard was clear. I couldn't see all of it; the bathroom extension butted out a good distance and somebody could be in the space beneath it, adjacent to the back door. If they'd hid there, they weren't the source of the voices. Again I realised the words came from over my shoulder, and now the hand that had earlier gripped my heart was back and it gave it a solid squeeze.

There was only one room I hadn't checked on this floor, the closet containing the dumbwaiter. Why did that narrow, webbed space fill me with such dread?

6

Jack in the Box

Irrational fear is every bit as debilitating as genuine fear, sometimes greater than. The symptoms are much the same, except that groundless distress can be magnified by the very nature of being afraid of something you don't understand, you don't grasp the full extent of the danger and therefore fear it all the more. It would explain why sweat poured down my back and from my hairline, cold and slick, and why I had to hang tightly to the hammer and chisel in case they slid from my wet palms. My breath was now coming in short, shallow gasps. I was shivering, but not from the cold.

I stood facing the closet door, and an absurd thought kept demanding an answer.

How the fuck could two people even fit in that small space?

I already knew the answer.

They couldn't. It was impossibility.

And yet I could hear their voices.

They were now just faint rasps, as if they knew only the door separated us, and had hushed their conversation as they plotted their next move.

What was the most absurd and irrational thing of all? I was convinced that the voices sounded familiar.

This had to be some elaborate hoax, a prank formulated by my workmates, and Sarah in particular. She was the only colleague who'd been in the house. Had she smuggled in a recording device or something, and hidden it in the dumbwaiter closet, with the intention of scaring the bejesus out of me? Had she deliberately concealed her iPhone in the bathroom earlier, then claimed it had been moved by invisible hands, to add validation to this intricate joke? Weirding me out, setting me up for when I was hit by this punch line?

OK. It was a ridiculous theory, but what the hell else did I have?

It was either a joke, there were a couple of burglars in my closet or...

I was making excuses for not opening the door.

Scared of ghosts, Jack?

I didn't believe in ghosts, for fuck's sake!

Setting my jaw I yanked open the door, the hammer drawn back over my shoulder. I roared like a lion.

Nobody was there.

How could there have been? The bottom half of the cupboard had been filled by a box-like structure, through which the dumbwaiter rose and fell, and the lift mechanism itself filled most of the top half. There was nowhere even a contortionist could hide.

The voices had fallen silent.

The sudden quiet was equally as disturbing as the whispering before. It told me that the conversation had not come from a recording device or anything like it: the voices had stopped because the speakers knew I was there, listening.

Dusty cobwebs formed a mesh over the opening to the dumbwaiter. The weave puffed back and forward, and I imagined some colossal black spider lurking just out of sight, teasing me with delicate movements of the web. Inviting me to closer investigation when it could leap out and grasp me in its skull-piercing mandibles. It took a moment to realise it was my own breath that stirred the web. And the realisation only added to my already growing sense of foolishness.

The dumbwaiter shifted side to side, very marginally, shaken by some breeze from below. As it moved there was a corresponding squeak, and in the next second it budged again and the creak that followed was deeper in tone. I stood there feeling like an idiot. The noise had a rhythm to it, a cadence, and if I stretched my imagination enough it sounded like the back and forward chatter of a male and female.

How bloody stupid had I been?

I'd not only allowed my imagination to get away from me, I'd allowed it to break down the gates of my scepticism and run loose like wildfire through a forest.

I laughed, telling myself it was not in relief, but at how easy I'd fooled myself. I took a swipe at the cobwebs with the hammer. Accidentally the hammerhead struck the base of the dumbwaiter, and it was all the force required to make the support ropes unfurl. The small freight elevator disappeared into the bowels of the shaft, shrieking all the way down like a damned soul pitched into hell. Irrationality had been a feature of the past five minutes or so, and things weren't about to change now. I made an ill-advised lunge, dropping the chisel in the process, and snapped a hand on the rope, intending to halt the dumbwaiter's fall. The rope zipped through my palm, scouring the flesh, before I had the sense to let it go. I swore as I jerked back from the shaft, inspecting my palm. It was red hot and beaded with blood oozing from the fresh burn.

Somewhere below me the elevator crashed to the bottom of the shaft. Displaced air and dust puffed upward. I leaned into the box structure, trying to make out the extent of the damage, but all I saw was an endless shaft of deepest black.

There was no light bulb in the closet, and I didn't have a flashlight to hand. But what separates man from the beasts is ingenuity. Shaking my stinging hand, I went into the bedroom and thought about dragging the lamp through to next door, but the flex wasn't long enough. Aha! I placed down the hammer, exchanging it for my mobile phone and carried it back to the closet. Leaning over the box, I pressed a random button and the screen glowed blue.

Using the phone's light to illuminate the shaft, I angled it back and forward, but the glow was too weak to reach even the next level down. Undefeated, I bent over the box, reaching down as far as I could, trying to send the light directly down the shaft.

Something moved.

Just beyond the extent of the dim blue glow.

'What the…?'

Lower in the shaft something swirled, then blossomed. Like ink in dirty water, it grew, pushing back even the glow of the light. It gained momentum and then geysered up at me, a frigid blast of stinking air enveloping me entirely. I pedalled frantically away, hands slapping at the gritty embrace. I screamed.

And something screamed back.

A screeching howl of mockery that dug at my eardrums and sent white flashes through my vision.

I collided with the doorframe of my bedroom, felt the impact deep in my shoulder joint, and my phone flew out of my hand and clattered across the hall. I didn't bend to fetch it; I was too busy hurtling down the stairs away from whatever nightmare creature was about to erupt from the shaft like a demented jack in the box, grasp me in its rending claws and drag me into those nighted depths where it preferred to feast.

7

Cold Light

Things didn't feel much better in the cold light of day.

My knee was killing me; my spine ached; my assaulted shoulder sent stabbing agony through my ribs; and the friction burn on my left palm stung as if I gripped a bunch of angry hornets. But they were physical pain. The mental pain of a bruised ego hurt worse. I was embarrassed that I'd allowed my imagination to get the better of me and began looking for alternative reasons for everything I'd experienced. I wasn't infallible: I could be caught up in the moment like any other person, but I didn't have to believe that there was a supernatural explanation for what had gone on. It was strange, but totally natural.

Yes, the weirdness of all that had happened could be easily explained when taken in rational steps: vibrations, subsidence, temperature changes, and deterioration of the structure. They were alternatives for the strange occurrences, and now that I'd had a chance to think about it I could even offer a fair explanation of what had happened in the dumbwaiter shaft.

Then why did I still feel shaky, even hours afterwards?

I couldn't come up with a *rational* reason for that.

I was walking around on tiptoes. OK, that's an exaggeration, but I was taking things slow and easy, some part of my mind listening for anything irregular, anything unnatural. I was sneaking glances over my shoulder, pausing before entering doors, and I'm not sure of what I expected to see. Actually, that's not exactly true, either. I feared seeing that bloody shadow man dogging my steps, or that he'd be waiting to jump at me the second I entered a room if I went unguarded.

> *"When I came home last night at three*
> *The man was waiting there for me*
> *But when I looked around the hall*
> *I couldn't see him there at all."*

As I moved through the house, shifting boxes of clutter from one room to another, that damn rhyme was tumbling around my brain once more.

"'Go away, go away, don't you come back anymore.'" I quoted Antigonish out loud. "'Go away, go away, and please don't slam the door!'"

I stopped, clutching a cardboard box to my chest. Listening. Not sure if I wanted to hear a slamming door or not. At least if the door did crash shut it might signify the banishment of the

71

shadow man and an end to all my problems. But the door didn't bang. In fact, the house was still and silent. Somehow that made me uneasier than ever and I went to the parlour where I'd temporarily set up my TV and turned it on. I hadn't yet organised a satellite TV provision, so could only access the free channels. I tuned to BBC 1, where a presenter was interviewing a politician. True to form the politician was couching his answers, neither agreeing or disagreeing with the presenter's point of view, and delivering over and over again his party line. It was typical obfuscation, a layering on of pile after pile of bullshit. Perhaps the politician wasn't so different from me in that respect.

I couldn't go on like that.

I turned up the volume on the TV, enough that it would offer a background soundtrack as I worked. Then I headed for the stairs. If I was going to regain any sense of normality I was going to have to confront the problem, not bury it under layers of lame excuses. I returned to where all this began: the small hallway with its four facing doors. I could remember my bedroom door and the one on to the stairwell had been open, and the one to the second bedroom. The dumbwaiter closet door had been shut. I arranged all the doors to reflect my memory, then slowly backed into my bedroom. I got two shadows for my trouble. One that was short, fat and very faint grey in colour that leaned into my bedroom, at about forty-five degrees to my position. The second was cast by the light coming in through my bedroom windows, and was like a very faint double exposure. It was more elongated, but it was apparent from the way it extended from my feet, across the threshold and into the hall, then only partially up the closet door, that it was nothing like I'd seen before. Another thing I had to consider: when I first visited the house it was raining, the sky was overcast and grey, unlike this morning, so the sources of light weren't as strong as they were now. Back then my shadows would have been less defined.

I plotted where I'd seen the shadow. If it had been mine – which it *had* to be – then I required a bright source of light directly behind me. I moved across the bedroom and peered out the window.

Directly opposite my house was a three-storey building that had been converted to bedsits. It was a long shot to suggest a light from one of those windows had been cast all the way across the street and into my room, but what if someone had been dicking around with a torch or something? They could have been scoping out what was happening having noticed Muir leading Sarah and I inside the house, after it had known no residents for a long time. The reason, I told myself, that the shadow had seemingly zipped out of view was that the torch beam had moved to check out the other windows. I couldn't credit my theory with much weight, but hey, it was still possible. As weak as it sounded, it was a more credible explanation than that I was sharing my new home with a living shadow.

Satisfied with my explanation, I went to the closet and barely paused before opening the door.

OK.

'This is just wrong.'

How the fuck could I put a logical spin on *this*?

The dumbwaiter platform had returned to its original position, and not by my hands.

8

Down the Chute

'I wondered if you'd come over,' I said into my phone. 'I need someone to convince me I'm not going out of my mind.'

'I'm having lunch with my parents, Jack.'

'Yeah, I understand. It's Sunday and all. But I hoped that maybe you could pop over after…'

'We were going to go out shopping.'

'Later then? Maybe this evening?' I was trying not to sound too needy, too over-demanding, but neither did I want Sarah to turn me down. She didn't answer, and was possibly searching for a way to let me down gently. She could be biting at times, and wasn't afraid of doling out sarcasm when necessary, but despite all that she was my friend. I was certain that she liked me, and hoped that her feelings went further than simple friendship. The incident with her phone had rattled her, and she was weirded out by my new home, and I didn't want any unease to form a wedge between us. 'I could get a pizza delivered, a bottle of wine?'

She still didn't answer.

I waited.

'I thought you'd given up drinking,' she said.

'I have. But a little wine with dinner doesn't count, does it?'

Now I waited her out.

The longer the silence the more difficult it was for her to find a plausible excuse.

'I'll come over this afternoon,' she finally said. Her voice was a dull monotone. 'I'm going into town with my parents, but the shops close at four. I suppose I could pop round for a while then.'

'Great,' I said.

'Don't bother with the pizza,' she said, a little of her inherent wit returning.

'Pinot Grigio?'

'Ideal. Do I have to bring my Marigolds with me?'

'No, you won't need your rubber gloves this time. I've got the cleaning done, ready for the carpets and furniture. All you need bring is your opinion.'

She laughed. 'Usually I'm told to keep it to myself.'

'I appreciate your forthrightness,' I said, putting on a plummy accent.

'You said you wanted me to convince you that you're not going out of your mind. Too late for that, Jack. It's confirmed: you're nuts.'

'You know, I'm beginning to wonder what would be worse. Part of me hopes that I am having a little mental wobble.' I avoided adding "again".

'What has happened?'

'I'll tell you when you get here.'

'Jack?'

'It's nothing...'

'You want my opinion on *nothing*?' Sarah scolded.

'I want a *second* opinion. Look, don't worry. There's probably a good explanation for it all. It's just that-' I paused, wondering if I sounded too whiney '-well, I can't figure this out and I'd value your opinion.'

'You haven't been seeing shadows again?'

'No. No, it's nothing like that. I figured all that stuff out. This is something different.'

Sarah exhaled. 'I wish you'd just tell me.'

If I did, I'd a feeling she'd suddenly recall that she had another more pressing engagement. But then again, she was into all that Ghostbuster stuff...

'All the spooky shenanigans will be explained when you arrive,' I said in that plummy, posh accent again. She didn't find it funny this time. She snorted.

'You're a jerk, Jack Newman.'

'Uh...'

'You've got my mind working on overtime now. I'll make my excuses to my mum and dad. I'll be over within the hour, OK?'

'I didn't mean to spoil your plans, Sarah.'

'Forget it. But you'd better make up for dragging me away from a shopping trip. Get two bottles of Pinot on ice.'

Once we'd made our short goodbyes I headed to a nearby Tesco Express store and grabbed the promised wine. Once home again, I parked my Volvo in the back service alley, but didn't immediately go inside. I wasn't putting off going in the house; there was something that I wanted to check out. I took the wine with me, in a cheap carrier bag, the bottles clinking, the handles threatening to snap under the weight at any second. I placed the bag by the back gate to the yard. From outside the gate couldn't be opened, an added security feature, but also an inconvenience for getting back and forward from the garage. I followed the boundary of the yard to the side of the house. The windows of the living room and those at the side of the parlour were on this wall, and faced directly onto the pavement. Mid-way along I found what I was looking for. At street level were two narrow windows, but planks screwed into the frame had blocked them in. Extending horizontally from the windows was a tin-sheet cover, sunk into a bracket in the pavement. The sheet was rusty, curled at one edge where someone had prized it up at some point in the past. I crouched, feeling the strain in my sore knee and got my fingers under the sheet. It was an effort but I hauled it up.

Directly below the windows I found an entrance to the basement Muir had spoken of. It was a coal chute, a feature of that type of building when the home was heated by solid fuel. Back in the day, the coal man would arrive with his horse and cart, and tip the coal down the chute, out of sight and hearing of the wealthy residents. A servant in the basement would then fetch coal from the hopper below the chute as and when necessary. In later days an iron grid had been fixed over the entrance to stop trespassers gaining entrance to the building, but it wasn't totally burglar proof. Somebody had hacksawed a couple of the bars free, leaving a wide enough gap for someone to slip inside. I was confident that there was no way someone could find ingress to the house from the basement, but they could play silly buggers with the dumbwaiter mechanism from down there.

If it were not for the fact I wanted to see Sarah, I would have called her back, told her to enjoy her shopping trip, as I'd solved the riddle. Or at the very least I'd discovered a plausible explanation for how the dumbwaiter had returned to its original position. I had a squatter living in my basement.

As I have already mentioned, I'm not an accomplished scrapper. Therefore I didn't feel confident about descending into the cellar alone. Discretion, they say, is the better part of valour, so I called Peter Muir.

'I'm having my Sunday dinner, man,' Muir said. It seemed as if a trend was developing.

I told him about my suspicions regarding a trespasser.

'Wouldn't surprise me if some tramp has sneaked inside. It wouldn't be the first time to be honest. But I thought I'd put a stop to that.'

'The hatch to the basement's insecure,' I told him. 'It has been prized up and you can see where someone's damaged the bars and made their way in.'

'Bloody hell.'

'I wondered if you'd come over and take a look with me.'

'I'm having dinner, man,' he reminded me. 'Just call the police. It's their job any way.'

I sighed, but he was probably right. Who knew who was down there, or how they'd react if they were cornered. It was better if someone trained and equipped to handle a belligerent drunk was on the scene if they required evicting.

I hung up and searched for the number for the local nick in my contacts. The police wouldn't appreciate a 999 call; this wasn't exactly what you'd call an emergency. So I brought up the number I'd saved for making general enquiries and low-level complaints. There was a time when I'd frequently called them. I got through to an operator after doing the run around of menus and such, and asked if an officer could attend at their first convenience. I didn't expect anyone to turn up soon. In the meantime I pushed the tin sheet back in place. I even thought about bringing round my car and parking over the escape hatch, but decided against it. The best scenario would be if the trespasser came out now that they knew they'd been rumbled and pissed off without any fuss. To encourage them, I opened the hatch again and propped it against the window. I then made it obvious I was walking away, whistling as I went to fetch my bag of wine. As I returned past the hatch I took a sneaky peek down to see if anyone lurked in the dimness ready to escape once I was out of earshot. I couldn't see a thing beyond the dim spill of light on the coal chute. But that suited me fine.

I went inside and made sure the door was locked. Making my way to the living room, I angled myself so I could spy out of the window without being seen. The open hatch was to my right, below my line of sight, but I'd spot anyone trying to sneak out.

There was a sharp rap from behind me.

I jumped, before realising that it was someone at the front door. It was the first time I'd heard the old iron knocker.

Expecting the police, I was instead greeted by Sarah. She was wearing a duffel coat over a white sweater and blue jeans. She looked really cute. She had forewarned me that she'd be there within an hour, but it hadn't felt that long – I'd been in the supermarket a bit longer than I'd thought. I invited her in and directed her to the living room, but placed a finger to my lips. 'I'm trying to see something,' I whispered.

'See what?'

'I think there's someone down in my basement.'

She frowned. She was probably wondering why the hell I was spying out the window.

'There's a hatch out there that I found. I was hoping they'd just come out and leave before there's any bother.'

As she shucked out of her coat, Sarah craned for a look. I urged her to keep back.

'Don't let them see you.'

'Why not?'

'They might get angry and cause a fuss.'

'It's probably some old tramp. You should go and shout down the hole at him to come out.'

'I called the police,' I said.

A flicker of disappointment danced in her eyes, and I immediately felt bad. She thought I was acting cowardly.

'I'm not frightened,' I blustered. 'You know what it's like with those type of people. If you bother them they take it personally, they might come back and smash the windows or something.'

'Trust me,' Sarah replied. 'They won't. They'll be too busy looking for their next bottle of cider to bother you again.'

Perhaps. Whoever was down in my cellar had pulled the dumbwaiter back up the shaft, whether intending it as a joke or some other deviltry I couldn't decide. But if they were prepared to mess about like that, then they might take things further if I pissed them off.

'Let's just wait for the cops, eh? They'll get their details and warn them against coming back.' I lifted the carrier bag. 'We have another small problem. I've no fridge yet. I couldn't chill the wine like you asked.'

'It was just a turn of phrase.' Sarah leaned for another look out the window. 'Do you want me to go and give them a bollocking? They won't mess with me.'

Grinning at her, I said, 'I wouldn't blame them.'

'Are you saying I look scary?' She mocked a hard face.

'Not scary. More "formidable".'

'Bloody hell, Jack, I've been called a few things in my time but never formidable. What is that? Man code for "ugly bitch"?'

'Now we both know that's not true.' I stared at her gorgeous features just a tad too long. She smiled, but it was with a hint of nervousness. She wafted a hand at the bag, deftly changing the subject.

'Tell me you have clean glasses, Jack. I don't fancy drinking wine out of the paper cups you were using yesterday.' She ushered me away. 'Don't worry, I'll keep an eye out if anyone tries to sneak out the cellar.'

I wanted to wait, to see whom my unwelcome guest turned out to be, but more so I wanted to please Sarah. Earlier I'd unpacked a box of crockery and drinking glasses and having washed them in the sink, set two glasses on the drainer. I opened one of the bottles and poured a good glug of wine into each glass. I carried them back with me to the living room. Sarah was watching distractedly out of the window. Apparently she'd seen nothing interesting while I was gone.

'Have you heard anything from the cellar?' she asked as she accepted her glass of Pinot Grigio. I shook my head. 'They've probably already left. If there was even anyone there to start with.'

While I was out at the supermarket, a trespasser could indeed have left the cellar. I hadn't considered that. But I still wanted it checked out. I told her about the voices I thought I'd heard, and how they turned out to be the rusty squeaking of the dumbwaiter. Then I told her of my ham-handed swing of the hammer and how the elevator platform had fell, only to return to its original position later.

'Someone had to have pulled it back up,' I said.

'Unless it's on a counterweight mechanism,' she pointed out, and took a deep gulp of wine, watching me all the while over the rim of the glass, her pupils dancing.

'If it was counterweighted it wouldn't have fallen the way it did. Look,' I said, showing her my grazed palm, 'it took the bloody skin off me.'

Sarah frowned at my palm, but didn't say a thing.

She thought I was being a wimp.

I closed my hand. 'It's nothing. I just meant that it was falling fast enough to spool out the rope. It burned me when I tried to grab it. A counterweight wouldn't have allowed that to happen.'

'So the obvious explanation is that some tramp living in your cellar heard the commotion and thought he'd do the neighbourly thing and send the dumbwaiter back up to you? Why'd he bother?'

'Who knows? He probably doesn't know himself. If he was pissed...'

'He probably wouldn't have even heard the thing falling.'

I'd asked for her second opinion, so wasn't going to argue. 'Maybe you're right. Do you think I should ring the cops back and cancel?'

'You've called them now; you may as well let them come. Even if it's just to put your mind at rest.' She finished her wine and held the glass out to me. 'Anything else strange happen last night?'

'Nothing.' I headed for the kitchen. Sarah followed me this time, and I had to hide the mild irritation. Who was going to watch for the squatter now? Sarah had written the incident off; she didn't believe me, only her opinion was correct. I shook the feeling off and avoided glancing through the parlour windows as we passed the open door. In the kitchen I refilled our glasses, telling her how I'd figured out the shadow man phenomena, how my own shadow had been cast when somebody in the opposite house shone a bright torchlight into the house.

'Dick head,' Sarah commented, and I wasn't sure if she meant my torch-happy neighbour or me. Then she delved in her handbag. 'That reminds me: I've something I want you to have a look at.'

Before she could go further, I glanced out of the kitchen window as a police car pulled to the kerb outside.

'The cops are here,' I said, suddenly feeling nervous. If Sarah was right and my squatter had already sneaked off, the police weren't going to be happy. They'd view me as a time waster. Huh, I thought, they'd probably berate me for making them miss their Sunday lunch too. Did coppers even eat Sunday lunch, trading Yorkshire puddings for doughnuts? I snickered at my own joke and caught another frown from Sarah.

'You feeling all right, Jack?'

'Yeah. Just nervous. They're probably going to be pissed off at me.'

'At least you don't have to worry about the police coming back and smashing your windows.' She smirked.

I put down my glass on the drainer, and went to greet the police officers at the front door. There were two of them, a woman and a boy who looked barely old enough to shave let alone wear a uniform. I wondered if it was "take your child to work day", and chuckled again. Drinking wine on an empty stomach obviously wasn't good for me. They both greeted me with dour expressions and I waved off my laughter, saying, 'Sorry, private joke with my friend.'

The female officer introduced herself and her colleague, but I didn't take in their names. To me they'd be "Officer", whichever one of them I referred to. I told them about my suspicions regarding the basement.

'How do we get down there?' asked the woman.

'There's no access from inside,' I said, and waved alongside the house. 'There's a hatch round there. I'll show you.'

As I led them to the coal chute, I explained that it was highly likely that the trespasser had already left. Arriving at the open hatch the two officers stood there peering down into the darkness. I could see the woman judging the narrow gap between the bars and concluding there was no way she was going to attempt squeezing through. She gave her colleague a meaningful look. 'Got your torch, Andy?'

The boy ratched about on his cumbersome utility belt and brought out a slim Maglite torch, and held it up. The woman gave him a second meaningful look and he hitched his shoulders. 'I'll take a look,' he offered.

The subject of who was going down the hole hadn't been in question: I took it that the woman was a tutor and the boy a probationer. He'd get all the shitty jobs.

'Do you think there are rats down there?' the young man asked.

'Probably,' the woman said. Bitch.

Before he went down the chute, the young cop shucked off his stab-proof vest and unclipped his utility belt. The woman held his belt for him as he shimmied his way through the narrow gap, then passed the belt to him. He fumbled back into the belt as he went down the chute.

Then we couldn't see him.

I heard his muffled voice, as he called out. Even faint, he sounded scared. I shared a glance with the female officer and she shook her head as if to say, "This is the kind of recruits we're stuck with these days". I made an apologetic face of my own. 'I'm sorry about this. Like I said, they're probably already gone.'

'Does no harm to check it out,' said the officer. Maybe if she were the one who'd had to go down the hole it would have been a different story.

'Anything?' she hollered down the chute.

There was a shuffle of movement and the young man's head appeared below us. He looked up, and though there still remained a note of fear in his features, his eyes shone excitedly. 'It's amazing down here. Like walking back in time.'

'Anyone there?' the woman snapped.

'No, it's clear.'

'Then come on then; we haven't time for a museum trip.'

It took the copper a minute or two to climb out, reversing the procedure with his utility belt. Finally he stood on the pavement next to us, and wiped at cobwebs stuck in his hair. 'Nobody there,' he reiterated. Then to me he added, 'Haven't you been down there, sir? It's crazy.'

I shook my head. 'I only moved in yesterday, I haven't had the opportunity yet.'

'You should take a look. Really interesting.'

The woman interjected.

'Was there any sign of damage?'

'No. Someone has been down there though. There was an old mattress in one corner with some empty beer cans and stuff. But it looks old; might even have been there for years.'

The female officer used the toe of her boots to kick at the bars. 'This looks like old damage too. We can take a report but…'

'No, no,' I said, cutting her off, and I saw the relief pass through her. 'If it's old it's pointless giving you a load of paperwork for nothing.' I thanked them both for coming, and made apologies again for wasting their time. The young cop grinned at me, said it was no bother. He'd actually enjoyed himself, and his enthusiasm intrigued me. They made their goodbyes and walked for their car. I heard the woman give an update over her radio, stating quite clearly that it was a false alarm, and no crime to report. Once they were gone I fitted the tin sheet back over the hole, resolving to come back and screw it in place later. Sarah was waiting for me in the kitchen when I got back. Whatever she wanted to show me before had been forgotten. I noticed that she'd turned her attention to her wine while I was with the police.

I went and fetched my hammer.

'Want to see something really cool?' I asked.

'What you going to do with the hammer, knock some sense into your skull?'

I laughed with her, but then left the kitchen, hoping that she'd follow. After a second or two she did.

9

The Chase

'Whoa! What the hell are you doing, Jack?'

I swung the hammer again, winking over my shoulder at Sarah who was shocked by my vandalism. The hammer punched a second hole in the wall and plaster dust wafted around me. 'I'm opening the basement,' I said, stating the obvious.

'How do you know you've got the right spot?'

'Where else could the entrance be?' Having cleared all the ground floor there wasn't anything that indicated a trapdoor entrance to the basement in any of the floorboards. A little detective work – not to mention recalling that Muir said the previous tenants had boarded it up – I realised that the only place the entrance could be was in the void beneath the stairs to the split-level landing. 'Look, you can see inside.'

The wall was plasterboard tacked to a flimsy frame of wood. Over it there were several layers of wallpaper and emulsion paint, indicating how long ago the basement had been blocked up. My two solid whacks of the hammer had already opened a hole large enough to fit my head through. I couldn't see anything in particular, only a dark emptiness but I knew I'd found the right location.

'Why would you even want to open it up? Isn't the house already too large for you?' Sarah had taken a few steps back, wiping plaster dust off her shoulder. She frowned at the dirt on her pristine white sweater the way she had at my palm earlier.

'Muir said I could use the space for storage.'

'Ehm,' Sarah said, with an expansive wave of her arms. I already had eight rooms and a closet, so take my pick, her expression said.

'Even if I don't use it, I still want to take a look.' I told her about how impressed the young copper had been after poking around in the basement for a few minutes. 'He said it was as if time had stood still.'

Sarah's complexion lightened a few shades. Not as a result of the two glasses of wine she'd gulped down. 'I don't think it's a good idea, Jack. There was a reason the previous tenants blocked it up.'

I offered her a patronising smile. 'You're not starting with those ghost stories again?'

'You hear of stuff like this all the time,' she said. 'People move into an old house. Everything is fine until they start renovating the place and the changes they make upset the spirits; it stirs them up. Then all hell breaks loose!'

'You watch too many horror movies for your own good.' I lay in with the hammer again.

'You can laugh, Jacko, but most of those films are based on some grain of truth. I seriously suggest you stop what you're doing.'

'Too late,' I crowed, ripping loose a full three feet square chunk of plasterboard. I leaned into the gap and found a set of stairs that descended into darkness. 'C'mon, Sarah: you don't really believe all that spooky nonsense?'

'It's not me who claims to have seen a shadow man.'

'And I already explained what it was,' I countered.

'Yeah, with the kind of bullshit theory sceptics always come up with. Who is going to be using a torch during the daytime, Jack? It was morning when we came here, not the middle of the bloody night.'

'It was raining, dull, that's why.'

Sarah shook her head in disbelief at my stubbornness. I offered another cheeky grin, then kicked loose some boards. Broken pieces tumbled down the newly disgorged stairs. There was now plenty room to step through on to the head of the stairs. I looked back at Sarah as I placed the hammer aside. 'Coming?'

'No way.'

'Aw, come on. I wanted to share this discovery with you.'

She relented. 'If I get possessed by some evil spirit I'm going to take it out on your ass!'

'Promises, promises,' I quipped, then reached out a hand for her.

'My sweater's going to get filthy,' she griped.

My eyes were drawn to her white sweater. The cotton was sheer and I could make out the outline of her push-up bra beneath. Her breasts were small globes that rose and fell as she breathed. I quickly averted my gaze before she saw where my scrutiny had got stuck, but was positive I'd been too slow. I told myself that was her purpose of mentioning her sweater in the first place.

'Once you're through the gap it'll be fine. The stairs are clear and I can just make out an open door at the bottom.' I looked around as best I could. 'How do you feel about spiders?'

'Spiders!'

'It's all right, I was just about to say there are none.'

'Tosser!'

'I love it when you talk dirty,' I said.

Sarah made a little dip of her chin towards one shoulder, and nipped at her bottom lip. God, she was gorgeous. I was tempted to forget about the cellar, and go for broke instead. But she spoiled the moment by delving in her bag and pulling out her iPhone. She fiddled about and got an app working. It was a torch light. Probably played havoc on her phone's battery life, but it was a handy tool. I took out my mobile and hit a button and the screen glowed blue. I beckoned Sarah again, and was happy when she slipped her fingers into mine. 'Careful,' I said, leading her through the gap.

She stood close to me, and I could smell her fragrance. It wasn't a heavy perfume, more a clean smell of soap and shampoo. I also caught a faint waft of wine breath as she gave a little gasp. She moved so close that our hips touched, and I didn't move away. I shivered. Jesus, you'd think she was the first girl I'd ever been close to. I'm certain she shivered too, but it was for another reason. An icy wash of damp air wafted past, and my skin crawled as if gossamer-thin spider webs adhered to it.

'Did you feel that cold draught?' she said, her voice catching in her throat.

'It's ages since the place was last opened. It's bound to be colder down there.' I surreptitiously wiped at my face with the back of the hand holding my phone, but it didn't make a difference; the webs were now the tickly sensation of static electricity. Even the small hairs on the back of my hand danced. Goose bumps climbed my arms.

Unconsciously, Sarah placed her free hand across her breasts. It was the same hand gripping her phone. The beam from the torch app played down the right side of the stairwell. I angled mine to the left. We went down, still - to my secret pleasure -

hand in hand. Sarah was trembling, and a little thrill went through me. Not long ago I was worried she thought I was a wimp, now I was her protector. I glanced at her, wondering if it would be going too far if I wrapped a comforting arm around her waist. I hoped for a hint that she'd accept such intimacy but couldn't read her expression. I chickened out, fearing she'd slap me.

'Exciting, isn't it?' I whispered for something to take my mind off the imagined slight.

'Is that what I'm feeling?'

'Are you scared?'

'You have to admit this is weird.'

'Yeah,' I said, as we exited the stairwell into larger space. It was weird *and* creepy, but aren't all deserted, forgotten places? The torch beams were ineffective here, and we had to turn left to play the light over the nearest feature. There was an open door and room beyond. Dim light played near the far ceiling and as my eyes adjusted to the darkness I understood that we were adjacent to where the coal chute entered the basement. The light leaked around the edges of the boards over the windows, and even at the sides of the tin sheet trapdoor. There was rubbish on the floor – leaf litter, ancient food wrappers, a couple of flattened tins. I could make out where the young copper had kicked his way through the litter as he'd groped his way into the basement proper. It smelled musty, and of wet iron and crumbling brick dust. Still attached at the hip, we shuffled forward, passing another pitch black room, and through another open portal. There we stood, and I had to admit: the copper hadn't been wrong.

It was gritty underfoot, and motes of dust danced in our phone beams, but there was no hint of the clutter that had found its way down the coal chute. But for the discolouration of the walls and flooring, you'd swear that the room hadn't been touched for decades. But that wasn't the biggest surprise. I had expected that the basement had been left as it had looked back in the 1980s, but I was out by about one hundred years.

'It's like a scene out of Downton Abbey,' Sarah said with burgeoning awe.

I'd never watched the TV period drama she referred to, but knew enough about it to agree. The room was like a set from the show, but one that had been left to the damp and must for decades.

'Look at the cooking range!' Sarah had forgotten her fear now. She released my hand so that she could play the torch light over the expansive range that dominated most of the wall on our left. It was huge, with two cast iron ovens, an open hearth at the centre, and hot plates to either end. Dusty spider webs netted the entire thing. Cupboards above the hearth on both sides were also formed of cast metal. They were probably once employed to keep prepared dishes warm, utilising the heat from the ovens below. Over the hearth were hooks and rods where pans still hung, ready for the return of the cook. Behind the fire, the wall was decorated with original glazed tiles, and even someone who was unfamiliar with their reclamation value could recognise their monetary worth. In fact the entire range was probably worth a fortune. Sarah *oohed* and *aahed* as she inspected it.

I allowed her to enjoy the find while I extended our treasure hunt, sweeping the glow from my phone over a table in the middle of the ancient scullery. It was a "butcher's block", a huge, sturdy thing. More pots and crockery sat on the table, dusty and spotted with fly crap. At the edge of my light, I saw a pot sink, ancient cupboards, and a welsh dresser, again stacked with grimy dishes. The floor was formed of Lakeland slate tiles, but beneath the table was an inlaid glazed tile mosaic. I couldn't be positive but I felt the pattern reflected the design of the stained glass window above the bathroom entrance upstairs.

I turned away, checking for new delights. There was another door to my right. I left Sarah to it, and moved for the door. I pulled it open and found a pantry. Inside was the old mattress the cop had mentioned. It was ancient, almost rotted through, stained and damp, and there was a scattering of trash on top of it, empty beer cans and liquor bottles. The scene was at odds with the ancient scullery and I shoved the door to in disgust. At a right angle to the pantry was another door. It was partially open, from when the young cop had investigated the basement. I opened it and stared into a wedge-shaped space that extended beneath the actual pavement and part of the road outside.

I took a step but faltered, and eased back.

The solid darkness was menacing.

Something scraped, like a heavy boot on paving.

Chewing my lip, I thought about closing the door, and forgetting all about the room. But I knew what Sarah would say.

I leaned, aiming the light. It didn't extend all the way to the far wall. Something monstrous could be lurking just beyond sight, about to lunge out and snap its teeth into my throat. I reared back again.

Jesus, Jack, the noise was probably just a mouse. Yeah, a fucking mouse wearing hobnail boots! I steeled myself, this time convincing myself that a pedestrian on the pavement above had made the noise.

Stepping inside, a cold chill descended over me. I could even taste the dampness in the atmosphere, and I spat it out. There could be poisonous black mold spores floating around. I pulled my sweatshirt up over my nose as I peered into the blue-tinged gloom. It was like a hidden dungeon, the domain of a sadistic torturer or serial killer. I pictured wraithlike victims hung to bleed out as knives and hot irons were applied, fleecing their skin from their bones. It was actually an old cold storage pantry, evidence of which was a long trestle counter to one side and a line of meat hooks on the opposite wall. Despite my unease the place fascinated me. I moved along, touching my fingertips to each meat hook. They were tarnished, spotted with rust in places, but the points were still sharp. At the narrow point of the wedge, I found the source of the dampness and cold. Rainwater had leaked in through a crack in the ceiling. The wall was slick and green with algae, or moss. I had the urge to poke my fingers into the filth but a shiver of revulsion trickled down my spine. I retreated, expecting the growth to suddenly leap at me, smother me, drowning me in its cloying embrace. Where I'd been shocked or disturbed by the previous unusual events in the house, now I experienced a level of disgust that fed a deeper nausea than any scare I'd had. My stomach twinged, and saliva flooded my mouth, a precursor to purging my guts.

Turning round, I grabbed at the trestle table for support as my gut heaved painfully. I fought down vomit. Sweat popped out along my hairline and poured down my face, pooling in my eye sockets.

'To hell with this!' I wanted out. I rushed for the exit, gagging down bile. The phone's blue glow blinked out, but light leaked from the Victorian kitchen where Sarah's torch app danced.

I picked up my pace, desperately wanting to reach that light.

But something moved faster.

A coal-black figure hurtled from behind me and through the open door. I stumbled to a halt. What the fuck?

The urge to throw up was gone, now clamped down by the contracting of my throat and chest. My legs turned to water. Instead of being sick I might have soiled my trousers, except I didn't get the chance.

A larger shadow zipped past me in the same direction, and I cried out. It was madness, but I made a defensive swipe at it. My hand passed through the inky black form, and my fingers tingled, as if I'd just touched an electrical charge. Then the numbness began, an icy coldness creeping up my fingers towards my wrist. I gawped, but only until I saw where the second shadow was running to. I croaked a warning to Sarah. Terrified, I lurched after the figure, chasing to stop it before it reached her.

I banged out of the doorway, my sore knee taking the brunt against the doorframe, and I shouted in pain. Sarah was in the far right corner, cringing at my unexpected yell. Her hands were at her throat, and the light of her torch scored unnatural highlights on her face.

'Look out!' I barked as the shadow figure raced directly for her. Ignoring it, Sarah stared at me, her eyes wide, her teeth clamped. She reared back against the closet door, as if I was the dangerous one. The figure loomed over her, blocking her from my sight, made a swiping grab for her.

The smaller shadow appeared, diving under the larger figure's outstretched arms, speeding past the cooking range for the exit door. The big one went after it. Both were screaming – one voice was raised in terror, the other malicious fury. I took a couple of steps after them before Sarah shrieked and collapsed in the corner.

10

Unattainable

Years before I met Catriona, and we had our two children, I was in another relationship. My first lover was called Naomi Woodall. We met in our final year of secondary school and were together almost seven years before things ended. It didn't end well. Despite trying hard to wipe that fateful night from my memory our final minutes together often intruded in my dreams, and left me calling out in regret, sometimes in sheer horror. Naomi was an attractive girl, still in the flush of youth, but in those last few minutes her face had taken on a different look all together, and it wasn't pretty.

Looking down at Sarah huddled on the basement floor, she wore a similar expression to the one Naomi had back then. Her mouth was contorted, and her eyes went from wide-open one second to screwed up tightly the next. Her arms thrust at me, shoving and pushing. She made little animal noises, whines and squeaks.

'Sarah? Sarah! Are you all right?'

'Get away from me!'

'What's wrong? Did it hurt you?'

'Get away, Jack!'

At a loss, I stepped away, my gaze going for the door the two shadows had disappeared through. I couldn't see or hear them now. Sarah scuffled around, looking for something. As she fell she dropped her iPhone. We were in almost darkness. I nudged the phone with my foot, bent and picked it up. I held it to Sarah and she snatched it out of my hand, fumbling with it until she got the beam going again. She shone it directly in my eyes. I averted my gaze, hissing, half-blinded.

Her demand came out of left field. 'What the hell were you playing at?'

'What do you mean?'

'Frightening the shit out of me like that! Do you think it was bloody funny?' Sarah struggled up. I offered a hand but she pushed it away. 'Get off me.'

'What do you mean I frightened you? It wasn't me…'

'You screamed like a little girl,' Sarah snapped, 'then came flying out of that room as if it was on fire. I almost had a bloody heart attack.'

I screamed?

Maybe I did but it wasn't to frighten her, it was to warn her.

'I, uh, I…'

Sarah scrubbed at a knee. Wiping off dust. She looked up from under her disarranged hair, then shook her head. 'Good one, Jacko,' she muttered. But then she saw the humour of the moment and let out an unsteady laugh. 'You got me good there, you idiot.'

'I wasn't trying to scare you,' I said, 'I was, uh…'

She shoved me, but it was playful this time. 'So what was all the screaming for? I thought you were being murdered.'

'Didn't you see them?' I asked, and I bent to scan the darkness through the open door to the stairs.

'See who? I thought you were right and there was an intruder the copper missed. I half expected a mad axe man to come running out behind you.' Sarah followed my gaze and shone the torch that way. 'What are you looking at?'

'Those two shadows,' I explained, 'they shot past me towards you. That's what I was shouting for.'

'You saw him again?' Give Sarah her due, she was such a believer in the weird and whacky that she didn't question their existence. This time even I didn't question myself. I knew what I'd seen. The first shadow was running in terror, chased by the second.

'There were two of them this time. A big one chasing a smaller one.'

'A child?'

'No, it was more like a woman. She was smaller, the other was about my size.'

'I warned you what would happen if you opened this bloody place.' Sarah was now bent at the waist, aiming her torch between the cold pantry and the exit passage. 'Something must've happened here, Jack. Something horrible. I've heard of stuff like this before. It's called a residual haunt.'

I'd never heard of the term. Still looking for evidence, Sarah went on. 'Some mediums and paranormal investigators have this theory that during a traumatic incident the negative energy can become trapped in the environment, and when the atmospheric conditions are right it can be replayed. It's like old videotape replaying the same scene over and over again. You just witnessed something that happened years and years ago. It could be why the basement was boarded up afterwards. Or maybe the previous tenants witnessed the same event and they shut the place up as a result. What did these shadows look like?'

'Shadows,' I said. 'Black.'

'But what about features, clothing, anything specific like that?'

'It happened too fast,' I explained. 'I didn't get a look at any detail. But I know what you're getting at and the answer's no. I couldn't make out what the figures actually looked like, they were just solid black shapes.'

She gnawed at her bottom lip, her tongue dancing in and out. Sarah had regained some of her composure, but one emotion had replaced the other. Her previous fear had morphed into excitement. Partly I was relieved, because she'd forgotten her anger – her fear – of me. On the other hand I felt extremely uncomfortable, because I was only adding credence to something I'd always argued against.

'Are you suggesting that I *actually* saw a couple of spirits?' I said, layering on a tone of doubt I didn't genuinely feel. 'And you find that exciting? I…I don't know what to think. *Real* spirits?'

'No. They're not spirits. It's like I said, they're just a replay. They're not sentient, have no intelligence. They're not actually there in the sense that they are real forms. Imagine them as a recording only, being replayed like a film projected on to a screen. They're no different than a mirage, but cast into the present from the past. It's just the same traumatic scene re-enacted time and again. They can't hurt you, Jack, because they're not really there.'

I thought of the static charge as my hand passed through the larger shadow, how my fingers had tingled as an unearthly chill had crept up my fingers, all of which contradicted Sarah's explanation. But I kept those details to myself. 'I thought that ghosts were supposed to be the spirits of dead people.'

'That's why so many people find ghosts so hard to believe in,' Sarah gripped my arm. 'Come on, as much as I'm interested in the paranormal, I'm not enjoying this creepy place. Let's go upstairs where it's light and I'll explain.'

She led me up the stairs. As we progressed I couldn't help glancing around, checking that the two spooks weren't going to come hurtling up the steps behind us. When we stepped into the vestibule again, I exhaled noisily.

'You're rattled,' Sarah said.

'Just a bit.'

'I think it's fantastic!' Sarah's toffee eyes flashed. 'I wish I'd seen what you did.'

'You didn't see anything of them?'

'No,' she said, heading for the kitchen and, I assumed, a replenishment of her wine glass. 'Tell me again what you saw.'

I narrated the scene as I followed her to where we'd left our glasses, telling how the smaller figure had raced past, followed by the other moments later. As I'd come out of the cold pantry I thought the bigger one was going for Sarah, but apparently he was after the one hiding behind her. 'I thought he was grabbing at you, that's why I hollered.'

'But she was hiding from him in the closet?'

'That's what it looked like. But she came out right through the door and ran off, with him giving chase up the stairs.'

'That's why I think it was a residual haunt. "Spirits",' she said, making double quotation marks with her fingers, 'can manipulate the environment.

They can open and close doors. Residual haunts don't need to. In her day the closet door was maybe open, and that's why it just looked like she passed directly through the physical one now. It wasn't closed then, so it wasn't closed to her in the replay.'

I frowned.

Sarah took my moment of confusion as a good point to tip the rest of the first bottle of wine into her glass. She didn't offer me any. That was fine. My stomach was soured from the incident and I wasn't sure I could keep it down. She leaned her hips against the worktop surface. 'Spirits-' again she gestured but this time in a wave that said she was doubtful '-if they do exist are supposed to be the life essence of a person who has died. They have left their bodies and are trapped in limbo between this plane and the afterlife. Sometimes they don't know they are dead, sometimes they do. They think, they can move around, they can, as I said, manipulate their environment. You've heard of *poltergeists*?'

'Yeah. The name translates as 'noisy ghosts', right?'

Sarah offered a wicked smile. 'You're not as daft as you sometimes make out, Jack.'

'Thanks,' I said. 'I think.'

She nudged me with her elbow, and it was only then I noticed how close we were standing. At least she wasn't holding the fright I'd given her against me. I smiled, and nuzzled in a fraction closer, and she didn't move away.

'I know you've never given this much credence before,' Sarah went on, 'and having given it little thought probably do what everyone else does. You lump all mention of ghosts in one pot. Because some stories you hear are a bit "out there" it's easy to say it's all a load of old rubbish, and to be fair I can't blame you. Some of the stuff people present as evidence is easily debunked, but because of that people with little knowledge of the subject think that means that everything has been debunked. That's not the case.'

'Nothing I've ever seen has convinced me,' I said, with the hidden caveat that my beliefs were being severely tested since moving into this house.

'Until now?'

'Well.' I squirmed, but got a half-inch closer. I could feel the warmth coming off her, got another waft of her clean soapy smell. 'I'm still not convinced. It could be my medication.' I briefly explained how the pills I was taking for my knee had stripped my stomach lining to a point my own digestive acids were attacking me. I had to take a second course of pills to halt the production of acids, but it was giving me added problems with indigestion, and disturbed sleep patterns.

'Some of the sceptics blame ghost sightings on sleep deprivation and sleep paralysis.' She was thoughtful. 'But then again they also blame sleep disorders for supposed alien abduction cases, Old Hag, the succubus and incubus phenomena and a whole host of other stuff. It's too easy a get out, if you ask me. It might explain seeing shadows out of the corner of your eye, we all have experiences of that, where you mistake a floating mote or even a natural shadow for something else. But the experience only lasts a split second. In my opinion it doesn't fit when you see something head-on.'

Nor did it explain how two figures could have run from behind me. To me that sounded more like a full on hallucination – maybe I was coming down with something, a bug or fever. I touched my forehead, checking my temperature and I was a little hot: but that could have been as much from my proximity to Sarah as anything. Apart from feeling queasy, I was otherwise OK.

'Other people blame the presence of high EMF and even infrasound for hauntings. They claim that some people are hyper-sensitive to naturally – or man-made - sources that cause them to feel creeped out, as if they're being watched, or even being touched.'

'Touched?'

'Yeah. Like a prickly sensation on the skin.'

I didn't comment. But I wondered if that was why I'd felt as if I'd brushed something electrical when swiping at the bigger figure.

'But I think it's a load of nonsense. OK, I'll admit that some people do have negative reactions to both, but it doesn't explain everything, does it?'

'I don't even know what EMF is,' I said.

'Electro magnetic fields.' Sarah was on a roll. 'They're all around us. Do you know what infrasound is?'

'Yeah, I think so. It's the inaudible sounds beyond our auditory range?'

'*Almost* correct.' Sarah laid her free hand on my forearm, and I felt a tingle. God, was she charged with EMF or what? 'It's low frequency sound cycling at less than twenty hertz per second. That's below the normal lower range of human hearing so we're usually unaware of it, but it can have an effect on our brain chemistry and even our bodies. Have you ever been near one of those Catherine wheels at a fireworks display? Sometimes you can feel the infrasound it makes in your gut, like a kind of buzzing sensation.'

'I've never had the pleasure.'

'Infrasound can be produced by various means,' Sarah went on. 'A ceiling fan oscillating back and forward as it spins can make it, or even constant traffic passing on a busy road.'

There was no fan in the basement, but I had to concede that when I was in the pantry I was beneath the road, so there could have been something in it.

Except, Sarah wasn't buying it. 'You need to be exposed to both for a prolonged period before you would be affected to the point of seeing hallucinations.'

'How do you know all this stuff? Did you study it at Uni?'

'Who said I went to university?'

'I just thought, well you being a manager at work. I thought you'd need degrees and stuff.'

'It's called aspiration, Jack. I went to Art College, and did get my degrees. One day I intend to be a graphic designer, but I also need to earn a living in the meantime. In this economy you have to take what you can, and I'm thankful of the job at BathCo, even if I'm not prepared to stay on the sales floor. I've worked hard, *earned* my management position. But I won't be staying: I hope to save enough money to set up a small business and go self-employed in a year or two.'

'Admirable,' I said. 'But it doesn't answer my original question.'

'The paranormal? I've just picked it up watching programmes on TV and reading and stuff. I've also been on a couple of investigations before, and have kept in touch with the event organizers on Facebook. They often post answers to people's questions about their paranormal experiences.'

'Experts are they?'

'Sarcasm doesn't suit you, Jack. How can you be an expert in something you can't hope to prove?' Sarah gave me a contrite smile. *Touché*. 'But they know as much, maybe even more, than any scientists, who won't even study the paranormal for fear of being ridiculed by their closed-minded colleagues. At least paranormal investigators are trying to find answers.'

'What's the point, if you can't hope to prove it?'

'It's the search for answers that's important.' Sarah finished her wine in one last gulp. 'There's an adage that to a believer no proof is necessary, to a sceptic no proof is possible. It's never going to be enough for them, but they keep asking: we seek "scientific" proof to hopefully shut the naysayers up.'

'So basically you're pandering to the sceptics?'

'They'll always find an alternative – usually equally disproven – explanation for anything we present, but while they're at it, I suppose it keeps them out of our hair. It lets us get on with seeking the truth.'

'Sounds counterproductive to me, like politicians who won't agree on any point.'

'I'm not bothered what they think.' She shrugged again. 'A sceptic once laughed at my belief in the paranormal. *When I hear the sound of hooves*, he said, *I think horse. I don't think unicorn.* So I said, *but wouldn't it be bloody great if it were a unicorn?* It must be awful going through life without a sense of wonder or imagination. Aw, what the hell! They can enjoy their boring lives with their rigid rules and regulations. I'm interested in the possibility of something else, something mysterious and *beyond* us. Aren't you, Jack? Haven't you ever reached for the unattainable and tried to grasp hold of it?'

Hell, yes.

And right then I was very tempted.

11

Night Terrors

I dreamed of Sarah that night. The dream was erotic, putting into action my waking desires, in a manner that Sarah hadn't yet done in reality, but had perhaps been hinting at. In my fantasy she was a coy temptress who led me by my hand to bed, and then when she was under the sheets she was a whore, willing to try *anything*. Hell, it had been many years since I'd experienced an adolescent wet dream, but even deep in sleep I was aware of my ejaculation and took pleasure from it. In some deep corner of my mind I felt guilty, but in another I wallowed in the titillation and longed for the dream to last the entire night. But as is the way of dreams, it changed and not for the better.

We were lying in bed together, and it didn't escape my notice that the room bore little resemblance to the empty space I actually slept in. This dream room was sumptuous, with a huge divan bed and satin sheets and drapes, candlelight and soft music. Sarah was urging me to make love to her again, and I was happy to comply. I squirmed on top, parting her thighs with mine as I prepared to enter her, all the while running my hands up the sides of her narrow waist from flaring hips to where

I could cup the outer swellings of her breasts. I peered down at her and her pouting lips were slightly open as she panted with desire. Her eyes were closed, and the dream so vivid I could see each individual eyelash tremble beneath my own exhalations. I leaned in and kissed her and her mouth was as soft as mist. She kissed back and our tongues entwined. That's when the minutiae altered. It was subtle at first, but my subconscious mind noticed the change and immediately a sense of dread flooded my guts. I pulled back from her mouth, but Sarah followed me, her lips now ranging over my face, and now they weren't so soft, but cold and slimy, and it was as if her need had changed from satisfying one hunger to another. In my mouth I tasted something unpleasant. I can't be sure if I honestly tasted rot or if my subconscious mind told me so. The rotten taste brought bitter saliva to my mouth, and I almost gagged. I tried again to pull away, but Sarah's hands were firmly around my head, digging sharp nails into my scalp. My ardour had fled, but Sarah wrapped her legs around my waist and bumped her pubis against mine, willing our conjoining to go on by force. I struggled to extricate myself, and now her pants had become grunts, then animalistic growls. The stench of decomposition wafted around us. Disgust flooded me, and I cried out, trying to break free.

Sarah's grip was unrelenting. She wouldn't let me go.

'*I want you, Jack,*' she said, and her voice was a hoarse rasp, the sound of something bestial.

Panic engulfed me, I tried to push her away, but she held on remorselessly. Her nails were now fisted in my hair, tearing at my scalp, her pubic mound battered at mine painfully, while her mouth now almost engulfed my face, sucking with enough tenacity to rip the flesh from my skull.

I fought her. I prized at her fingers, but she clenched all the more and I could feel clumps of my hair ripping loose. She squirmed her groin against mine, serpentine, and in my mind's eye her legs were far too long to be those of an ordinary woman but the long tentacle–like appendages of a creature from the deep. They wrapped around my legs, coiling, constricting, and I cried out in agony as my bones began to snap under the pressure. I tried to shriek again, but her mouth engulfed my entire head and I found I could barely breathe let alone scream.

Abruptly the scenario changed once more. I've no words to describe how I extricated myself from that horrible embrace, but in my mind I was now standing. Sarah was on her back on the bed. It wasn't a plush divan and satin sheets she lay on now but a patchy lawn, and sprinkled among the tufts of crushed grass were nuggets of glass and chunks of plastic and torn metal. She stank of smoke and

118

petrol fumes. Sarah was no longer naked, but dressed in a red dress and black boots. She lay peering up at me, dreamy eyed as she again spoke those same words. '*I want you, Jack.*'

'No, no, noooo…' I moaned.

'*I want you.*'

I backed away one slow step at a time. But caught in the nightmare it made no difference because I gained no space between us.

Sarah rose from the ground plank straight and was immediately before me.

No.

Not Sarah. As if it was wax under a blowtorch her face deformed, dripped, changed. Now her's was a face of another woman. A face that I knew. But even that familiarity was fleeting because in the next instant her flawless skin split, open wounds gouging furrows into her brow and cheeks, across her nose, and almost detaching her bottom lip so that it hung like a torn rag against her jaw. Blood flooded from the awful wounds. Her teeth were broken stumps, bloody and sharp. A hand came up, reaching for my face, and I watched yellowed bones erupt from the flesh of her forearm. Her skin began to discolour, purpling, then growing a mottled brownish green. Again the stench of rot shrouded me, and I turned away in disgust. The hand touched my face, and despite reason howling at me to run, I turned back to the woman. Her fingertips caressed my cheek. And deep inside me I felt a pang of longing, of regret, but again the sensation was fleeting, because she hooked in her nails, digging them deep into my face.

'*I want you,*' she croaked, and mucus dotted with blood poured from her throat.

'No!' I pushed at her, and my hands sank almost to the wrists in a chest that was now a puss-filled cavity. 'Get away from me! Get away!'

'*I…want…you.*'

I tore loose from her grip, falling backwards.

The woman advanced now, step by careful step. Her pretty dress was now a discoloured rag, her boots were falling apart, flopping round bony ankles. As she approached her flesh continued to blister, then peel from her bones, so that she bent to look down at me with a skeletal grin. Her throat was now a loose wattle of decomposing flesh, her windpipe exposed, pinholes growing in it as it rotted at an unnatural rate. No way was it possible that she could form words now, and yet she spoke in a sputtering exhalation. '*I…want…you.*'

When my thoughts had been consumed by eroticism some small part of me had recognised them as a dream, and yet now, as events had grown nightmarish I was fully engulfed, lost in this otherworld. Even in its absurdity I could not recognise its *wrongness*. To me a monstrous undead corpse stood over me, its clawed hands reaching to tear me apart, mouth opening so that it could bite down on my throat with its cracked and broken teeth. And yet something told me that something was not right. This was not how things had happened. This was a lie.

I found my voice, but now my scream was more of denial than horror.

The skeletal thing didn't hear me, or if it did it ignored me, because it continued to lean in, to clutch me again in its embrace. I knew if it got its bony fingers in my hair again that it would drag me down with it to whatever grave it had crawled from.

'No! Get away from me! Get away!' I slapped at its grasping hands. My arms were no barriers to it though and it reached for me, taking hold of my head in both its palms. The exposed metatarsals of its fingertips drove into my flesh, ground into my skull with unrelenting strength, even though the ligaments and tendons, and the muscles required to form a grip, had already disintegrated to rotting fragments, adding to the miasma of stench shrouding us. I squirmed in agony, feeling the sharp bones dig deep into my brain, but I couldn't get free. She lifted me from the ground as if I weighed nothing, pulling me close. The broken teeth chattered an inch from my face.

'*I want you to die.*'

Those words broke the spell...

…I kicked free of her hold, freefalling momentarily as my mind tried to make sense of the sudden detachment from the nightmare to wakefulness. My body spasmed, as if jolted by a stun gun, and I jerked upright to a seated position, my legs kicking as I attempted to propel myself further from the dream. My sleeping bag entangled me for a moment more, and in those last intangible moments of nightmare I thought that those serpentine coils had again been thrown around me. I screamed, fought free of the sleeping bag and fell naked on the bare floorboards.

It was cold, dusty and the rough boards chafed my skin. But I was glad to be back in the real world. I clawed my way a few feet across the floor, finally pushing the last clinging folds of my sleeping bag off my feet, and sat there shivering, bathed in cold sweat, my heart beating like jungle drums inside my head.

It was still dark outside, though some meagre light etched the windows against the blackness. I blinked, wiping at my face, half expecting to find the torn skin where the skeletal thing had sunk in its claws. Sweat ran in rivulets off me. I jerked my gaze around, seeking but dreading to find that the monster had followed me out of my nightmare into the here and now.

There was no lurking creature.

No shadows that moved with a will of their own either.

An unsteady laugh broke from me. In the echoing room it sounded tinny and not a little insane. I'd probably inhaled spores from that horrible fungus down in the basement, poisoning my dreams. I stopped laughing, pushing myself up to stand there, shaking not just from the sweat chilling on my skin, but from the adrenalin coursing through me, a lingering consequence of the nightmare.

That's all it was, I reassured myself. A fucking bad dream, a side effect of my bloody medication or hallucinogenic mold. Nothing about it was real. But I knew I was lying to myself. There had been some truth in those final words of the skeletal thing, except in the real world it hadn't been a woman who'd uttered them.

12

Show and Tell

Working at BathCo was as mundane as ever that week. Unlike my previous career as a teacher, it didn't challenge my mind to sell bathroom suites and plumbing accessories. The company I worked for wasn't even a genuine plumbing supplies store; we were simply a showroom, the baths and taps and stuff being delivered wholesale from overseas. It made me laugh when a customer came in looking for a replacement washer for a dripping tap and we couldn't even sell him one. Hell, I wasn't sure without checking on the internet what size of washer he actually required, and then had to send him elsewhere to buy one. We were the fast food equivalent of bathroom suite retailers. But that was the nature of the job, and I just had to get on with it. The only benefit I could see was the fact I got to spend more time with Sarah.

Following our weird weekend we barely touched on the subject of ghosts or anything else. Perhaps it was because she'd picked up on the less than subtle vibes I'd been sending her way after she'd posed that question about grasping for the unattainable. She wasn't normally the shy and retiring type, but she'd grown self conscious, began pushing at her scruffed up hair, pawed at the dust on her sweater, then made an excuse to get home. I offered to drive her, but she would have none of it, reminding me that I'd been drinking. The fact I'd barely touched my second glass and that she was responsible for downing the majority of the Pinot didn't make a difference. She headed off with the promise she'd see me at work on the Monday. She came through with the promise but had kept her distance since. Thankfully when we did meet at the coffee machine in the staff room she hadn't brushed me off, but she did blush a little. Handily by then I'd mostly expunged from memory the horrific nightmare I'd endured, but chose to recall the earlier dream that led to it, and what Sarah and I had got up to in that boudoir. I'd blushed too, and then we'd laughed and she'd put her hand on my forearm and allowed it to linger tantalizingly before she carried away her coffee. I smiled all day after that, despite the boredom of the job.

After I finished on Tuesday, I was away early enough to visit a local carpet fitter and arranged for floor coverings for the parlour, the adjacent living room and my bedroom, plus the one next to it for when the kids stopped over. My bank balance decided that the other rooms could wait. Wednesday evening saw me at a used furniture depot where I ordered in the basics; hell, I wasn't made of money. And I ordered two beds off the internet, a double for me, and bunks for the kids – some things just had to be new. I intended furnishing enough of the rooms to make them habitable, and decorating the other rooms as time went on.

Thursday evening saw me wielding paintbrushes and rollers as I tidied up the walls of the parlour. Maybe it was because my mind was otherwise engaged, but I seen neither hide nor hair of shadow people or anything else weird. By the time Friday came round I'd put the oddities to the back of my mind, and was beginning to feel more comfortable in my new home.

It was about seven o'clock on Friday evening when my mobile rang.

'Hello?'

'It's me.'

'Hi, Sarah.' I'd seen her name come up on the screen.

'Hi.' She fumbled with her phone by the sound of things. 'Ehm, I was just wondering what you were doing.'

'Watching Emmerdale.'

'I didn't take you for a soap opera fan.'

'I'm not. I still haven't got satellite set up. I just put the TV on and Emmerdale was playing.'

'You don't have to make excuses,' she said, and added a short laugh. 'I watch Emmerdale too.'

'You should come over and watch it with me.' I made the invite sound like I was joking, but hoped she'd take it up any way.

She laughed through her nose. But she didn't let me down. 'It's why I was ringing: to see if you were going to be in.'

'You want to come over?'

'Is it inconvenient?'

'No. It's just I expected you to be hitting the town. TGIF and all that.'

'When I was at yours on Sunday, there was something I wanted to show you. I forgot because of all the excitement. I think you need to see it…'

I recalled her delving in her handbag just before I'd gone at the wall with my hammer. I too had forgotten until now.

'Want me to pick you up?'

'No, it's OK. My dad will drop me off.'

'See you soon then.'

'Yeah, I'll pick up some nibbles on the way there.'

As soon as she hung up, I made a quick scout around the room, tidying as I went, moving my dirty dinner plate to the kitchen, hiding my discarded work shoes in the next room. I hit the bathroom, washed, shaved and brushed my teeth. Gave myself a squirt of aftershave endorsed by a world famous footballer.

As I exited the bathroom I sensed eyes on me, and I juddered to a halt. That prickling sensation was back, but now centred on the back of my head. The small hairs crept on my neck.

It was early evening, but not dark enough that I'd turned on the lights. There was still enough to see by coming in through the stained glass window above the bathroom door. Because of the dominance of red glass in the pattern the landing above was bathed in dim pink. I stared at it, tracing the pattern the reflected light made on the wall, and was again sure I could make out a familiar face in it. The face was watching me.

'No,' I snapped. 'You're not real. If you are, then why didn't you come when I begged you to?'

The face stared, unmoved by my demand.

I screwed my eyelids tight, rubbed my hands over my face. When I opened my lids spots of colour danced across my vision. The image of the face was broken and I used the chance to turn away, discount it as a figment of an over-active imagination, telling myself that I was only seeing that face because of that hellish nightmare I'd experienced.

As I went down to the ground floor, I was sure those glaring eyes observed me the entire way, but I stubbornly refused to check.

EMF, I convinced myself. The wiring in the old house was ancient. It was probably unshielded and was leaking energy into the halls. Maybe I suffered that hypersensitivity-thingee that Sarah told me about and, fuelled by the recent nightmare, I'd conjured a hallucination. Maybe, I concluded with a disparaging laugh, I was simply going nuts.

The knocker sounded.

Sarah had arrived.

It was the distraction I needed.

My walk along the hall was rushed. I pulled open the front door, opened my mouth in greeting.

It wasn't Sarah.

There was nobody there.

First there were the visual hallucinations and now auditory ones? I genuinely was going squirrel shit.

There was another knock, but this time I caught its source. Bloody TV. A quick glance showed me some character called Zack knocking in fence posts with a hammer, while a pretty Scots woman in a boiler suit jabbered in his ear.

There were more noises, but now that I was thinking clearer, I understood they were coming from next door. Someone was finishing late at the insurance office. I poked my head out the front door and saw a woman locking the front door. She was dressed in a tabard and was carrying cleaning products in a bucket. She noticed me watching and raised her chin in greeting. I gave her a wave, and a smile. She walked away without reciprocation: that's all the attention from her I could expect. I thought about calling her back and asking if she'd ever experienced anything unusual in the adjacent building. But I didn't want her to think I was crazy, so didn't.

While I was at the front door, a car pulled to the kerb. It was a late model Citroën Xsara Picasso, pale blue. The kind of car an older man drives. Sarah was sitting in the front passenger seat, but I couldn't make much out of her father, but for his thick-fingered hands on the steering wheel. Sarah turned to speak to him, and then opened the door. 'Thanks, Dad. See you later,' she said by way of goodbye. I expected him to lean down and check me out, but he didn't. Probably because Sarah hadn't told him I was her boyfriend. Sadly I was *just* a workmate, and an underling at that. Her father waited for a gap in the traffic and pulled out. I waved, being sociable, in case he did take a glimpse back in his mirrors.

'You're keen,' Sarah said as she walked up the short path.

'Eh?'

'Meeting me at the door like this.'

'I just wanted to check what nibbles you'd brought,' I assured her. "You only get in if they're to my satisfaction.'

She held up a carrier bag. 'Hope you like chocolate? Three bars for a pound at the petrol station. I got six.'

'Great.'

'Don't worry, I've got other stuff too.'

'Then you may enter,' I said, in a plumby way and sweep of my arm.

She was carrying a laptop computer under her other arm. She was dressed in black jeans, boots and a grey sweater. Her hair was pulled into a ponytail and she wore only a touch of makeup. I got a waft of warm air as she stepped close and handed off the bag; it had that same aroma of soap from before. There was something about the simplicity of her dress, make-up and perfume that worked for me.

Ushering her in, I closed the door and followed her to the parlour. Emmerdale had finished and Coronation Street was just coming on. I turned down the volume. Placed down the bag of goodies, then held up a hand. 'Before we get started, there's something I'd like to show you.'

'It isn't down in the basement again?'

'No. Here, I'll show you.'

She put down her laptop, then followed along the hall to the stairs.

'This isn't some devious ploy to get me to your bedroom I hope?' Sarah said the words like she meant them, but the cock of her hip hinted otherwise. 'Want to show me your etchings?'

'No. Of course not.' I too flavoured my tone with the suggestion that I would take her up on the offer if she wanted to.

Sarah laughed and it broke the moment. 'My mum always warned me about guys like you.'

I forced out a chuckle. 'I thought women liked their men to be bad boys?'

'Not all of us: I prefer dorky geeks. Go on you silly beggar. What do you want to show me?' She pushed me up the stairs ahead of her.

Now that I was heading for the half-landing I suddenly felt stupid. What the hell had I been thinking bringing this up? It wasn't as if the face would be familiar to Sarah. Working hard I tried to come up with a feasible excuse for turning back. But by then it was too late. Stopping outside the bathroom, I checked the wall on the landing to the first floor. While I'd been distracted by the noises and Sarah's arrival, the night had settled further in, and the pink glow wasn't as evident now. I searched but I could no longer distinguish a face in the faded pattern on the wall. 'Hmmm,' I said.

'What?' Sarah had stopped alongside me, obviously wondering why I'd paused.

'It was just something I noticed before. But it isn't visible now. Here…turn round. Did you notice the stained glass window when last you were here.'

'Yeah. Nice.'

'The coloured glass: is it just a random pattern to you, or is it meant to signify something?'

Sarah peered up at it. 'Looks vaguely geometric.'

'You don't see any faces in it?'

'Faces? No. Can you?'

When I studied it now, my answer had to be no.

'Maybe it just depends on how the light is shining through it,' I suggested. 'I thought that I saw a face earlier.'

'In the window?'

'In the light it cast on the wall over there.' I thumbed towards the upper landing. 'Aah, it's nothing. Probably just matrixing.'

'Ooh, *matrixing*? Get you, Jack Newman: Paranormal Investigator. You do know some of the terminology we use.' Sarah looked pleased. Maybe she thought I'd been studying, but it was a term I'd already been familiar with. She gestured at the window. 'We also call it *pareidolia*, but that's a catchall phrase. It's where a vague or random stimulus is perceived as significant, but includes both images and sounds. Actually, both terms are slightly misused, because the actual term is *apophenia*.'

I held up a hand. 'You're losing me now, Professor Van Helsing.'

She hip-bumped me.

'Stick to matrixing, numbskull,' she said.

We went downstairs, and part way down I hip-bumped her in return. Not enough to send her sprawling, but enough that she grabbed at my hand to steady herself. We laughed together, and didn't let go until we were at the bottom of the stairs, and only then reluctantly. At least, for me it was.

'Come on.' Sarah sped for the parlour. 'It's my turn to show you something interesting. And you might want to keep the subject of matrixing in mind, and try to tell me that's what you're experiencing then.'

She set up her laptop, and fiddled in a dongle device so she could access the internet. It was slow to load but she brought up a video-sharing site. She tapped the legend "SHADOW PEOPLE" into the search bar and hit the return key.

Hands fisted on my hips, I peered at the screen as it loaded. 'You do realise that half the crap on there is faked?'

'More than half, nearer ninety-five per cent,' Sarah said. 'But not all of it. I know where to look, and which uploads are from a reputable source. You can usually tell when the tag line says something like "genuine", "one hundred per cent", or "real". Generally they aren't. But I know this name here, it belongs to a reputable parapsychologist who's been conducting a study of the phenomenon, and this is what I wanted to show you.'

She clicked on a link in the sidebar and the screen shifted so that the video was now centred at the top.

The video buffered slowly, but within ten seconds it began to play.

'The connection's a bit crappy,' Sarah scowled, 'but it should do for now. This is a compendium of some of the shadow people that have been caught on tape.'

I viewed various snatches of recordings. Some of them were hard to make out, having been filmed on infrared cameras in the dark. Others had been caught on mobile phones and were grainy. Having my sceptical head firmly screwed on I could dismiss most of the images as misidentification, shadows from exterior sources, and even matrixing. But then there were others.

'Jesus!'

'Impressed?'

'Unless that's a fake it's pretty undeniable,' I said.

I'd just viewed a scene where some paranormal investigators were standing in a tunnel, filmed by a locked-off camera on a tripod. The investigators, two men and a woman, were in clear shot, and easily definable down to their individual clothing and hairstyles. The IR light cast their shadows beyond them, and they too were obvious. What happened next was dramatic, but only because whatever had cast the shadow that moved between them and the camera must also have been between them. But nothing tangible did move into that space. Yet a full human figure walked from right to left, pitch black and solid, blocking each investigator out as it moved past them. The figure looked male, and I could make out the sharp delineation of its silhouette, but that was all. Details should have been crystal clear if it had been a living person. It also moved in a way that was in contravention to the norm. It was as if it stuttered at a very fast rate. In and of itself, the scene – a few seconds at most – was unusual to say the least. And then it turned stranger. Before the figure moved out of left frame it halted and turned to peer at the trio of humans beyond it. And in that instant of turning it blinked out of existence. Just as the shadow figure in my parlour had that time.

'Play that again.'

Sarah held up a cautioning hand. 'Hang on, there are more. I'll go back through them all in a minute, but you should see the next ones. If you were impressed by that one…'

The next scene was shot by a CCTV security system. It was filmed in broad daylight, in colour this time. The camera was positioned on a residential street, attached to the front wall of a house so that the owner could view those approaching the front door and the car parked on their drive. But the shot was wide enough that it also encompassed part of the roadway outside, the opposite pavement and a grassy meadow. To the extreme left there was a cross street on which traffic moved. A young couple walked arm in arm on the opposite side, heading for the busier road.

'There!' Sarah became animated, pointing at the screen. 'Did you see it?'

I thought I'd caught a flash of grey, but that was all – I was too busy watching the young couple amble by.

'Don't worry. The scene is repeated in slow motion,' Sarah said. I hunkered closer to the screen. As she'd promised the same clip came on again, slowed by about five times. And this time I did see it.

A single shadow figure moved along the pavement behind the couple, as if following them, its head cocking to and fro as if enthralled by them. At one point it moved off the pavement and part way across the street, before it zigzagged after them. It flickered in and out, solid one instant then vaporous the next.

'Watch here.' Sarah indicated the bottom of the shot, where the car was parked on the drive. Another vague shadow figure materialised as if out of the very atmosphere, and came up the path. It stood for a moment directly below the camera, its head tilted up at the lens as if aware of the camera's scrutiny, then it turned and was gone. A few seconds later it reappeared, standing at the rear of the parked car, before it too moved off, crossing the street and following in the path of the first.

'And you're positive this isn't CGI, Sarah?'

'I can't attest to its authenticity, but it looks real to me. But if it were computer graphics, it would be evident. The parapsychologist has had the film checked by experts who confirm that the film is original and hasn't been tampered with.'

I just hunkered there, fuddled.

'Let me see those last few clips again.'

Sarah worked the computer and I watched in silence this time.

After the second run through Sarah paused the movie clip. 'Well?'

'I don't know what to say. The problem is they *could* be fakes.'

'Spoken like a true sceptic,' she said.

'You know what I'm getting at. All those "found-footage" movies are so popular now. "The Blair Witch Project", "Paranormal Activity". People watch them and then decide to make their own videos for the fun of it.'

'I just told you, the last one was verified by specialists.'

'But how do we know that? We have to take the word of this parapsychologist?'

'She's renowned in her field,' Sarah iterated. 'She isn't going to put her name to anything that can't be verified. She'd be ridiculed by her peers if she did. I'm not talking about someone who has done a correspondence course here, Jack. Doctor Kiera Ross is from the Consciousness and Transpersonal Psychology Research Unit based at Liverpool John Moores University. She first began studying the shadow people phenomenon as part of a wider study into the effects of sleep deprivation and sleep paralysis, and has written a thesis on both. But then she grew aware that there was more to the subject than she could easily explain away: especially when she began receiving video and photographic evidence. Dreams don't cast shadows in the real world.'

'If I hadn't seen them with my own eyes…'

I caught myself.

'So they are the same as what you've witnessed?' Sarah stood up, peered down at me.

'The second video was different,' I explained. 'Those figures were mistier. The shadows I saw were more like that one in the tunnel in the first vid.'

'Don't forget that the street view was filmed in daylight. They would appear less sharp, fainter in colour. The first was shot in darkness with a special camera. There might even be some possibility of artefacts adding to the depth of shade in the first.'

'The ones I've seen have been full black, in daytime, too.'

'It was dark in the basement,' Sarah began. 'The one you saw here in the parlour was in daylight.'

'So was the first one.' I stood up and eyed her. Trying not to blink.

'You saw another? You didn't tell me.'

'It was the first time we came here. Upstairs, near my bedroom.'

'You saw a shadow figure when we came to view the property? Why didn't you say anything?'

'You'd have tried to talk me out of taking the place if I had.'

'Not necessarily, I'm interested, remember.'

Sadly she meant she was interested in paranormal stuff, not in me per se.

Gesturing at the now idle computer, I said, 'You thought those shadows I witnessed in the basement were…what did you call it, a residual haunt? But you said that it was just like a moment in time replayed over and over, the ghosts were just projected images not real. Those shadow people on the video looked as if they were aware of the living people. They were watching them, following them. They looked real enough.'

'That's an entirely different subject.' Sarah went to the bag of nibbles and hauled out some Dairy Milk. She was shivering and I didn't think it was from low blood sugar. 'Let's sit down and talk about it. I think this calls for chocolate, don't you?'

We sat. I'd only the one settee for now, so it meant we were side-by-side, but we turned so that we could converse without getting stiff necks. Our knees were almost touching. Sarah handed me a bar of chocolate, and I broke chunks off, allowing them to melt slowly in my mouth. She chewed hers, thinking hard as she ordered in her mind what she knew on the subject. Finally, she gestured at the laptop.

'Dr Ross hasn't published her findings on the shadow people phenomenon yet, but there are plenty of others who have. Some of them are a bit "out there" but hey! Who's to say they're wrong?'

Not me. I'd seen them. But I still hadn't a clue what the hell I'd borne witness to.

'Some people call them ghosts,' Sarah went on. 'But I've already established that there are different types of ghost, the most common being residuals. There are spirits, and there are other types too: poltergeists, crisis apparitions, and harbingers. Although they share similarities the term "ghost" isn't an adequate description of what the shadow people are.'

'What's the most common theory?'

'Hang on. I'll get to that. There are even different types of shadow figure, so I think it's best we separate them, and try to come up with which one you've been seeing.'

The chocolate was silky in my mouth, but flavourless. I popped in another chunk, just going through the motions as I listened to Sarah.

'The sceptics will have it that they're simply figments of an over-active imagination. We're seeing things.' She laughed. 'But as I said, you can't photograph or film your dreams. So they say that we are misidentifying natural phenomena, shadow play caused by passing headlights and such.' The very theory I'd put down my first sightings to. 'Most ghosts that are witnessed tend to be vaporous, usually white or greyish, and even if they are described as transparent they are often sharp enough to define their features, their clothing *etcetera*. Some people say that the shadow people are demonic, or other negative spirit entities, and it usually depends on their religion - Catholics see demons, Moslems see Djinn – and base their theories on the dogma they've been raised on.

'Have you heard of out of body experiences?'

'Yeah,' I said. 'You're talking about astral projection?'

Sarah smiled. I wasn't as ignorant at this stuff as I'd originally made out. 'The very thing,' she said. 'There's a theory that we're witnessing the astral projections of other people who are undergoing an out of the body experience. Some people say they are aliens, extra-terrestrial visitors using some kind of cloaking technology-' she laughed at that whacky explanation '-while others have surmised that they are visitors from our future, time travellers who are observing us going about our day to day business in our timeline. Some people have even hypothesized that they are guardian angels.'

'What do you believe?'

'I don't think it's any of those,' Sarah replied, and offered a conspiratorial wink. 'But I'll get to my theory in a minute. First we have to look at what you've seen and try to decide what type of shadow figure we're dealing with.'

'I told you already. They are human-shaped, full black. They look solid, with clearly defined edges. But when they turn side-on they disappear, almost as if they are only two dimensional.'

'They sound very similar to the video we watched of that investigation in the tunnel.'

I nodded. They shared some characteristics with the others we'd seen in the street view, but were also different. My shadows didn't move at high speed, except for when they disappeared.

'There are various manifestations that have been recorded. Some look like black smoke, or oily masses, and tend to be without shape, but they can morph into something resembling a human being. They tend to be two dimensional, often to be seen following the contours of a wall or some other feature; when they leave the object they tend to turn three-D then, but are usually seen to take on a spherical formation. Most paranormal investigators believe these to be the manifestation of some form of negative energy. Then you get the flickerers; like in the video, where the entity is shadowy, but seen as if you're looking through one of those old zoetrope devices – you know that cylinder thing with slits in the side, and a sequence of pictures on the inner surface? When the cylinder spins it gives the illusion that the sequential pictures are moving.' I had seen them before, so nodded, and Sarah went on. 'You have Hat Man. Basically, he's a shadow man that is often seen wearing a hat.'

'Mine wasn't.'

'No,' she said, and looked ready to tell me more about this Hat Man, but decided it wasn't important. 'You have shadow figures described as having glowing red eyes, but you already said yours were featureless. Can I ask you something?'

'Go ahead.'

'When you saw the shadow man, what did you feel?'

'It has been different each time.' I moved an inch or two closer to her. 'First time I was surprised, confused. Second time, in here, I was a bit freaked out because of what had just happened with the door.' I hadn't told her about that, and I noticed her eyes widening. 'In the basement I was more frightened for you.'

'You had no sense of foreboding, an uneasiness?'

'Well, yeah. I suppose I did. But it was as much through not knowing what I was looking at as anything else.'

'The reason I ask,' Sarah said, 'is because most people who see them describe them as being malignant in nature, they sense that the shadow has evil intent towards them.'

I said nothing.

'You know what I don't get?' Sarah asked.

'What?'

'My phone being moved by unseen hands. Your story about the dumbwaiter platform going up and down by itself. And now…what's this about a door?'

I briefly narrated my escapades with the jammed door, and how it had led to my second sighting of the shadow man. I was even bold enough to suggest that I heard it laughing at me as it held the door shut, denying me exit, though I didn't mention that it then went for my throat. 'It was as if it was taking the piss,' I added.

'That's what bothers me most.' Sarah placed a hand on my knee and leaned in. Her breath tickled my cheek. She was trembling, and so was I. 'As far as I know, that kind of phenomena hasn't been recorded coinciding with shadow people sightings before. It's different again…'

'Trust me to have a bloody unique kind of ghost living in my house.' I said it for a laugh, but Sarah was a little awestruck by the idea. Her mouth hung open, her bottom lip pulsating slightly.

'You said you saw something else, Jack. Earlier. You said you saw a face on the landing. You put it down to matrixing, but there's more to it than that, isn't there? You recognised it?'

'No,' I said. 'It was just a faint image in the light shining through the window. It was nothing. Nobody.'

But I was lying.

13

Collision

'The house isn't ready for the kids yet. If you hang on a few more days I should have their bunk beds set up. They can come over then.'

It was the Thursday following Sarah's visit, and I was standing on the front step of my marital home, and wasn't going to get any further inside. Catriona, my estranged wife, stood with her arms tightly crossed beneath her breasts. She wasn't a big woman, but she somehow managed to fill the entire doorway, barring entrance. She was wearing a bathrobe over pyjamas even though it was after mid-day, and the sour grimace she usually aimed at me these days.

'You promised the kids they could come and stay a few nights, and that was a fortnight ago,' Catriona reminded me. 'Now you're going to let them down?'

'Their beds haven't arrived yet. You want them to sleep on the bare floorboards?' I was exaggerating. The carpet fitters had been and decked out the spare room on Monday. Also, I'd had a message to say the bunk beds would be with me by tomorrow. It wasn't that I didn't want my children to come over; just that I wasn't sure it would be the right thing to do. Not with all that had been happening recently.

'You could give them your bed for the weekend.'

My double bed was also due to be delivered. 'Where am I meant to sleep?'

'Ha! Are you telling me that you're uncomfortable on the floor in your sleeping bag? You've slept like that the first few weeks you've been there, I bet.' Catriona has a way of being sarcastic that has none of the fun that Sarah manages. 'I'll just tell them you aren't interested, shall I? What's wrong, Jack? Someone else staying that you don't want them to see?'

'There's only me,' I said, and tried not to sound as bitchy as she did. Maybe my tone sounded more disappointed than intended.

'Doesn't surprise me, really. I don't know why I put up with you for as long as I did.' She lifted her nose and sniffed, as if I was something nasty to be wiped off the sole of her slipper.

'You didn't though, did you?' I reminded her, giving in to base instinct. 'And while we're on the subject, it's you who's probably hiding someone in your bed from them. The way you hid Mark from me.'

Mark Wilson used to be my best friend. But after I caught him in bed with my wife our friendship had soured. If I'd been a fighter I would have given him a hiding, but I wasn't. I hadn't even given him a mouthful; I'd just turned away and walked out of the bedroom, as equally betrayed by them both. Mark had shown enough grace in not trying to apologise for screwing my wife, and had sneaked out. He never called after that, unless it was to Catriona when I was at work. I'd never seen the son of a bitch since then, and didn't want to now. 'Is he still sniffing around or have you moved on to another of my old friends?'

'Who I choose to sleep with is my business,' Catriona said. 'We're divorcing, remember, you don't have a say in it any more.'

I wanted to respond that who I slept with was my *fucking* business too, but what was the point? I was attracted to Sarah, and was keen to have her as my lover, attested to by the dream I'd had of her before it turned nasty. But as yet, apart from a little flirting, our relationship hadn't progressed beyond handholding and the occasional touch of knees. Even then, I was aware that I was possibly reading more into those small intimacies than Sarah was.

I shook my head. I had no desire to argue and just wanted to get away. 'Look, I'll make it up to them. I'll still come and get them on Saturday and take them out for the day. But I'll have to bring them home before evening.'

'I was planning on going out on Saturday night. You said you'd have them all weekend.'

'I'll get them again Sunday morning,' I said.

'And what am I supposed to do about my plans?'

'It can't be helped. You'll have to cancel. Stay in and watch the X-Factor like everyone else.'

'Bastard,' she snapped. 'You always were a selfish prick. I should have known what you were like when you first started obsessing about-'

'Don't fucking start on about that again,' I growled.

'Fuck off,' she said and slammed the door in my face.

Happy families.

I stamped my way back to my Volvo. Slammed the door, trying to make it louder than her parting shot. I scrabbled to get the key in the ignition and missed. I swore, then commanded myself to get a grip. I exhaled, long and hard, venting my anger. I peeped out of the window and saw my daughter watching from behind the curtains in her bedroom. Forcing a smile on my face, I waved. Gemma offered me the same kind of tight-lipped scowl her mother was good at and disappeared from view. I felt like a piece of shit. Gemma and Jake had both been excited about coming to stay with me at the weekend, and I had promised them a great time. But that was before all the stuff I'd learned about shadow people. I was afraid that an entity capable of moving a phone unseen from one room to another, or indeed locking a grown man in a room, might be capable of hurting a child. No way was I prepared to subject either of my kids to harm – not physical harm at any rate. Gemma was obviously upset – the reason she'd scowled at me – and was likely now curled up on her bed sobbing her heart out. Jake had taken the news that I had to break my promise of a stay with stoic resolve, but that had only been on the surface. He too had quickly scuttled off to hide in his room, and I bet that he too was weeping.

Jack, you are a bastard.

Was I was being too cautious? Hell, maybe there was nothing to the strange incidents I'd witnessed, except for a trick of the eyes, a poorly maintained home, and a willingness to please a woman I was attracted to. Should I go back, cap in hand and tell Catriona I'd take the kids for the weekend after all?

Why? So she could go out on the town with another man? Not fucking likely!

I started the engine and peeled out at speed.

Catriona called me selfish. Well, to hell with her. She could stop in and watch TV like I had to. She – I convinced myself – was the one in the wrong, the way she'd been in the wrong when wrapping her legs around Mark's waist. It wasn't me being selfish then, was it? If I didn't like the fact my wife, the mother of my children, was bonking with my best mate, and that made me selfish, then fuck it. I was selfish, and justifiably so.

You need to get a grip, Jack.

Fuck, I needed to get a grip of Catriona's throat and throttle some fucking respect out of her!

I was driving like something demented. Far too wildly for those streets and the time of day. I spun around one corner, the back end of the Volvo almost hitting a parked car in the opposite lane. It didn't stop me from putting down my foot and pushing the car harder along the road. I punched the steering wheel. It hurt, so I slapped it instead. That hurt too, my abraded palm not having fully healed yet. I swore again.

Frigging Catriona would never be pleased. She'd got the house, the kids, everything in our marital home, and more than half our savings. I was going to be paying child maintenance until Gemma and Jake were grown adults. Even though she was the one who'd done wrong, it wasn't enough for her. Now she wanted me to take the kids so she could go trawling for sex! 'Who's the fucking selfish bastard, *bitch*?'

Fifty feet ahead of me a woman stepped off the pavement between two parked cars, as if readying to cross. She was a blur of red.

It hadn't occurred to me that I was crying.

I was so angry with Catriona that tears were misting my eyes, and as I batted them away, that was when I saw that the woman had continued out into the road. Hearing the roar of my engine, or maybe my scream of fury aimed at my estranged wife, she'd turned to face the oncoming vehicle. The car's bonnet was now less than thirty feet from her. If she lunged back the way she'd come, she'd be safe. But she didn't. She stood there, trapped in indecision.

And yet, that wasn't it.

She lifted her head and looked me dead in the eye.

I hit the brakes, hollering, and wanted to avert my attention from the inevitable. But I couldn't. It was as if her accusing gaze held mine in an unrelenting vice. I couldn't look away, and in that moment I knew that face, and my yell of warning morphed to one of horror.

The car hit her at the tops of her thighs, rucking up her red dress, and the impact went through the structure of the car as a deep shudder. She was catapulted on to the bonnet, her face slammed the windscreen, and though it couldn't have been for more than a split second, her gaze still bore into mine. Then she hurtled up and over, her limbs floppy, windmilling wildly as she was pitched over the roof, and onto the road behind me. I fought hard to keep a grip on the wheel, the car slewing, and I felt the collisions as the back end side-swiped a parked vehicle on either side before coming to a screeching, juddering stop.

I knew that this couldn't be happening.

How could it?

But I still leapt out of my seat, almost falling out the door, as I screamed for her. Begging her to be all right.

But how could she be?

I'd already killed my first love Naomi Woodall more than ten years ago.

14

Lies and Oxymorons

'Have you drunk any alcohol today, sir?'

'Uh, no. Nothing. I'm on my lunch break from work, just been to see my kids…'

I was standing on the pavement opposite my parked car. It had been moved out of the carriageway by one of the police officers that'd turned up following my call. It was drizzling with rain, but I wasn't offered the dry comfort of a seat in their car – but perhaps I should have been thankful for that.

The officer speaking with me held up a breathalyser device and explained that it was procedure to procure a specimen of my breath because of the damage I'd caused to the other vehicles.

'I swerved to miss a dog,' I lied. 'It just ran out without warning.'

Whether he believed me or not, he didn't let on. He was a guy in his mid-forties, stocky, looking constricted by his stab-proof vest. He wore a hangdog expression, but his eyes were feral, a pit bull straining at the leash. He made it clear to me that it was an offence to fail to give a specimen of my breath, and that I could be arrested if I refused to do so. He rattled out some other procedural statements, but to be honest I was too shaken to take any of it in. He fixed a white tube to the device, and offered me the job of pulling off a plastic coating: for my hygiene, he told me. He explained what an array of lights on the device meant, before warning me that if the lights turned red it would be off to the nick for me.

'Seal the end of the tube with your lips, then blow until I tell you to stop.'

I sucked in a couple of deep inhalations, then leaned to the tube. I puckered and blew.

'Keep going, keep going, keep going…' the cop's words blended one into the next as he watched the flickering lights on the device.

They didn't progress past green.

'OK, sir, you can stop now.' The policeman took the device, pressed a couple of buttons, then gave a little nod. He held out the breathalyser, his eyes still glaring, and I feared the worst. 'You've passed.'

'I haven't had a drink for days,' I reiterated, even though it was obvious to the policeman.

'Did you strike the dog, sir?'

'No. I missed it.'

'Must have run off,' said the cop, sounding disinterested now. Both officers had already checked the front of my car for damage and found none. He looked across at his colleague who was busy noting details of the cars I'd hit on some sort of pad.

'We'll make an effort to contact the owners of those vehicles and pass on your details,' the cop explained, 'so this can be sorted via your respective insurance companies.'

He then asked me for my name, address, date of birth and a bunch of other things relating to my car. He transferred those details to a pad identical to the one his colleague worked on. He handed me the form, which turned out to be a HO/RT 1. 'This is a producer, sir. It requires you to produce the documents listed upon it at a police station within seven days of midnight tonight. If you fail to produce those documents, you will be committing an offence. Do you understand?'

I looked at the form without seeing it and nodded dumbly.

The cop then moved away a few feet, indiscreetly speaking into his radio. He was running a check on my details. His colleague walked over, holding some papers he'd pulled from his pad. I was known to them, but didn't have any outstanding warrants or unpaid fines. They didn't need to tell me as much, and only shared a nod as they received confirmation from their control room.

The second copper, a younger man, who had a southern accent, handed me copies of the forms he'd filled in. 'You'll probably need those details for your insurance.'

That was it.

Nothing else to be concerned with, the police officers returned to their car. They didn't drive off; they sat filling in their notebooks. They were possibly relieved that they hadn't earned a massive pile of paperwork with this collision. But who knew? It was highly likely they had a mass of reports to get on with that I'd never see. The stocky policeman glanced up and noted that I hadn't yet moved from the pavement.

I was studying the road where I was positive there should have been a body.

It was clear, but for the greasy rain. No corpse. No blood. No nothing.

When I'd hurtled from my car after the collision, I was positive I'd find Naomi lying crumpled on the road. If not Naomi – how could it possibly be her? – then some other woman bearing a passing resemblance to my old girlfriend, dressed in a similar red dress and black boots. But there was nobody there. No *body*.

I couldn't understand how it was possible. I'd felt the impact, watched the woman's face smash against the windscreen, before she was catapulted over the roof. Horrified, I'd widened my search, checking behind the parked cars on both sides, even in the adjacent gardens along the route. Finding no sign of the woman, I'd returned to my car. Both rear wings were scratched and dented from hitting the parked vehicles, but on the front there wasn't as much as a scuff. Nothing on the windscreen or roof either. It made no sense. What disturbed me most was that I'd hoped to find a stranger lying in the road, because the alternative was sheer madness. How could I have hit some one who'd simply disappeared?

I was shivering. Shock had forced bile from my stomach, and it burned my throat. I had no idea what to do, and would have jumped in my car and sped off, if I hadn't noticed an elderly lady watching me from a bedroom window. No way I could make off, so I'd brought out my mobile and phoned the police, saying only I'd had an accident. It seemed like forever before they'd arrived on scene, and throughout the wait my thoughts had tumbled wildly as I tried to make sense of what had gone on.

One thing I couldn't tell the police was that I'd just run down my ex girlfriend, who had already died years ago. If I had they'd have had me back at the police station for certain. I could expect tests for drug misuse and maybe even a visit from a doctor. Swerving to miss a stray dog was a feasible enough excuse, though I'm not sure I was believed.

Now, standing in the road like that, I might just pique the suspicions of the officers and bring them back out of their vehicle. I gave the stocky cop a short wave, then hurried to my car. The young cop had left the keys in the ignition.

I drove off carefully, got a few streets away, then parked alongside some metal railings at the boundary of a park. Empty wrappers from a nearby take-away were caught in the undergrowth next to the fence. My Volvo was under some overhanging tree branches. Drops of rain made a drumroll on the roof. Clenching the steering wheel, I sat; but my mind was a blank. I'm not sure how long I sat there, or when or how I made it back to work. My first conscious memory afterwards is of being hailed by my boss, Daniel Graham, and he made a sharp gesture towards his office. I'd already done so for the cops, now it was time for me to pucker up and blow for him.

Still numb, I walked in the office and he closed the door behind me. The office was small, with barely room for his chair and desk. He pushed by me, sat down. I stood in front of him, my back touching the wall, thighs nudging the desk. I felt trapped.

'What time do you call this?' Daniel asked without preamble.

Honestly, I had no idea. Daniel made a show of looking at his watch. 'Three forty,' he informed me.

I should have been back at work for one thirty.

I didn't say a thing. My eyes darted for the door, for a way out.

'Nothing to say for yourself, Jack?'

I mumbled something.

'What? I can't hear you.'

'I said I was in a car smash.' My voice was barely audible.

Daniel frowned, checked me up and down. His gaze settled on my haunted eyes. My proclamation had thrown him for a moment.

'Are you hurt?'

'I'm…I'm OK.'

'Was anyone else hurt?'

Only Naomi.

Of course, I couldn't tell him that. 'No.' I pictured a mangy dog running off between the parked cars. 'I hit a couple of cars. My Volvo's a bit banged up.'

'Hell! At least you're all right.' His tone didn't match his sentiment. 'What happened?'

I related the same lies I'd told the police.

'Some pet owners are irresponsible, letting them run around like that,' Daniel said. 'They should be fined or something.'

'The dog ran off, no way of tracing it or the owner.' I had no desire to speak with my boss, certainly no intention of doing so for longer than I had to. 'I had to wait for the police to come because of the damage to the other cars.'

Suddenly Daniel clicked back into his managerial role again. He put on his caring face. 'You should have called and let me know what was going on. I was worried about you.'

Sure he was.

'I was too shocked. I…I wasn't thinking straight. I thought I'd be arrested or something.' The desk was digging into my legs. I adjusted my body. I wondered if he could feel my trembling emanating through the furniture.

'You didn't have a drink or anything?'

What was this? Trying to catch me out? 'I'm not allowed to drink on my lunch break,' I reminded him.

He shrugged as if he didn't care about rules. 'Some of the other guys have a couple of pints with their pub lunches.'

'I don't.'

'I'm not accusing you of anything, Jack. But it remains to be said that you're late back by -' he checked his watch '- two and a quarter hours. I'm going to have to dock the time from your wages.'

I could have argued that I'd been back for ten minutes or more, but no way was I going to win. 'I understand.'

'Or you can make up the time. We're doing stock taking this Saturday evening, you could stop back…'

I shook my head, and a lie jumped easily enough to my lips. 'I've got my kids on Saturday evening. I'm off all weekend remember.'

Daniel snorted. He made it sound as if he was offering a lifeline, but he wasn't. He didn't have children, or a demanding ex wife, and lived for the job. If he was going to be in work on a weekend then so should his staff. 'I'm going to have to put a note on your employment record,' he went on. 'Don't worry it's an "unofficial warning".'

That was an oxymoron if ever I'd heard one. So what was the bloody point? 'I'd no intention of getting back late. Events kind of overtook me.'

Daniel looked down, scribbling notes on a pad. Those policemen had been more forgiving than the prick.

'Sorry, Dan,' I held my stomach. 'Are we finished? I need to be sick.'

He blinked at me, alarmed. Not that I was going to throw up, but that I might have the temerity of doing it in his presence.

My stomach flipped, and the insides of my cheeks watered. I slapped a hand over my mouth.

'Get to the toilet,' Daniel commanded, even as he reared back out of the splash zone. If I did vomit, there would be no escape in this confined space. I grabbed for the door handle and let myself out. I raced for the men's room, and banged through the door. I wasn't really going to throw up if I could help it, my act a ploy to get out of the office. But I only made it as far as the washbasins and my stomach purged itself without bidding.

163

Leaning on the edge of the sink, I retched up the meagre contents of my stomach. The purging was so violent that it shot pains through my insides, and even between my legs. I shuddered and spat out the last strings of bile. Sweat poured from my hairline, and my eyes were swollen and distended from their sockets. Turning on the taps, I sluiced away the vomit, then cupped water and splashed it on my face. Distractedly I wondered how bad I looked, but I was scared to check in the mirror for fear I'd see Naomi staring back.

15

Is There Anybody There?

'Why now?'

I stood on the half-landing peering up at the stained glass window above my bathroom.

'Why now?' I asked again, this time louder. 'Come on, I know you're there. Why won't you answer me?'

As hard as I tried, I couldn't make out Naomi's face in the mish-mash pattern of glass. When I'd asked Sarah what she saw in the window she'd said it looked geometric. To me it was chaos. It was random, with no hint of repetition other than in the proliferation of the colour red in the swirl of colours. Outside it was dark, almost nine o'clock, and with no source of light from outside, the colours didn't bleed onto the landing wall.

I turned and looked down the stairs to where Sarah stood. She was holding a digital voice recorder. Our gazes met and I shook my head. She pursed her lips.

'Keep going,' she urged. 'Just because we can't hear the replies the recorder could be picking something up.'

I directed my question at the window again. 'You showed yourself to me before. Why won't you show yourself now?'

Sarah moved cautiously. She said something for the purpose of the recording, noting her movements so they wouldn't be misconstrued later when we listened back. She'd also warned me to "tag" any undue noises I made too, but I'd forgot.

'Naomi? Are you there?'

As mad as it sounds, coming from a confirmed disbeliever, I didn't feel foolish calling out to my dead girlfriend. Part of me even wanted to hear her reply. Sarah had cautioned that it was unlikely we'd hear any disembodied voices in the audible range, but it was possible we could pick up EVP's. She was referring to electronic voice phenomena: supposedly spirit voices imprinted on digital recording media. I was doubtful about the value of such an experiment, offering my theory that we would probably just pick up on interference from a passing taxi radio or something like it. Sarah was adamant that EVP's didn't appear in the radio bandwidths; usually they were seated in the white noise below. I hadn't a clue about that kind of stuff, so had to take her word for it.

I waited until she joined me on the half-landing.

'Maybe she doesn't want to speak to me,' I said.

'She obviously wants to contact you,' Sarah said, 'otherwise why keep presenting herself?'

After throwing my guts up at work, I'd waited a few minutes before showing myself on the shop floor. Having cleaned myself up I thought I was presentable enough to face customers, but as soon as Sarah spotted me she informed me I looked like hell. I briefly told her about the crash, and the joyous ear bashing from Daniel. I might have hinted that I'd seen something unusual that had caused me to lose control of the car.

'Not another shadow man?'

'No. Someone else.'

After that she wouldn't let the subject lie, and I'd finally given in, telling her I was positive that my deceased girlfriend had stepped out in front of the car. I also admitted it was not the first time I'd seen her, hers being the face I'd seen on the wall, and who'd attacked me in my nightmare - though I never mentioned that Sarah had at first featured in that particular dream.

'Maybe we've been approaching your haunting from the wrong angle. I thought we were only dealing with shadows, but now you tell me you've seen a full figure apparition.' She was energised anew. 'How's about I come over after work? There's something I'd like to try if you're OK with it.'

I didn't know how I felt, but I agreed. To tell the truth, I'm not sure I wanted to be alone in the house. Not until I'd shaken the uncanny sensation that hadn't left me following the incident earlier. We went our separate ways at home time, but Sarah had turned up at my door by seven o'clock. She was carrying her laptop and her digital recorder, and that was when she'd brought up doing the EVP experiment, explaining the methodology and the hoped for results.

Before we got started I made some early supper, and we sat in the parlour with the TV playing, but the sound muted. Sarah wanted to wait until the traffic died down outside, and the adjoining building was empty of cleaning staff. It was a good idea, she said, to get a feel for the ambient noises of my house before we began the EVP session so we could discount any natural knocks and creaks.

She didn't ask how Naomi died, and I didn't tell her. I'd already mentioned that my girlfriend was killed in a car crash, and she was respectful enough not to demand the gory details now. She also knew that my split from my wife was acrimonious, and was astute enough to guess that I'd been emotionally frustrated after my visit with Catriona. She hinted that Naomi had perhaps chosen to show herself to me now that I was in a low state, that she was there to offer spiritual support.

It was rubbish.

Of course, I hadn't mentioned that I ran Naomi's ghost down and she'd been catapulted over the roof of the car. As far as Sarah knew, Naomi had simply stepped out in the road, and I'd reacted by jamming on the brakes and tail-ending the parked vehicles.

She had explained how to ask questions of the spirits and to leave a pause after each, in order to allow them to gather enough energy to answer. It all sounded like pseudo-science to me, but I went with the flow.

On the half-landing, Sarah held the digital recorder nearer the window. She nodded at me to continue.

'Naomi, if you can hear me, please answer,' I called out. 'Just let us hear your voice.'

We waited.

Then, as if by some telepathic agreement, we moved up the short set of stairs to the next level. I continued calling out. The house was dead still.

When we'd finished a sweep of that floor, Sarah decided it was time to listen back to our recordings. She set them going, and we huddled, heads almost touching, as we listened. I heard my voice and thought how strange it sounded compared to what I heard inside my own head. 'I didn't realise I sounded so lame.'

'Shhh,' Sarah cautioned.

We listened, but I could make out nothing beyond our own voices. At one point there was a faint hiss and crackle, and Sarah replayed that section three times before discounting the sound as the scuffing of her clothing as she walked along the landing. 'I'll remember and keep the recorder held well away from my body next time.'

I raised an eyebrow.

'I'm impressed at your professional style,' I said.

'I'm an amateur at this stuff.'

'You could have fooled me.' I was bulling her up, complimenting her in a way I knew would appeal. She wasn't as much acting professionally as she was copying what she'd seen in all those TV ghost hunting programmes she watched. 'I wouldn't have known where to start. I'm only happy I've got a good friend like you.'

She looked at me for a moment and I couldn't figure out what she was thinking. In the end she slipped on a slither of a smile. 'Do you want me to call out this time?'

'Go on. You know more about this stuff than I do.'

'Open the door for me.' She indicated the door that led up to the bedrooms. I felt a little thrill go through me at her command. The first nice feeling I'd experienced since arriving at Catriona's door earlier.

I pulled open the door as she set the recorder going again. I was about to go up, but Sarah put a hand on my arm. 'Wait,' she said *sotto voce*, 'let's allow things to settle down first, that way we've a better chance of catching something.'

We waited, listening. I could hear the soft rasp of Sarah's breath. She was breathing faster than normal and I wondered if her anticipation was at hearing something strange, or for her first visit to my bedroom. She glanced at me and offered a sly grin, and I hoped she had read my mind. 'OK,' she announced, not exactly dashing my hopes, 'let's go up.'

There were too many creaks and groans from the stairs, and the swish of my shoulders against the walls as we went up, to try to capture an EVP. I tried to avert my gaze from Sarah's swaying backside as she climbed, but it was unavoidable. Sarah waited until we were in the small landing before she introduced herself, said she was a friend of mine, then launched into a pre-set list of questions. She entered my bedroom, and the first thing I noted was how quiet things were now that the carpet had been fitted. My sleeping bag was rolled up against the wall opposite the windows, next to the lamp. Not exactly a romantic boudoir. I stood in the doorway, watching her as she patrolled the room, taking short steps, the recorder held out at arm's length. She asked her questions, paused, asked again.

'What's that?'

Her question was buried in with the others, and it took a moment before I realised she'd addressed me, not the spirits in the ether.

'What's what?'

Without answering she approached the walk-in wardrobe.

'It's only my clothes in there,' I said, trying to deter her. My shoes and trainers were in there too. Catriona once made the glib remark that I was the only person who'd ever received a refund from Odour Eaters.

'Sometimes spirits will keep out of the way of the living by hiding in seldom used spaces,' Sarah pointed out, and pulled open the doors. Thankfully she didn't step away from the assault of sweaty trainer smell. In fact, undeterred she stepped into the wardrobe and asked a couple of questions. Wanting to divert her, I indicated the crawl space.

'If she's anywhere she's likely to be in there then.'

Sarah headed for the little door in the eaves next to the window. I discreetly closed the closet behind her, while she crouched to access the crawl space. 'Hello, is there anybody there?' she asked in a singsong voice. She asked another two or three standard questions. Then she backed out, shivering. 'I think the only living things in there are spiders.'

She turned off the device, brought up the latest file and played it. This time she listened to it herself. By the disappointment on her face there were no anomalous voices calling out from the after-life. She looked up. 'We may as well do the other rooms before we hit the basement.'

I led the way into the spare bedroom. It smelled of new carpet, a warm scent of fibres, rubber underlay and glue. Behind me, Sarah had entered the room, fiddling with the recorder. She opened her mouth to tag the beginning of her latest EVP session, but the words caught in her throat. 'What the bloody hell?'

I didn't need to ask what had surprised her. I knew that there was graffiti scrawled on the walls, but had never taken much notice of the writing: I took it that it would be the usual tacky stuff that people of low intelligence scrawled on walls, and had pointedly ignored it – planning to paint it over before the kids ever came to visit.

Nevertheless, I was speechless.

All over the walls was the same repeated message.

I WANT YOU.

That wasn't the worst of it.

Some of the writing had been scraped deeply into the plasterwork, and it was obviously new damage, because the crumbling plaster dust made small piles on the brand new carpet beneath.

'How did this happen?' I wondered aloud.

Sarah stared at the walls, then accusingly at me. 'Is this some kind of Joke?'

'If it is, it's in bloody bad taste.' I looked at her, and she was in total agreement, but her mouth was set in a slash of disdain for me. 'What? It wasn't me!'

'Who else could it be?'

'Not bloody me.' I darted a look around the room. A carpet knife could have done the scoring of the walls. 'The bloody carpet fitters. I knew I should've been here when they were in the house.'

'Jack, who in their right mind are going to come in, fit your carpets and then vandalise your property on the way out?'

She was correct. I knew the fitters weren't responsible. 'Who else could it be?'

'Well if it wasn't you, there's only one feasible explanation.'

The ghosts? I left it unsaid, but that's exactly where Sarah's mind was drifting.

'I don't like this, Jack.' Sarah looked ready to run. 'It's getting a little out of hand now. I haven't the experience to deal with *this*.'

'Hold on,' I cautioned. 'Let's not get ahead of ourselves. There's a rational explanation. We have to think before jumping to conclusions.'

'OK, convince me then. If it sounds plausible I won't bugger off. But I'm warning you, Jack, if this is down to a poltergeist I'm out of here. If it can scratch a wall like that, it can scratch us too.'

I gave it my best shot. 'There was already graffiti on the walls. I saw it, even if I didn't pay it much attention before. Here's what I think happened. When the fitters were in, the carpet was probably much bigger and had to be propped against the walls while they cut it down to size. The stiff carpet must have rubbed at the writing, made it look newer than it is, maybe loosened the edges and made more dust fall out. Once the carpet was laid some of the plaster dust fell and settled on top of the carpet. It makes sense when you think about it.'

'It makes more sense than the fitters doing it,' she concurred. 'And, OK, I'm sorry for suggesting it was you. It would be a poor idea of a joke if it were.'

'Yeah,' I said. 'It would.'

But someone was having a nasty laugh at my expense.

Despite persuading Sarah with my lame theory of carpets gouging the walls anew, I hadn't convinced myself.

Whoever had scratched those words into the wall had sent me the text message, and perhaps who'd spoken them in my nightmare.

Taken in that context, it made more sense to me. It threw me back more than a decade to when those words had been screamed in despair.

16

I Want You Back

I wanted to see *Gangs of New York*, but Naomi didn't, electing instead to coerce me into watching some Reese Witherspoon vehicle about a woman who ran away from her husband in Alabama to reinvent herself as a New York socialite. It was a romantic comedy, not exactly my cup of tea. It was possibly a decent movie, but I deliberately didn't enjoy it, and made it obvious throughout, grumbling and moaning. By the time we left the cinema, Naomi was decidedly frosty and declined my suggestion of going on to the pub even though she'd dressed for a night out in her red satin dress and new black boots.

'Take me home,' she commanded when we were back at my car. Back then I drove a Vauxhall Corsa, a sporty model with tinted windows and "go faster" stripes, just the thing to suit the boy racer in me.

I was six months older than Naomi, and she was still early in her twenty-third year. We'd been together since school. Long enough to have progressed beyond that first flush of infatuation, and settled into a place where we were comfortable arguing about the mundane and the ridiculous. In my mind, couples did that sort of thing. My parents had been arguers, and I doubted they could have lasted as long together without constantly bickering: otherwise they'd have had nothing to say to each other. I wasn't being serious when I suggested that Naomi was like that character out of the movie, a spoilt bitch that didn't appreciate the good in her man. 'What you going to do, run away to New York too?'

'I should for all you care,' Naomi had snapped. She scrunched down in the front passenger seat, as far away from me as she could get in the small car.

'I do care,' I said, peeling out with a squeal of rubber. We'd parked in a public car park, which even at ten in the evening was still full. I roared along the aisles, heading for the exit. There were undulations in the road surface, an attempt at slowing down traffic, but my Corsa skimmed off them, jostling on the downslopes.

'Slow down for God's sake!'

'I thought you were in a hurry to get home?' I gave the throttle another nudge.

'Stop being stupid, Jack. You already spoiled the movie, don't go on or you'll spoil everything.'

'What do you mean by *everything*?'

'You know fine well what I mean.'

I barely gave way at the exit, pulling a sharp left on to the main road. An approaching vehicle almost ran into the back of us. The driver hit the brakes, and his horn a second later. It blared.

I flipped him a two-fingered salute out of the window and roared off, exceeding the posted speed limit.

'You're talking about finishing with me because I didn't like a bloody soppy movie?' I snapped across at Naomi. 'I told you I wanted to watch Gangs of New York.'

'You know I'm not interested in all that violent stuff.'

'Leonardo di Crappio was in it. I thought you liked that pretty boy? You've watched the flaming *Titanic* enough times.'

'It's DiCaprio,' Naomi said, and not for the first time that evening. She knew I was deliberately mispronouncing the actor's name.

'Crappio,' I sniped.

'If he's so crap why did you want to watch a movie with him in it?'

I fumed. Caught out by the old double twist.

We were fast approaching a crossroad and the light was on green, but about to change. I put my foot down. We were ten metres off the lights when they went amber. I sped up. The amber flicked to red, and we breezed through, beating the traffic waiting to pull out from the adjoining streets. I emitted an angry laugh, exclaiming my disregard for the other road users.

'Jack, slow down.'

'No. You wanted home. I'm taking you home.'

'You're just being a dick.'

'You're just being a bitch.'

You wouldn't think we loved each other, not if you heard the course our argument took next. There was lots of swearing, name-calling and screams. Naomi was crying before we'd finished, and I was hammering at the steering wheel with my hands, shouting like a lunatic. The only good of it was that I'd lost some of my forward volition and had slowed down to around forty miles per hour. It was still too fast for the conditions. I flew through another red light, this time earning an angry blare of horns from a van driver and a truck driver, both of who had to brake to miss us. I turned my anger on them, flipping them the 'V' sign out the window, screaming threats at them. I knew they weren't in a position to follow so was safe enough from a beating.

Looking back, that's what I would have deserved. If those guys had followed, cornered me, then dragged me from my car and gave me a good kicking, I'd have asked for it. I was being a dick. More than that, I was being reckless, not to mention a purely selfish and immature dick. Naomi told me, but I didn't listen.

'That's it!' she finally howled. 'We're finished! Stop the car and let me out.'

'No. I'm not fucking stopping.'

'Let me out, Jack. You've gone way too far this time!'

'I'm not stopping for nobody…' To prove the point I stamped the throttle hard. 'And you aren't going anywhere til we get this sorted.'

'There's nothing to sort. I told you: *We're finished.*'

'No we're not. We are going to sort this. Fucking hell, Naomi?'

'You're always the bloody same. If you don't get your own way, you just go off on one. Well I'm sick of it. I'm sick of walking on eggshells around you. I'm not putting up with it any longer. Stop the car, Jack. Stop right now.'

'No! You're not finishing with me.'

'Like you can stop me?'

My anger had deflated, now shrinking to a cold slice of panic that speared my heart. I had gone too far. I was just too woodenheaded to admit it. 'I won't let you,' I cried, and my voice was a high-pitched whine.

'Ha!' Naomi's face grew harder. 'Don't dare start with your usual threats. I don't give a shit if you kill yourself. Go on. Commit suicide, see if I care.'

'Who says I'm going to kill myself?' My eyes were extending out their sockets.

'It's what you usually say, Jack.' Naomi lowered her voice, doing a pretty decent impression of my voice. '"Oh, don't leave me. I couldn't live without you, Naomi. I'm going to kill myself!"'

'I was just a stupid kid back then,' I challenged.

'The first time, yeah. What about the others? You tried it only four months ago. And I know you, you'll try it again.' Naomi pulled at her seatbelt, unclipping it. 'Go on. Prove you won't. Stop the car and let me out.'

'No. Put your belt back on.'

'If you don't stop the car, I'll jump.'

'Now who's being an idiot?'

'It's called emotional blackmail, Jack, and you're a bloody expert at it. Well, sorry, but two can play at that game.' Naomi pulled at the door handle.

'What are you doing? Stop it!' Jumping from the car at that speed she'd break her neck. I began to assert some pressure on the brake pedal.

Naomi got the door open. I grabbed her with my left hand, held her elbow.

'Get off me, you psycho!' Naomi yanked free, made to push the door open further.

I could never be sure if she was bluffing or not. It wasn't something I was about to allow happen. I grabbed her by her hair, a good handful and yanked her towards me. I was trying to save her life, for fuck's sake! Naomi screeched, clawed at my hands and I let go, but only so I could reach across and grab for the partly open door.

That was when Naomi went for my face. She screwed her nails into my cheek to a point I thought she'd draw blood. In response, I screwed my eyes shut, shouting out.

The sound that followed was the loudest I'd ever heard. It was as if a grenade went off inside my skull. A white blinding flash seared my vision, even behind my screwed eyelids. I felt weightless. No up, no down, no left or right. In contradiction a terrible force rammed my guts. I was too confused to scream.

In the next second my eyes were open, and I cast glances around, but could make no sense of the colours I saw in hyper-clarity. Reds, oranges, yellows, and the deepest black I could ever imagine. My hearing was compressed down to a faint whistle. I was numb from the neck down. Except for in my right leg – there was a furnace of heat brewing in my knee.

I knew we'd crashed.

I just didn't see it coming, had no idea of what we'd crashed into.

Grey dots swirled across my vision. I shook my head, and my ears popped. There was a screeching sound coming from somewhere and it took me a minute to realise it was rising from my throat. I tried to shift in my seat, looking for Naomi.

Where was she?

I was too disorientated to understand the severity of what had happened. I expected Naomi to be seated beside me. Her seat was buckled forward, the headrest touching the dash. Naomi wasn't a big girl. She could fit in the space beneath the buckled chair. I reached, pressing it back, and found that the supports had sheared and the chair back was loose. I pushed it away, gritting my teeth against a fresh burst of pain that came from my core.

Sparks popped.

The stench of burning rubber filled my senses.

'Naomi? Naomi!'

The left side of the windscreen was shattered. On my side it was starred from where my forehead had impacted it. Only my seatbelt had halted me flying headlong through the glass.

'Naomi? Naomiiiii…?'

Naomi had unclipped her belt.

I clawed at the steering wheel. It pinned me. The entire bonnet was crushed, everything forced back by a foot. The dash had warped at the centre, and more sparks fizzed and crackled. I pulled and shoved, crying out in alarm. My belt was tight. I fed down a hand and hit the release mechanism. Thankfully it popped open and I'd a little more room to move. I twisted as best I could, checking the rear seat as if I'd find Naomi there, having spotted the impending collision and leapt in the back for cover. Absurd, I know, but the hope was there. Naomi wasn't.

My worst fear was realised. Naomi had been catapulted through the windscreen when the car had come to such a violent and abrupt stop. That screeching noise began to leak from me again. I fought to get free of the steering column. My door was jammed. The door's structure had twisted. The window had exploded. I pulled and pushed, trying to find a way out the window. I got my torso out of the gap, but couldn't free my right leg. The steering column was jammed against it, and my foot was caught under one of the misaligned pedals. In that moment I would have ripped my leg out of the socket, so I threw my weight this way and that, and finally pulled free. Agony flared through my knee, shot to my foot and ricocheted up my entire body to my brain. I screamed, and tears flooded my features. I fell on the road alongside my car. I held on to the car, scrabbling at the paintwork for a handhold to help me rise; I made it to my left foot, but the right wouldn't bear any weight. I hopped along the car, calling for my girlfriend, hanging on where I could. I fell twice, grazing my palms on nuggets of shattered windscreen glass and unrecognisable bits of metal and plastic. Both times I rose, and limped in agony for the wall we'd smashed into.

These days, if anyone notices my limp and are shameless enough to ask about it, I reply equally barefaced. I lie. I tell them that the gimpy knee was down to an accident on the rugby pitch. I wouldn't mention the crash, because they would then demand the gory details: I didn't want to tell them how lucky I'd been. Not after what happened to Naomi.

As we'd struggled, and my attention was off the road while I tried to close Naomi's door, the car had swerved left, mounted the pavement and struck a garden wall. The garden belonged to a corner lot, and we'd hit the worst possible place where the wall formed a right angle. The sandstone wall had largely defied the car's forward volition, stopping it dead. The bonnet and engine compartment had folded around the sharp wedge of stone. Naomi had been thrown headlong through the windscreen, catapulted over the wall and twenty feet into the garden.

It was possibly no more than thirty seconds since we'd smashed into the wall, but already neighbours were leaning out of their windows, or had come to front doors, checking on the commotion. Lights had come on in the bedrooms of the house the garden belonged to, and the oblong cast from one picked out Naomi's crumpled form as if she was in the spotlight on a stage. I screamed her name.

I scrambled over the partly collapsed wall, and fell among flowers and shrubs. I fought free, partly crawling across a previously well-tended lawn that was now littered with blood-dotted glass, debris and shards of sandstone. My gaze never shifted from Naomi, limned as she was in the yellow glow from the bedroom light. Her dress was rucked up around her waist, her stick thin legs deathly pale above the black boots. She was dead still.

It seemed like a mile across the grass, and felt as if it took an eternity to reach her, but then I had her cradled in my lap, pushing down the hem of her dress in an effort at protecting her modesty. I stroked hair back off her features. It was clotted with her blood. Her face was unrecognisable, torn to tatters as she'd gone through the exploding window, as red as her torn dress. I moaned her name now.

Naomi stirred.

She mewled like a kicked dog.

'Naomi, baby, it's going to be OK.' Even I didn't believe my words. I touched her face, and she pulled away. It was reflex, I'm sure. 'Naomi? Can you hear me, babe?'

She gave a second mewl, and her body shuddered in my hands.

'Naomi?'

One eye slid open. It was unfocussed. The pupil moved rapidly around in a flicking motion. Blood pooled in the corner, barely watered down by the thick tear that oozed out. Using a thumb, I smoothed away the blood. My action was enough for Naomi to focus on, and I watched her pupil dilate as she peered up at me. Perhaps she experienced a similar clarity that I did. Perhaps not. I was so tortured that every detail hit me in sharp relief.

'J…Jaaa…' Her voice came from some distant place. 'Jaaack?'

'Yes, it's me, babe. It's Jack. I'm going to look after you; you're going to be all right. I…I promise….'

Bystanders had begun to gather. Some had even come into the garden. I viewed everything with stark clarity, and yet those people were insubstantial to me. Grey shapes against the darkness.

'Why won't you help her?' I screamed. 'Somebody. Please! Call an ambulance, for God's sake!

A man crouched alongside me, his hand on my shoulder. His face was next to mine, but I couldn't see him. All I could see was Naomi's ruined face, her one open eye now centred on my face. The man said something, perhaps reassuring me an ambulance was coming, but his words were a muffled sequence of nonsensical sounds. In contrast Naomi's words were sharp, even though they had a distant quality to them, like she called to me from across some great gulf.

'Why didn't you stop, Jack?'

'Shhh, don't talk. Save your strength.'

As guilty as it makes me feel these days, I didn't want the bystanders to hear the truth behind the crash. I didn't want them to know we'd been having a blazing row. All they need hear was how much I loved Naomi.

'Babe, everything's going to be all right. An ambulance is coming. They'll make you well again in no time.' I leaned and kissed her gently on the forehead. I tasted her blood, but it didn't matter.

Naomi squirmed away from my lips. Her features twisted in revulsion. Pain, I told myself, it's the pain she's turning from. She pawed at me, her fingernails digging into my cheek. She didn't realise it was me, I hoped, she was oblivious.

Gently I moved her hand away, and leaned in. 'Everything's going to be fine soon,' I reassured her.

'No.'

'Honest, Naomi, you're going to be OK. I'm going to look after you.'

'Noooo…' Her face turned to mine, and her open eye was blazing. A bubble of mucus burst from her left nostril and more blood poured out. She champed her teeth, and spat frothy blood at me. 'Get…away…from me.'

'I'm going to keep you safe.' I was crying, shameless in the face of the group of bystanders now peering down at us like ghouls.

'G…get away from me…' Her face contorted and there was no denying the terror in her gaze as she peered up at my face. She shuddered, and I knew it was from revulsion. 'You...you did this to me.'

'No. No, Naomi, that's not fair.'

I could feel hands on my shoulders. Someone was attempting to ease me away. Voices were low but commanding.

'No! I'm not leaving her. She needs me!'

Naomi pushed at me, her limbs as light as gossamer. The other hands were more substantial but I jerked free, pushing back with an elbow.

'I'm not leaving her!' My scream was more forceful than my attempts to shove the bystanders away. But it did no good.

'I'm leaving you, Jack.' Her voice was surprisingly clear.

'No, Naomi, you can't. I want you...'

Her eyelid drooped shut.

'Naomi! No. Don't leave me! I want you, babe. I want you back!'

'I'm...going...' a smile slid across her mouth and it signified a calm stillness to her entire body. 'I'm going...sweet...home...'

Her final words were confused, random firings of her memory as she slipped from this world into oblivion. The last thing she said were words from the title of that damn film. Why hadn't we just gone to see that other movie?

Naomi was dead. I knew it. Yet I wasn't prepared to let her go.

'Naomi,' I wailed. 'Don't go. Come back. I want you to come back. Please, babe. I want you. I want you.'

Apparently I was still mumbling the same phrase when the paramedics arrived on the scene minutes later. I was still mumbling them when I was carted off to hospital. They sent a different ambulance for Naomi.

17

Caressed by a Ghostly Hand

Sarah looked strange. Actually, that's incorrect; she was looking at me in a strange way. I was the one with the odd expression on my face.

'What's wrong?'

I blinked out of my awful reminiscence.

'Sorry, did I zone out for a minute?'

'You were mumbling something.'

'I was?'

She held up her digital recorder. 'If you don't believe me, I can let you hear. We're still recording.'

'I was just, uh, reading those words,' I said. I was positive that if we did listen back I'd have been repeating the same mantra as I had the night Naomi died.

'Yeah,' she agreed, but she didn't relax her odd perusal.

'What?'

'Nothing. Just forget about it.'

'Forget about what?'

Sarah pushed back her hair. Rocked her balance from one foot to the other before settling herself. 'You had this look on your face: you looked ready to murder someone.'

I stared at her, didn't say a word.

The atmosphere grew palpable.

I let out a slow exhalation. 'I've never hurt a soul in my life.'

'Didn't say you had,' Sarah replied, 'I said you looked ready to murder someone. And seeing as I'm the only one here…'

She was only kidding, and offered a conciliatory smile to show it. She said into the recorder, 'EVP session ended.'

Studying the scrawled words on the walls again, I made myself a promise that I'd fill them in with Polyfilla or some other spackling paste before painting them over. A coat of emulsion wouldn't hide the words, and I didn't want my children seeing them. I'm not sure how easy a lie would come to my lips if Gemma or Jake asked what their significance was.

'Should we go and get a cuppa before we tackle the basement?'

'You still want to go down there?' I asked.

'Yeah, we should cover all bases.'

'I thought the basement creeped you out.'

'It does. But so do you and I'm still here.' She stuck her tongue in her cheek.

'That's what I like about you, Sarah. You never mince your words.'

'Oh, so you like me then?' She moved from foot to foot again.

'Well, yeah, of course. I thought that was obvious.' My face warmed by degrees.

'So there's a chance I will survive the night, after all?'

I looked away quickly. I'd misconstrued her question, got my hopes up. 'I'd never hurt a soul,' I reassured her. Then I had to wonder if I had indeed misinterpreted her meaning. Was she suggesting she stay the entire night? I glanced at her, but she'd already headed out of the room.

'We'll leave the recorder running in the dumbwaiter cupboard,' she said, 'may as well be productive while we're supping tea.'

I joined her as she set the recorder on the dumbwaiter platform. She stepped out the closet and closed the door. Her back was against my chest, and I could feel the contours of her body, the warmth of her skin radiating through her clothing. She didn't step away. She looked over her shoulder at me. Our gazes held for a second longer, then I cleared my throat, and gave her room to move. When she did I was positive she deliberately swept her backside across my groin. My scrotum tingled, and I felt a stirring down below that had been absent since I'd walked in on Catriona and Mark months ago. Jesus, I wanted to pull her back to me and to let her feel my desire, but I didn't. I was afraid that she'd reject me, slap my face and storm off. I coughed again, turned to hide my growing erection by pretending to check the other doors were firmly shut.

My face was furnace hot now, and I daren't look back in case Sarah guessed what I was trying to hide. I fiddled with the door handle, until I was sure she was going down the stairs. I couldn't swear but I thought I caught a soft chuckle at my expense, and it was no disembodied voice.

I followed down the stairs, going slowly, adjusting the front of my pants.

What was wrong with me?

You'd think I'd never been with a woman before.

Why didn't I just let Sarah know how I felt and see how the rest of the evening panned out? I liked her and was sure she liked me too. What was the worst that could happen?

Rejection.

OK. But it wasn't as if I was a stranger to that, was it?

Catriona's face intruded in my mind, set in a scowl. It morphed to that of Naomi's. She was laughing, but it was bitter and harsh. I forced the memories away, though it was a struggle.

By the time I alighted the bottom step into the landing, my penis was flaccid again.

Sarah was ahead of my position, passing the spare rooms, almost to the short flight of steps to the half-landing. Beyond her was the stained glass window. I tore my gaze from it, afraid of the face I might see staring back, scorning me, and concentrated on the sway of Sarah's backside. In her trainers her step was accentuated, and her bum jiggled nicely. I could still feel the sensation of how it had rubbed against me, like the caress of a ghostly hand. It was the only lingering spirit I wanted to concentrate on. I hurried after her, and avoided looking at the window.

Sarah made the tea.

I opened a packet of HobNob biscuits, piling some on a plate.

We sat next to each other on the settee. The TV was still on, but muted. Neither of us gave it more than a cursory glance.

'I think we might be going about this the wrong way.'

My mind was still on making love to Sarah; at least planning the manner in which I might romance her into my bed. But that's not what she meant. She caught my dumb look.

'EVP's,' she said. 'When I think about it, we might be better served trying to catch visual evidence that something's here.'

Other than the unexplained movement of her phone, Sarah hadn't witnessed anything visually. Not first hand. OK, she'd been there when I watched the shadow man chase the smaller figure through the basement, but she'd only my word for that. She hadn't even been aware of anything unusual, apart from me howling and stumbling around. So I was secretly glad that she brought the subject up. It said a lot that my word wasn't being questioned.

'There's different phenomena happening here,' she went on. 'You've seen a full-bodied apparition of your old girlfriend, as well as the matrixing events in the window. Then there are the shadow people. We've had an apport, and also that stuff with the dumbwaiter. They're all activity that could be picked up by the right kind of equipment.'

'What's an "apport"?'

'It happened with my phone. It's a term paranormal investigators use to explain the transference of an object from one place to another. Sometimes – especially where a poltergeist is concerned - articles have been witnessed materializing out of thin air. Stones, nails, flowers, and even small animals have suddenly popped out of nowhere. I even know a married couple who swear a four foot rag doll they owned disappeared from its usual resting place in a rocking chair in their bedroom and has never been seen again.'

'A thief probably stole it.'

'Nothing else was taken. I doubt a burglar would sneak in and take nothing but a knitted doll.'

'A kid then.'

'They had no kids and no visitors to the house. They're both adamant, and I've no reason to doubt them. I mean, if they were going to make a story up, they'd choose something more believable than a rag doll going walkabout.'

I shivered at the image. There was something freaky about all dolls in my estimation. Let alone those that got up and walked away. Taking a glance over my shoulder I was relieved not to see a rosy-cheeked devil leering at me over the back of the settee. Grabbing a biscuit, I concentrated on chewing.

'We could set up some trigger objects,' Sarah suggested. 'Put a camera on them and see what we catch.'

'What kind of camera are you talking about?'

'It works best in night vision,' Sarah explained.

'You have one?'

'No. But remember that paranormal group I told you about, the one I'm friends with on Facebook…?'

'They'll lend you a camera?' I asked, doubting already that's what she meant.

'Probably not. But I'm sure they'd love to investigate this place.'

My headshake was emphatic.

'Oh, go on, Jack.' She leaned in close, her shoulder touching mine, and she rested her hands on my thigh. 'Be a sport.'

'I'm not sure I want a load of strangers roaming about the house,' I said, my eyes flicking from her hands to her face. Her eyes twinkled, and her fingers danced up my leg. Their touch was like an electric jolt. 'I'm happy doing this with you, but…'

'I promise you,' Sarah said, and her bottom lip pouted in that enticing way of hers. 'Let me bring in my friends some time, and you get me all to yourself tonight.'

Hell, if she had asked me to hand her the moon and stars I would have.

I nodded, the small gesture infinitely small, but it placed my lips marginally closer to hers. Her breath tickled my face.

Sarah peered deeply into my eyes. Then her eyelids crinkled at the corners and she craned up. Her mouth met mine, and we both sighed as we gently kissed. It was like the flutter of butterfly wings in my mouth, a soft gentle buzz. But then we leaned in closer and kissed with passion and hunger.

18

Things That Go Bump in the Night.

'Jack? Are you awake?'

'I am now.'

I reached for Sarah, my head stuffed with warm cotton wool as I surfaced from the deepest sleep I'd known in months. We had made love snuggled close together in my sleeping bag. It was slow and languid, almost tentative, but when we'd climaxed it had been together and more wonderful even than the first time downstairs. Then the sex had been frantic, rushed, and we'd barely got half of our clothes off before I had her stretched out on the settee and was hammering into her like a sixteen year old virgin in a brothel. We'd both been voracious, a bit too eager, and we knew if we left things at that, then we would probably never look each other in the eye again. Sarah had taken the lead, just as she had in my dream. Dressed only in her sweater, her coffee and cream legs flashing, her paler bum swaying, she'd led me from the parlour, up the stairs to my bedroom. I was without my trousers too, and was a little self-conscious. Sarah gave my goofy appearance no heed, going up the stairs in full view of my lascivious appraisal. She paused only to open the dumbwaiter closet and switch off the digital recorder. Disembodied moans were sure to follow and not the kind she wished to document.

I momentarily lamented that my new bed had yet to be delivered, and this wasn't the boudoir of my fantasy, but it was a fleeting concern. Sarah switched on the lamp. She bent to spread my sleeping bag on the carpet, and I watched, transfixed. Then she patted the sleeping bag and commanded me to lie down. I did as ordered, first pulling off my shirt and socks and tossing them aside. I must have been panting like a dog.

'Slow down,' Sarah said. 'Take things easy, Jack. We've all night remember.'

I lay back, watching her as if she was a veritable goddess.

She peeled off her sweater and gently set it aside. She stood there, her breasts lifting and falling. They were small, pert globes that barely filled the cups of her push up bra. My breath caught in my throat as she arched her spine to unclip the straps. The mound of her vagina was presented to me, a small strip of pubic hair all that had been spared the razor. Her labia were slightly swollen, pouting, as had her mouth before we'd taken that first kiss. I wanted to reach up and touch, but Sarah angled slightly away as she slipped out of her bra. She wasn't being coy; she turned back and straddled over me, then lowered down and took my newly engorged penis inside her. The entire time I'd been holding my breath. My head was throbbing, and scarlet flashes darted across my vision – I exhaled long and hard, pure elation.

I began to thrust inside her, but Sarah pressed her fingertips to my chest, whispering again for me to slow down. It took some control, and some guidance from her, but I managed. Soon I slipped into that same languid rhythm as she, and that second conjoining lasted and lasted. We came together, and then Sarah leaned in, her head fitting into the hollow of my shoulder. I pulled the sleeping bag around us, before our sweat could chill in the night air, and we'd finally rolled arm in arm onto our sides, where, spent and wrapped in the muzzy afterglow of shared orgasm, we slept.

But now Sarah had wakened, and I wondered how fantastic a third time would be. Never had I gone three times in one night, but the stirring in my loins told me this time would be my personal record.

Bang! Bang!

'Can you hear that, Jack?' Sarah's voice reached me as a hushed rasp.

I tensed.

The bang was repeated.

I sat up.

I had no idea of the time. Outside it was still dark. But it might have been morning, with people on their way to work. Was the noise from outside?

'It's coming from inside the house.' Sarah was also sitting up. I think she had been since before she'd woken me.

Bump! Bang!

'Shit,' I said. 'What *is* that?'

'Is someone inside the house?' The streetlamps cast enough of a wan glow within the bedroom for me to pick out Sarah's features. Her eyes were wide and moist.

'Burglars,' I hissed.

I didn't remember either of us switching off the lamp. I clicked it on.

Bang! Bump!

'Jesus,' Sarah said, 'it sounds like they're wrecking the place.'

I grabbed for my clothing. It was only after scrabbling around that I recalled my jeans and boxer shorts had been discarded at the foot of the settee in the parlour. No way was I prepared to face a burglar with my balls swinging; I went to the pile of laundry I was yet to place in the walk-in wardrobe. I wriggled into a pair of paint splattered jogging pants, even as Sarah pulled on her sweater. I found her a pair of clean boxers and she yanked them up.

'Phone the police,' Sarah said.

It was a sound strategy but for one thing.

'My phone's downstairs.'

'So is mine,' Sarah moaned.

As far as weapons went, I could see nothing to use. A tremor of fear went through me. Burglars often carried the tools of their trade: a screwdriver, a hammer, a crowbar, sometimes even a knife. I had no wish to meet a desperate thief with only my bare hands. I grabbed the lamp, unplugged it. If we were faced with no other option, I'd throw the damn thing at the burglar's head.

'Wait here,' I told Sarah.

'Like hell! I'm not staying here on my own.'

She was probably right. If I got in a tangle with a burglar I'd need her to run to our phones and get the police there ASAP.

'OK. But stay behind me.'

'Don't worry about that.' Sarah tucked in, holding onto my waist with her left hand. She'd bunched the knuckles of her right.

Bang! Bump! Bang!

'Holy shit!' I wheezed.

The bangs and crashes sounded as if they were emanating up the narrow stairwell. I flicked on the hall light and peered down. The door at the bottom was shut. I couldn't tell by the angle, because the stairs twisted left and met the facing wall. But it was inky dark, with no light spill from the landing below. I remembered leaving the doors open from the spare rooms on the first floor when we'd been progressing from one to the next on our EVP hunt. The streetlamps outside should have cast enough light to leak into the stairwell. I didn't recall shutting the door on the way up. I was too busy watching Sarah's bum and other delights as I'd followed her up to the bedroom. Maybe I closed it on autopilot. Could have. But I didn't think so.

'I think they're on the first floor,' I whispered.

As if to confirm it there was another loud bang, and it did sound as if it came from just beyond the closed door. We came to a halt on the stairs. Sarah's breath was hot on the back of my neck. I juggled the lamp, preparing for a throw if someone suddenly entered the stairwell.

'We don't want to get trapped up here.' Sarah's voice was equally faint.

We went down again, one slow step at a time. Where the final few stairs turned towards the door, I halted and Sarah bumped against me. She took a firmer grip on my waistline. I peered back at her. My lips were taut, and I attempted to hide my trepidation by asking if she was OK. Diverting my fear on her. She nodded, gave me a gentle shove forward. I held my breath as I took the door handle in my free hand. Counted to three.

Bash!

I flinched from the door, nearly falling on Sarah. She yelped. Once I'd worried that she might think I was a coward, and I wasn't doing much to change her mind now. The thought galvanised me to action. I grabbed the handle, yanked it open and threw back the door. I jumped out on to the landing.

'Hiiyyaaaa!' I yelled, my best Bruce Lee impression. I hefted the lamp, prepared to crown anybody in throwing distance. I searched everywhere at once, eyes darting.

The landing was empty.

Bang, bang, bang, bang-bang!

The racket came like a drumroll.

But not from the first floor, it came from downstairs.

At least, that's what I thought.

I indicated to Sarah that we should check and she nodded in agreement. Then I held up a finger. I'd stored my tools in the first floor junk closet. We quickly grabbed a hammer for me, and a chisel for Sarah. I'm not sure either of us would have enough moral outrage to physically use them as weapons, but it made us look more formidable. I left the lamp behind, a little more comfortable now that I appeared to mean business. We padded along the hall barefooted, and I was glad I'd had the foresight to knock in the protruding nail heads. Once more, I avoided looking at the stained glass window, going down quickly to the bathroom landing. From there we could see down into the ground floor vestibule. There was no one to be seen, but we could both hear the continued banging. Sarah was the first to look back the way we'd just come, but we'd already ascertained that there was nobody there.

I pointed the hammer downwards.

'It sounds as if it's coming from the basement,' I whispered.

Sarah frowned. Shook her head.

I set off down the stairs anyway.

At the bottom I switched on the lights. The front door was firmly closed. Twisting to look the other way, the back door into the yard was also shut. The bolts were thrown over: no way had anyone entered by that entrance. Positioning myself so I could guard her, I watched while Sarah rushed for the parlour. She paused briefly in the wedged open doorway, then nipped inside, fetching her mobile.

'Nobody there,' she said by way of greeting on her return. She was holding her phone poised for action, but hadn't yet called for help.

'Don't ring the cops yet,' I said.

The banging had stopped.

'Do you think they heard us and left?' Sarah wondered, her voice still barely above a whisper.

'It'd be best if they have,' I said, 'but we should still check the other rooms.'

We did so, a quick glance in the kitchen and the living room. That left the basement, and to be honest, I wasn't looking forward to going down. I'd since replaced the hatch with sturdier tin sheet and timber, and was confident that nobody could have got in via the coal chute. Then again, the racket they'd been making, they might just have.

We edged towards the entrance to the basement.

As a temporary measure, I'd set a large sheet of plywood up against the wall, blocking the hole I'd smashed through the plasterboard. I'd used a pile of loose bricks I found in the back yard to prop it up. The plyboard hadn't been disturbed. Just about to jostle it aside, Sarah halted me.

'Listen,' she said.

'What?'

'Shhh.'

We listened.

Bang!

The noise didn't come from below but above us.

'Bloody hell, what's going on around here?' I demanded.

'I thought the noise was coming from up there. It's hard to tell in this old place. The acoustics are crazy.'

Returning to the bottom of the stairs, I peered up. From that angle I could just see the edge of the bathroom door and a portion of the stained glass. We hadn't checked the bathroom for interlopers.

'Do you want to stay here while I check things out?'

When Sarah replied in the negative I was secretly relieved. Not that I expected her to do much more than I could achieve, but having her presence at my back did help firm up my spine.

'OK, but if there's anyone there, I want you to run down and out the front door. Call the police when you're outside.'

'That's if there's *actually* anyone there,' she reminded me.

Until then the thought that our noisy visitor could be anything but a real person hadn't entered my mind. Now that uneasy feeling that whom we had been seeking to hear from earlier had finally decided to introduce themselves sent a qualm through me. The short hairs bristled on my neck. Suddenly I lost the resolve to go up the stairs. I looked at Sarah again, and saw her chew at the corner of her lip. She nodded me on. Her hero.

Swearing under my breath at my idiocy, I planted my foot on the first step.

The banging continued, an intermittent knocking.

An air blockage in the water pipes, I hoped.

Arriving at the bathroom door, I sneaked a glance at the nearby landing wall, but my vision must have been too pinpointed for it to matrix any images. Thankful for small mercies, I leaned so my ear was next to the bathroom door.

'Go on.'

I jumped.

How Sarah had climbed the stairs without me realising is no surprise in hindsight, but at the time I almost messed my jogging pants. 'Jesus,' I hissed.

'Go on in,' she urged.

'It isn't coming from the bathroom.' I pointed upward.

'But we've already checked those rooms.'

'Yeah.'

But we'd have to check again.

Braver now about looking in the bathroom, I turned the handle and pressed open the door. Nobody was in sight. I quickly went in and checked the toilet cubicle at the end. Shook my head as I returned to Sarah, and again pointed upstairs. 'Do you hear it?'

Catching her bottom lip on her eyeteeth, she nodded.

We backtracked, and again I sneaked glances in the rooms on that floor. I needn't have bothered, as it was evident from where the knocking originated. I stood at the foot of the narrow stairwell, peering up.

Yesterday upon the stair I met a man who wasn't there...

He wasn't there now, and it was a relief.

Going up, I held the hammer ready to bash out the brains of anyone desperate enough to try to run past me. Did I have it in me to deliver a crushing blow? Right then, right there, the answer was yes. Whether a burglar would give me the opportunity to get in the first strike was debatable. The hammer shaft was slick with sweat.

Bangbangbang!

The knocking came like a volley of machinegun fire.

'What the hell *is* that?'

I spared a glance at Sarah who was following close on my heels. The question was pointless because I had no answer.

Gaining the tiny hallway, we stopped. Sarah pressed tightly against me, one arm around my waist. Her touch gave me the courage to lean into the bedroom we'd recently shared.

Boom!

The previous sounds had come like gunshots; this was more of a mortar blast. We fell back against the dumbwaiter closet door. Our language was choice.

'Did something blow up?' Sarah managed.

I couldn't be sure, but my first instinct was that the sound had simply been a forceful knock from within the bedroom. Briefly I wondered if the racket had come from above, from the roof itself, but I knew it hadn't. That was no clubfooted bird at roost. It was been a deliberate knock on the wall to the right. Cursing the fact I'd unplugged the lamp, and left it downstairs, I took a look at where I believed the sound came from: the walk-in wardrobe door.

We'd neglected to check the wardrobe earlier.

All this time while we'd searched the house, whoever – whatever - was stuck in the wardrobe had continued their incessant banging. It was as Sarah had pointed out, the acoustics were crazy. Banging on the back wall of the cupboard would make a noise in the first floor landing – which would then be carried back up the stairs and through the bedroom door.

'Put your phone light on,' I whispered.

Sarah complied and cast the beam over the cupboard doors.

Bang!

The doors moved a fraction.

Bangbangbang!

They rattled in the frame.

'Who's there?' I demanded.

No answer.

'Who's there? I've got to warn you, we've called the police and they're on the way here. You've got seconds at best to come out and give yourself up.'

Bangbangbang!

'Right,' I shouted. 'Don't say you weren't warned.'

Rushing to the doors, I jammed my foot against the central gap so that the doors couldn't be pushed open.

Bang! Boom! Bang!

I rammed my shoulder to the doors. I could feel the solid thumps through the wood.

'I warned you. Now you're not getting out. The police will be here any second.' Looking for Sarah, I motioned for her to make the call. But she didn't stab the buttons.

'I don't think we should,' she warned. 'I don't think they're going to find a person.'

To be fair, I didn't either. But if there was a wild animal in my cupboard I wanted someone on hand to capture and take it away.

'Open the door, Jack,' Sarah urged.

'What? Are you crazy?'

'We can't go on like this all night, can we?'

There was no need to think it through, she was correct. The logical thing to do was open the bloody doors and put an end to the mystery. If some stray cat had found its way into the cupboard, then releasing it was the thing to do.

'OK. But keep back. There's no saying how it will react.'

B-b-b-b-bang!

The door rattled under the impacts. They were weaker than before but no less disconcerting.

I steadied myself, the hammer ready, my foot still jamming the doors. A quick check with Sarah earned me a nod. She held her phone in one hand and the chisel the other. She didn't look as if she had it in her to stab anything, but her support was better than nothing.

I yanked open the doors, stepping quickly aside. I expected a sleek critter to come flying out the cupboard and seek exit. Nothing moved. So it was probably huddled in a corner now, fearing for its life. I moved closer, waving Sarah over with her phone light. She shone it into the cupboard. I'd hung some of my clothing, piled some more on the floor. There was nothing else in there.

Nothing visible.

Cautiously I probed through the clothing on the floor with my feet. Nothing moved. I shifted the hanging garments with the hammer. Nothing.

It made no sense. There was nothing physically there.

Something else was missing.

The banging had stopped the instant I opened the doors.

'This makes no sense,' I said.

BANG!

I screamed and threw myself out of the wardrobe, sprawling on the floor at Sarah's feet. She did a little dance of fright, eyes and mouth wide open. We both craned to look at the open wardrobe door, which still rattled from the forceful impact.

19

Dream on, Casanova

'We asked for proof and we got it.'

Sarah was pale from the shock. We'd reconvened in the parlour on the ground floor, the nearest room to the exit door. I'd made tea to settle our nerves while Sarah dressed, adding plenty of sugar to the brew. Apparently sweet tea was a good antidote to shock. I was on my second mug but Sarah still cupped her first, her elbows on her knees as she rocked slowly back and forward.

'I only wish I knew what the hell it was.'

'It's common to hear knocking during hauntings,' Sarah explained. 'Sometimes it's the only way a spirit has of communicating with us. We asked it to speak, it replied the only way it could.'

'By scaring the living daylights out of us?'

'Just because the sounds were loud doesn't mean it was ominous. Maybe it was just frustrated because it couldn't find a way to let us know what it really wanted.' Sarah moved her mug to her lips, but paused before sipping. The cup went back to her lap untouched. 'There's a theory that ghosts manifest using the available energy in the atmosphere. There was little for it to draw upon, so it couldn't find the strength to speak as we asked.

So it knocked. Maybe it wanted us to respond in kind.'

'By using Morse code?' My tone was sarcastic.

'More like "two knocks for yes, one knock for no". It's a method of communication that's been used for years during séances. By asking certain yes and no questions you can usually determine who the spirit is and what they want from us.'

Now that we were downstairs and the sky lightening outside, I wasn't as frightened as before. As my nerve returned, so did my doubt. 'It was probably nothing to do with ghosts. The house is old, the wardrobe door was probably just contracting or something.'

'Jack, how can you say that? You know the banging wasn't a result of the bloody wood shrinking. Stop all this denial, will you?'

I shrugged. 'I'm only saying.'

'Well don't. The longer you keep coming up with alternative excuses, the longer it will take to get to the bottom of this.'

'Maybe I don't want to get to the bottom of it: maybe I only want it all to stop. Jesus Christ! We're talking about a bloody haunting here.'

The very fact we were on the subject severely challenged my belief system. When challenged, I was the type to grow defensive. If that meant me coming up with alternative theories for everything that had happened then Sarah would just have to live with it.

'It's so frustrating.' I'm not sure if she was referring to the situation or the fact I was being as stubborn as usual. 'What was it trying to tell us, Jack?'

'I haven't got a clue. But I don't like the idea that it was spying on us from the bloody closet. Heard of any pervert ghosts before?'

'That's not funny.'

'But it's true. Do you think it was watching us when we were…well, you know?'

'Having sex.' She said it perfunctorily. I noticed her mouth twist slightly at the thought. 'If it was an actual spirit, then maybe it was watching. They're the essence of a deceased human with all the same likes and dislikes.'

'A lecherous ghost: who'd have thought?'

'But maybe not,' Sarah went on. 'If it was there when we were having sex it didn't let us know. Why wait until hours later?'

'Maybe it was enjoying the peepshow and didn't want us to stop. Who knows, maybe it started all that banging to wake us up hoping for another show.'

'You're sick.'

'And horny,' I said.

She shook her head. 'It's almost morning. We need to start thinking about getting ready for work.'

'I'm not going in.'

'What?'

'I'm going to throw a sickie. You should too.'

'I can't take a sick day. I'm management, Jack.'

'Of course you can. Daniel's always spouting on about how much he loves being at work, so let him roll up his sleeves and get stuck in for a change.'

'No. I'm not doing it. It will fall on our workmates to pick up the slack if we don't go in.'

'Shit. You're making me feel guilty now.'

'Yeah, right.'

I grinned. 'I've jobs to do here. I'm having the beds delivered and stuff. After what happened with my car crash and getting sick at work I've a good excuse for not going in.'

'I haven't. And it's not going to happen: I'm not good when it comes to lying.'

'I'm not lying, just being conservative with the truth. I was sick yesterday, so should get away with it.' I understood I was putting her in a bad position, her being management and all. 'You wouldn't grass me up would you?'

'I'm not going to tell.' Sarah placed down her untouched tea, frowning. 'You've got an excuse, yeah, but if it were me I couldn't do it. I don't think you should either.'

'I'm not being dishonest, Sarah. We've a sick pay scheme in place, and I haven't been off once this year. Not even when I was genuinely ill: I don't feel bad about taking my allowance.'

'Once this year?" She looked momentarily confused, but chose to ignore the way her mind was going. 'Sick pay's not an allowance, Jack. The scheme's there to help when you're poorly, not to be abused.'

'Now you do sound like a manager. I don't see it as abuse, Sarah. I pay my national insurance, it's time I got something back from it.' I waited for her to start quoting the importance of business ethics and loyalty to our employer. 'It's not as if you work in pay roll, or HR: it doesn't affect your team's staffing levels if I don't go in.'

Sarah shook her head. 'We're just going to have to agree to disagree. After last night, I don't know how you can still doubt me.'

I offered a lecherous wink. 'Talk about things going bump in the night, eh?'

'Typical man,' she said, but I got a shy grin from her. 'Seriously though, with all that knocking going on I wish I'd left the recorder running. It would have been incredible proof.'

'At least we can corroborate each other's story.'

Sarah made a face. I guessed what it meant. She didn't want anyone knowing that she'd spent the night with me. What was wrong if the story got out, she was my girlfriend, and it was no business of anyone else? Was refusing to stay off work really because she didn't like to lie? It was a bit of a contradiction if she wasn't prepared to admit she'd been with me all night.

'Do I embarrass you?' I said before thinking things through.

'What do you mean?'

'Do you regret sleeping with me now?'

'No, Jack. Why would you think that?'

I shrugged. I knew it made me look like a petulant teenager, but I didn't care. Disappointment soured my guts.

'You sound as if you don't want anyone to know about us,' I said.

She stood, and I thought I'd pushed things too far too soon. But Sarah face-planted a kiss on me. She held the back of my head, twining her fingers through my hair as her lips roamed over mine. I tasted her breath – hoped that she didn't get the sour tang from mine. Finally she stepped away and looked up at me. 'Did that feel like someone who regrets anything?'

I leaked air like a deflating balloon. It was all it took to dispel the discomfort of the last minute or two.

'Can you give me a lift back to my house?' Sarah asked. 'I can't very well go into work dressed like this.'

'Yeah, just give me a minute to fetch the car round.'

I bustled. Found my keys, and headed out. I fetched my Volvo from the back lane and halted at the junction. Sarah was waiting for me at the front door. If I turned out on to the main road towards her I'd be facing the wrong way up the one-way street. I waved her to the car and she pulled the door shut behind her. She got in the front passenger seat.

'I don't agree with what you're doing, but suppose I could cover for you at work,' she offered as I pulled out. 'I could tell them I called to check and you were poorly.'

Just about to ask why she wouldn't admit to staying at my house, I realised she was right. If I'd the strength to make whoopee all night, I'd have no excuse for throwing a sickie. 'Yeah, if it doesn't offend your morals,' I said, but I weighted my words with a cheeky grin. She elbowed me in the shoulder.

'Go easy,' I said. 'I don't want to lose control again.'

'Three times in one night? Dream on, Casanova.'

'I meant of the car,' I said. 'But if you want to see if I'm good for a third time in the sack, I'm willing to give it a blast. I can soon take us back.'

She smiled, but shook her head. 'Take me home.'

With those words my reinvigorated desire popped like a soap bubble, and my mind was again cast back to that fateful night when Naomi died. I drove Sarah home slowly, taking care to watch for my dead girlfriend stepping out between parked cars.

20

Crimson Teeth

'I'm really sick, boss.'

'So I heard.'

'I take it you spoke with Sarah King, the manager from Store Ops? She, uh, called me earlier and I told her I wouldn't be coming in.'

'Yes. She said. I'm only surprised that you're feeling so unwell. I mean, it was only a minor collision you were involved in yesterday. Nothing to fret over.'

'I've been having stomach problems for a while.' The lies sounded more plausible when laden with a sprinkling of truth. 'With throwing up at work, I really upset it and it has flared up. I had a really bad night.'

Daniel Graham said nothing.

'I'm going to try to get a doctor's appointment,' I went on, 'to see if he can prescribe me something. I'm just not confident it'll be today.'

'If anything changes, let me know. But, Jack…'

'What?'

'I expect to see you in on Monday.'

'I'll be there, boss. I promise.'

'In fact, if you're feeling up for it, you can come in tomorrow evening for stock take. You can make it up for letting me down today.'

Now I said nothing. I was fuming.

After a beat Daniel must have realised he sounded like a bully. He quickly backtracked, saying, 'It was a stupid suggestion. If you're unwell you're unwell. Just take today off and I'll see you after the weekend. You have your kids this weekend don't you? Still a good idea to have them over if you're not feeling too good?'

What a fucking saint.

'It isn't catching,' I said, trying not to sound too scathing. 'The kids will be fine. I'm sure I will be too, but right now I feel as sick as a dog. Sorry, boss, but the toilet calls.'

I hung up before he could respond.

Standing in the parlour, I held my phone by my side. Staring off into space. When I told him I'd had a bad night the silence from the other end of the line was palpable. He'd confirmed to me that he'd spoken to Sarah. I wondered what she told him, and if she had admitted to being with me all night. I used to think that Daniel was a closet homosexual, but lately I'd noticed him eyeing Sarah in a way that proved otherwise. Was he jealous of us? Was that the reason why he was such a dick towards me? Then again, if Sarah had told him about our night of passion he wouldn't have bought my sickness as an excuse for being absent from work. No, Sarah couldn't have told him. But then I wasn't sure if that made me happy or disappointed. I looked at my phone. No reason to: it wasn't as if I'd find the answer there.

I ate breakfast, drank more tea. Hung about waiting on the delivery guys. By mid-day they hadn't turned up so I went upstairs to my bedroom and stood looking at the wardrobe doors.

'Knock, knock,' I said.

There was no response.

'Naomi? Was that you knocking earlier?'

I listened.

'Two knocks for yes, one knock for no,' I commanded, feeling mildly foolish.

Stepping up to the door, I rapped my knuckles on it. The sound was identical to those I'd heard in the early hours. A bone-aching chill descended over me.

'Did you hear that, Naomi? Can you knock like that for me?' I rapped again in demonstration. Waited.

Considering the implications of all that I'd seen and heard, what I'd done, I posed another question. 'Are you mad at me?'

No reply.

I pulled open the doors and looked inside. The wardrobe was large enough to accommodate me plus half a dozen ghosts. Stepping inside, I waited then repeated my question. 'If you are angry, then tell me. Knock like you did last night.'

Minutes passed. Another idea struck me.

'If I'm not speaking to Naomi, who am I speaking to? Is it somebody else?' The shadow figure had been a male, no doubt about it. If I could touch him, then maybe he was more corporeal than his insubstantial form suggested. Maybe he could make a fist and pound on a door. 'If I'm speaking to the shadow man, then let me know. Knock twice. Let me know what you want from me.'

Again I received no reply.

But then I got to thinking. Sarah said that ghosts were believed to manifest using the available energy, and there was little for a spirit to feed off in this room. Maybe I was receiving answers, just not in a way that I could comprehend. I went to the dumbwaiter closet and found Sarah's digital recorder where she'd left it after turning it off. Unfamiliar with how it worked, I fiddled around a bit, then set it running. I placed it inside the wardrobe and closed the doors. From outside, I said, 'If you have a message for me, then speak into the device. Tell me who you are and what you want.'

A knocking from below caught my attention, but there was nothing sinister about the sound. It had a different, natural resonance as it echoed up two flights of stairs, and I immediately recognised the clack of the front door knocker. The new beds had arrived.

I greeted the deliverymen at the door. They'd parked their truck on the street, its hazard lights blinking to stave off any over eager traffic wardens. It was an older man, skinny, about eight stone wet through, huge Adam's apple, and a younger guy who looked as if he'd got the job on his muscular build alone. Despite my initial impression of them, the younger one seemed to be in charge, and it was the older bloke who was the hired muscle. I showed them in, pointed out the rooms I wanted the beds delivered to and left them to it. My bed would be easily assembled. The kids' bunk beds would take a little longer to erect, coming in about a thousand parts and twice as many fixings. I wondered if I bunged the boss a few quid he'd make his pal put the bunks together for me. In the end I decided that the job would keep my mind off the weird goings on in the house. I thanked them kindly and ushered them out of the door at first opportunity.

The young man paused on the step, as if he was waiting for a tip. But instead of sticking out his hand he offered a funny look, and made a nod towards the stairs. 'Has summat happened in this house, mate?'

'What do you mean?'

'Up there? Y'know on the landing next to the bathroom?'

'No. Not that I know of.' I kept my features straight, so as not to betray the lie. Or my excitement. Had he seen something too?

'Ah, man, it was probably just my eyes playing tricks on me.' The man shook his head, abashed to have brought it up.

'Why? What did you see?'

'Probably nothin'.' He peered past me, again looking up the stairs. 'Just, well, when I turned the corner I thought I saw a woman on the landing. I thought it was your missus. But when I looked again she was gone. Didn't see her in any of the rooms.' He held up a hand. 'Not that I was going through your place, like, the doors were all open and I could see the rooms were empty.'

'Well,' I said. 'That's strange.'

'Aye,' he agreed.

I shrugged.

'Summat else,' he added. 'She looked as if she had blood on her face. I was gonna give you a shout, but when I couldn't find her…'

We stood looking at each other for a slow beat. He shook his head. 'Probably just me,' he said, and handed me the delivery note for signing. He took the papers back without comment and turned for his truck. The older man had already got in and started the engine. By the look on his face, and the rapid bobbing of his Adam's apple, he too had seen something and was keen to get away. I didn't bother

227

waving them off, shutting the door quickly and heading along the vestibule for the stairs.

I went up to the half-landing, a buzz of adrenalin in my gut. Daylight streamed through the stained glass window, casting colours on the wall on the left of the adjacent landing. Standing at the vantage outside the bathroom door I looked up at what had alarmed the deliveryman. At a glance it was easy to see how he'd conjured the image of a woman out of the splash of pattern on the wall. The bloody face was in bold relief. In the next instant the clouds must have covered the sun because the image faded and disappeared. A second or two later and the sun poked out its head and the woman was back again. Definitely a case of *pareidolia*. Or was it?

Moving up the short set of stairs, I noticed my own shadow projected before me. I went close to the wall so that my head and shoulders were cast adjacent to the woman's face. This near it had lost much of its definition, the way an oil painting does when viewed up close, but having concentrated on it as I approached I could still make out the features. More than ten years after the event, I could still clearly picture Naomi's face in those last moments we spent together, but I could also recall her from calmer times. Lifting my right hand, I directed its shadow twin so that it lay over the face. I stroked and my shadow played its fingers down her right cheek.

A tear oozed out of my left eye and ran down my jaw.

My shadow fingers stroked her hair, made a soft caress of her cheek. After Naomi's death I'd honoured her memory with a form of subdued grief, only once weeping for her at her burial as I watched her casket lowered into the grave. The rest I bottled inside, and kept to myself. Grief for me was a private thing. I'd buried it as completely as the six feet of dirt that covered her coffin. Only recently had it resurfaced, and it had proved the undoing of my marriage to Catriona. My bitchy wife hadn't understood. My doctor told me it was best to grieve, to let Naomi go with an outpouring of emotion, but my wife hadn't seen things that way. She couldn't understand my sudden weepy periods, or my heart-broken sobs as we lay together in bed. She thought my love for Naomi diminished her, pushed her to a lesser place in my affections. She was angered, grew bitter, said I was obsessed with a fucking corpse. Perhaps my riposte wasn't well thought out when I replied that sex with her was like screwing a corpse, so where was the fucking difference. Maybe my scorn was what pushed her into the willing arms of Mark Wilson, Catriona's attempt at showing that she wasn't the one with a problem in the bedroom.

The main reason it had taken so long for me to release my pent up grief was this: who exactly would listen?

How would crying for Naomi do any good? It wasn't as if she could hear me. I was brought up in the Church of England faith, but was largely agnostic. I barely believed in God, let alone Heaven. I didn't think that a haloed Naomi was sitting on a cloud somewhere, strumming a harp and watching over me. All that remained of Naomi was a collection of stained bones and tattered funeral raiment, buried two yards beneath the earth. How could she hear my heartfelt cries? Oh, I did try to speak to her. I asked her to respond, let me know she could hear me. Give me a sign. But her response had been as cold as her decomposing body.

My faith in God and an afterlife at His side was already built on shaky ground, and when I failed to receive communication from my dead girlfriend it plunged deep into the earth, swallowed wholly, and I'd come to realise I was a confirmed atheist.

That was then.

Tracing the outline of that face on the wall, I wondered - had I seen it back then - would I have accepted it as the sign I longed for? Would this pattern on the wall, this result of apophenia, have swayed me down a different path? It was hard to say, but I thought that I'd been too closed down to accept anything as proof that my girlfriend's spirit endured. But now? Since moving into my new home, having witnessed both unnerving and perplexing events, and having engaged with a person who helped explain my way around the weird and wonderful goings on, I was beginning to accept *possibilities*.

One thing I was certain of, before now a pattern on the wall wouldn't have brought me to tears.

'Jesus, Naomi, I miss you so much.' I physically touched the face now. 'I love you and I want you back.'

Speaking out loud like that caused a twinge of guilt to shoot through me. Hell, I was with Sarah now. I shouldn't be dwelling on my love for another woman. It almost felt like cheating. The way Catriona had cheated on me.

The clouds shifted.

The face faded.

Had Naomi felt my guilt, and withdrew from me?

'Don't go, babe, please.' I reached for the blank wall.

The sun stabbed light through the stained glass.

The face reappeared. Vivid red. Blood poured fresh from the eyes and mouth. I touched the lips. To smooth away the hurt. The crimson teeth snapped, gnashing at my fingers like a savage beast.

Recoiling from those teeth, a scream leaped from my throat.

My fear took me backwards. My left heel skidded off the top riser, and then I was weightless. I fell.

It was only a few short steps down to the bathroom's half-landing, but from the top of my head to the floorboards it was at least ten feet, and my skull made a perfect arc all the way down.

The back of my head felt as if it imploded, and a wash of scarlet agony swept across my vision. I lay crumpled on the half-landing, with my feet propped up the stairs. Black edged my senses, floated in like ink on water, and then all was a foggy swirl through which I could define neither detail nor sense. All senses fled but my hearing was the last to fade. I could hear the pounding of my heart in my veins, and the cackle of bitter laughter.

21

The Writing's on the Wall

My palm stung.

There was also a dull throb at the base of my skull, but it was nothing compared to the burning sensation in my hand. I peeled open my fingers allowing the screwdriver to drop with a dull thud on the new carpet. My abraded palm had mostly healed from when I stupidly grabbed at the falling dumbwaiter rope, but my new exertions had reopened the graze, raised blisters, and the salt in my own sweat had invaded the wounds. Plasma oozed from the ruptured blisters. I shook my hand, ran it down my T-shirt to dry it and only then blinked in confusion.

'What the bloody hell?'

I'd been busy.

The kids' bunk beds stood against the wall, fully erected but for the mattresses yet to be placed in the frame. Flattened cardboard boxes and white polystyrene packaging was strewn around me. My toolbox was open, some random tools spread around it. I checked the time on my watch. I'd been very industrious in the – what? – two hours or so that I'd lost. Squinting in confusion, I checked my watch a second time. Two bloody hours!

The beds were proof that I'd been hard at work, and yet I'd no recollection of building them. Hell, I must have completed the job lost in the murk of a fugue. My last waking memory was of rearing back from those snapping teeth, falling...bitter laughter.

This wasn't right. Worrying.

All I needed on top of everything else was a bloody concussion. With some trepidation I touched the sore spot at the back of my skull, and winced at the size of the egg I found. As loath as I was to discover further injury, I gently pressed my skull around the bump, terrified that something would move. The distance I'd fallen, smacking my head against the bathroom door, I was lucky I didn't smash my skull open, or break my neck. It was little wonder that I'd come round in a daze, and somehow found my way to the children's room, applying myself to the task of erecting their beds.

Earlier I'd lied to Daniel when promising to go to the doctor, but now I thought that I had a genuine reason to do so. For all I knew my skull was fractured, the bones pressing on my brain, suppressing my memory. Maybe I was bleeding inside. Jesus, I could be dying. A flurry of panic washed through me and I clutched at the bedframe for balance. To add to my concern, pain sang a lament from my damaged knee. I stood there breathing heavily, feeling sorry for myself.

When I didn't collapse it was a relief. It took a few more calming breaths before I was ready to test my legs for stability. I was OK, but for the fog when I tried to recall anything after my fall. Bending, I retrieved the screwdriver. Checking it over, I could dredge faint recollections of using it to fix the screws that held the spars on the uppermost bunk. I worked backwards from there, could vaguely recall splitting the cardboard packaging and disgorging the dozens of pieces of wood on the bedroom floor. Before that, there was nothing. But maybe it would come back. I was relieved that the motions I'd gone through were there somewhere, and would need a little teasing to bring to the fore, but at least I hadn't been totally brain dead for the past two hours.

A selfish, lazy part of me was smugly pleased that the beds had been erected. It wasn't a task I was looking forward to, and I was happy that the mundane job was behind me. However the manner in which the task was completed remained troubling. Again I worried that I'd caused myself some serious injury. I touched my head again, hissing between my teeth. It wasn't as sore as I told myself it was. Puffing out my cheeks, I laid the screwdriver down, and turned for the door, intending finding some painkillers. That was when I saw the walls.

'Oh, fuck!'

It was undeniable this time. The words written on the wall weren't old graffiti, neither were they given a fresh look through the edge of a carpet scraping the loose plaster from their edges. These words were scoured a half inch deep into the wall, huge ragged letters a foot and more tall. Three words. Repeated time and again.

I WANT YOU

'Jesus, what the hell's going on in this bloody place?'

I was afraid to approach, but my feet had other ideas. I stumbled to the wall, goggling at the lettering gouged into the plaster. Fresh dust was on the carpet. I had a clue when this had happened, but not how. It was an illogical terror that held my fingers from the wall. If I touched the lettering would those crimson teeth again snap at them from the very fabric of the wall? Yes, my fear was idiotic, but it was there and I couldn't shake it. I stepped back. In my mind there was only one person who could be responsible for the vandalism.

Turning fast, I hollered through the door, into the hallway, down the stairs to the landing where last she'd laughed at me.

'Naomi! Why the fuck are doing this to me?'

When I'd begged her to give me a sign, when I was at breaking point and my grief was at it rawest, when I was destroying my marriage to Catriona, my ex girlfriend had kept her silence. Now she was being most vocal. Why now? What had caused her to come out of the shadows to haunt me like this?

'Why, Naomi? Are you trying to punish me for some reason?'

As ever when I demanded a reply, I got none.

Exasperated, I grabbed the screwdriver, then in a fit of anger, I ran at the wall and jabbed the tip into the plasterwork. I began ripping and tearing with it, attempting to obliterate those infuriating words. I cut and slashed, wedged the tip under a loose portion of plaster and yanked it off the laths beneath. I dug in again, and something stayed my rage. The tip of the screwdriver fit neatly into the groove of a letter "I".

'Uh,' I said, or something equally less than eloquent.

The tip of the screwdriver was an exact fit, and when I placed it into other grooves it fit there too. I looked at the screwdriver, back at the wall, then at my trembling hands.

'Fuck.'

Dropping the screwdriver, I stepped away. I didn't take my eyes off my hands. They were shaking. So were my insides.

Naomi wasn't the one responsible for scraping that phrase into the wall. How could she? That left only one other, and I was horrified at the realisation.

What was worse: My dead girlfriend haunting me, turning her wicked poltergeist hands to leaving crazy messages on the bedroom wall, or that I, dazed after the fall, had scraped the words into the plaster, my hands guided by some impulse to torture me? In that moment I couldn't really say. Both scenarios were equally as insane, and horrific. Marginally, cutting out those letters myself was preferential to the knowledge that my ex was back and she had brought a sense of misguided vengeance along with her. My excuse was that I was stunned from the fall, confused, disoriented. Maybe I'd picked up the screwdriver, read those other words previously scraped into the wall and simply copied them. Hell, it was obvious I'd no clue what I was doing. How could I be expected to act rationally in such a situation?

I fled the room.

But in the tiny hallway I paused. There was one act I remembered doing earlier.

Entering my bedroom I stood in front of the wardrobe doors.

'If that wasn't you who wrote on the walls, Naomi, then it stands to reason you didn't leave your voice for me to hear either.' My words were a challenge of sorts, reverse psychology you might say. I opened the wardrobe and recovered the digital recorder I'd set running earlier. I fully expected it to have run its course, and it had. The batteries had died. I took the recorder with me and went downstairs where I searched for fresh batteries. I found some in the miscellany that I'd dumped in one of the kitchen drawers days earlier and fed them into the device. The read-out on the front indicated various time stamped files – those Sarah had recorded yesterday, plus the latest one I'd initiated. I ignored the first ones and brought up the file on mine. I clicked "play" as I went and sat in the parlour.

For a few seconds all I heard was the soft hiss of white noise, then my voice, strangely distorted from the voice I recognised in my own head said 'If you have a message for me, then speak into the device. Tell me who you are and what you want.' Clunks and clicks followed as I closed the doors. A faint rattle I recognised as the door knocker, then the sounds of my feet going downstairs to greet the deliverymen.

There followed conversation too muffled to understand, me talking to the men. There then came the occasional indistinct click but that was probably nothing, just ambient noises made by us moving about on the lower floors, and then came more solid thuds and bumps as the beds and the boxed bunks were carted upstairs. The deliverymen talked to each other, but it was inane crap, nothing of value. But then there was a good half-minute of white noise.

'Hello?' The voice was faint, but I knew it was that of the younger deliveryman. 'Hello? Missus? Anybody there?'

The questions coincided with the boss' story of having thought he'd seen an injured woman and searching for her through the house. He must have come again to the top floor because this time his voice was louder, and it had an uneasy tone to it. 'Hello, missus? Do you need help? Should I fetch your husband? Uh…'

Another voice joined his. The old guy's. 'There's naebody here, Mike. I don't understand it, man.'

'Nah…neither do I.'

There was one last attempt. Judging by the rise in volume, the young man had stuck his head in the bedroom itself. 'Halloo? Nah, nobody there either. I don't get it, Ronnie. I'm bloody sure I saw a woman.'

'Wishful thinking, eh?' replied Ronnie, his voice more distant. The men grumbled out uneasy laughter. Then Mike the boss said, 'Never mind. I'll mention it to the bloke downstairs, see what he says.'

'Ask him if he's gonna give us a hand while you're at it,' said Ronnie.

'I'd rather he didn't. He looks like a right divot.'

Hearing that I leaned away from the digital recorder, giving it a hard glare. 'Fucking divot? I'm not the one lifting and carrying for a living.'

Speaking like that I almost didn't hear it.

Three faint rasps followed by a breathy exhalation.

There was more noise as the deliverymen made their way downstairs. Muffled conversation from below. I ignored it, rewinding the recording to a few seconds before.

'…like a right divot.' The recording kicked in.

Then the trio of faint rasps.

I couldn't make out what they were, but there was a cadence to them like spoken words. I rewound the recording, again hit "play", then thumbed up the volume to its highest setting. I strained to listen, but when they came the words were easy to define.

Not…safe…here…

The words were spoken haltingly, as if delivered over a great distance. But there was no denying the message. Or in whose voice they were spoken.

Naomi's.

22

Chinks in the Crimson Glass

I want you. I want you. I want you...

The faint strains of my voice came from Sarah's digital recorder. She was sitting with it in her lap, cupping a pair of earphones with her palms, dazed as she listened to my mantra. When I'd called her and asked her to come over on the Friday evening after work to listen to the EVP's we'd captured this was not what she had expected to hear.

'I promise you I've no recollection of saying that,' I said for about the umpteenth time.

At first she'd been sceptical, perhaps believing I'd made the recording knowing full well that she'd be intrigued by it. But after explaining my tumble down the stairs, the bump to my head, and my subsequent blackout for the best part of two hours she was now listening more keenly. I'd even allowed her to check my bump to validate my tale. Pressing me to go to A&E she argued I should have my head checked out: she feared I might have a concussion. I too had been concerned but had later decided not to go to hospital; what were they going to do? Tell me to take some painkillers – which I'd already done – and try not to fall asleep until someone else was around to watch over me? I just cut out the middleman.

'I can't stay over tonight,' Sarah had said.

Trying not to show my disappointment, I'd replied, 'I'm sure I'll be OK. So no worries.' I'm only glad she couldn't see the way I'd bit my lip as I said those words. 'Are you off out tonight?'

'Yeah,' she said, 'I just made the plans today at work. There's a bunch of us going out for a meal and drinks.'

'Daniel going?'

She nodded.

'Which means I can't,' I said. 'Not after calling in sick and playing it for all it was worth.'

'You wouldn't have come any way,' Sarah said, and it was the first real sign of reproof she'd shown me in days.

I'd no argument. So I brought up the subject of EVP's instead, steering her away from the jealous streak that threatened to consume me. I let her listen to the first EVP: the female voice saying "not safe here", but then forwarded the recording to what had caused me such dismay when I'd first heard it. The recording had caught my tumble as a series of thumps. Silence had followed but for only a few seconds. Then there had come the dull creaks of me ascending the stairs and entering the spare bedroom. There had been another short period of silence, and then my voice had rung out.

Considering the recorder was in the closed wardrobe in the adjacent room I must have been shouting as I scored those words into the wall with the screwdriver.

'What, or who, is it you want?' Sarah asked.

'To be honest I haven't a clue. I think I was just repeating what was already scraped on the wall.'

Her look was one of consideration. It metamorphosed into one of concern. 'It isn't rational behaviour.'

'I'd just knocked myself out. Hardly likely I was going to act rationally after such a bump to the head.'

'That's why you need to see a doctor. You could have done yourself serious damage.'

'I'm fine now. The bump hurts, but only where it got scraped.' I touched my head. 'I'm all there, if that's what you're worried about.'

Normally she'd come back with a swift retort on the subject of my mental stability, but didn't.

'Really. I'm fine. OK, so I was dazed, but I'm thinking clearly now.'

'You built a set of bunk beds in a daze?'

'Yeah. Sounds ridiculous, but it's true. Usually I can't follow those instructions for love nor money: maybe next time I've a chore to do I'll bang my head on a wall first.'

'You can laugh, but I don't like it, Jack. You need to get checked out.'

Rubbing my hands over my skull, then across my face, I said, 'I need to get to the bottom of all this. We've established that was my voice while I was in the bedroom, but whose was it that answered the deliveryman?'

'You said it sounded like your ex,' Sarah pointed out.

I shrugged. 'Maybe I'm just making her voice fit. It's ten years since I heard Naomi speak. How can I be sure? It's so faint, distant.'

'Let's listen to it again. Here sit down.' Sarah adjusted the earphones so I could sit alongside her and listen. We propped our heads together, while Sarah took the recording back to the first voice.

Not…safe…here…

'Not safe here,' Sarah repeated.

'Some kind of warning?' I suggested.

'Yeah. Possibly. But for who?'

'That's what I wondered about. Did she speak to the driver, or because she knew I'd be the one to listen to the recording?'

'So we're in agreement it's a "she" at least,' said Sarah.

The voice was barely more than a whisper, but the pitch was higher in tone, and sounded female, but could even have been that of a young boy. Hearing it again I couldn't really say that it sounded anything like Naomi's voice, it could equally be

Sarah's or of any other female or prepubescent boy. I chose not to dispute Sarah's decision.

We listened to the EVP again.

'Wait,' Sarah said. 'I hear the three words, but what is that afterwards?'

To me it was an indiscernible sigh or breathy exhalation.

Sarah's eyes were wide when she pulled away.

'Did she just say *my* name?'

'No. It's just a, uh, breath or something.'

'Sarah shook her head, then leaned in so I could listen again. 'There,' she said as she replayed the EVP.

'Sounds more like "essair" to me,' I said.

Sarah pulled off the headphones and handed them over. 'Put them on. Listen again.'

…not…safe…here….essair…uhhh…

'Well?' Sarah demanded.

'I can't make it out. Essair? Rewind it and let me hear again.'

'Never mind. Let me listen.' She took back the earphones and settled them into place. I watched her face. It grew stony.

'It's just an exhalation,' I repeated.

She shook her head, unconvinced. 'Why would it be saying my name? Why warn me?'

'I'm not sure it's your name,' I said. 'The warning was probably for me. After all, I'm the clumsy git who fell down the stairs shortly afterwards.'

'Yeah,' Sarah agreed without conviction. 'You never really explained how that happened.'

'I tripped.'

'You said; but how did you trip?'

'Kind of fell over my feet.'

Sarah eyed me from the other end of the settee. Waited.

'OK. I thought I could see that face on the landing wall again. You know the matrixing effect I told you about. I took a step back to get a different angle and slipped off the top step.'

'You saw Naomi's face again?'

'I saw a face, yeah, but it's nothing. Just the way the light comes in through the stained glass. I thought we'd already established that?'

'Bit of a coincidence that her voice comes through warning you and then a few minutes later you take a tumble down the stairs.'

Waving off her comment, I said, 'It wasn't her face and wasn't her voice. It's like I said, I just heard what I wanted to hear.'

'And saw what you wanted to see,' she finished for me. She shook her head in denial. 'Nu-uh, I'm not buying it. I can't say it was Naomi: I didn't know her, haven't seen a photo of her or heard her voice, but this goes beyond coincidence for me. I'm…I'm beginning to get frightened, Jack.'

'Frightened of what? You haven't been hurt; I'm the only one with the bump on his head.'

'About *you*! God, what a thicko you are at times! I'm worried that you're going to get hurt. Jesus, I told you it was a bad idea moving into this house.' Sarah pulled off the headphones and stood. She bent at the waist, standing over me, her face a picture. 'You should move out before things go too far.'

'I've paid the full lease,' I reminded her.

'But that was before you knew the place was haunted. Under the circumstances you could demand your money back; Muir should have warned you.'

'About *what* exactly? I only tripped.'

'So you say, but there's more to it. Tell me the truth, Jack.'

I reached for her, putting my hands on her hips. I gently tugged, but she resisted, pulling back and away.

'I am telling the truth,' I said as she fidgeted from foot to foot. She drew a stray lock of hair between her fingers and twiddled it.

'No you're not. I'm not comfortable with lies. Maybe you are.' She wasn't referring to the fact I'd blatantly lied to our boss to get a day off work. 'But if we're going to be friends I need you to stop lying to me.'

How quickly the tide had changed. She had gone from concerned, to frightened, to angry all in the space of a few minutes. All of those emotions aimed at me.

'I haven't lied to you,' I tried.

'Just been selective with the truth,' she finished. 'Jack, if you want help you need to tell me everything that has been going on.'

'I have told you.'

Sarah shook her head, and now she looked desultory. She began looking for her bag and jacket, huffing and puffing in exasperation.

'Don't go,' I said.

'I have to. I told you I'm going out.'

'Stay with me. Let's talk this through.'

Sarah snorted.

'Don't leave while you're still mad at me,' I said. 'It makes coming back difficult.'

'I'm not mad at you, I'm mad at your reticence to talk.'

I sat there, numb. Finally I managed to say, 'I am speaking to you.'

'I'm talking about you being frank with me. Telling me the truth. Not sharing only what you think I need to hear and keeping the rest a secret. We can't base a relationship on *lies*, Jack.'

I'd no comprehension of having stood, or following her towards the front door, but we were in the entrance vestibule when I put an arm around her. She felt small, fragile, my arm encircling her waist like that. I held her from opening the door. 'Don't go.'

'I have to.' Her eyes were hard.

'I…I will tell you everything if you stay.'

'I can't stay. I'm going out. I already told you.' Now a film of moisture made her eyes gleam.

A fist clenched around my gut and gave it a squeeze. Going out with Daniel was more important than talking about our relationship, was it? No, I understood that wasn't what she meant. She needed to leave now before we both said something we'd later regret.

'Will you come back tomorrow?' I asked softly.

'Don't you have the kids over?'

'Only during the day. I'll be taking them home tomorrow evening.'

'Maybe I should leave it til Sunday,' she said, and it was enough to put off the nagging doubt she'd ever return.

'Yeah, Sunday's good. I'm getting the kids again, but they'll be home with Catriona by tea time.'

Sarah pushed her hair behind her ear. 'OK. So you're adamant you're not leaving this house, then? If that's the case we need to do something. Do you remember we talked about bringing in some people with more experience about the paranormal?'

'Your Facebook mates,' I said, trying not to sound derisory.

'I spoke with them earlier, and they're free Sunday evening.'

My pause was palpable.

'I was thinking that we could maybe get a bottle of wine and a Chinese take away,' I began, but I could see Sarah wasn't giving me a choice. It was Sarah and her Facebook buddies or nothing. 'But I suppose we can do that another night.'

She nodded, lips pulled tight.

'How many of these friends are we talking about?' I had visions of a mob invasion: weirdoes with dousing rods and crystal pendants.

'There are three of them available, but it should be enough.'

Only three. That was something, at least. I nodded, sealing the deal.

'Sunday evening, then?' I prompted as Sarah opened the door.

Acquiescing to her plan seemed to have thawed her. She leaned in and kissed me. Not as passionately as she had last night, but I was just as glad to receive it.

'Sunday evening,' she agreed. 'I'll come over a little earlier than the team. You can tell me *everything* that's been happening before the others get here.'

Taking her fingers in mine, I held on. She stared at me, waiting. In the end I promised. 'I'll tell you everything.'

She bobbed her head around my shoulder. 'Just checking you haven't got your other fingers crossed behind you,' she said, and offered a smile. I laughed without much humour, and felt her fingers slip from mine. She went out the door without looking back. I didn't watch her along the street, just shut the door.

That evening I was consumed by bitterness.

Not about the electronic voice recording, or my crazy mantra as I scraped the same words into the bedroom wall. I was thinking about Sarah and how much she was enjoying her night out, away from me. With Daniel.

By the time I fell asleep, fully clothed, on the settee in the parlour I'd grown to hate my smug boss with a passion. I dreamed about Sarah again, and it was erotic. The only problem was that it wasn't me I watched her screw, but my limp-wristed boss. In the dream it was as if I was on the other side of a stained glass window, spying on them through chinks in the crimson glass. I screamed and beat at the glass with my balled fists, but except for a disdainful turn of Sarah's head, I received no response. Not even when I smashed bodily through the glass and pulled Sarah away from him. Daniel just lay there, nonplussed, while I wrapped my fingers round her throat and throttled the life out of an equally unresponsive Sarah. All the while I screamed in her face: 'Why, Sarah? Why? I want you. I WANT YOU!'

I think I was shouting the same thing when kicking my way off the settee, sweat lashing down my face, my hands held in a rigor mortis-tight grip.

23

Bloody Old Dive

'Why can't we see your new house, Dad?'

It was a fair question my daughter Gemma asked. I didn't have an honest answer.

'I thought you liked Mickey D's,' I said.

We were sitting at a table in our local McDonalds, Jake and I on one side, Gemma opposite. Piled between us were three trays overflowing with stuff off the food outlet's saver menu: French fries, assorted condiments and sauces in sachets, burgers wrapped in greaseproof paper. I'd got a cup of coffee, the kids had elected for Diet Coke and Fanta orange. The children had also asked for a round of sweets – a Smarties McFlurry apiece – but I'd told them they must eat their dinners first. The restaurant was busy, families sitting at the tables, those without time to waste standing in the queue in an effort to grab and run. It was noisy and smelly. I hated the place, but knew the kids loved their weekly visit. Catriona didn't allow them to indulge in fast food, but screw her.

'I do,' Gemma said with a self-satisfied nod to a nearby kid who was chomping down on a ketchup-dripping bun. 'But we could take it back to yours.'

'You'll get to visit soon,' I promised.

'How soon?' Jake was my mini-me. He even had the same type of cowlick in his hair I'd struggled to control most of my life. 'As soon as we finish eating?'

'Not as soon as that, Son. Maybe next weekend.'

'Awk!' Jake said. That was a word I'd only ever read before in comic books. It made me chuckle. Jake gave me a searing look of reproof. 'It's not fair,' he said.

'I'm still decorating your room.'

'We don't mind. Mum said your house is a dump, but I don't care.' Gemma reached for her cheeseburger but picked up my mayo chicken. I swapped them out.

'Your mum say that did she?'

'Yeah. She said it's a right old dive.'

'What's a dive, Dad?' Jake asked.

'Something you do in a swimming pool,' I retorted and received another reproving glance, this time from both my kids. 'Your mum's right in one respect: It still needs some tidying up before you can stay over.'

'We could help you clean up.' Gemma's offer was delivered without conviction.

'Like you're always keen about cleaning your bedroom?' I looked at her.

Gemma shrugged, and transferred her energy to unwrapping her cheeseburger.

Jake burst a sachet of salt over the table. He picked up some grains and tossed it over his shoulder; superstitious in a way I never was.

'Mum said you don't want us to stay with you.' Gemma managed to mouth the accusation without releasing her bite on her burger.

'I do. Your mum must have mistaken what I meant. I just said I couldn't take you this weekend.'

'Mum says you're more interested in your new lady friend than us.'

Typical of Catriona, being spiteful like that, but I wasn't going to say anything bad about her to the kids. 'Like I said, your mum misheard me. I told her you could come and stay but after I've got the house ready.' I paused. News sure did travel fast these days. Maybe Sarah had mentioned our intimacy to some of her friends at work, after all, and it had got back to Catriona. That was the way of small towns, even without the assistance of social media networks. 'What "lady friend" are you talking about?'

'Your new floozy.' Jake quoted Catriona without shame.

I shook my head. It was time to change the subject. 'OK. After we finish here, what next? Cinema or bowling?'

'Bowling,' said Gemma.

'Cinema,' said Jake.

'We can't do both,' I said. 'Not today. I'll tell you what; we'll go bowling today, the cinema tomorrow. How does that sound?'

'Awk!' said Jake, but Gemma grinned showing a mouthful of cheesy teeth.

'You can choose which film we see,' I offered as a conciliatory gesture to my son.

Jake fist-pumped the air. 'Yes!'

With the children sufficiently appeased, we continued our meal then headed off to the bowling alley. We had a fun time. Then we spent some time at the public park in the shadow of Carlisle's Norman era castle, taking a walk along the paths where the River's Eden and Caldew converged. Not too long ago, those rivers that once served as protection against raiders from the north had proved the undoing of this part of the city. They'd flooded, bursting their banks and sending a large part of the city under water. There was no sign of the devastation now, but new flood defences had been erected, embankments where previously there had been none, and they felt unfamiliar to me who'd regularly played there as a kid. We returned to the car, and I followed the dual carriageway to the central hub of the city's roads. Called Hardwicke Circus, the huge roundabout was built on the ground where the northern exit to the city once stood. The huge and ugly edifice of the Civic Centre – thankfully Carlisle's only tower block – dominated the skyline to one side, and on the other was the Sands Centre – Carlisle's main leisure complex. We headed north over the bridge spanning the Eden on the unimaginatively named Scotland Road.

I dropped the kids at the front door of my old home. Catriona didn't come to meet them. She stood glaring out the living room window at me. Her arms were crossed beneath her breasts. Her mouth was pinched around a half-done cigarette. She was probably pissed that she didn't get enough time to finish it before the kids returned. I gave her a wave, mouthing, "I'll pick them up at ten in the morning." Catriona only plucked out her cigarette stump and turned away. 'Enjoy your night in front of the telly,' I said aloud.

I didn't enjoy mine.

In fact, I didn't stay in. I had no desire to see or hear anything unusual; because there was enough I'd to relate to Sarah the following evening, and to come up with feasible half-truths about, without gathering more. I walked to a nearby pub, ordered myself a pint and sat quietly in a corner where I wouldn't be bothered. It was the first beer I'd had in a long time, and I wondered why the hell I'd denied myself the pleasure. I had a few more pints. When I arrived home near midnight, slightly worse for wear, I made sure that I looked straight ahead as I went upstairs and then flopped in my bed. I slept. This time without nightmares.

In the morning I went out for a walk, spending some time wandering around the grounds of the cathedral, the reason why Carlisle was named the Border City and not known as the glorified town it really was. Returning for the car I went north over the Eden Bridge and picked up Gemma and Jake. Catriona gave instructions to have them back by three. The movie we watched – the latest Pixar cartoon – didn't finish until three twenty, but again I decided, screw her. I got them home by four o'clock and my estranged wife was almost volcanic. Mark Wilson's car was parked on the drive.

'Say hello to *your* floozy for me,' I said.

If Catriona had been holding something heavy or sharp she would have thrown it at me as I retreated up the path. I got in my Volvo and sped off before she could fetch something applicable.

I headed home to wait for Sarah.

My day out with Gemma and Jake had proved enjoyable, all but for those last few minutes while dropping them at home. It might sound as if I took some selfish glee in upsetting Catriona, but really I was hurt. I could never throw a decent punch, but I was all right with pointed barbs. It's never good for a man's ego when he knows that the man now sleeping with his wife is sitting comfortably in his house, and he has to return to some rented dwelling in much need of repair. I paid for that fucking house he was in, that fucking furniture he'd settled his arse on, that fucking drive Mark had parked his car in, and I was the one forced to drive away. I didn't wrong my wife; it was Catriona who'd cheated on me. Where was the justice in any of it? She was sitting pretty. I was sitting in – as she'd aptly called it in front of my son - a bloody old dive.

I turned on the TV.

Nothing playing on it caught my attention.

I was too angry.

I turned it off.

Sarah hadn't set a time for her visit. She'd only said she would arrive before her Facebook pals, but with no idea when to expect them I couldn't approximate her arrival time either. I thought about ringing her. But didn't. I didn't want to sound needy. Not after our uncomfortable moment on Friday. Maybe if I pushed her for a time it would give her an excuse to pass. No, she wouldn't do that. Despite being a bit miffed with me and with my lies, she had also been excited about bringing round her friends to do a full paranormal investigation. She'd subdued her excitement, but I didn't require any outward signs to tell she was practically jumping up and down at the opportunity. I could see it behind her eyes when she made that joke about me crossing my fingers behind my back. She was anxious to get back in the house, but if I sounded like I was being too controlling she might hold off until her friends arrived. I wanted some time in private with her before those weirdoes joined us.

To kill some time, I went and dragged out some spackling paste and mixed up a batch in a bucket. Equipped with a small trowel I headed up to the top floor.

In the children's bedroom I stood before the vandalised wall, reading the repeated phrase. For a second I considered putting off the job, maybe it would be helpful to show Sarah's friends the writing on the wall, but decided no. There was nothing paranormal, supernatural or even mildly unusual about the words. Not anything I was about to admit to them any way. In fact, I made up my mind that, despite my promise to Sarah, there were still some things I wasn't going to come clean about. I began filling in the scrapes and gouges, smoothing extra Polyfilla on the walls around them so that they could no longer be read.

The oldest letters were easily covered, but those words I'd scored into the plaster after my fall were deep. I'd also added to the problem when later attacking them and prizing off chunks of plaster. Before I was done I ran out of spackling paste. The words weren't decipherable, but I knew what they'd said. Looking at them, I felt a trickle of unease run through me. Remembering whom I'd said those words to ten years earlier.

'I want you,' I said softly.

The air chilled around me. I thought I'd be able to see my breath if I exhaled, but it was caught in my throat. I backed away. Dropped the trowel into the damp bucket and fled the room.

I was almost to the ground floor when the front door knocker resounded through the house.

24

Nuisance Neighbours

'How you doin', Mr Newman?'

Expecting Beauty, I got the Beast. OK. Maybe that's a little unfair. Peter Muir, my landlord, wasn't exactly a beast, but neither was he a vision easy on the eye. What little hair remained on his head looked greasy, his skin dull, and he hadn't stood too close to his razor that morning. His white moustache looked bushier than I remembered. His clothing was rumpled and there was a gravy spot on his shirt collar. He looked as if he'd aborted his late Sunday lunch to come visit. I noted wariness to his question, not the pleasantry he intended it to sound.

'I'm, uh, good,' I replied. Notwithstanding the uneasy shiver that still played down my spine, of course. 'Is there some kind of problem?'

Muir glanced once towards the insurance brokers' office next door. He rubbed his nose with the palm of one hand, sniffed snot back. 'You mind if I come in?'

He was my landlord; I didn't have much of a choice in the matter.

'Sure. Come in.' I held open the door for him. As he moved past me I got a whiff of body odour and cigarettes off his clothing. Behind his back I puffed out my cheeks. He hadn't prepared for this visit; it was obviously off the cuff. I leaned outside, checking that Sarah wasn't approaching. Thankfully she wasn't and I closed the door. Muir had naturally headed for the living room, but had paused at the wedged open parlour door. It didn't take a great detective to deduce that it was my main living space.

'You want a cuppa or something?' I kind of figured that having come inside he wasn't planning on leaving immediately.

'Nah, I'm awright, Mr Newman.'

'Just Jack,' I said. 'When you call me Mr Newman it sounds as if I'm in some kind of trouble.'

My comment was loaded. What other reason was there for Muir to abandon his Sunday afternoon on the sofa to come and perform a visit? When signing the lease, Muir had told me he reserved the right to do spot check visits, but had also been relaxed about it. He said that if he ever intended coming over he'd give me ample notice. I hadn't checked my mobile phone for an hour or two but was certain he hadn't called or left a message. Even engaged in spackling the bedroom wall I'd have still heard the phone in my pocket.

Muir rubbed his face again. Almost knocked off his spectacles, which he had to settle on his nose as he took a brief glance around the parlour. 'You're not in any kind of trouble,' he intoned. 'But there is…well, somethin' I have to mention.'

I indicated the settee, but he pointedly ignored my invite to sit. I stood too, my thumbs tucked into my waistband. There was dried spackling paste on my knuckles. Muir smoothed down the edges of his moustache, obviously ordering the words in his mind. He took another look around as if checking for evidence of something.

I waited.

Finally, Muir took off his glasses and cleaned them on the front of his shirt. He put them back on and blinked at me through the thick lenses. There was a little rainbow coming off the right corner, grease working as a prism. 'You've been here, what, two weeks already?'

'Yeah,' I agreed. 'I moved in a fortnight ago yesterday.'

He nodded as if confirmation added weight to whatever he wanted to impart.

'Like I said: is there a problem?' I gave him my wide-eyed innocent look.

'I've had a few complaints.'

'Complaints?'

'Uh-hu. About noise.'

'I've been moving in, doing some decorating…'

Muir waved a dismissive hand. 'No. It's not that. I told them in the office next door to expect a little noise while you got settled.'

'So what's up?'

'The other stuff.'

'I don't know what you mean. I've been doing most of the decorating during the weekend or on an evening, after the office is closed. I'm out at work most of the time they're there.'

'Have you had your lady friend around?'

I wasn't aware of anything in the lease agreement that forbade visitors. It was odd that he'd used the same words to describe Sarah as Gemma had yesterday. Stranger again that he'd said it with the same undercurrent of reproof. 'Sarah's been round a couple times. Why?'

Muir looked at the floor, as if he'd find the right words etched in the grain of the skirting boards.

'There have been a few complaints about her.'

'Hold on! What are you talking about? I can't even think of a time when she's been here when the office was open.' I could feel my cheeks growing hard. My thumbs slipped free of my waistband and I was conscious of making fists. I struggled to uncurl my fingers. 'What exactly are they saying about her?'

'The screaming, man,' Muir said, and this time he was more pointed. He straightened his back. He was bigger, heavier than me. He was the one in charge.

Shoving my hands in my jeans pockets, I turned partly away from him, looking in the general direction of the neighbouring building. 'Whatever they complained about they're talking bollocks. Screaming? There's been no screaming.'

'I've had two telephone calls from them. Once last week, again on Thursday.' He looked up at the ceiling, but I knew he was picturing what might have been going on in one of the bedrooms overhead.

'I can assure you there's been no screaming,' I said. 'Not from Sarah, not from anyone that I know of.'

'I'm only saying what I've been told. The first time, the manager said it was bad, but I kind of appeased him, telling him you'd just moved in. Probably christening the place.' He offered a leer to get his meaning over. I didn't reply. 'On Thursday when he called he was angry. He said the screaming had been going on for hours.'

'Thursday? I wasn't even in on Thursday. I was at work, and so was Sarah.' I didn't think it pertinent to mention the car crash I was involved in during Thursday lunchtime, or that I'd gone back to work after. 'Sarah didn't come over until the evening and the office was already shut by then.'

'This was just after mid-day,' Muir said.

I jiggled my hands out and showed him my palms. 'We weren't here then.'

'I know. I came round.'

'You did? Why didn't you let me know?'

'I was passing, so I called by. When I got no answer, I, uh, let myself in.' His eyelids flicked down at that last admission. He was about to launch into how he reserved the right to enter the property at any time, but I cut him off.

'So you know that Sarah wasn't here. Neither was I. So it couldn't have been either of us causing the racket.'

He nodded. 'I thought I might've just missed you.'

'We were at work,' I said again, this time coolly.

I thought about something. 'Remember when I thought someone was down in the cellar? Maybe someone got in again…'

'I thought about that, but nobody could have got in. I checked the hatch outside. You did a good job of securing it.'

'Yes,' I said. But that only made the alternative sound more plausible, that Sarah and I had been home and causing a lot of noise. Screaming. 'It wasn't us,' I reiterated.

He shrugged, brushing off the issue. 'Maybe someone was out in the lane at the back. They mistook the noise for coming from the house.'

'That's probably it,' I said. 'Sure as hell wasn't us.'

Muir scuffed his feet on the new carpet. 'I'll let them know.'

'I'd appreciate it if you did,' I said. 'I don't want any trouble, especially with my neighbours. I…I like living here.'

Muir waved down any concern. 'There's nowt to worry about, man. I just wanted to clear things up. Give you a friendly head's up.'

'Except it wasn't us.'

Muir paced to the front window and looked out over the street. The traffic flow had died down this late on a Sunday afternoon. He turned and looked at me, gave a brief nod to himself. 'We'll leave it at that then.'

I was about to agree, show him to the door, but something was troubling me. 'When you came in the house on Thursday, how far into the house did you get?'

Muir frowned, made it look as if he was racking his brains. 'I got as far as the first landing. I just called out from there.'

'You didn't go all the way up to the top?'

'There was no need. I already knew the house was empty. I could, uh, feel it.' He looked at me quizzically. 'Why do you ask? I wasn't poking around your belongings if that's what you're worried about.'

Now it was my turn to wave down any concern. To be honest I wondered if he'd been in the kids' room and was the one responsible for rubbing at the edges of the faint lettering making them more

269

visible to Sarah and I during our EVP session on Thursday night. If he had been there, he might have brought up the subject of the lettering, blaming me for it. 'No. It's nothing. I was just wondering if there had been someone else in the house and if you checked the full place. Nobody else has keys, have they?'

'Just you and me, Jack.'

'What about previous tenants?'

'There haven't been any for years. And any way, after that small business moved out, I had the locks changed.' He stood eyeing me a moment. 'Has there been something else goin' on?'

'Like what?'

'I dunno. It sounded like you wanted to ask me something.'

'Why haven't there been any other tenants? You just let the place sit empty for years?'

He allowed a self-deprecating laugh, but his expression was guarded. 'You're not worried the place is haunted or anything?'

I also gave a laugh. 'I don't believe in all that tripe. But there has to be some reason the place has stayed empty?'

'Personal choice and private business,' Muir said, tapping a finger alongside his nose. Then he shrugged. 'I didn't buy this building. It was left to me in a will: my grandfather's. But I didn't have sole ownership. My sister also had a part share. I wanted to sell, she didn't. So we came to an arrangement where we'd lease it out. We did for a while, but when that business moved out we started squabbling again. My sister wanted to keep the place as a family home, I didn't. So it just sat empty all those years til she died.'

'She died recently?'

'Year or two ago.'

'I'm sorry.'

'Don't be. We didn't get on. She was an old cow, if I'd to be honest. She didn't have any family, and I was her sole heir. I got the building back. It was mine to do with as I pleased, but I was in no rush. First time I put it up for lease I had a bunch of job seekers around. A young couple came close to renting it, but backed out at the last minute. They signed the agreement and everything, but after staying for one night they left. Didn't say why, but I got this impression the wife didn't like the place that much. You know what she said?' He waited for me to ask, and when I didn't, he went on, 'She said it creeped her out. Said there was something *wrong* with the place. I guess she did believe in ghosts, eh?' he chuckled at the absurdity of it. 'Me, I just think she was jumping at her own shadow.'

'Shadow?' I said, trying not to show my discomfort.

'It's an old house; the light comes in at funny angles. That's all.'

'Yeah.' I grinned, though I suspect I might have looked a little manic.

'You were the first person I showed the house to after they did a bunk. To be honest, I thought your lady friend was gonna put you off movin' in. I got the impression she didn't like the place either. Must be summat to do with lasses, that "women's instinct" thing they go on about, eh?' He made it sound as if he was joking, but I'd gained the impression that he knew more than he was letting on.

'The house has grown on her,' I lied.

We were going round in a circle. Had he really come around to warn me about the noise, or was he searching for answers to another mystery? Was he trying to determine if I'd heard anything strange, and did it threaten the promised rental payment going into his account at the end of each month?

'Like I said: we'll leave things at that, eh?'

'Fine by me.' Sneaking a look at my watch, I wanted Muir out of the house. 'When you speak to the manager from next door, tell him there'll be no more noise. Not coming from us, any way. But if he's got any problem in future he should just come and knock on the door. He can find out for himself that I'm a good neighbour.'

In hindsight my words did sound like a less than subtle warning, and from the rapid blinking of Muir's eyelids he thought that the manager might not be the only one who'd be an unwelcome visitor at my door should the issue be raised again. He cleared his throat, adjusted his spectacles, then gave me a nod. 'I'll be off then. Oh, before I do.' He gave a satisfactory tilt of his head at the room. 'You've got the place looking nice already.'

I'd thrown around a bit of paint, got a few new carpets and some second hand furniture. But it was his way of making peace. I said, 'Thanks.'

I walked him to the door.

Once out on the street he looked back at me, before his gaze slid to the adjoining building. 'He's a miserable twat, the manager. He should think himself lucky I didn't rent to a bunch of dole boys instead of a decent bloke like you. He'd know what "nuisance neighbours" meant then.' Muir winked conspiratorially then walked off. His tiny Nissan Micra was parked under a tree about thirty yards away. It was dotted by bird shit. I could hear the starlings in the tree as they came in to roost. Evening was on its way, and so should Sarah be. I checked she wasn't walking towards me from the other direction, but she wasn't. I was thankful. I'd rather Muir left before she arrived and gave him reason to wonder if I'd been lying to him about how often she visited. As he drove by, Muir honked his horn and waved as if we were old pals.

Smiling, waving at him, I said under my breath, 'Fuck off.' And I meant it literally.

Not so much at his coming round to tell me off, or perhaps to dig for information on something else, but that he'd placed another burden on my shoulders. I didn't doubt that the manager of the insurance office had heard screaming, and that it had come from my house. I'd heard plenty of strange things myself since moving in; saw things that were very odd indeed. I thought of the shadow man chasing the female figure through the basement and up the stairs. Sarah's description of a residual haunt took on more meaning: perhaps the ghostly figures played out that scenario time and time again. Sometimes they would appear as insignificant shadow beings, silent and insubstantial, but maybe on other occasions they were full-blown apparitions given voice. It was something else I was going to have to tell Sarah about, alongside everything else I'd only offered half-truths on to date.

25

Vengeful Spirit

To get into her good books and help smooth over our little moment of unease the other night, I elected to tell Sarah about Peter Muir's visit the minute she arrived. I even told her the manner of the complaint, that the office workers thought that it might have been her screaming.

'Unless they worked very late on Thursday night, I doubt they'd have heard more than a yelp out of me.' She'd winked coyly, and I was pleased to find from her remark that I was forgiven. 'Maybe we should pop back one lunchtime and give them something to really talk about.'

'I'm up for that,' I said eagerly.

'Ha! Steady on there, stud. I'm only joking.'

'I'm not.'

'I know.'

She pecked me on the cheek. Then slapped me on the butt, and headed for the parlour. We sat on the settee.

I told her about the previous tenants doing a runner after only staying one night, and how Muir had alluded to the woman jumping at shadows.

'You think he was quizzing you? To see if you'd had any similar experiences?'

'That's the impression I got.'

'He knows more than he's letting on,' Sarah concluded.

'He gave me some lame excuse why the house hasn't been let for years. I think there's more to it. I think he knows the place is haunted and that's why he couldn't get a tenant to move in.'

'The way things are these days a haunting might be a real selling point. He's missing out on a huge marketing opportunity. Any way, get you! I notice you aren't embarrassed admitting that the house is haunted now.'

'How can I be? Not that I'm fully convinced we're talking about ghosts – uh, spirits, I mean – but there's definitely something weird going on.'

'Hopefully tonight we'll find out exactly what. My friends should be here-' she grabbed my wrist and tilted my watch towards her '-in about an hour.'

My eyebrows raised an inch or two.

'You're still uncomfortable about them coming over?'

'No. Not really. Just, well, it would've been nice to have the time to ourselves.'

'We'll get time afterwards,' she promised. 'But don't you want to know the truth about what's going on here? Oh, wait! Is it because you're afraid they'll find concrete proof and then you'll have to believe in ghosts?'

'I'm already coming around,' I pointed out.

'You're still in denial. You told me about seeing Naomi when you crashed your car, and how you've seen and heard her in the house. Yet you still won't accept the possibility of life after death.'

'After hearing that voice on the recorder it has made me think.'

'The other day you made excuses, said you couldn't be sure.'

'I'm allowed to change my mind.'

'No. That's a right reserved for women.' She nudged me with an elbow and I laughed on cue. She grew serious. 'There's a lot more you haven't told me, Jack. I'd've thought I could be trusted by now.'

'I haven't held anything back. What haven't I told you?' I began to list the phenomena, beginning with the shadows, the sticky door, the laughter, the matrixing of faces from the reflection on the landing wall, even my nightmare. 'You were there when the bumping in the wardrobe happened, and when your iPhone got teleported to the bathroom. And I told you what happened after my fall.'

'I still don't buy your story about how you fell.'

I hung my head. 'OK. I didn't tell the entire truth and I'm sorry. I was trying to make out Naomi's face in the pattern, but I was closer than I admitted to. I just didn't tell you because you were concerned enough about the bang I took to the head, if I'd told you the full truth then you'd have definitely thought I was off my rocker and dragged me to hospital.'

'So tell me now.' She moved a little closer on the settee, her thigh touching mine. She rested a hand on my knee and I folded my fingers over it.

'I touched her face.'

'That was all?'

'No. She tried to bite my fingers off.'

'What?'

'Don't laugh. See, that's why I didn't tell you. I knew you'd bloody laugh at me.'

'I'm not laughing.' She was. She was sniggering.

'Sarah!'

She placed her free hand over her mouth. Stifled her chuckles. 'I'm sorry. I'm not laughing at you. It's just, ehm, nervous laughter.'

'Now you're taking the piss.' I pushed her hand off my knee, but in a way that told her I didn't really mean it. She slapped her hand back in place, digging her fingertips into the nerves either side of my kneecap. I jumped about three feet in the air.

'Oh, sorry! Was that your bad knee?'

'Yes. But it's OK. You didn't hurt me.' I quickly gave her knee a squeeze and now it was her turn to leap. 'Just made me jump.'

We laughed together, and I felt better about it. Sarah was first to mellow. 'So Naomi tried to bite your fingers?'

'Yeah. Her teeth were all bloody and she snapped at my hand like a rabid dog. I got such a fright I fell off the top step. I wasn't lying about that. I smacked my head on the doorjamb on the bathroom door. But before I blacked out I was sure I heard her laughing at me. Not in an amused way either.'

'She sounded nasty?'

'Yeah, as if she took pleasure in seeing me hurt.'

Sarah sunk back into the cushions. Warm air wafted up and I was enveloped in her scent. Ordinarily she smelled of soap, but this time I got the faintest hint of sweat. She hadn't showered after work, but had come straight over. It only then occurred to me that she had been in work doing stock take; holding the fort where I'd refused to go in. Bitterly I thought that she'd spent more time in Daniel's company than mine the last few days. I squinted sideways at her. But she misconstrued my envious look.

'You think that Naomi's being a little vengeful?'

'No. Why would she be?'

'You said she was killed in a car crash, that you were the one driving.'

'Yeah, but I wasn't to blame.'

Sarah didn't say anything. She wanted to hear the full story, but I wasn't prepared to divulge the minutiae just yet.

'It wasn't my fault she died.' I clamped up on the last word.

Silence reigned for a minute.

'I get that it's painful. But maybe all it takes to put her at rest is to talk about it. I'm not going to be judgmental, Jack.'

I shook my head.

Naomi rested her hand on my knee once more. The time for fooling around had passed. 'It's too much to ask just now; I get that. We don't have to talk about the crash itself. But what about her? What was Naomi like? As a person I mean.'

'Not as pretty as you,' I said diplomatically.

Sarah smiled, gave my knee a gentle squeeze. 'You know that isn't what I mean.'

I didn't know what she wanted me to say. I hadn't ever been in a position where a woman was happy to talk about my ex girlfriend. Whenever Naomi's name was raised with Catriona, it was usually uncomfortable at best, a screaming match at worst. 'We were just kids,' I said. 'Naomi was a kid. I'm sure if she'd got the opportunity to mature she'd have been a very different person.'

'She was immature?'

'No. That's not really fair. Not immature, just that she was a young woman with a young woman's ideals and dreams.' I laughed uncomfortably. 'Sometimes we were at cross purposes.'

'You argued?'

'Not much, but yeah…sometimes. To be honest, I was probably young and immature myself. When I think back I can't give you a good example. It was all inane stuff. Like what movies we liked, stuff like that.'

'No change there, then,' Sarah teased.

'That's not exactly true, is it? We're both in agreement about Emmerdale on TV.'

'Not the best of examples,' Sarah said, 'but yeah, we do have some things in common.'

'The difference between you and Naomi is your willingness to roll with the differences. You're a total believer in all of this paranormal stuff. I'm surprised with me having this sceptical streak you haven't run a mile.'

'It's not really something that should come between us. It's not like a staunch religion where you're forbidden to have relations with someone outside your faith. And any way, it's actually healthy to be sceptical about it all. Otherwise you begin to believe everything you see or hear is a sign from the other side. Sadly a lot of the evidence presented as paranormal is mundane, everyday stuff, with a natural explanation. When people present evidence along those lines it just makes the scientists laugh. That's why I prefer scepticism. If we can be totally sceptical, try to come up with a logical explanation but fail, then what we *might* have is the real deal.' She nodded as if coming to some kind of self-agreement. 'See, the thing with the paranormal is, once you come up with a logical explanation – whatever that might be – then it's no longer paranormal. It's just the norm. I like that much of the phenomena can't be explained: where would the mystery be if we understood it?'

'So you'd prefer never to learn if there's a life after death?'

'Sooner or later we'll all find out the truth, Jack. We all die. If we then ascend to some other realm or dimension, then we'll know the answer. If we don't, if we simply cease to exist then, well, it won't matter will it?'

'Wouldn't you like to know for sure? Wouldn't it give you comfort if you knew that we did go on after this life? It'd take away the fear of death.' I was growing quite philosophical, and I scrubbed at my jaw with my left hand. It's what intelligent people did during contemplation, I'd noticed.

'It depends. If we go on to some kind of heaven, then fair enough. But what if we don't? What if we just go to some other plane of existence where we have to live our lives over again, with no memory of the last? What'd be the point of that? Or what if we were stuck here?' She looked around the room and didn't seem overly impressed by the prospect of hanging around my parlour for all eternity. 'It's something I've always wondered about spirits that haunt prisons and old ruins and draughty castles and stuff. Why would you hang around horrible places like that if you still have a sense of free will? Who'd want to live forever if we don't have free will in the after life? If we can become trapped in a place we hated in life, I think I'd prefer if there was no afterlife, that we did just disappear into nothingness.'

'So your reason for seeking the truth about ghosts is to reassure yourself that you aren't going to get stuck somewhere nasty?'

'Can you imagine an eternity of hanging around at flippin' BathCo? Thank God I plan on leaving that dump. Hell, it's bad enough being there thirty-eight hours a week, let alone til the end of time.'

We both had a chuckle. I could imagine Daniel haunting our showroom, rattling bath plugs and turning on and off dry taps: he spent so much time there in life, it wouldn't surprise me if he chose to stick around after he popped his clogs.

Sobering, I was right back to the subject of my dead ex again. 'Supposing what I've seen is real, why would Naomi choose to hang around me? Not only that, but why now? Why wait more than ten years to show herself?'

'Unresolved business,' Sarah suggested. 'Maybe she just needs to send you a message before she can find rest.'

'That's what I can't figure out: what's the message?'

'It could be that she loves you and needs you to know that.'

'She has a funny way of showing it. Causing me to crash my car, trying to bite my fingers off, knocking me out when I fell down the bloody stairs.'

Her eyebrows rose. 'Did you finish on bad terms?'

'She was killed in a car accident.'

'Yeah, but how were the two of you at the end? Did you get to say goodbye?'

I couldn't answer. Not at first. I still hadn't told the entire truth about how we'd ended up smashing through that garden wall with enough force that Naomi went through the windscreen and into the garden. Sarah surprised me by touching her fingers to the corner of my right eye. I hadn't realised I was crying.

'Were you having one of your arguments?'

'You wouldn't believe what it was about,' I said, wiping the smeared tears from my cheeks. 'Bloody Leonardo DiCaprio.'

'Did Naomi fancy him or something?'

'That's the stupid part. I wanted to watch Gangs of New York, but she made me go to some chick flick: Sweet Home-bloody-Alabama! We kind of fell out and Naomi kicked off big style.' I touched my face; I could almost recall the burning sensation where her nails had raked my cheek.

'She attacked you?' Sarah eyes were huge.

I flicked an embarrassed grimace. 'I probably asked for it. I was being a dick.'

'And that's how you lost control of the car?'

'Yeah. There was nothing I could do to stop it. The worst thing was Naomi wasn't wearing her seatbelt. It wasn't pretty: she got cut up bad, broke loads of bones. Took me years to shake the image from my mind.'

Exhaling deeply, Sarah sank back in the settee. When she looked at me again it wasn't in sympathy. 'And now she's back and trying to hurt you. To me, Naomi does sound like a vengeful spirit. I think she blames you for her death, Jack, and wants to punish you in some way.'

'Why punish me when she caused the crash? It wasn't my fault!'

'Sadly she might not see things the same way.'

'Bloody hell,' I said, trying to lighten the mood. 'That's all I need; another vengeful woman tormenting me. I thought Catriona was bad enough.'

26

Trust Your Senses

I was expecting a trio of dudes like those Lone Gunmen off the X-Files TV show, or geekish lads with greasy hair and T-shirts with strategically torn holes, baggy jeans. I was wrong. Two of them were a couple, sharply dressed and middle-aged, the man looking like a retired professional sportsman, the woman his WAG. The third was a young woman who could have been aged anything from her mid-twenties up to late forties. She dressed like an older woman but had a seamless complexion and clear eyes; her voice was mellifluous. She was only about five feet tall and slim built, mousy hair in pigtails, kind of frail.

'Steve and Brianne Walker,' the bloke said, sticking out his hand to shake. His wife offered a smile from beyond his shoulder as he crushed my hand in his mitt. Steve held my gaze, an eyetooth glinting against his perma-tan, a silvery wink of light a similar colour to his expensively cut hair. It was as if he peered into my soul, judging me.

'Jack Newman,' I said, trying not to wince.

The small woman was named Hilary. An unfashionable name these days, so I began to think of her in terms of my upper age-range estimate. She laced her fingers and shrugged by way of greeting.

Steve – he even looked like a *Steve* – gave Sarah a hug. His hands lingered on her hips even after he took a step back. I shared a glance with Brianne and thought she was probably as jealous as I was. Before the atmosphere grew too bitter, Steve had moved into the house, eyes darting everywhere, as if he could tell where the hotpots were without direction.

As Brianne and Hilary followed him inside, I stage whispered to Sarah: 'Is he a psychic or something?'

Sarah only chuckled. Then she followed the group to the parlour while I was left to close the front door. Steve had parked his car – a big Range Rover - on the front street. Being a Sunday night he wouldn't be troubled by traffic wardens. I guessed their ghost hunting equipment was locked in the car, because they'd brought nothing in with them. When I joined them in the parlour, Brianne and Hilary were perched on my settee. Steve had his elbow propped on the fireplace, posing like the lord of the manor. Sarah stood in front of the TV. Without preamble Steve nodded at the propped open door. 'How about removing that wedge, Jack? Let's see if the spirits will perform for us.'

I'd grown used to having the door propped open. When I removed the wedge and pressed it closed I suddenly felt hemmed in, claustrophobic.

Steve moved me aside, tried the handle. The door opened easily.

'Sarah told me you had trouble with the door. As if it resisted you,' he said. He pronounced her name "Sah-rah", making her sound almost as pompous as him.

'Yeah.' I related the incident in full, explaining it only opened after I threatened to kick it down.

Steve grunted, as if he'd heard it all before. Without asking for anything to happen he opened and closed the door a few times. He then leaned his shoulder against it, trying deliberately to jam it in the frame. I was silently pleased when it opened without hindrance to a gentle twist of the knob. Not because it partly validated my story, but that he hadn't found a way to debunk it. I was beginning to dislike Steve and he'd only been in my house minutes. Hell, I'd hated him on first sight.

'There's supposed to be a shadow figure you've witnessed, too,' Steve went on.

I narrated the few times I'd seen the shadow man. I told him how the figure had been in this very room after the incident with the jammed door and that it had lunged at me. I caught a blink of surprise from Sarah. Had I told her that or not? I couldn't recall. Maybe she was simply adding to the gravitas for Steve's sake.

'Normally shadow people are elusive beings that try to avoid human contact. Shadow Man is sometimes belligerent, and those that see him believe he means them harm.' Steve turned down his mouth. 'There's no way of saying which it was, I guess. Odd though that a shadow person interacted with you like that.'

"Shadow people". "Shadow Man". "Hat Man". These were all terms I'd grown used to from my discussions, and her video show-and-tell, with Sarah. But to hear them coming from this relative stranger sent fresh qualms up my spine. Going by what Steve said, it was apparent that he classified shadow people as harmless entities, but Shadow Man was to be feared. 'There was also a shadow woman,' I pointed out.

I told them all about our trip down to the basement and how I watched a woman flee from a man. I was pretty certain that the male figure was the same one I'd seen in the parlour and on the top landing the first day I looked the property over. Sarah added to the story here and there, but made it clear she had neither seen nor heard the figures at any time. It was apparent that they'd already discussed what had been going on in the house, because Steve and his companions had already come with some ideas in mind.

Hilary was the equipment technician. She explained that they had brought night vision cameras, digital recorders, motion sensors, and something she called a lux metre. The other stuff was commonplace, but I hadn't a clue about the lux metre.

'Basically it's a shadow detector. It measures the ambient light and can tell if there's any disturbance to it. I couple it with an infrared trap camera. If the lux metre detects a shift in the atmosphere, the camera shoots a series of pictures. We've had good results from it before on other shadow people cases.' Hilary ended her explanation with an almost embarrassed flicker of a smile, a quick shrug.

'You've carried out other investigations like mine?' I said, surprised.

'Not with this level of activity,' Hilary admitted, glancing at Steve as if she'd spoken out of place.

'Alleged activity,' Steve said, and raised a finger to emphasise the point.

'I'm not making anything up,' I said.

'I'm not suggesting you are.' It sounded exactly like that to me. 'It's just that the human memory is very untrustworthy and prone to elaboration. We sometimes hear reports that are so outlandish they're laughable. I prefer facts over fabrications.'

'I'm not lying.' My throat had grown tight. I looked quickly at Sarah for support, but she only shook her head softly at me.

'That's not what I said, Jack: I'm saying that your mind might have added detail that was not originally there.' Steve gave me a patronising nod. There, his gesture said, that's you told.

'If you think I'm talking crap, why bother investigating the place at all?'

'I don't think that; I think there's enough going on here that we might find some proof. If we do I'll happily put my name to it. But I must warn you...'

I just looked him in the eye.

'If I can debunk your story I will. If there's nothing here I will say so.' He turned to his wife. 'Brianne and I have a reputation in the field of paranormal investigation and are keen to maintain it.'

I made myself a silent bet Steve had a reputation all right, but it was one of smug arrogance, and rarely mentioned to his face. I nodded at his challenge. 'Let's hope you find something,' I said.

Steve grinned. The rules were out of the way. He clapped his hands together. 'Let's get stuck in then. You want to join the investigation, Jack? I'm sure Sarah will be keen to get some more experience.'

Sarah smiled eagerly. I noticed Steve's gaze lingered on her a beat too long. Brianne gave a little cough and his attention slid slowly to her. His grin didn't slip, just hardened. What a prat, I thought.

'I'd like to be involved,' I said. What I didn't add was that I wasn't about to let Steve out of my sight, not when he was going to be in darkened rooms with Sarah. My girlfriend was going to require protection from the smarmy son of a bitch.

'Sounds good to me,' Steve announced. 'That way we can be sure you aren't playing any pranks while the investigation is underway.'

What a cheeky bastard!

Again I sought support from Sarah, but she was too far beneath the big brave Steve's thrall to take my side. I caught a smile from Hilary; as if she knew the conclusion I'd come to about their leader, and secretly agreed with me. Steve led the way to collect their gear. Brianne and Sarah followed, Hilary hung back long enough to whisper, 'He's all bluff. He's actually supposed to be all right when you get to know him.'

'He's a big-headed twat.'

'Yeah,' she smiled. 'I haven't fully got to know him yet either.'

Hilary winked, then sped off after her colleagues.

I instantly liked Hilary.

It took an hour or two to get all the equipment up and running. There was more in their kit than Hilary had mentioned. They also came armed with K2 metres for measuring electromagnetic fields, and something called an SB-7 – allegedly a way to speak with spirits in real time – that was like a detuned radio that rapidly scanned through white noise. In addition to the infrared cameras, lux metre and trap cameras, they also set up extra full spectrum digital cameras that Hilary told me could capture in photographs "things beyond the capacity of human vision". Digital voice recorders were left in rooms where no other recording medium was placed. They covered the house from top floor to basement, setting up an electronic dragnet. I was impressed: if there was anything spooky in my house they had to catch it.

'Don't just rely on the equipment,' Brianne told me, the first time we'd had any real interaction. We were at the foot of the stairs on the ground floor; the others were down in the basement. 'Sometimes our best investigative tools are our own senses. We see, hear, smell, taste and touch things that the recording devices never will. Don't be afraid to say something if you experience anything odd.'

'I've experienced a few weird things lately. It's only a shame that my senses will never be accepted as proof, or my word. Steve made it quite clear he's doubtful of what I told him. I'm almost frightened to say if anything happens for fear he'll bite my head off.'

'You really shouldn't pay too much attention to my husband. He doesn't intend to be personal. He comes across as pushy, yes, but that's him aiming to present a business-like front. Really he's determined to prove the existence of spirit, and he is frustrated by some of the supposed evidence some of the other paranormal groups present. He only hopes that the evidence he comes up with is beyond reproach. He likes to set the boundaries so that our clients know what to expect from us, but also what is expected of them.'

'Yeah, he made that abundantly clear,' I said.

'Once he relaxes into the investigation, you'll find that he's not such a bad guy. You might even get to like him.' Suddenly a shard of diamond settled in her eyes. 'Your girlfriend does.'

Hilary ascended the stairs from the basement. I'd removed the temporary plywood door and placed it aside. She offered us the thumbs up signal. Steve and Sarah were alone downstairs in the dark. I wanted to charge down there, and I could sense Brianne shifting too. Trust your senses, she'd more or less said, and we were both worried about the same thing. But it was short lived. Sarah came out the stairwell a couple of seconds behind Hilary. She looked from Brianne to me, and announced 'Almost ready to start. Steve's just setting the cameras off then we're going to lock this area down so there's no contamination.' To me she added, 'All exciting stuff, eh?'

I gave her double thumbs up and a little quirk of my shoulders. Not because I was excited, but because I was relieved she'd resisted Steve's charms.

27

White Noise

The evening passed in a blur and segued through the witching hour without any fanfare. Both Sarah and I had to be up for work for seven in the morning, but we were caught up in the chase. Sleep wouldn't come for hours yet. As a group we'd conducted various experiments, but with little tangible result. At one point a faint knocking came in response to a prompt from Steve, but we tracked it back to the kitchen and an airlock in the water pipes. Steve aimed an arched eyebrow at me. The knocking was nothing like the banging we witnessed when Sarah stayed over on Thursday night, but to Steve it was the obvious explanation. He was sceptical, critical in places, and very much like I had been only a couple of weeks ago. Insufferable. But he was also funny on occasion, and having relaxed into the investigation hadn't once cast further aspersions on my integrity.

We took a short break, converging in the kitchen where I poured us all strong coffee. Hilary popped outside with her cup, going for a sly ciggie. I could tell Sarah wanted one too, but thought it more important that she stay behind. Steve and Brianne stood at one side of the kitchen, Sarah and I the other, facing each other over the scuffed linoleum.

'It has been an interesting night,' Steve offered, but he was vague enough to remain noncommittal.

'Can't say as I've seen or heard anything strange tonight,' I said.

'It can often be the way,' Steve said, 'when we first arrive. Think about it: if you were a spirit and a bunch of strangers invaded your home would you be happy performing parlour tricks for them?'

'Sometimes we have to do repeat investigations before we come to a final conclusion about a case,' Brianne said.

'Ghosts can't be expected to perform on command,' Sarah also chipped in.

To me they all sounded defensive. As if the lack of phenomena was their fault, but they weren't prepared to accept the responsibility. Funnily enough, I wanted to argue that there was definitely something there, even if it hadn't showed its face yet. Quite a turn around. I was supposed to be the sceptic, these guys were the believers and it was as if there had been a complete about face in our attitudes.

'We've a stack of devices running, all recording,' Steve added, 'that will require checking over the next few days. If it's there, we've probably caught it. We won't know until a full analysis of the footage has been completed.'

'You'll let me know?' I asked.

'One way or another.'

Steve nipped his bottom lip between his teeth. Despite his boldness earlier he now sounded reserved about his judgement. Brianne mentioned he was determined to prove the existence of spirit, but I was beginning to think that a more appropriate choice of word was *desperate*. He wanted to find something in my home as much as I did, and I gained the opinion he had been hoping for much more than we'd experienced until now. He wasn't ready to pack up his ghost hunting kit yet.

'So what's the plan for the rest of the night?' I asked.

'Once we're refreshed I think it will be a good time to run a spirit box session. We've recorded interesting results from it in the past. From what I've heard from both you and Sarah the predominant activity here is in the form of noise and voice phenomena – the SB-seven should confirm it for us.'

Hilary had given me a brief run down on the SB-7 device, but to be honest I wasn't fully conversant with how it worked. Steve must have noticed something in my expression.

'I know that results from the spirit box is subjective but the theory behind it is sound. The device rapidly scans through white noise, performing a sweep through the bandwidths at a rate of approximately four channels per second. Because it only pauses on a specific frequency for a quarter of a second it shouldn't be possible to hear any full words, certainly not any phrases or sentences and yet we do. The idea is that the spirit can manipulate the white noise to allow its voice to be heard.' Steve placed down his coffee and folded his arms. 'As wacky as the idea sounds, the device is proving very popular with paranormal researchers these days. But the idea is certainly not a new one: Thomas Edison, who also invented the phonograph, allegedly worked on the first 'spirit phone'. In the nineteen twenties radio had recently gained huge audiences, but prior to that the very notion that voices travelling wirelessly through space could be heard was deemed impossible. With his phonograph Edison had already performed a miracle - showing that through recordings he could preserve the voices of the dead for future generations - and it was his opinion that, with a radio, if you could hear living people speak through a box then why not the dead?'

'I think I watched a programme on the Discovery Channel about that,' I said.

'Quite possibly. There have been other precursors to the modern device. William O'Neill's *Spiricom* and Frank Sumption's *Ghost Box* are probably the best known. Sceptics say that the device is picking up random radio chatter, or voices from CB radios or even baby monitors, and we must take this into consideration. The other argument they use is that we're all suffering the effects of auditory pareidolia: basically we have an expectancy to hear voices and therefore form words from random noise. Again, I have to agree to some extent. But what I've found through my own studies is that their arguments don't offer a full explanation for everything that's heard.'

Brianne also laid credibility in results gained from the spirit box. 'Isn't it ironic that the scientific community claims that research into EVP and Instrumental Transcommunication is carried out by amateur researchers-' she indicated her husband '-who lack the training or resources to conduct scientific research, and who are governed by subjective motives. Yet their scientific opinion is wholly subjective on claiming we're either misguided loonies or that we fake the results ourselves. Can I just remind everyone that these are the same people that burned *heretics* who claimed the earth was round.'

'If only they were prepared to think outside the spirit box, eh?' Sarah quipped.

'Anything that challenges accepted science is always ridiculed,' Steve said forcefully. 'I'm surprised that the human race has made any advances from cavemen when faced with such closed minds. They work between such rigid parameters that they try to fit everything inside them. Then again, we probably don't help our own credibility in the eyes of the wider scientific community. There are too many paranormal groups out there using dubious methods to capture equally dubious evidence – and I use the term "evidence" very loosely.'

'To a sceptic no proof is possible, to a believer no proof is necessary.' Brianne raised her sculptured eyebrows at me. 'You've probably heard similar phrases bandied around when it comes to the study of the paranormal. Our ethos is that we should sit between those opposing viewpoints; sadly, because of our stance we're sometimes looked upon as "fence sitters" by both sides. But that's fine: it also makes us trend setters.' She smiled, happy at the notion.

'Particularly if we snag some evidence that is irrefutable,' Steve added, and it was the unofficial signal to put down our cups and get on with the next experiment.

Hilary appeared in the kitchen doorway. She put down her cup on the counter, began rubbing her palms together, feeling the chill outside. I caught a waft of breath from her, acrid with smoke. 'We all ready for round two?' she asked.

There was no single location in the house that was more active than another, but a few where nothing unusual had happened. I'd experienced activity of some sort in all the top floor bedrooms, the landing and bathroom on the first floor, the parlour on the ground floor and the basement. The first floor rooms and living room next door to the parlour we could largely ignore. Hilary collected the SB-7 and portable speaker, plus a digital voice recorder, while Steve led us up the stairs to the very top. Although we'd been in the bedrooms already I was a tad uneasy when Steve arranged us in the kids' bedroom, in full sight of my slapdash attempt at covering up the words on the walls. I made a mental note to pick up extra spackling paste at my first opportunity.

Hilary set out the equipment. She placed the spirit box and speaker on the top bunk, and to ensure a clear recording of the experiment, she placed the recoding device on the lower bunk. Sarah had carried up a digicam to visually capture the scene.

'We're rolling,' Hilary said, and switched on the spirit box. The harsh white noise dug a dagger inside my skull. It was constant, periodically under laid by a soft blip, a single syllable or note of music snatched from the ether.

Steve introduced the group and because the others made their hello's I too offered a quick 'Hi'. Steve continued with the routine, time and date stamping the experiment for evidential purposes. He then asked if there was anyone else in the room, encouraging them to use the energy from the SB-7 to speak to us.

Ksshhhhhhhhaaaaaksshhhhhaaaaaa…

The white noise made the skin on my skull shrink. I moved to the far wall, propping my hips against the windowsill. It had no discernible effect on the volume, but at least it didn't feel as if ants were crawling all over me.

'Let us know your name,' Steve called.

White noise. A blip. White noise.

'Was that a voice?' Brianne ventured.

We all shrugged, but Steve picked up the pace a little. 'We think we might have just heard your voice. Try again. Use all the energy in the room, use the energy from the device,' he touched his chest, 'or use *our* energy. Just let us know your name.' He paused.

"*Mwa…*"

'Was that 'Mike'?' Sarah wondered aloud. Her statement confirmed the subjectivity of using such devices to supposedly communicate with the dead.

"*Bob…*"

'Bob?' offered Brianne.

They were snatching syllables from the white noise and making them fit. To be fair, Steve didn't rise to their suggestions. He wore a frown as he listened. Softly shaking his head.

'Come into this room,' he said. 'Let us know you are here. Tell us your name.'

White noise reigned.

'OK. If you don't want to tell us who you are, tell us who is in this room.'

"*J-ack.*"

All eyes turned on me. Shifting uncomfortably, I could only offer a shrug.

'It just said "Jack",' Sarah said needlessly.

'It sounded like "Jack", but might not have been,' I said. 'It sounded more like a part of a word.'

Sarah eyed me over the top of the camera's viewfinder. Her mouth made a frustrated shudder.

'Come on. Did you just name Jack? Say "Yes", confirm to us that it was you speaking." Steve's voice had grown in volume, in direct competition with the white noise blaring from the speaker.

"*Mwa…*" the same noise came as before.

'Say it clearly for us,' Steve commanded. 'Say "yes", or name another in the room.'

"*Essair….uh…ksshhaahhh….*"

'Sarah,' both Brianne and Hilary intoned together. They both turned to look at my girlfriend, but her attention was still on me.

'Where have we heard that before?' she asked.

Remaining noncommittal, I stayed silent. Sarah swung the digicam off me towards the device.

'You try speaking with it, Sarah,' Steve said.

Sarah pinched her lips. She took a few unnecessary steps towards the bunk beds. If there was indeed a ghost listening, I doubted it needed to stand beside the SB-7 in order to project its voice through it. 'Are you trying to tell me something?' Sarah ventured. 'Please make it clear.' She extolled the spirit to use the energy from the box. 'Speak through this box or give me another sign, show yourself in front of this camera.'

"*Essair…*"

'That's right. That's my name,' said Sarah, 'but what are you trying to tell me?'

White noise.

'Come on, gather all the available energy and speak.' Sarah adjusted the camera, as if by doing so it would offer the supposed spirit a better angle to come through.

"*Not.*"

'Not? Not what?' Sarah called.

"*Safe here.*"

'Not safe here,' I said, parroting what I'd just heard. It was the self-same phrase caught on the digital recorder when the deliverymen conducted their search for the mysterious bleeding woman. The words burned my throat as if laced with acid. I clamped my teeth, swallowing hard.

Sarah turned and peered at me. Her eyes were huge. Frightened. 'Oh my God,' she mouthed.

I shook my head. 'It's not the same. That's a man's voice.'

Steve interrupted. 'The voices we are hearing are those that the spirits are able to manipulate. They pick up on the available voices on the various airwaves and use them as necessary. It could be male, female, or anything else that is speaking.'

Anything else? What the bloody hell did he mean by that?

'Not safe here?' Steve called loudly. 'Who isn't safe here?'

"*Essair...uh...*"

'Sarah!' Again the name was spoken by more than one in the group.

'Do you mean Sarah harm?' Steve asked.

White noise.

'Tell us,' Steve commanded this time. 'Do you mean to do Sarah harm?'

"*Murrrd...*"

'You're making no sense,' Steve said.

"*Murrrd...*"

'Murder? Is it trying to say murder?' Now Brianne's eyes were as large as Sarah's.

Steve held up a hand for silence. He addressed the unseen spirit. 'Is that what you're trying to say? Murder?'

White noise.

'Speak to us.'

"*Murrrd....J-ack....murrrd...*"

'What the fuck?' I whispered. 'It wants to murder me?'

Before anyone could comment the white noise was shattered by a static crackle. The voice that then emanated from the box was unmistakable. "*Want you...Want you...I...Want...YOU...*"

Before any of us could absorb what we'd just listened to, Steve took a hurried step towards the bunks. He leaned, seeking the buttons to silence the spirit box. 'Ending session,' he announced.

28

Lies, Damned Lies and Fantasy.

'That ended much too soon for my liking.'

Sarah's naked body was slick against me. We were twined together, one of her knees between mine, an ankle hooked around my left foot. Her breasts were pressed to my chest, her face nuzzled in my neck as she spoke. I played distractedly with her hair, running it between my fingers, letting it float and fan out across the damp pillow.

'I tried to hold back as long as I could...but you're just so hot I exploded.'

Pushing up on to one elbow Sarah eyed me in wide-eyed scandal. 'I didn't mean the sex. I meant the spirit box session!'

Smug as hell, I said. 'I knew what you meant.'

Sarah tweaked one of my nipples and I jerked back with a yell that was part giggle part scream. 'Don't,' I cried, 'I'm ticklish.'

That was like waving a red rag to a bull. She tweaked at my nipple again and I almost went over the side of my new double bed. We both laughed. Sarah got up on her knees, then straddled my stomach. Her pert breasts were barely pendulous. I reached for them, but Sarah grasped my wrists and pressed them down either side of my mussed hair. Her face grew serious.

'Don't you agree? We were only just starting to get the answers we were looking for and Steve called a halt.'

'You ask me, he was afraid of what might be said next.'

'Further proof that harm was going to come to you?'

'No. The opposite. Up to that point the voice we heard said some pretty profound things. Steve can present it as positive proof of the SB-seven's efficacy in speaking with the dead. But if he'd allowed the session to go on, what next? What about when it just started speaking gibberish? It would throw doubt on everything he'd already recorded. The names it mentioned, the talk about harm and murder, it'd all have been buried in whatever crap came out the box next. See that's the problem with any of this paranormal stuff.'

'To a sceptic no proof is possible; to a believer no proof is necessary. But Steve's a fence sitter.' Sarah conceded my point. 'He wanted something he could present without anything that would cloud the validity of the evidence.'

'In other words, he's a bloody faker.' It gave me great pleasure getting those words out. I watched her face for a reaction, and was glad to see only a wry turn of her lips. 'How can you like that bighead, Sarah? He's a pompous arsehole.'

'Jealous, Jack?' Sarah sat back. Her vagina pressed against my belly, slick and warm from our lovemaking. I reared my hips an inch or two, my newly reinvigorated penis bumping against her backside.

'Need I be?'

She didn't answer. She bent forward, pressed back with her hips and I slid inside her. We were languid at first. Until Sarah leaned into me, her hair covering my face and I grabbed her butt cheeks with both hands. We jostled and bumped gracelessly, and I shuddered out my final dregs. Sarah squirmed around on me a few more beats, but I was done, my penis going soft. She lay on top, allowing a sigh to leak from her mouth. I wasn't sure if it was a sigh of contentment or one of disappointment. I continued to jiggle around, attempting to get some life in my limp dick, but my head was full of damp wool and I couldn't get it up. Sarah said something I didn't hear.

She slid off me sideways, leaving a glistening trail across my lower belly. She laid facing away from me.

I could feel the chill on my skin now that she'd moved aside, and I pulled at the duvet to cover us. I rolled on my side, went to spoon Sarah against me, but she shifted, and her body suddenly felt wooden.

I held back an inch or two, just looking at her messed up hair.

Something had happened that I didn't quite comprehend.

I'd meant my words as a tongue in cheek challenge, but maybe I'd hit a raw nerve.

Was she fantasizing about Steve when she mounted me for round two? When I failed to last, had I burst her fantasy bubble? Was she pissed off that I hadn't set her alight while she dreamed about another man? I shifted back another inch or so. Then, without thought, I was standing by the bed. 'I need to take a leak,' I announced, but it was only an excuse. I quickly left the room, going down the narrow stairs, my bare heels banging on each step. Our bodily secretions felt icy on my belly and tops of my thighs.

Anger is particularly debilitating to logical thinking even when there's a good reason for it. I didn't have any reason, other than what my imagination tormented me with. I pictured Sarah riding Steve, crying out with joy each time he thrust into her. His whitened teeth flashed with each flexing of his loins, grins of triumph at my expense.

I banged through the door at the bottom and was halfway along the landing before I asked the question: 'What the fuck is wrong with you, Jack? You're acting like an insecure kid.'

It was only in *my* mind that Sarah and Steve were making whoopee. There was nothing real in it. So what the bloody hell was I worried about? For all I knew Sarah hadn't given the pompous bastard the slightest thought when she'd guided me back inside her. Maybe she was simply spent, and wanted nothing more than to relax for the last few hours before we had to get up for work.

Yeah, that was it. She was tired. I worried that she was betraying me inside her mind when all she wanted to do was sleep. I blamed Catriona for my jealous streak. Catriona had betrayed me, no question, but it didn't mean that Sarah would. Sarah was a better person than my ex. Much better. It was why I loved her, I realised.

Is that why you're acting like a green-eyed monster? You've fallen for her, Jack. You love that girl and it frightens you.

The thoughts bounced around my skull like a pinball as I stood at the toilet and urinated. I hadn't needed to piss, but now that I stood poised over the bowl, it came in a torrent. I was mildly embarrassed that Sarah might hear me all the way upstairs. I nipped my bum cheeks, trying to control the flow. Now I peed in stops and starts, and that was the rhythm my thoughts took. In one instant I pictured Sarah's lovely toffee-coloured eyes blinking up at me in dreamy adoration, the next the man hammering into her was Steve and they were both

311

laughing at how his capacity for satisfying her made me look like a eunuch in comparison. Then Sarah was telling me how much she loved me too, but when I checked it wasn't me she said those words to but Daniel, our uptight boss. My right hand was still engaged in directing the sputtering flow of urine into the bowl; my left hand rubbed at my face. I jammed the base of my thumb into my eye sockets in turn, trying to force the images out of my skull.

'Fucking bitch,' I muttered to myself.

I bit down on the words.

What the hell?

I hadn't meant to utter a thing, especially not concerning Sarah.

This was my insecurity, nothing to do with her!

'Fucking bitch!'

I punched the wall with my left fist. Mad at myself. Mad at Catriona for making me so insecure. Mad at Sarah for offering the cold shoulder. Didn't women expect to be cuddled after sex? Hell, I was being the ideal gentleman and she'd turned from me. Fucking bitch. Fucking bitch. Fucking bitch.

I flushed the loo. Turned. Stood in the cubicle exit, peering the length of the bathroom.

A woman stood in the far doorway, on the half-landing. She was a silhouette.

Naomi?

She stepped forward into the dull light bleeding from the toilet cubicle behind me.

'What are you doing, Jack?'

It was Sarah. She was naked but had pulled a sheet around her shoulders to ward off the cold.

I massaged my red knuckles, as I stared back at her. I was like a kid caught jacking off over his dad's porn mags. My face flushed, I could feel the heat rising up from my throat, my scalp prickling. I had no excuse for my crazy antics or for my words. I dreaded that she'd heard me.

'I, uh, knocked my hand on the doorframe,' I lied.

Sarah watched me. Then she reached for the cord and switched on the bathroom light.

I showed her my reddening knuckles. But she knew I was lying: to a sceptic no proof is possible.

'Why did you get out of bed like that?'

'I needed to pee,' I said.

'That much?'

'I don't know what you mean.'

The length of the narrow bathroom still separated us.

'I thought I'd done something wrong,' she said. 'You jumped out of bed like a scalded cat and ran down here.'

'I was bursting. Must've been all that coffee we drank.' I was self-conscious standing like that with my shrivelled penis displayed in all its miniscule glory. I lowered my hands over my groin. Sarah wore a perplexed expression but at least I could detect no anger. She hadn't heard me swearing thankfully. She adjusted the sheet on her shoulder.

'It's bloody freezing,' I said, 'we should go back to bed.'

'It's after five. We need to get up soon. I think I'll just stay up and have a bath. Is that OK?'

'Yeah, sure.' I took a step towards the tub. 'I'll run it for you.'

Sarah looked me up and down. She allowed the sheet to fall from her shoulders and it pooled behind her. 'Why don't you get in with me?'

I was happy that I'd not got round to fitting a new bath yet. The tub was old, cast iron, large enough to accommodate us both. 'Who gets the tap end?'

'You. No question about it.'

I ran the water. Put in some foaming bubbles. Helped Sarah to step in the tub. She oohed and aahed at the heat as she lowered herself. I got in, again self-conscious about the proximity of my shrivelled member to her face. Bathing together was supposed to be romantic, but it was anything but. It was difficult to lower myself without knocking Sarah around, and my dodgy knee gave me hell as I tried to get settled. The taps were at extremes of temperature and both touched my shoulders in turn. I oohed and aahed for different reasons, and a bit sharper.

Once we had found a modicum of comfort, things got better. I forgot all about my momentary wobble of minutes ago: Sarah sponged me down and then I took a turn at her. I spent more time on her boobs than was perhaps necessary, to a point where I felt a couple of pleasant ticks of my penis, and I wondered what it would be like doing it right there in the warm water. It didn't come to that. Once I'd shampooed my hair, Sarah made it obvious that it was time for me to get out. She wanted to lie prone in order to soak away some of her fatigue.

I got out, dripping on the linoleum. After wrapping myself in the discarded sheet, I stood there admiring her as she lengthened herself out in the bath, slowly massaging shampoo into her locks. Her breasts and the mound of her pubis were elevated above the suds. I began to grow hard. But Sarah didn't notice; her eyes were shut and she was murmuring with pleasure. I wondered whom she was thinking about. My guts clenching, I went to find some fresh towels.

Collecting towels from a clean laundry pile in the ground floor kitchen, I shucked off the bed sheet and wrapped myself in a cotton bath sheet. It was more absorbent than the bed sheet and warmer. I carried two more towels with me as I headed back to the bathroom. My feet wanted to move faster, but I denied the urge to run back to Sarah. I conjured images in my mind, and they weren't nice ones, where Sarah was pleasuring herself while murmuring Steve and Daniel's names in turn. Partly I wanted to catch her in the act, but another part of me was terrified what it would mean for us if I did. I chickened out in the end, making sure that I made enough noise as I ascended the stairs to alert her of my approach. I'd left the door partly ajar, but I still gave a gentle rap of my knuckles before entering.

I stood looking down at Sarah for a moment too long.

It was because my breath had caught in my throat.

She was lying stretched out in the soapy water as I'd left her, but she wasn't murmuring in pleasure now. She wasn't doing anything. She was totally inert, and her head was beneath the surface. Her mouth was slightly open, and it was awash. A single stray bubble popped from her right nostril.

Without thought I lunged for her, hooking one arm under her knees and one beneath her neck. As I yanked her from the bath I hollered her name; it sounded more like a ragged howl of animalistic horror. Water splashed everywhere, my gimpy knee gave way and I fell back against the wall, still hugging Sarah's limp body in my arms. As I began the slide to my butt cheeks, Sarah gave a violent start. Her eyes sprang open and she emitted an ear-piercing shriek.

316

We ended on the floor, with Sarah on top of me. Her eyes were wild, her soaking hair lashing my face as she shook to get free.

'It's OK, it's OK!' I cried.

'Jack! What are you doing?' Her voice was pitched between terror and rage. She tried to pull away from me. Her elbow dug me in the groin.

'It's OK. Jesus, I thought you'd drowned!'

'Hell! I was only relaxing,' Sarah croaked. 'You almost gave me a heart attack!'

'I'm sorry.' I tried to help her to a more comfortable position. Sarah continued to squirm, trying to free herself of my grasp. I received another dig in the groin and this time it made me feel sick. Or maybe that was my response to thinking she had drowned. 'Bloody hell, Sarah! You need to be more careful. You fell asleep and slipped under water. Shit! I thought you were *dead.*'

Sarah began weeping: it was a conditioned response to the terror of the moment. My eyeballs were bolting from my head, prickling like crazy. Perhaps I cried too.

29

Ghost in the Machine

It was an uncomfortable few days that followed. My attempts at saving Sarah from drowning had proved counterproductive in that it almost frightened the life out of her. Neither of us knew how to respond. I'd been trying to help, but you wouldn't think it. Once she'd dried herself, got dressed, she called her dad to pick her up and had fled home rather than travel in to work with me. She called in sick that day. When Daniel asked if I'd seen her the previous evening I lied. She was in work on Tuesday but avoided me as best she could. I thought about cornering her in the staffroom and asking what was wrong with her, but decided it was best to give her some distance. On Wednesday Daniel sent me to work in the stockroom for the entire shift. He kept Sarah busy with managerial duties in the office. He even ensured that Sarah and I were on different lunch hours, so he had her all to himself the entire day. I fumed silently, thinking evil thoughts. I've never been overtly violent, but I did start to wonder what shaped dent a spanner would put in my boss's head.

It was raining on Wednesday evening when I left the showroom and headed for my Volvo. A brisk wind swirled the raindrops around beneath the security lights at the rear of the warehouse where I'd parked. I thought it was cold enough for snow, and the rain was a little flinty where it struck my exposed face. Turning up my jacket collar, I made the decision it was time to get my winter coat out of storage: a task for when I arrived home. Sliding into the driver's seat, I shivered at the rain running down my back. The windscreen misted the second I turned the engine, and I fiddled with the heater blowers to clear it. The engine grumbled, damp, and I gave it some throttle to get things moving. I drove around the building in time to see Sarah come out the customer exit. She threw up her hands in exasperation at the weather, then dug in her handbag for her collapsible umbrella. I pulled up, wound down the window.

'I can give you a lift home if you want?'

In that moment it was as if the uncomfortable atmosphere had lifted and she smiled pleasantly at me. Sarah trotted over to the car and leaned down at the window. 'I'm glad I caught you, Jack.'

About to respond that there had been ample opportunity to seek me out the last few days, I clamped down on it, saying instead, 'I'm glad you did too.'

'Brianne called. There's stuff to go over with you. Is now a good time?'

'They found something?' I asked, not sure how I felt about the news.

'I think it's best I let Brianne tell you herself. Can I call her and let her know she can come over?' Sarah clambered into the passenger seat, alongside a swirl of damp wind.

'What about Steve?' I asked.

'He's busy with something,' Sarah replied. I was happy that he wasn't busy with her. Maybe something in my face told Sarah so. She looked across at me. 'What's wrong with you? You've been acting funny since the other night.'

'Things did end on an awkward note,' I pointed out.

Abashed, Sarah nodded. 'I did over react a little.'

'Only a little?'

'Jack, put yourself in my shoes. I was snoozing away nicely and you hauled me out of the bath like a sack of spuds. I thought I was being attacked. I thought you were trying to…well, after that loony spirit box session, I thought you were trying to kill me. No wonder I acted a little crazy after that.'

'I was trying to help you,' I countered.

'I know that now, but at the time? I don't know, maybe I was dreaming or something, but when you first grabbed me by the throat I thought you were trying to force my head under the water.'

'I didn't grab you by the throat. I put my arm under your head to lift you out.'

Sarah leaned over, placed her fingertips beneath my chin and closed my mouth.

'I know. But at the time I was confused. I was scared.'

'I'm sorry,' I said, wondering why I was the one apologizing.

'It's nothing. Forget about it. I'm the one who's sorry. Hell, Jack, I should be thanking you. If I did fall asleep and slipped under water, it's highly likely you saved my life.'

I sat holding the steering wheel.

'Can we just put it behind us?' I finally ventured.

Sarah mimed balling something up and tossing it on to the back seat. 'There. Forgotten.' But then she leaned to place her lips against my cheek. 'But I still want to say thank you.'

I nodded, allowed her to buss her lips against my cheek, then I drove for the junction to the main road. While I steered us towards my house, Sarah got on her phone and called Brianne Walker to organise a meeting.

'Brianne said she'll be over within the hour,' Sarah said after hanging up.

'What has she told you about the investigation?'

'Not a lot. But to be fair we didn't get much chance to talk earlier. Daniel was on my case when she rang me, and then gave me a bollocking for using my personal phone in company time.'

'What a dick,' I said.

'Tell me about it. There aren't too many people I find insufferable, but Daniel Graham is one of them. I can't wait to leave and see the back of him.'

Her words were music to my ears. Yet a nagging thought bothered me: there was truth in that old saying that guilt is ill veiled when you protest your innocence too much.

'What about Steve "the fake" Walker? On the scale of insufferability he rates very highly in my estimation,' I said.

'Steve's not that bad. Not when you get to know him.'

'So I keep hearing, but there's nothing about the smarmy git I find endearing. Not enough that I care to get to know him any better.' I made a face. 'Brianne's OK, I guess. And Hilary was cool.'

'Huh,' said Sarah, 'Hilary's cool, eh? Have I got some competition for your affections?'

'Trust me, when I look at Hilary I feel no romantic inklings. But you have to admit she's an interesting little thing.'

'You want her for her mind, and me for my body?' Thankfully Sarah was teasing, but if I knew women the way I thought I did then she was fishing for a compliment.

'I get the full package with you. Beauty and brains.'

'Shame the same can't be said for you,' she quipped. I mock scowled at her, but after a beat we

322

laughed. It was good to have the old sarcastic Sarah back.

Once back at the house, I left Sarah to prepare sandwiches and a cup of coffee each for us while I went to the parlour and phoned Catriona, intending to set a time on Saturday when I could collect my children.

'So it has started again,' was my estranged wife's opening statement.

'What's started? What are you talking about?'

'Your *obsessing*, Jack. What the hell do you think I'm talking about?' Instead of her usual bitter self, Catriona sounded weary. 'You need to see a doctor before it's too late.'

'What are you going on about?'

'You know, Jack. It's the same as the last time.'

I looked at my phone, but it didn't help.

'You've lost me, Catriona.' Fateful words. 'I haven't a clue what you're talking about.'

'That's exactly why you need to speak to your doctor.'

'At least give me a clue: what do you mean? I only phoned to say I'll pick the kids up-'

Catriona cut me off mid-stride. 'You're not getting the kids. Not while you're like this.'

'Come again? Like I'm *what*?'

'Obsessing.'

I didn't answer.

'Are you still taking your medication, Jack?'

My Naproxen and Lansoprazole? What the hell had that to do with anything?

'Yes, I'm taking them. What's this about, Catriona?'

'First it was Naomi. Now it's me?' she sounded defeated.

'Catriona, you'd best start making some sense or you'll have me thinking you're the one who should see a bloody doctor.'

'Twenty-seven text messages,' she stated.

'Pardon me?' Again I looked at the phone.

'You've texted me the same message twenty-seven times today, Jack.'

'I haven't even messaged you once!'

'Jack. They're from your phone. Hang up and check your sent texts if you don't believe me.'

'I don't need to bloody check. I haven't sent you a damn thing. This is the first time I've phoned since the weekend.'

'On the same phone,' she said. 'It's the same number, Jack.'

'I can bloody well reassure you they didn't come from me. I've been at work all day and I left my phone at home on charge.' My statement wasn't exactly true, but if it helped shut up her accusations then so be it. 'Any way, what exactly am I supposed to have said?'

'The same thing every time,' Catriona said.

'You what?'

'You repeated the same message twenty-seven frigging times, Jack. Are you telling me you've no knowledge of sending them, you don't remember?'

'I don't have to remember. I didn't bloody send them!'

'Jack…please…'

'No. It's fucking *you*, Catriona. You're just trying to piss me around. What is this? Some stupid attempt at getting back at me for spoiling your weekend with Mark?' That had to be what she was up to. 'You're telling me I can't see my own kids? Why: to force me to beg and plead with you? Then you can make out you feel sorry for me and relent, so that I take the kids off your hands all weekend. Just what you hoped for all the time? Well fuck you, Catriona. I'm not playing that game.'

'Jack, listen to yourself.'

'No! You listen to me. Fuck off you twisted bitch!'

I hung up.

When I turned around Sarah was standing in the parlour doorway. She had a sandwich on a plate in one hand, a mug of steaming coffee the other. Her eyelids were downcast; she wasn't able to meet my gaze, dismayed at the vitriol of my conversation with Catriona.

I wanted to throw the phone away, maybe kick something. Instead I felt deflated. 'I, uh, I'm sorry you had to hear that,' I whispered.

Sarah didn't comment.

'It was my ex. She's trying her hardest to make things difficult for me.' I wondered if I should say what was on my mind, and thought that it was probably best to do so. 'I think she knows about us, Sarah. That we're a couple, I mean. I'm not sure she's very happy. It's all right when she's sleeping with someone else, but I'm not allowed to have a relationship without her getting jealous.'

Placing down my sandwich and cuppa, she retreated to the kitchen. Perhaps it was too soon to proclaim our status, but I'd done it. I just wasn't sure that Sarah was on the same page. Yet when she returned a moment later, she was carrying her sandwich and coffee and placed them on the table next to mine. She sat without speaking, but patted the cushion next to her. I joined her on the settee.

'I heard what Catriona said. I wasn't being nosey, but I couldn't help but hear…'

'She can be a real bitch at times,' I said.

Sarah shifted on the settee.

'Did you hear what she was accusing me of? She's making me out to be some kind of bloody stalker.'

'The text messages?'

'Yeah. She said I sent her twenty-seven texts…I haven't sent her a single one!'

'Can I just see your phone?'

'Why? Don't you believe me?'

'It's not about believing you, it's just that we can sort this out quickly if you let me.'

I was reluctant to hand over my mobile, though for what reason I couldn't say. There was nothing incriminating on it. It was some survival instinct kicking in, as though by Sarah asking she doubted my honesty.

'It's just that you might have hit a few buttons by accident and accidentally sent the same one you sent me at work today.' She must have recognised the dumbfounded expression I tried hard to conceal, because she added: 'You did send me it, didn't you?'

'What did it say?'

'I want you.'

The same words that I'd repeated over and over again while attacking the bedroom wall with the screwdriver. I felt sick. Perhaps I was going nuts and had sent the texts after all.

'I didn't send you a text,' I said, sounding as lame as I felt. 'I do want you, Sarah, but I didn't send you that text.'

She frowned. 'It's not the first time,' she said.

'What?'

'That day we had coffee in town. You sent me the same text then. I thought you were shy, and I was waiting for you to make the first move. I thought that by sending me the text it was your way of letting me know you liked me. I thought you sent me the same text today because it was just your way of making up.'

I recalled the incident at Starbucks. But I didn't send her the text; it was the other way around. 'I do like you. A lot. And I was dying to tell you but Sarah, I didn't send that text. In fact, I got one from you saying the very same thing. I thought *you* were making the first move!'

Sarah shook her head. She was perplexed, and not the only one.

As a conciliatory gesture I held out my phone. 'Take a look. I'm not making this up.'

She paused, but then accepted my phone. She brought up my message log. I watched her the entire time, saying nothing. Sarah grunted.

'Did you clear your history?' she finally asked.

'Nope.'

She held my phone out so I could see the screen. On it was the text I'd received while standing in the queue in the coffee shop. I WANT YOU. The proof was right there in my inbox.

'Very strange,' she said. 'I'm not kidding you, Jack. I didn't send this.'

'I didn't send one to you.' I felt vindicated, as this was all it took to show that I wasn't guilty of sending the message to her again today, or the huge number that Catriona accused me of sending to her. 'Check and you'll see. And there are none to Catriona either. You'll find where I telephoned her last weekend, and then again just now, but that will be it.'

Sarah didn't reply. She thumbed through the message lists but there was nothing else there.

'Strange,' she said again. I could tell she was figuring out if I'd deleted the incriminating evidence or not. But that wouldn't explain how my phone would show a message received she was equally adamant she had not sent.

'Remember when my iPhone went missing that day?'

Anticipating where she was going with this, I held up a hand. 'Your phone went walkabout after we came back from the café,' I reminded her. 'Check the time the message was sent to my phone, it was on the afternoon when we were in town. Your iPhone went missing later in the evening: I didn't take it and send my own phone a message so I had an alibi for when things turned really weird now!'

Sarah's cheeks coloured. 'I wasn't accusing you of anything,' she said, 'just wanted to make the point that phones have featured in all the strange stuff that has been going on in your house.'

'You're saying it's my ghost that has been sending the texts to us all?'

'I've heard of stranger things. If you believe the reports, some people have received telephone calls from deceased friends or relatives, some of them have had message pop up at random on their computer screens, some have even had the voices or images of their dead loved ones come over TV programmes. If we believe that the spirits can communicate with us via devices like the SB-seven and through EVP's on recording devices, then is it a long shot to say they might be able to manipulate a mobile phone?'

I laughed, sounding manic. 'You think that Naomi played cupid in order to get us together?'

She smiled at the notion, but her expression remained fixed, and didn't extend to her eyes. 'It's a romantic notion, but why would she then send the same message to your ex wife? It sounds more of a vindictive act, if you ask me.'

Yeah, I had to agree, very vindictive.

30

PK Nuts

We were still puzzling over the issue with the mobile phone texts when Brianne Walker arrived. To my surprise she'd brought Hilary with her. When I first laid eyes on Brianne I'd designated her a trophy wife for Steve Walker – her grooming and her attire were all top end – but today she looked down to earth in jeans, a pale pink Hello Kitty sweatshirt, white trainers, her mane pulled back in a plastic head band and only a gentle application of make up. It didn't make her a Plain Jane; she was still hot. Hilary looked much the same as she had last time, reminding me of a cute librarian or social worker: kind of a Miss Jean Brodie with a laptop-type.

I made way on the settee, allowing them to sit alongside Sarah while I went and posed with one elbow propped on the fireplace. With the trio of women all eyeing me with expectancy, I felt like Charlie surrounded by his Angels, during downtime between missions. Being stared at by three lovely women made me more than self-conscious, and I could feel the warmth off my body rising out the back of my shirt collar. My mouth was gummy, and

I had to take a sip of my now tepid coffee to get it working.

'Anything interesting from the other night?' I prompted.

Brianne and Hilary looked at each other. I knew instantly they had come together for mutual support. Being Steve's second, Brianne was the spokesperson, but Hilary had come along to offer her technical opinion, and also to offer backing to her friend. I guessed they hadn't come to give me good news. After a short nod from Hilary, Brianne turned her attention on me, lifting both empty palms in a "Well, what can I say?" gesture.

'You know what we did; we came in with an open mind and were determined to document any anomalous phenomena in order to give you some answers to what has been going on here. We placed our equipment throughout your home and conducted an extensive investigation, including various experiments.'

It sounded as if Brianne had practiced that delivery, and had probably used a similar line on all their previous clients, but this time she sounded tongue-tied, enough that her entire statement sounded garbled to me. I got the gist of what she was saying – laying all of their cards on the table – but over it all I could detect a very large BUT coming.

'You didn't catch any evidence,' I said.

'I'm afraid not,' said Brianne.

Hilary said, 'I've conducted a full analysis of all of our equipment – video, digital recordings, photographs, data loggers – and except for a few subjective voices caught during the S-B seven session in the top bedroom there was not a grain of evidence on any of the other recording devices. Unfortunately there's nothing to support a haunting in your home.'

'Oh,' I said, unsure how that made me feel. I'd long been a disbeliever, but that was then. Now that I was standing there like a plum ripe for the picking, I felt somewhat defensive about everything both Sarah and I had experienced. I must have appeared ready to argue my case because Brianne quickly interjected.

'We're not suggesting that there is nothing going on here, only that during our investigation we didn't gather any proof to support your claims of activity.'

I glanced at Sarah and saw that she was as disappointed as me.

'Sometimes it's necessary to conduct follow up investigations,' Hilary went on. 'The ghosts don't always come out on command as we warned. We've investigated well-known highly active locations before with negative results. But on a second or third attempt we've recorded some truly stunning activity.'

'So you want to do it all again?' I asked.

Silence reigned for too long. Again the two investigators stirred to look at each other before Brianne said, 'We'd love to, but Steve has made an executive decision: I'm afraid there will be no follow up investigation of this house.'

Again I was left feeling dejected by the announcement. When Sarah first suggested bringing in a team of paranormal investigators I'd been less than enthused, but now they were brushing me off it came as a kick in the teeth.

'So what's *his* fucking problem?' My mouth engaged before I could stop it, and my tone was bitter.

Brianne blinked in dismay. Sarah's mouth fell open. Hilary on the other hand dipped her chin to her collar to conceal a tiny smile.

'Steve hasn't got a problem.' Brianne was now the defensive one, even though if she searched her heart and mind she probably knew she was lying on his behalf. 'It's just that we are busy, we have time constraints, and other cases demand our attention.'

'Your husband made it clear when he first arrived that he suspected I was lying. I take it this "lack of evidence" only helped him make up his mind about me.' I took out my mobile phone, was about to display the latest evidence of my haunting but caught a discrete headshake from Sarah. I pushed away my phone, sliding it along the fireplace as if that was all I'd intended. Looking directly at

334

Brianne I asked, 'What about you? Do you think I'm making this stuff up? Sarah has witnessed most of what I told you all about too. Do you think she's lying?'

'None of us think you're lying, Jack,' Brianne said.

'But you're ready to walk away and leave us to it. What happened to these supposed investigation groups helping people suffering hauntings? Don't you do house cleansings or exorcisms or stuff like that?'

'We're a science based outfit,' Brianne explained. 'We don't go into all that spiritual nonsense.'

'Pseudo-science more like!' I was gritting my teeth so hard my jaws ached. 'You all talk a load of old bollocks if you ask me!'

'Jack!' Sarah stood bolt upright off the settee. Her face was as livid as mine, but it wasn't aimed at her friends.

'Well,' I said, like a petulant child, 'they're just giving us the brush off and we're supposed to take it. I allowed them to come into my house to do their investigation, but because it isn't as interesting as the other cases "demanding their attention" then we've been dropped like a bag of shite. I knew all of this was a waste of bloody time and energy.'

Sarah grasped me by an elbow. She pulled me round so I was looking directly at her. 'It's not their fault they found no evidence. Hilary said it: the ghosts don't always come out on demand. They're not saying there's no haunting, and are not accusing us of lying. You're being very rude, Jack. These people are my friends.' She released me, her movements brusque as she turned to the other women. Brianne and Hilary were standing up from the settee. 'Please, don't be offended. Jack had some bad news earlier and isn't acting like himself.'

She was right. I was acting like a complete dick, but there was nothing I could do about it. When the red mist descends it plays havoc on the sensibilities. 'You don't have to apologise for me,' I snapped.

'No, I shouldn't have to,' Sarah countered. 'You should do it yourself.'

I wasn't in a mood for apologizing to anyone.

'Maybe we should just agree to disagree,' I said, aiming my words at Brianne. 'We both know what this is really about. Steve doesn't like me and I sure as hell don't like him. I can understand you taking your husband's side, Brianne, but I think the rest of us know the truth. He's a self-serving bastard. He doesn't want to come back here because he doesn't think there's anything in it for him, that's all. And he's a coward. That's why he didn't come with you to tell me the bad news. He was too afraid. He sent you women along because he didn't have the guts to come and tell me himself.'

'Jack! For God's sake!' Sarah cried.

'It's all right, Sarah,' Brianne told her. 'We're used to this kind of reaction: some people get passionate about their beliefs when we have to deliver disappointing results. We don't take it personal.'

Sarah wasn't mollified. Brianne despite her words was angry, while Hilary was taking all the drama with a faint sense of amusement. As a knot the three women headed for the exit door. I was happy to let Brianne and Hilary go, but was now fearful I'd gone too far, that Sarah would follow them out the front door.

When conducting his debunking exercise of the parlour door, Steve had removed the wedge. It still lay on the floor behind the open door. As I turned to follow the women, about to attempt some consoling of Sarah, the door jerked away from the wall. It wasn't a result of a loose floorboard, misaligned doorjamb, or errant breeze that closed the door. It was propelled violently and with speed, almost too fast to see, and the noise as it slammed shut was like a grenade going off. The trio of women all stumbled back, crying out in a mixture of alarm and confusion. I too jumped about a foot in the air.

'What the hell?' It was the first time I'd heard Hilary squeal in fear – or perhaps it was delight. 'Did you just see that?'

Brianne wasn't filled with the same awe. She turned and stared at me, suspicious. I held up my hands. Look no strings.

'Still think there's nothing here of interest?' I asked.

Ignoring my comment, both Brianne and Hilary approached the door. Fingers crossed it would resist them. But when Brianne turned the knob, the door swung inwards. She gave it a test push back and forth. It creaked gently on its old hinges, but moved barely a few inches one way or another. Hilary looked around, as if she had the capacity for visually identifying breezes and draughts. The windows were shut. We crossed gazes, and I could see her pupils jumping wildly as she tried to make logic out of the illogical.

'PK,' she said to herself.

Brianne glanced sharply at me, before closing the door again. The door reacted exactly as an ordinary door should. 'Maybe,' she concurred.

'What's pee-kay?' I asked.

'Psychokinesis,' Hilary explained. 'You've probably heard of the term telekinesis, but this is the most accepted term for the ability to move or manipulate an object with the power of the mind.'

I tried to absorb what exactly she meant.

'Are you saying I'm some kind of psychic and that I slammed the door?'

Hilary shrugged, her way of showing she believed anything was possible.

'In certain poltergeist cases it has been shown that the activity was probably caused by PK energy rather than a spirit. Most times a prepubescent girl was in close proximity to the activity and that her latent PK ability was the cause of the unnatural movement of objects. It's all subconscious, so there's no trickery or deliberate manipulation of the environment involved...'

She stopped talking because of the scowl growing on my face. 'I'm neither a girl nor prepubescent,' I pointed out.

'Those cases aren't unique; there have been others where adults were involved. Usually they were under some kind of stress or duress when the phenomena manifested.' She raised her eyebrows, pursed her lips.

'The door closing had nothing to do with me.'

Brianne looked searchingly at Hilary. 'Maybe we *could* convince Steve to come back.'

'No,' I said. 'He can go to hell. He's not coming here to study *me*!'

Brianne said, 'But if we can document proof of your PK energy-'

I snatched my mobile phone off the mantelpiece, swiping it through the air between us and letting it go. It arched over the top of the settee and clattered on the carpet beyond. 'Do you think I did *that* with my fucking mind alone?'

My outburst was met by stunned silence.

Brianne broke the spell, pulling open the door and rushing into the hall. She stood there in the threshold peering back at Hilary, her gaze exhorting her to get out of harm's way. She looked from her friend to me and I could tell what she was thinking: she believed that I was potentially dangerous to them all.

But I knew otherwise.

Standing behind Brianne was the same coal black figure I'd witnessed before. It peered over her shoulder directly at me. Its face was featureless, an inky blot, but I could sense it was grinning manically back at me. I just couldn't tell if it was taking enjoyment at the women's reactions or that it could continue to torment me in this way.

I had no real dislike of Brianne – it was her husband I took umbrage with – and definitely wished her no harm. So when the shadow man loomed over her, his arms coming round to envelope her head and perhaps drag her off to the hellish world from where he came, I hollered loudly and pounced to protect Brianne.

She had to have been aware of the otherworldly hands enclosing her face, but she didn't react to them. Her eyes widened, her mouth elongated, but her expression was all aimed at me. I grasped her by her shoulders and yanked her towards me. Brianne screamed. So did Sarah, as she grasped me in turn and attempted to tug me away. Hilary was out of my sphere of notice, and I've no idea how she reacted. As I tried to haul Brianne to safety, Sarah screeched loudly at me, and I felt her hands enfold my face – the way the shadow figure grasped Brianne. We all stumbled together and went down on the floor, partly inside the parlour, partly in the hall. We tangled, all pulling at each other, until I could get a foot under me and rise up. A gunshot of agony flared through my busted knee, and I moaned. Maybe my moan was more at the misunderstanding the women had of my rescue attempt. They were shouting and screaming, all of them – Hilary included – to stop what I was doing. I staggered back into the parlour, and Hilary showed there was more strength in her fragile-looking frame by shoving me hard. I bounced off the wall and went down on my knees on the hearth. A second flash of agony went through my knee.

I rolled on my side, pulling my knee to me. I emitted a noise like a pan of water boiling over.

When I blinked away the pulsing pain that starburst behind my eyelids I found Sarah standing over me. She had her legs splayed, her torso angled towards me. Tendons stood out harshly against the coffee cream skin of her neck.

'What the hell do you think you're doing?' she squawked.

'Didn't you see?'

'You attacked Brianne!'

'No! No, I was protecting her. Didn't you see?'

Sarah looked back at Brianne. She had made it to her feet and was leaning on the doorjamb while Hilary consoled her. Brianne peered fearfully back at me. I pointed beyond her to the empty space of the hallway. All eyes in the room followed my gesture. The shadow man had gone. The trio of women, a consolidation against my apparent aggression cast doubtful eyes down on me.

'He was right there!' I was adamant, and jabbed my finger at the dead air beyond Brianne. 'He grabbed *you*! I was only trying to stop him!'

'Who grabbed her, Jack? Who are you talking about?' Sarah demanded.

'Who do you think? The bloody shadow man I've been seeing.'

Again their heads swivelled for the hall. Hilary even took an exploratory step into the hall before thinking better of it and returning to Brianne's side. Sarah shook her head in regret.

Struggling to my feet, holding on to the fireplace for support, I said it again, 'Didn't you see? Any of you? Hilary. You were behind me, you must have seen him?'

'I didn't,' she said quickly. 'All I saw was you going for Bri's throat.'

'I didn't touch her throat. I grabbed her by her shoulder, that's all. I pulled her out of the way.' Turning my pitiful expression on the injured party, I said, 'Didn't you sense him, Brianne? He had his hands around your face. You had to see his hands!'

'I think we should leave,' she responded.

'You're right.' Hilary glared at me. 'Somebody needs to get a grip of themselves.'

'I swear to you,' I cried. 'I wasn't trying to hurt you! I was trying to protect you. Sarah, please! You know what's been going on here: tell them!'

Sarah had tears on her face. She hugged herself. Her world had imploded in the last few minutes. I reached for her, but she stepped away, avoiding my fingers, shaking her head.

'Don't,' she said. 'You've done enough already.'

Watching her, open-mouthed, I didn't know how to react.

Sarah moved quickly past me, joining the other two at the doorway. They huddled together like the three witches out of Macbeth, bent over their cauldron. Words passed between them but not for my ears. I still stood dumbfounded. Why was I the bad guy here? I'd only tried to help.

There was a flicker of red beyond the women.

It was a bloody visage that formed then dissipated in a stutter before solidifying. A fourth set of accusing eyes glared at me.

I threw up a hand, pointing at the spectre of my dead girlfriend. But none of the women were having any of it. They moved in their huddle for the front door. The image of Naomi blinked out, but not before a smile of satisfaction formed on her pulped lips.

Panic swelled inside me.

I could understand why Brianne and Hilary might make a hasty get away, but what about Sarah? Why was she leaving? I took a pace towards the door and a jagged lightning rod of pain shot from my knee almost to the crown of my head. I put out my left hand to stop my stumble, and got a grasp on the doorjamb.

And that's where Hilary's nutty theory of psychokinesis being behind the unnatural movement of the objects in my home held no substance. The door slammed, trapping my fingers, and I sure as hell had no intention – conscious or otherwise – of smashing my fingers. I screeched in torment, sinking down as all strength momentarily failed me. I found reserves of energy somewhere, because in the next instant I was scrabbling at the doorknob with my other hand, trying desperately to free my trapped hand, while I hollered and moaned for help. Blood streaked on the paintwork told me I'd sustained a nasty injury.

Beyond the door I heard the women's response. There was a clatter of footsteps, garbled voices and then the front door was yanked open and they spilled out on to the pavement. I cared little at the time; too busy fighting to free myself. But I caught movement in my periphery. I took a hurried glance that way, and let out a howl. The shadow man had returned. He stood there watching me, rocking on his heels as he laughed at the spectacle. It was a familiar cackle that rang inside my skull.

'Bastard!' I screamed. 'Why are you doing this to me?'

The door opened abruptly, and for the third time in minutes I found myself on the parlour floor. This time it was my damaged fingers I nursed. Again Sarah was standing over me. I pointed urgently beyond the settee. 'Look, Sarah! If you don't believe me, look there!'

In reaction she did look.

But she just stood there shaking her head.

I too looked, but all I could see now were Brianne and Hilary peering in through the front window at me. Their expressions of revulsion said it all.

31

Mortar Shells

If I thought that the last few days had been uncomfortable those that followed were even more so. Sarah didn't abandon me. Not immediately. She'd gone to join the others on the pavement outside, trying to make amends on my behalf, but I knew that there was no way either Brianne or Hilary would ever come back inside my home. At least Brianne had agreed to take my supposed assault of her no further, but I bet when she got home that Steve would have other ideas. I almost welcomed him coming round, because I would smack him in the face, busted knuckles or no busted knuckles.

'Stop that kind of talk,' Sarah had warned when she came back inside and I told her what would happen if Steve showed up. 'You've done enough damage already.'

Showing her my smashed hand garnered no pity, even though I was the only one with any physical signs of injury. She was brusque in the way she led me to the kitchen and made me run my hand under the warm water. I hissed and scowled as the water stung the abrasions and Sarah told me to stop being a baby.

'Is that what you think of me? That I'm being childish?'

'I think you over reacted, yes,' she said, then rubbed her thumb over my cuts and grazes.

'Aah!'

'Hold still,' she snapped curtly. 'I need to check for any broken bones. She again rubbed her fingers over my hand, checking for unusual lumps or bumps. 'Can you make a fist?'

I tried. Tentatively. Pain boiled up my forearm. I swore.

'Try again.'

I did. This time I was able to form a loose fist, but it was a struggle to unfurl my fingers.

'I don't think you've broken anything.'

Only her heart?

'I…I think I'm all right,' I said.

Sarah's face was sad. 'You're not all right, Jack.'

'What do you mean?'

'Do I need to explain?'

'I'm sorry about that. I was still angry over what happened earlier, the way Catriona accused me of sending those messages like I was some kind of crazy stalker. When Brianne told me that Steve was writing me off as some kind of nut job, well, I admit I might have seen red.'

'They aren't writing us off. They simply said there was no evidence, and they didn't think a follow up investigation would gather any either.'

'Same difference. They're clowns.'

'They are *my* friends, Jack.' Sarah stood away, folding her arms beneath her breasts.

'Are they though? By doubting me they also doubt you.'

'You weren't listening to what they were telling you.'

'I thought it was pretty clear. I was a liar, they weren't going to waste any more time on me.'

Sarah shook her head again; it was becoming her default option whenever I tried to defend myself. 'Well they sure as hell aren't going to have anything to do with us now.'

I was happy to hear she said "us": we were still united.

'There's no reason for you to fall out with them,' I said.

'I haven't, but the feeling might not be mutual.'

'Well, if they're as shallow as that they're not your real friends. What's the worst they can do? De-friend you from their Facebook group?'

'It isn't a laughing matter, Jack.'

'I'm only trying to lighten the mood.'

Sarah threw her hands in the air. 'It's about an hour too late for that!'

'Sarah. Look. I'm sorry. I acted like an idiot, but it's only because I felt we were being made fools of.' I went to hold her, but her hands formed wedges against my chest. She eased away, walking without comment for the parlour. 'Where are you going?' I asked, following on her heels.

'To get my coat. It's time I went home.'

'Don't go,' I said. 'Not like this. Not while you're mad at me.'

'I'm not mad, Jack.' Tears shone in her eyes. 'I'm disappointed.'

'There's stuff we have to talk about,' I argued. 'The texts. The slamming door. Don't say you blame me for any of those things happening. Psychokinesis, my arse! They're making me out to be frigging *Carrie* or something.'

Sarah didn't reply. She pulled on her coat. Fished out her umbrella from her handbag, and with it a pack of cigarettes. She pre-empted my offer of a lift home. 'I want to smoke,' she said.

Then she was gone.

I was left standing in my parlour feeling like a steaming pile of shit.

Sleep didn't come easy that night. That damn Antigonish poem kept running through my mind. Finally I shouted at the darkness, 'Go away, go away, and please don't slam the door!'

Absurdly I found my antics funny. I laughed, laughed some more, and somewhere along the way my laughter turned to hiccups, and then sobs. I think I cried myself to sleep.

In the morning I didn't feel any better. My hand was sore, as was my knee, but they were simply physical pain. They paled in comparison to the gnawing pain in my chest and guts. I downed my meds, plus four paracetamol, which I dry swallowed. When finally I made it to the bathroom and caught my reflection in the mirror above the sink, I averted my gaze in disgust. Not because I couldn't look at my swollen eyelids or mussed hair, but because I couldn't bear to look myself in the eye. I knew that I was in the wrong last night, and whichever way I dressed up my excuses, cast blame on the members of the paranormal group, it was my behaviour that was inexcusable. I'd acted like a petulant, selfish dick, and it was no wonder I'd turned them all against me. I could live without Steve, Brianne and Hilary in my small circle of friends, but not Sarah.

I phoned in sick for work.

Thankfully Daniel didn't answer the phone. He was on another line to head office, so I got one of our colleagues instead. Lee Colman worked the customer information desk: he wasn't a bad lad, and promised to pass on my message. I was glad that I hadn't been put through to speak with my boss. The mood I was in, I would have told him where to shove his job so far that he'd need drain cleaner and rods to ease it out again. Breakfast was off the menu: I downed a few cups of coffee, one after the other, then headed out to my car. Yesterday's rain had subsided during the night, the skies clearing, the temperature falling. There was a soft coating of frost on the windows that I scraped clear with the edge of a CD – it was one of Catriona's discs that had been inadvertently left in the car when I left home.

It took around twenty minutes to negotiate the roads, the traffic heavy for a Thursday morning in town, particularly around Hardwicke Circus and the road north over the bridge. When I pulled up outside my old family home it was too late to see my children. They would have already gone to school by now. Mark Wilson's car wasn't on the drive. I wondered if he was so entrenched that he now did the school run. I didn't immediately get out of my Volvo, just sat there looking at my former house. It was alien terrain: I felt no attachment to it any more. A light was on in the lounge, and also in the front hall.

Standing by the car, my breath misted in the air as I steeled myself. Then I strode purposefully for the front door. Catriona didn't know it, but I still carried a key to the house on my keyring. I could have let myself in if I wanted to. Instead I banged my undamaged fist on the door. Waited.

I watched the lounge window. Catriona didn't peek out. Therefore it was a surprise when she called from behind the closed front door. 'What do you want, Jack?'

'I want to speak to you.'

'You're not coming in.'

'Why?'

'Because I'm not letting you in.'

I stared at the door. Then I craned so I could look through the glass at the top. It was too opaque to make out anything except a blur of colour as she shifted. I heard the security chain rattle in place: I took it she wasn't taking it off.

'This is ridiculous,' I snapped, rapping my knuckles against the glass. 'Open the bloody door.'

'I told you yesterday you weren't seeing the kids while you're like this.'

'That's the thing, Catriona. I don't know what you bloody mean.'

'You've started again,' she said.

'Started what? Oh, wait! You said I was obsessing again. What the fuck are you going on about?'

'All those texts, Jack.'

'That's the thing. It wasn't me who sent them. I can prove it if you take a look at my phone.' I pulled my mobile out of my pocket. It was dead. After I threw it across the room I'd retrieved it and checked for damage, it was fine. I'd used it to call work. But now the screen was dull black, lifeless. I pressed buttons but it didn't power up. Dead battery, I assumed. Not that it mattered; Catriona wasn't prepared to check it out.

'Just go away, Jack. Mark will be here any minute.'

I snorted. Was that supposed to be some kind of threat?

'He'd better not have my kids,' I snapped.

Catriona didn't answer, but her silence told me everything I needed to know.

'He's never going to replace me as their father!'

'Jack, just go away.'

I banged the door again. 'Open the bloody door, Catriona. We need to get this sorted.'

'There's only one thing needs sorting. Go to your doctor, Jack. Tell him it's happening again.'

'What the hell do you mean?'

Again silence reigned.

'Catriona!'

'You haven't been taking your meds. Your behaviour is growing erratic. Don't you see it yourself, Jack? It's the same as last time. When you wouldn't stay away from the bloody cemetery.' Catriona made a noise like a long, stuttering sniff.

Now it was me who was lost for words.

The silence was palpable. Gusts of frigid breath wreathed my face.

The security chain clattered as Catriona eased open the door. She peered out at me from between the doorjamb and door, a space of only a few inches. Tears made her eyes red.

'You don't remember, do you?' she said.

I still had no words.

'It's what finished us, Jack. Jesus Christ, you wouldn't stay away from her. You thought more of her than you did me or the kids.'

'You're talking about Naomi?' I finally managed to say.

'Yes. Who else? You spent all your time sitting by her grave begging for her to come back to you. You don't remember any of that? "I want you, Naomi. I want you". It's why we broke up.' Catriona forced a little iron into her stance. She dashed the tears off her cheeks. 'I couldn't compete with a dead girl, Jack. I put up with it all that time, but I couldn't take it any longer. I had to put the kids before our problems. I couldn't take care of you as well, not while I was second best in your eyes.'

It was true that I'd visited Naomi's grave on occasion, I couldn't deny it, but it was two or three times at most. I'd asked her to give me a sign that she could hear me: when she remained tight-lipped I gave up the ghost, literally. 'It wasn't me who treated anyone as second best,' I reminded her.

'You did, Jack. You were obsessing about Naomi. Constantly.'

'Talking about obsessing, you soon jumped into bed with my best mate. How long had you been planning that?'

'It wasn't like that and you know it.'

'What was it like then? You didn't fucking hang around, did you?' I caught myself tugging repeatedly at my earlobe and dropped my hand by my side.

'We'd been split up for more than a year, Jack. You'd been…away. I had no idea if you'd ever come back again. And even if you did, *how* would you be? That's the only reason I got with Mark. *You know that.*'

Mortar shells were exploding inside my skull, the ringing concussions mentally staggering me with each revelation. I shook my head, but it didn't help clear it.

'More than a year? What are you talking about? We only split up when I caught you humping Mark!' Even as I made that proclamation, something uneasy wormed its way through my chest. An image flashed through my memories, one where I was sitting motionless in an upright vinyl-coated chair, peering at walls that were an institutional mauve colour. I didn't recognise the chair or the room. I blinked hard to clear away the fog.

'After your breakdown…' Catriona stopped.

She must have recognised the look of panic that almost tore me in half. She shook her head morosely.

'Jack, please, I can see you're confused. It isn't for me to tell you all this. You need to go and see your doctor, OK?'

'I'm not going anywhere!' My voice came out harsh, and I lurched at the door, pounding it with the flats of my palms. The chain held, but the door rattled wildly back and forth. Catriona squeaked in dismay. 'Tell me what the fuck you're going on about or so help me I'll…'

I'd do what?

I tell myself that it was frustration that motivated my aggression. Confusion maybe. Definitely panic. I slapped my palms against the door again. Yelling wordlessly. The security chain held, but I recalled fitting it: it was a cheap thing bought at a flea market, with only tiny screw fixtures. If I wanted to I could easily burst my way inside. Catriona must have come to the same conclusion because she threw her shoulder against the door to close it. I pushed against her. 'Let me in!' I commanded.

'Jack! Jack! Stop it!'

'Let me in, for God's sake!' I withdrew my palms to give another shove, except Catriona was quicker and slammed the door to. There was a clack of the bolt being thrown. Futilely I pounded my palms on the door. I took a kick at it but my foot merely skidded off, leaving a dirty footprint, and a jolt of pain in my knee. I swore savagely.

'Go away! Now, Jack, or I'm going to call the police.'

'Call the bloody police. I don't care.' I gave another kick at the door but with much the same paltry effect as before.

Mark's timing was impeccable. He pulled up directly on to the drive alongside me just as I went to the lounge window and peered in, banging my balled fist on the glass to attract Catriona's attention. I spun to glare at him as my old friend got out of the car. He was biting his bottom lip, wary, and kept the open car door between us.

'What are you doing here, Jack?' he asked, trying to sound reasonable.

'What am I doing here? Don't forget it's *my* fucking house. That's my wife inside, not yours.' I approached him, and he surprised me by slamming the car door and coming to meet me. We stood only feet apart.

'Jack,' he said, again reasonably. 'There's no need for any trouble between us.'

'Is that right? You're screwing my wife and I'm supposed to take it lying down?' I made a fist, but it hurt too much. I flexed my fingers. Mark noticed, and took a half step. Not away. His hands curled into fists.

'You need to get out of here,' he warned.

'I'm going nowhere.'

Mark craned to see past me. Behind me, Catriona had opened the door again. She still hadn't released the chain. 'You all right, Cat?'

'I've called the police,' she replied. 'They're on their way.'

Rounding on her, I hollered, 'Let them bloody come! I haven't done anything yet.'

'You're not going to do anything full stop,' said Mark. His tone was no longer reasonable. I quickly turned to face him, and was late. Mark grabbed hold off my jacket and pushed me towards the path.

'Get your fucking hands off me,' I snarled, yanking out of his grip. Mark held up a warning finger.

'Go away, Jack. Last warning.'

'Why? What are you going to do?'

Catriona made a cautionary noise for Mark's sake. But it seemed that my old pal had suddenly found his balls. He stepped up directly in my face, our noses only inches apart. The tendons in his throat were taut.

'I'm telling you, Jack. Don't try me. I'm not a young girl you can beat up.'

'What?' I shoved him in the chest, but he barely shifted. 'What are you talking about?'

'Mark,' Catriona cried. 'No. Don't.'

But Mark was on a roll. 'We all know what you did, Jack, even if you won't admit it.'

'You *what?*' Again I pushed Mark in the chest, this time with a bit more of my weight behind it.

Mark shoved back and I almost tripped over the edge of the path. I staggered to find my balance.

Mark came after me, shoving again. 'That night Naomi died? Those bruises on her face? They weren't a result of the crash and we all know it. You were hitting her, weren't you, you fucking coward? Are you going to hit me? Go ahead. I'll have you arrested, but not before I knock you on your bloody arse first.'

Another mortar shell exploded in my vision. I screamed like a wounded animal and went for him. Mark caught me in a headlock, under his elbow, and he pushed me down. He might have punched me with his free hand, but I can't be sure now. We kind of scuffled along the path, and then I was free, but backpedalling towards the gate. Catriona was screeching at Mark to come inside. I swore at him, told him to listen to her, but Mark wasn't having anything of it. He took another couple of steps after me, his hands coming up.

I swiped at him, but he danced back. He loaded up a kick, but I too skipped back.

'Get out of here, Jack. I mean it.' Mark stamped his foot, and I jerked back. 'If you don't piss off I'm gonna get you done for assault.'

He was the one who got me in a neck lock and got a few digs in, not me. He must have read the expression on my face because he added, 'You came at me first; I was only restraining you.' He flung a gesture in Catriona's direction. 'I've got a witness.'

'Of course you do!' I spat back. 'And it wouldn't be the first time she betrayed me.'

'Get out of here, Jack. Last time I'm telling you.'

I swore, ranting like someone not right in the head. In a fit of frustration I bent to the drive and grabbed a fistful of gravel.

I didn't hear any sirens, but suddenly faint blue lights were bouncing off my old house and Mark's parked car. I glanced around and saw two police officers scrambling from their car. One of them was huge, and he adjusted his equipment belt as he came towards me. The other was a blond female, her slim form swathed in high-viz yellow. She had her hand poised over her CS gas canister like some old time gunslinger. I looked at her, saw the warning in her gaze and allowed the gravel to trickle from my fingers. It was kind of pathetic when I think about it.

Everything was a whirl after that. I proclaimed my innocence, while Catriona and Mark countered me with allegations. It didn't matter what I said, because there was only ever going to be one bad guy here. Next I knew I was sitting in the rear of the squad car, handcuffed, arrested in order to prevent a further breach of the peace.

32

The Twisted Truth

According to the constitutional laws of England and Wales, a breach of the peace is not an offence punishable by either fine or imprisonment, and thankfully the intention of the police officers was to only remove me from the scene before an actual criminal offence could be committed. Actually, once we were clear of the housing estate where Catriona lived they grew more relaxed in my presence, and lightened up on the stern voices and looks they'd cast my way earlier. Their duty was complete once I was no longer in a position to continue the breach of the peace; therefore I was now just an ordinary Joe in their eyes. The big cop made it clear he understood it took two to have an argument, and didn't hold my behaviour against me. Then he grew officious again stating that I should not return to Catriona's house or I would be arrested and taken to the nick next time. He warned me that if there was a next time I would be dealt with under the Public Order Act, and this time I could expect a day in court. I'd cooled off by then and made him a solemn promise to be a good boy. They dropped me on the corner next to my house, where the cuffs were removed.

'What about my car?' It was still parked on Catriona's street.

'It'll be safe there, sir,' said the female cop. 'Don't go to collect it today; just stay away. Do you understand me?'

I nodded, but I was pissed off. 'I need it to get to work tomorrow,' I explained. Not that I'd any intention of going in, but they didn't need to know that.

'Call for a taxi,' the female cop said. Then they drove off.

Taking a furtive glance around, I checked out the level of attention I was receiving from passers-by in the street, but if anyone noticed me getting turfed out of the police car nobody let on. Either they hadn't noticed, or were prudent enough to keep their noses out of my business. Maybe they thought I was a hardened criminal and had no desire to attract my attention. It was laughable if they knew what had actually gone on. Now that the fire had gone from my belly I was mildly embarrassed and I made a quick two-step dance to get off the street. I unlocked my front door and went inside, placing my back to the door as I took in the still atmosphere in my house. From that position I could see all the way to the back door into the yard. Something caught my eye.

On automatic I walked the length of the vestibule, bypassing the kitchen, parlour and rarely used living room, until I was standing adjacent to the entrance to the basement beneath the stairs. After the paranormal investigation on Sunday night, I had replaced the plyboard covering to block the opening, but while I was out the board had fallen and was lying flat on the floor. As I bent to pick it up, my muscles protested. The scuffle with Mark had been brief and hardly a full-blown fight, but I'd apparently used muscles I wasn't used to. I grunted as I hauled up the board and went to place it over the basement entrance.

Something stopped me.

Out of the corner of my eye I thought someone stood over me, their arm raised as if to strike me in the back of the head. But as I turned the image was gone.

Shaking off the vision as an after-effect of my brawl with Mark, I propped the board against the wall to one side of the opening. Then I peered through the hole, craning my head left to see down the short flight of stairs. It was the proverbial black hole. I couldn't make out even the faintest glimmer of ambient light, but little wonder seeing as I'd re-secured the hatch over the coal chute. Yet that didn't strike me as odd, but the wind blowing in my face did. It was gusty enough make me blink, and screw up my face. If there was nowhere for light to get into the basement, well, in my opinion there shouldn't be any way for a draught to get in either.

The breeze lessened, but the aroma it carried grew. I put a hand over my nostrils and mouth against the sickening stench of mold, decay, and rot. There could only be one place the stink was coming from: the wedge-shaped room at the far end of the basement. I hadn't gone in that small room since the incident with the shadow figures. Even when the big brave Steve had entered the room during the investigation I'd stayed back in the Victorian scullery. I wasn't about to enter it now.

Grabbing the plyboard, I rapidly secured it over the hole in the wall, and kicked the bricks into place to keep it upright. I backpedalled away, then swung round and headed for my kitchen. I filled a glass with water and downed it in one. I refilled the glass, using it as a prompt to go fetch my medication. My pills were in a drawer in the parlour, and I fished out packets of Naproxen and Lansoprazole and downed two of each. Placing the packets back in the drawer I noticed another box shoved at the back. It was white with a printed label, unlike the prescriptions you get from a pharmacy, and more like those unbranded boxes prescribed at a hospital. Frowning, I picked up the box and checked the label. It carried my name, and my old address, but the lower right edge had been picked off so there was no hint of what sort of pills it had contained. I shook the box. Empty.

I was about to toss the box in the waste paper bin, but it got me thinking.

"Are you still taking your medication, Jack?" Those had been Catriona's words. "You need to go and see your doctor."

Unease washed over me like a cold, wet blanket.

Studying the label again, it told me nothing extra. I pulled open the flap and checked inside. The box sounded empty when I shook it, but I hoped that maybe there was one of those folded sheets of instructions inside that would hint at what kind of medication the box once held. There was nothing.

"After your breakdown…" Catriona's words again.

A shiver wormed its way through my bowels as I considered the importance of what she was about to say.

Then Mark's accusations impeded in my mind: "We all know what you did, Jack, even if you won't admit it…That night Naomi died. Those bruises on her face. They weren't a result of the crash and we all know it. You were hitting her…"

I studied my damaged knuckles as though the nicks and grazes were proof of the crime. A whirl of images spiralled through my mind. They took away my strength and I slid down, my bum on the floor, my back against the drawer unit.

'Oh, God…' I moaned as I remembered that night.

Jack, slow down.'

'No. You wanted home. I'm taking you fucking home.'

'You're acting ridiculous,' Naomi cried.

'I'm not being a dick. You're just being a fucking bitch.'

I swore at her, called her a fucking whore. Naomi cried out in alarm as I hammered at the steering wheel with my hands, shouting maniacally. The car had slowed, and I jammed my foot on the accelerator, shooting through another red light, and forcing the traffic on green to brake. Horns blared. I stuck up my fingers, leaning out the window to scream insults at the drivers of a van and a truck. 'Come on you bastards, you think you can stop me, then fucking try it!'

'That's it!' Naomi howled. 'We're finished! Stop the car and let me out.'

'No. I'm not fucking stopping.'

'Let me out, Jack. You've gone way too far this time!'

'I'm not stopping for nobody…you aren't going anywhere til we get this sorted.'

'There's nothing to sort. I told you: We're finished.'

'No we're not. We are going to sort this. Fucking hell, Naomi?'

'God, I'm so sick of walking on eggshells around you. I'm not putting up with it any longer. Stop the car, Jack. Stop right now.'

'No! You're not finishing with me.'

'You can't stop me?'

'Can't I?' My voice was a dry rasp. *'I won't let you go. I'd die before I let you finish with me.'*

'No!' Naomi's features folded in dismay. *'Please don't start making those kind of threats. You shouldn't even kid about killing yourself.'*

'Who says I'm only going to kill myself?' My eyes were extending out their sockets. *'You know what would happen if you left me. I couldn't live without you, Naomi.* I want you...*I'm going to take you with me! Don't you remember last time? I warned you then what I'd do if you ever left me.'*

'You were just being stupid back then,' she cried. *'And you're being stupid now.'*

'I'm not being stupid. I'm deadly serious. I'll prove it.' I yanked down on the steering wheel sending us angling for the opposing traffic. At the last second, I hauled the wheel the other way and the car swayed and jounced before I got it under control.

Naomi tugged at her seatbelt, unclipping it. *'Stop the car and let me out. Please, Jack!'*

'No way.'

'If you don't stop the car, I'll jump.'

'Now who's being stupid? Emotional blackmail only works when there's a valid threat. If you jump you'll be killed. I'm going to kill you. So where's the fucking threat?'

Naomi pulled at the door handle.

'What do you think you're doing? Stop it!' I thumped her in the face with my balled left hand.

Naomi got the door open. I grabbed her with my left hand, twisting my fingers in her hair.

367

'Get off me, you psycho!' Naomi yanked free, and a clump of hair was left dangling from my fingers. Desperately, she pushed the door open and I was sure she was about to leap from the car. Now way would I allow that to happen. I grabbed her hair again, a good fistful and yanked her inside. Screeching like a wild cat Naomi clawed at my hands. I released her to grab for the partly open door. Naomi went for my face, screwing her nails into my cheek. I clenched my eyes shut so she didn't blind me. I warned her to stop but she wouldn't. So I hit her. I hit her again, my balled fist pounding her face. I felt her grip loosen and began to open my eyes. I saw the wall on the corner plot. I pulled down on the wheel, aimed for the sharpest point at the corner.

Baaddoooom!

There was a starburst of colour and movement. No up, no down. Blackness. Whistling from inside my skull. Pain in my trapped leg. I let out a screech of anguish. I knew we'd crashed, had intended it. But it had never been my intention that either of us would survive.

Where was Naomi?

Her empty seat had collapsed, the support bolts having sheared away, pushing the headrest against the dash. Naomi wasn't in the space beneath it.

Sparks popped.

The stench of burning rubber filled my senses.

'Where the fuck are you, Naomi?'

The left side of the windscreen was shattered. On my side it was starred from where my forehead had impacted it. Only my seatbelt had halted me flying headlong through the glass. Naomi had unclipped her belt.

'No!' I had to find her before anyone else arrived.

The steering wheel pinned me. The engine compartment was shoved back, warping the dash. More sparks fizzed and crackled. I pulled and shoved, got out of my seat belt, and made a cursory check of the rear seat, but Naomi wasn't there.

Naomi had been catapulted through the windscreen. At the realisation that she might have survived, I fought to get free of the steering column. The door's structure had twisted, the window had exploded. And I tried to scramble from it. I wormed my upper body out the gap, but couldn't free my right leg. My foot was caught under one of the misaligned pedals. I was desperate enough to rip off my leg, throwing my weight this way and that, and finally pulled free. Agony flared from my knee to my brain. I screamed. I fell on the road alongside my car, knowing I'd done myself serious damage, but there was nothing for it. I had to get to Naomi. I used the car for support, but fell twice. Both times I rose, and limped determinedly for the garden wall I'd smashed into.

It was no more than half a minute since I'd smashed into the wall, yet already neighbours were leaning out of their windows, or had come to front doors. They could spoil everything. Lights had come on in the bedrooms of the nearest house, illuminating Naomi's crumpled form. For effect, I screamed at her as I scrambled over the partly collapsed wall, and fell among flowers and shrubs. I fought free, partly crawling across a previously well-tended lawn that was now

369

littered with bloody glass, debris and shards of sandstone. My gaze never shifted from Naomi. I was relieved to see she was dead still. But I had to make sure.

It felt an eternity before I reached her, but as soon as I did I cradled her head in my lap, pushed her dress down to cover her exposed thighs. I stroked hair back off her features. It was clotted with her blood. Her face was unrecognisable, torn to pieces as she'd exploded through the window. I whispered her name.

Naomi stirred.

I mewled like a kicked dog.

'Naomi, baby, I warned you.' I touched her face, and she pulled away. 'Naomi? Can you hear me? I fucking warned you what would happen.'

I checked behind me for observers. No one was near enough to clearly see us. I shifted my hand, placing my palm over her nostrils and mouth. Her body shuddered.

'I have to do this, Naomi.' Nobody could learn the truth behind the crash.

One of Naomi's eyes slid open. It was unfocussed. The pupil was dilated, and moved rapidly around in a flicking motion. Blood pooled in the corner, barely watered down by the thick tear that oozed out. Using a thumb, I smoothed away the blood. My action was enough for Naomi to focus on, and I watched her pupil widen as she peered up at me and recognised me as her killer.

'J…Jaaa…' Her voice came as a wet sputter in her throat. 'Jaaack!'

'Yeah, it's me, Jack. I promised what would happen if you tried to leave me....'

Bystanders had begun to gather. Some had even come into the garden. Not close enough to see my hand firmly clamped over her face, but that might change any second. I panicked.

'Don't just stand there,' I screamed, all the while clamping my palm in place. 'She's choking! Go and call an ambulance, for God's sake! Go on!'

A man ran over and crouched alongside me, his hand on my shoulder. I ignored him. All I could see was Naomi's ruined face, her one open eye now centred on my face. The pupil was still, and the light had gone from her vision. I wiped at the blood around her mashed lips, as if attempting to clear her airways.

'She's gone, lad. Best you leave her alone now,' the man said. 'There's an ambulance coming, they'll look after her.'

'Why didn't you stop, Jack?' Naomi's words had a distant quality to them.

'Shhh, don't talk.' I didn't want the bystander to hear the truth behind the crash. Apparently he hadn't. He looked down at us sadly, shook his head in resignation.

'She's gone, lad,' he repeated.

Perhaps I'd only imagined her words, but I had to be sure.

I leaned over, as if embracing her, close enough to smother her. 'Babe, everything's going to be all right. An ambulance is coming. They'll make you well again in no time.' I kissed her gently on the forehead, tasting her blood. 'Everything's going to be fine soon.' It sounded like I comforted her, but really I

371

reassured myself. Beneath my hands and lips she was inert. Dead.

'Honest, Naomi, you're going to be OK. I'm going to look after you,' I went on for effect, crying, shameless in the face of the group of bystanders now gathered around us. 'I'm going to keep you safe.'

I felt hands on my shoulders. Someone attempted to ease me away.

'No! I'm not leaving her. She needs me!' I jerked free, pushing back with an elbow. 'I'm not leaving her!'

'I'm not leaving you, Jack.'

Naomi's voice was surprisingly clear. Fear clamped my throat in a vice-like grip. She was still alive?

'No, Naomi, you can't...' No one else had responded to her.

Naomi was dead. I knew it. Yet she wasn't prepared to let go. She wasn't prepared to let me go.

'Naomi,' I cried. 'I want you...I want you...'

My final words were for my ears only, but I trusted that her ghost would hear. 'I want you to just die.'

33

Guilt of the Heart and Mind

It was a different set of memories I recalled than those I'd related during my statement to the police after the crash. I had been taken to hospital, and my torn knee joint had meant a night on a ward. The police had arrived then and I gave my first account of the accident, swearing that Naomi had flown off the handle during an argument, and had attacked me while I was driving. I told them she was threatening to leap from the moving car, and as I'd tried to stop her, I lost control. The scratches on my cheek were obviously made by fingernails and added some validity to the lie. I kept to the same statement when interviewed under caution at the police station a few days later. I was facing a "causing death by dangerous driving" charge, which carried a custodial sentence, but in the end I must have convinced the police officers that I was the hurt party and the accident was not my fault. There were some small bruises on Naomi's face, but the pathologist responsible for her post mortem examination couldn't separate them from the cuts and contusions sustained when she went through the windscreen. I walked away without charge. There were some questions raised during the subsequent inquest into Naomi's death, but where there was doubt, I couldn't be held responsible. The fact that Naomi had unclipped her seatbelt, and partially opened her door, supported my version of events and went in my favour.

When all came to all, I'd got away with murder.

But in my heart and mind, I knew I was guilty.

It played on me, and at the young age of twenty-four I had my first nervous breakdown. I spent some weeks enjoying the hospitality of the local mental health facility. Sometimes people block out the trauma that afflicted them so badly, as I did. When I finally returned home to my parents' house, I believed the bogus tale concerning Naomi's death as much as everyone else did. I met Catriona and moved on. A fresh relationship, marriage, and the births of two children helped keep my mind off my guilt for a number of years.

But now, as I sat feeling despondent in my haunted bachelor pad, I began dredging up more recent

memories. I'm not sure what the spark was that had ignited my earlier memories, but I began to dwell on what had really happened to Naomi. Secretly I began visiting her gravesite, where I'd talk to her in the hope that I would receive a reply. I can accept now that I was seeking absolution of my sins, and the only one who could offer forgiveness was Naomi herself. My deceased girlfriend never replied, or if she did I wasn't ready to hear her. My need for peace of mind led to obsession, and I ended up spending more time at Naomi's grave than I did at home, or at work. I lost my job – back then I was actually a TEFL teacher, imparting my knowledge of the English language to the Eastern European immigrants flooding into Carlisle - and things grew strained between Catriona and me. It didn't help that – more than once – I called her Naomi during our arguments, and even once during sex. A second nervous breakdown struck me and I was again held in a secure mental health facility. I trust now that it was my doctors who convinced me that my belief in ghosts was nonsense, or that the certainty that I must make contact with my dead girlfriend was squashed under the fog of medication, because when I was finally kicked loose I was a staunch sceptic. To me ghosts weren't real. There was no afterlife. Dead meant dead. Ergo I didn't have to seek forgiveness from a dead girl. I was happy to absolve myself of all shame.

If things had been left at that then everything might have turned out well: instead I arrived home to find my wife and my best friend in bed together. I walked away. The trouble was I was once more found at Naomi's graveside crying "I want you, I want you" - it was a short hop from there back to the secure ward at the nut house, and another round of powerful drugs.

It was only a few months ago since I was discharged. My parents took me in at first, but I wanted my independence back. It wasn't a teaching job, I could no longer get the necessary clearance to work with students, but I found the job at the bathroom showroom, which despite being less than aspirational brought in a steady income, and I settled back into normality. I found myself a new home and a new girlfriend. Jesus, my first visit to this decrepit old house had been enough to set my feet once more on the rocky road to downfall.

Finding the empty medicine box, I studied it again. It had obviously held the drugs necessary to suppress my mental illness. When I'd last finished my course of meds, I hadn't ordered a fresh prescription, or if I had I'd promptly forgotten all about collecting them. That or I'd buried my memories of my illness the way I'd previously buried not just a murder but also my subsequent breakdowns and incarceration in mental health units.

I should make an appointment with my GP, I told myself.

In a sudden fit of anger I threw the box across the room. I was all right; I remembered everything now and I was still in control. I didn't need any fucking drugs to keep me sane. My irrational behaviour earlier had been through Catriona's mistreatment of me. Hell, if she'd opened the door as I asked we'd have had a civil conversation, and she could have helped me gain the answers I required without me having to go through this turmoil. But no. She'd chosen to lock me out, and then Mark thought himself the big hard man who was going to see me off. That clown thought he could throw me off my own frigging property, did he? Well he wasn't man enough, and Catriona knew it. So they got me arrested, the bastards!

I just bet that they were having a good laugh at my expense. "Poor crazy, Jack! Hardy-fucking-har-har! Now it's off to bed we go to celebrate ridding ourselves of that burr in our hides."

'Yeah, well, we'll just see about that!'

It didn't occur to me that my phone had been on the blink earlier, but now it was working fine. I took it out and phoned for a taxi. I waited on the front street for it to arrive, but lost patience and set off on foot, striding out. It probably took me twenty minutes to walk to Catriona's house. It was mid-afternoon. The kids wouldn't yet be home from school, which suited me. Mark's car was still on my drive. My Volvo was sitting on the roadside. I wouldn't put it past Mark to puncture my tyres for badness, but a quick check over told me I'd beaten him to the idea. I unlocked my car and took from the glove compartment a Philips screwdriver and returned to my drive. It was getting on to an early winter's evening, but it hadn't begun to grow dark yet and the lights in the house were off. The windows reflected the street outside, and I couldn't tell if I was observed or not. I didn't really care.

Hunkering down, I drove the screwdriver into the nearest tyre, stabbing in near the rim so that the tyre couldn't be repaired. The car dipped as the tyre deflated slowly. I made my way around the car at a squat, repeating the process until the car had settled on all four rims. I was still sitting there, listening to the last satisfying hiss of deflating tyres when the first snowflakes adhered to my hair. I touched one of the flakes, lifting it from my scalp on my fingertip. I studied the snowflake as it melted. When it was a tiny puddle of moisture I stood. I wasn't done yet.

With a flurry of white swirling around me, I walked the length of Mark's car, dragging the tip of the screwdriver along the paintwork. Then I dragged it over the bonnet a couple of times for good measure. Only then did I return to my Volvo and get inside.

The air was frigid in the car. Condensation had built on the inner side of the windscreen, while fresh snow piled on the outer. I turned on the engine, set the blowers to demist, and waited. I watched my old house, hoping that Mark would come out and discover his vandalised car before I left. It would give me great satisfaction to see the look of defeat on his face. More snow piled up and

I hit the wiper switch. The wipers made clear arches in the snow. Melt trickled on the window. It made me think of how transient a form a snowflake was. How easily it was transformed from one form of energy to another. The snowflake died and in its place existed a droplet of water. The droplet would sooner or later be absorbed back into the atmosphere, to again perhaps form into a snowflake to fall again and go through the same transformation. Death follows life follows death…on and on, eternally. It was probably metaphorical if I thought harder about it.

In the end I must have seen sense. It wasn't a good idea to hang around until Mark found the damage to his car. He'd have the cops on to me in an instant, and this time I'd committed a punishable offence. I drove away, fiddling with my phone. I called Sarah at work. Fuck Daniel and his rules against taking private calls in work time.

34

An Effigy of Straw

'I'm not sure this was such a good idea,' said Sarah as I let her in the front door of my house. She was swaddled against the snow in a parka with a fur lining, a knitted hat pulled over her hair. The snow was still falling, and had already laid down a good three inches or more. Snowflakes stuck to the wool fibres of her hat and on the shoulders of her parka. Her *café au lait* skin was more milk than usual. She stamped her boots on the hall floor – I'd yet to buy a welcome mat. I could smell tobacco smoke on her breath as she moved past me with not as much as a peck on the cheek.

'I'll run you home after,' I promised. 'I managed to get my car back.'

Sarah turned and eyed me. 'Eh?'

She knew nothing about my arrest or what had happened since. She didn't need to know.

'I'm not talking about coming out in the snow. I mean coming here.' She didn't move to take off her coat or hat. 'Not after the way you were the other day.'

I hung my head in shame. 'I don't blame you for feeling that way. I was a complete idiot. I owe you an apology.'

'It's not me you owe the apology. It's Brianne and Hilary. Steve too if they told him what you had to say about him.'

I shrugged. 'Probably.'

Of course I'd no sooner apologize to Smarmy Steve than I'd eat fresh dog shit scraped off his shoes. But if it pleased Sarah to watch me eat humble pie, then so be it. I could pretend. I'd had plenty of practise over the past ten years.

'Why don't you take off your coat? Go and sit down, I'll stick the kettle on.'

She looked into the parlour without entering. She turned back to me and she pulled her parka tighter, guarded.

I said, 'You'll get more benefit from your coat later if you take it off now. You'll soon warm up. I've got the fire on.'

Sarah pursed her lips, gave a short nod. She pulled off her woolly hat. Her hair retained the shape of the hat for a moment before a few stray locks tumbled. Sarah pushed them behind an ear as she entered the parlour. I had indeed got the decrepit gas fire working, and though it sputtered and guttered with dirty orange flame, it had done its job of warming the parlour.

Anticipating Sarah's arrival I'd already prepared cups with instant coffee granules, sugar and milk. The electric kettle was full, and I switched it on. Then I followed to the parlour, checking that Sarah hadn't slipped out while my back was turned. She had discarded her coat, hanging it over the corner of the settee, and sat down. She wasn't relaxed, not if the way she sat forward, her hands clenched on her knees, was any indication. She studied me from under hooded eyelids, and clenched her hands tighter. She trembled.

'Is everything OK?' I asked.

She didn't reply.

'Sarah?'

'I overheard something today that I didn't like,' she said.

A pang went through me. Had she heard about my little meltdown at Catriona's place?

I sat beside her. She budged over an inch. But it was away from me. The smell of tobacco smoke on her clothing was strong. She'd been smoking heavily on the way over. She unclasped her hands, her fingers played over her knees like spiders' legs.

'I can explain,' I began.

She cut me off. 'I know why you phoned in sick. I already explained that it's not something I'm happy with, but who am I to say anything?'

I was a bit lost. She obviously hadn't heard about my scuffle with Mark. 'What's wrong?' I ventured.

'I overheard Daniel on the phone to head office,' she explained. 'He was talking about you, saying he didn't believe that you were genuinely poorly. He was asking how he should progress with a disciplinary case against you. He suggested that you should be sacked for gross misconduct.'

I bit my lip. Despite my cavalier attitude to work, I really needed that job. 'They can't sack me for being off sick.'

'They can if it's shown there was nothing wrong with you. It's not as if this is the first time, is it?'

'So I'll go and get a doctor's note. What are they going to do then?'

Sarah was still for a moment. Then she peered at me. Lines crinkled at the corners of her eyes. 'I think…well, I think that might be a good idea.'

'Aye, that'll put a spanner in the works for Daniel. I might even sicken him and take a full week off work. I'm sure if I play up to the doctor he'll give me a note for as long as I need.'

Tears welled and dripped down Sarah's cheeks. Her sadness probably had nothing to do with my possible sacking, but what else could it be?

'I'm only kidding,' I consoled her. 'But it's probably best if I stay off at least tomorrow and then come back in after the weekend.'

She reached over and placed one hand on my knee. I patted it, covering her hand with mine. Her fingers didn't relax, so I couldn't twine them with mine the way I wanted to. Gently she extricated herself and clasped her hands in her lap once more.

'I mean you *should* go to your doctor,' she whispered.

'And I will.'

'Not because you need an excuse for being off work.' She sat still, allowed her silence to add import to her words.

'What else did you overhear?' I was equally as still after mine.

'I heard Daniel say: "I knew no good would come of hiring a psycho-loony".'

'Not what you expect to hear from someone as politically correct as Daniel Graham,' I quipped, but it didn't earn me as much as a flicker in response.

'Whomever he was speaking to in HR must have said much the same. Daniel backtracked, but said he was only stating the truth. He said that you had recently been released from the Cayton.'

'"The Cayton" was a derogatory name given by locals to the mental health hospital I'd been in. Officially it hadn't been called that for decades, but that was the way locals referred to the old insane asylum that predated the modern NHS facility.

Sarah was waiting for me to admit to Daniel's story. I just sat there. I felt numb inside, like I'd been cored out.

'I wasn't in the Cayton. You know that, Sarah. I've worked beside you the last...what? Six years?'

'Six weeks,' she corrected.

'What?'

'Never mind: you're obviously confused about that.'

I ran a hand through my hair; plumbing the depths of my memory for the denouements I'd come to earlier. Six weeks? Shit…

'I…' Sarah rubbed her hands over her face. She balled her hair in her hands. 'I did something I'm not proud of.'

I didn't answer. Whatever was coming I wasn't going to like it.

'I Googled your name,' Sarah admitted.

'Googling me wouldn't tell you if I was a patient at the Cayton,' I told her matter-of-factly.

'That's not what I was looking for. Suffering mental health issues isn't the taboo it once was. It isn't something I'd hold against you, Jack.'

'So what's the big deal, then?' At the centre of my empty core, a spark ignited. I felt tendrils of fire creeping through my body, up my chest. The short hairs on the back of my neck stood up, and painful electrical charges danced on the crown of my head.

'I read about what happened to Naomi.'

My eyes felt flat.

'I read that you were suspected of causing her death.'

'Did you also read that I was later cleared of all charges?' Despite how hard I tried I couldn't keep the venom out of my voice. I stood up quickly. Looked down at Sarah. She squirmed.

'Yes.' Her voice was a tiny squeak.

'It was all vicious lies!' I went on. 'Can you imagine how terrible I felt? I'd just lost my girlfriend in a horrible accident and people were making those fucking accusations about *me*!'

Red crept into Sarah's cheeks. What I could see of her throat was blotchy. Her hands knit a pattern, clasped in her lap once more. She was struggling to get her words out, and no wonder. 'Do you promise me that you had nothing to do with Naomi's death?'

'Do I even need to?'

'Please, Jack, don't shout at me.' Sarah's clasped hands had moved to her throat. 'I read some pretty horrible things today, and am only looking for some reassurance from you. Tell me you had nothing to do with her death and I'll accept it.'

'I had nothing to do with her death,' I said in monotone.

Sarah continued to eye me, and I noticed that her pupils were trembling. A small moan leaked between her lips.

'I had nothing to do with her death,' I intoned again, leaning closer to add weight to my denial. My breath snapped the hair back from her forehead. Sarah flinched with each syllable. 'What? You don't believe me?'

'The coroner's report said that she had bruises on her face that weren't-'

I cut her off with a slash of my hand. 'Yeah, and I had fucking scratches on my face. It was her that attacked me, not the other way round.'

Sarah placed an elbow on the arm of the settee for support, about to get up. I loomed over her, pressing her down and back by force of presence. 'Who have you been speaking to?' I demanded.

'What do you mean?'

'How would you know what the fuck the coroner's report said? It isn't in the public domain. You couldn't have got those kind of details from the news reports.'

'Catriona and Mark said-'

'And you listened to *those bastards*?'

'Catriona was worried about you. After that thing with all the texts, she just wanted to make sure that you were OK. She'd heard you were seeing a manager from work. Seeing as I'm the only female manager there, I didn't take much tracking down. She phoned and asked for me. She said she suspected you'd stopped taking your medication. She, uh, said that you were diagnosed with an extreme form of bi-polar disorder that you'd been receiving treatment for. She said you previously suffered manic-depressive episodes, exhibiting delusional ideas, causing you to become aggressive, intolerant, and even intrusive. She said your illness made you grow obsessive in the past, and sending multiple numbers of texts was something you used to do.'

I hardly listened to a word she'd said. Only one thing bothered me. 'When did you speak to them?'

'Yesterday.'

'So you won't know what those two did today? Do you know that when I went over to explain about the texts – that they weren't even from me - Mark attacked me? Then Catriona called the police and had *me* arrested? I bet she didn't tell you that. Yeah, Catriona's really worried about my welfare, isn't she? Really concerned. Fucking shit-stirring, you mean!'

'Jack! Please!'

When I looked down, Sarah's hands were braced against my chest. I'd leaned in so close to her that she felt I'd invaded her personal space. My mouth fell open and I stepped back. 'Uh, I'm, uh…'

Sarah struggled up from the settee. Tears were pouring down her cheeks. 'Catriona was right. There is something wrong with you. You've real anger management issues, Jack.'

I reached for her, but she jerked away, grabbing for her parka.

'No! You can't leave. Not yet. We have to clear the air, Sarah.'

'There's nothing more to say. I'm going.' She began feeding an arm into a sleeve. I grabbed the sleeve and yanked it away.

'Jack! For God's sake!'

'You're not going.'

'I am. You need to cool down. Then you need to phone your GP and make an appointment. Can't you see it, Jack? The way you're behaving? You're acting irrational.'

'Like a psycho-loony, you mean? Is that it, Sarah? Have you been in cahoots with Daniel as well?'

'Don't be ridiculous.' She attempted to step by me, but I blocked her.

'It stands to reason: you've listened to Catriona and Mark's lies. Why not Daniel's, too? And what about Steve-fucking-Walker? What exactly did he have to say about me?'

Her jaw hung open.

'What's really going on, Sah-rah?' I mimicked her name in a sanctimonious voice equating that of Steve's. 'Why is everyone teaming up against me, eh? I understand why Catriona and Mark would want me out of the way. Obviously Daniel and Steve too, because they want to get into your knickers and I'm already there! But you? Why you, Sarah? Is it because you want them in your knickers, too?'

Suddenly any fear in Sarah dissipated, replaced by a flash of anger.

'How bloody dare you!' she snapped. 'You are so filthy minded! It's your paranoia, Jack; it's sending you nuts. How can you think that about Daniel and Steve? How can you think that of *me*?'

'It's true though, isn't it?'

Sarah began stuffing herself inside her coat, like pushing meat into a sausage skin. I grabbed her parka and tore it away. Sarah set her mouth in a grimace and yanked the coat back again. 'Get off me.'

'No. You're not going.'

If she walked out the door I'd never see her again. There was no way she would forgive and forget. I had to change her mind.

'You're not going,' I repeated, even as she pulled on her coat. She cast around looking for her woolly hat. It had fallen to the floor. I kicked it away from her groping fingers. If I couldn't change her mind with words, I'd have to find another way to make her stay. Sarah glared at me, then bent to retrieve her hat. I pushed her and she fell against the settee. My intention was to stop her grabbing the hat, as if by depriving her of it she would be resistant about going out in the blizzard. Sarah over reacted, howling at me as if I was about to strike her or something. I stepped towards her, keen to offer a hand to help steady her. She slapped my hands away. Her nails broke the scabs on the damaged knuckles, and I hissed in pain as blood dripped.

'Get the fuck away from me!' Sarah rushed for the door still half bent over. But even with my gimpy knee I was that much quicker. I caught the edge of the open door and swung it closed. The door banged noisily. Sarah couldn't halt her momentum. She crashed against the door and rebounded. As she stared at me in horror, I could tell she was dazed as much by surprise as pain.

'You're not leaving me,' I told her, pulling her away from the door. 'Not like this.'

Sarah had always struck me as a strong, independent woman, but right then she was as fragile as an effigy of straw. 'Please, Jack, don't be like this.'

'Like what? Oh, angry you mean? Because the one person I care about is as bad as all the others. I thought we had something special going on, Sarah. I thought of all people you would take my word. I didn't have anything to do with Naomi's death. Why won't you fucking believe me?'

She didn't answer my question. Instead she said, 'That's enough, Jack. Let me go now.'

'No.' I folded my arms on my chest, standing guard at the door.

'I'm phoning for my dad,' she announced, and began to rake through her bag for her iPhone.

'No, you're not.'

'OK, then. You've had your chance, Jack. I'm phoning the police.' She pulled out the mobile phone. I took a single step forwards and slapped it out of her hand. It fell between us, and I reached for it, fending her away with my other arm.

'Give it back! Give it back, Jack.'

'No way.' I threw it down the room and watched it smash against the wall. The back popped loose, and the battery went flying. The screen and electronic components flew in the opposite direction.

'Are you fucking insane?' Sarah screeched.

'According to you I am,' I countered.

'You've gone too far now.' Sarah ran at me, and I flinched expecting a flurry of blows. Of course, she wasn't like that. She dodged to get under my arms and grabbed at the door handle. I caught her around her waist, hauled her backwards and dumped her on the settee. She jumped up immediately, feet scrabbling for purchase. I pushed her down again. Sarah began screaming.

Behind me my TV came on. The volume was at maximum. I turned to gape at it. On screen was some programme about antique hunters. But that wasn't what caught my eye. Reflected on the screen was the face of a woman. Dead Naomi screamed at me, and the speakers amplified her voice. I clasped my palms over my ears. It didn't help; her scream pierced me. I spun away, lurching for the door. I grabbed it and hauled it open, lurching into the hall and slamming it behind me. Sarah was hot on my heels. She grabbed the knob, twisting it, trying to force open the door. I held the knob from the opposite side, thwarting her. She screamed and swore.

'If you don't open this door I'll knock it off its hinges,' she threatened. She pummelled the door with her free fist.

I laughed at the absurdity of her threat. And then the laughter caught in my chest. I recalled saying something similar when I was stopped from opening the door: *You're going to open this time or I'll kick you off your bloody hinges!*

From within the parlour I could still hear Naomi's ghostly voice. It repeated the same phrase over and over: *Not safe here*. It was doubtful that Sarah could hear, because she was too busy hollering at me to open the damn door. She'd stopped banging. Moments later I caught the sound of a clatter as she repeatedly slapped her palms on one of the front windows. Was she trying to catch the attention of a passer-by? I quickly went to the front door and slapped the bolts in place. There was also an old-style brass snib on the drum lock and I pressed it to the locked position. It wouldn't stop Sarah escaping, but it would slow her should she get past me. Anyone outside would have a hell of a time getting in though.

Returning to the parlour, I opened the door and allowed it to swing open. Sarah had her back to me, craning to see out the window. The snow was a falling blanket, yellowish in the glow of the streetlamps. The blizzard helped quash Sarah's yells for help, and maybe that was good because it was still early enough for the workers in the insurance brokerage to hear.

'Are you going to calm down?' I asked.

Sarah spun round. Her face was set. She held her hands fisted across her tummy.

'There's no need for all this shouting and screaming,' I told her. 'You're going to piss off our neighbours.'

'You're off your head, Jack,' she responded.

'I'm off my head in love with you,' I said.

'No. You're not. How could you be and treat me like this?' She slashed her fists down by her sides, her head forced forward on a taut neck. 'You have to stop this now, Jack. It has gone way too far as it is.'

'If I let you go now, that will be it. I'll never see you again.'

'You can't keep me here. This is false imprisonment, Jack. You can get in a lot of trouble for this.' She softened along the jawline. 'But not if you let me go. I won't tell anyone what happened. I promise.'

I rocked my head on my shoulders, working on a kink in my neck. 'See, that's the problem, Sarah. I don't believe you. You went behind my back and listened to the lies told to you by my worst enemies.

How do you expect me to accept your word when you'd do that to me?'

She opened her hands, showing me her palms. 'I told you what happened. Catriona got in touch because she thought that you'd listen to me. You haven't been taking your medication and she thought you'd agree to go to your doctor if I asked you.'

'I've been taking my meds,' I told her. I lifted my aching knee and took a couple of pathetic little kicks. 'Look. I'm working just fine.'

'Not the medication for your knee, Jack,' she said in a soft keen.

Not safe here.

Sarah's attention flicked towards the TV. Had she heard Naomi's warning?

Not safe here, essair-uh…

If it wasn't bad enough that the living had conspired against me, now Naomi was putting thoughts in Sarah's head. I lunged at the TV and sent it crashing to the floor. The screen didn't explode dramatically but the picture immediately went off. Not the sound, though. It continued. *Not safe. Not safe. Not safe.* I scrabbled over the wreckage and yanked the power out of the socket. Finally the TV was silenced. Behind me, Sarah swerved past, heading for the door.

'No,' I screamed, going after her. Naomi left me. Catriona left me. 'You're not doing the fucking same!'

She reached the front door, slapped in desperation at the handle, but missed the bolts and snib. I was only a second behind her. My fingers sank into her curly hair and I hauled her backwards. Sarah's neck was craned in agony, and her fingernails scratched at my hands to free herself. Blood spattered on the floor from my old wounds. I barked angrily and threw her along the hall. She went to her hands and knees, wheezing.

I stood over her, my arm ramrod straight as I aimed it at her. 'You're not leaving me like all the others did.'

She didn't reply. She propelled herself along on her hands and knees until she gained the momentum to come to her feet. She headed directly for the back door, seeking escape through the yard. The door was locked and barred. She bounced off it, turned with her shoulders braced against the wood as she stared at me. I hadn't moved.

She opened her mouth to speak, and I watched a bubble of snot pop in her right nostril. She retained enough dignity to swipe at her nose with her sleeve.

'Ha!' I said.

'Jack, please. You have to stop this.'

'So you keep on saying,' I replied. 'But it isn't going to happen. Not until you see sense.'

'Sense?' she screeched. 'Sense? It's you who isn't seeing sense.'

'I see someone who has lied to me all along. I thought you liked me, Sarah. I thought you were my girlfriend. But I see now it was all an act. You were working with them to discredit me... you were working *against* me.'

'No, Jack! Listen to yourself. Can you even hear what you sound like?'

'Yeah, a psycho-loony,' I replied. 'But isn't that what you wanted me to sound like. That's why you brought in Steve and the others. You wanted to show I was fucking nuts. Is this so that Catriona gets full custody of the kids?'

Her head shook in desolation. I knew that I must be on to something.

'You almost had me too,' I went on. 'You had me believing all that shite about ghosts. It was all trickery, wasn't it? You were behind the noises and the voices.' I thought about things for a moment. Yeah, the texts, the EVPs, the voices during the spirit box session: Sarah could have planted all of those. The noises I'd heard too; they could have been made via hidden speakers or something. The movement of items was harder to explain, but not impossible. 'I must admit: I've no idea how you made me see Naomi. And those shadow figures: hell, that's some magic trick you pulled there.'

'What are you talking about? You think I set you up? How could I do all *that*? You're wrong, Jack. You're not thinking straight.'

Actually, I think it was the first time I'd thought clearly in a long time. 'You wanted me to feed on my guilt. Was that it? You played on my guilt over killing Naomi?'

Sarah's features folded in on themselves. She wasn't pretty when her face was scrunched up like a wadded rag. 'You *did* kill her.'

So I'd admitted it. So what? I shrugged. 'She was leaving me, threatening to kill herself. I just helped her on her way.'

'Oh my God…'

'And now you plan on leaving me.'

I shook my head slowly.

'Talk about history repeating itself,' I said calmly.

35

Professing my Love

A small part of me urged caution. It told me that I was acting irrationally, that everything I accused Sarah of was wrong, a figment of my paranoia and fucked up bi-polar disorder. How in God's name could she be responsible for any of the odd events I'd borne witness too, half the time she hadn't even been present. It warned me to stop, to allow Sarah to leave before things went too far again. But it was a distracted part of me, a third person voice that whispered from a far distance. A much larger portion of my psyche blustered and screamed, bolstering my madness, as it had the night that I'd smothered the life from my seriously injured girlfriend. That part of me was a raging monster by comparison, and it overwhelmed the voice of reason whispering to me from the darkest corner of my mind. Earlier that day the monster had tasted freedom when I'd punctured Mark's tyres, drew the screwdriver over the paintwork of his car, and it wasn't ready to go back in its box. Maybe it would never be ready again.

'I want to show you something.'

I took Sarah by a wrist.

She squirmed, twisted her arm, but my grip was relentless.

'Wh-where are you taking me?'

'To show you something.'

I led her along the hall. Sarah was reluctant to follow. With her free hand she grabbed at the plyboard I'd set over the hole to the basement. It was too flimsy to offer any resistance, and was simply dragged along with her. Sarah released the board and it clattered to the floor – in the exact place it had fallen of it's own volition that time. I studied it a moment, thinking, but then shook away the thought that had already germinated in my mind while holding shut the parlour door on her earlier. We made it to the foot of the stairs and I shoved Sarah ahead of me. 'All the way to the top,' I commanded.

'Oh, God, Jack! What are you doing?' Sarah attempted to push against me, digging in her heels on the bottom step. I pressed my groin against her backside, and immediately grew hard. You'd think I'd jabbed her with a cattle prod the way she jerked away.

'Don't you listen? I want to show you something.'

'You're not going to rape me…'

'Is that a hint of longing I hear?' I laughed at her squawk of dismay. 'Don't worry, Sarah. I'm not going to touch you. Unless that's what you want? Is that what was wrong with you the other night, why I didn't satisfy you: I wasn't rough enough?'

Sarah moaned something, but I couldn't make out her words. I laughed again. 'Don't worry. Despite what you think of me I'm no rapist.'

'Just a murderer,' she whispered.

I shoved her up the stairs.

Studiously avoiding making eye contact with the stained glass window and the faint pattern it cast on the landing wall, we bypassed the bathroom and I pressed Sarah along the hall to the entrance to the uppermost floor. Sarah again dug in at the doorway. She braced her hands against the jamb. 'Go on,' I warned her. 'Almost there.'

'Please let me go…' Tears danced on her lashes.

'Go on,' I said again.

She went up, and I followed.

In my pocket my mobile phone chirruped.

'Go in my room,' I said.

'Why?'

'Just do it.'

I pushed her towards the walk-in wardrobe, and pulled open the doors.

'Get inside.' My phone was still ringing, the tone urgent.

'No. Please, Jack, don't make me go in there.' Her eyes were huge. Terrified of the dark almost as much as she was of the consequences of refusing me.

'Get inside. It won't be for long.'

She opened her mouth to refuse, but I simply pressed a hand to her chest and shoved. She went backwards into the closet and banged up against the back wall. I shut the door, wedging my foot against it. I pulled out my phone. It still rang incessantly. Sarah hammered on the door. I banged my fist on the wood. 'Shut up. Let me answer my damn phone.'

I hit the button.

'Hello?'

'Mr Newman? Jack?'

'Yeah. Who is this?'

'It's Peter. Your landlord.' I recognised the Geordie twang then.

'Uh, hello, Mr Muir. How can I help?'

'Are you at home?'

I was about to reply in the affirmative. Not a good idea. 'No. I'm out. Is there a problem?'

'Those screams again. I've had the staff from the insurance brokers on the phone saying all hell's breaking loose in the house.'

I uttered a croak of disbelief. 'I thought we'd cleared this up the last time? There were no screams then and there are no screams now.'

'How can you be sure if you're not in?'

'They claimed the same the last time and it turned out to be nothing. It's probably just kids in the back alley like the last time.'

'Maybe...' Muir wasn't convinced. 'But if you're not home, I think I'd best call round and check. If nothing else I'll need to do some damage control with your neighbours.'

Behind me Sarah hammered on the door. She hollered. I thumped the door to quieten her.

'What was that?' Muir demanded.

'Nothing,' I said. 'I'm in town. It was just some stupid kids running by.'

'You're in town?'

'Aye.'

'Maybe you should go back to the house; I'll meet you there. Probably best if we cleared things up with your neighbours together.'

'I can't go home now.'

'Mr Newman: I think you should.'

Sarah banged again and I knew Muir had heard her plaintive cries from the way he fell silent. Rather than offer another flimsy excuse, I said, 'OK. I'll head back now. Give me twenty minutes and I'll be there. No need for you to go, I'll speak with the insurance lot myself.'

'Best-'

I hung up before he could say anything else. As I fed my phone into my pocket, I relaxed my guard. Sarah burst out of the closet, and I stumbled back, falling on my backside, my spine against my bed. History repeating. As she fled by, I shot out a hand and got a hold of her ankle. Sarah plunged headlong through the open door dragging me with her, and struck the door of the dumbwaiter cupboard hard. I clawed my way up her body, got my arms around her waist and forced her into the children's room chest-to-chest as if we were engaged in an ungainly dance.

Inside the room I clasped my hands on her shoulders. Met her gaze. At least I stared into hers, because her pupils were jumping around, seeking escape from her predicament. 'I told you I wanted to show you something.' I held out a hand, indicating the wall. Where I'd worked with the spackling paste the wording was largely obliterated, hidden under the thick white paste. But there were areas where I'd been more liberal with the covering, and still words that were stark on the wall after I ran out of Polyfilla. 'Think of it is my love letter to you,' I encouraged her.

She'd seen them before, but her lips moved silently as she read the words. Then her chin dipped and fresh tears dripped off the end of her nose and made damp splotches on the new carpet.

'You did this after all,' she said.

'Who else could it have been?' I repeated her own words back to her from the first time she'd witnessed the writing. Those were probably my first sensible words in the past ten minutes or more. 'If you ask me, that knock to the head when I fell down the stairs helped wake me up to the truth.'

'I should have recognised your problem then,' Sarah muttered. 'I should have made you go to the hospital; they would have fixed it before it got out of hand.'

'How's it a problem? I love you. *I want you*, Sarah.'

She looked me in the eyes now, but I could see the fog of deceit pooling deep behind them like a miasma. 'You still can have me. But not like this.' She reached up and touched my face, her fingertips trembling. 'We can start again, Jack. But first we have to stop this. We need to go to your doctor, OK?'

'Promise?' I asked.

'I promise.'

She'd promised before and I'd told her exactly what I thought of her word. After conspiring with Catriona it wasn't worth shit.

I sniffed in disdain.

'Sorry,' I said. 'No can do, I'm afraid.'

Sarah stiffened, but she attempted her wily female charms again. She stroked my cheek. 'Come on, Jack. You know this isn't really you. You said you loved me. Well if you really love me you wouldn't want to hurt me.'

'That's the thing,' I said. 'I do love you. But it's because I love you that I can't let you go. You'll tell the police I admitted to killing Naomi-'

'I won't. It'll be *our* secret.'

'Sarah. Credit me with some brains. It's one thing calling me insane, but don't call me stupid.'

'I promise-'

I held up a finger to stop her.

'It's because I love you so much that I can't let you go. Don't you get it, Sarah? I need you.' I waved a hand at the words on the wall. 'I want you. Nobody else can have you.'

Those words were the tipping point for both of us. I knew it. Sarah knew it. But she was first to respond. Her hand hadn't moved far from my face as she'd gone through the charade of actually caring for me. She immediately hooked her fingers and drove her nails into the skin of my forehead and cheek. She made a fist, and the uppermost nails scoured me almost to the bone. Her thumbnail dug into my eye socket, and for the briefest moment I shrieked, expecting my eyeball to pop out, skewered on her nail like a cherry on a cocktail stick.

'Bitch!'

Sarah slapped her way past me, her right hand catching me painfully across the side of my neck. Sparks exploded across my vision as I staggered. In reflex I snarled her hair in my fist, but she drove hard for the door, almost yanking my arm out of its socket. I was left with a few stray hairs jammed between my fingers. I went after her. I'd only taken about four steps and I was on the small landing outside the dumbwaiter cupboard. There I paused, listening as Sarah scrambled down the stairs. Illogically I stood there, peering into my bedroom and was positive I could make out a pale shimmer of light in the form of a human being. I looked left, right, took a step closer to the translucent image of myself, but then I realised that Sarah was almost to the bottom of the stairs and lurched after her. I skidded down the flight of stairs, my shoulders rubbing flakes of paint from the walls, my heels bumping off each riser. The door at the bottom was wide open, Sarah rushing along the landing. Again I paused for the briefest time to glance up the stairs. That same shimmering glow of light peeked around the doorjamb above me – and I knew that my suspicions concerning the secret of the shadow man were true.

It was a profound moment, but it was engulfed by panic. I couldn't allow Sarah to escape. I needed to put things right and if she ran out into the blizzard screaming that a maniac was after her then I'd be finished. I raced after her, ignoring the flashing pain in my knee at every step.

Sarah was running so fast that she overshot the top stair of the half-landing. She went down the short flight of stairs and crashed into the wall next to the bathroom door – exactly where I'd taken my tumble that time. The difference here was that I'd fallen backwards, but Sarah had flown headlong. Her forehead smacked the wall and she sunk to her knees groaning, her hands flat against the wall above her head. Seeing her hurt like that gave me pause. I stood on the top step, my hands pulling at my shirt as I thought about what my actions had led to. Above her something moved.

My attention jerked to the stained glass window. I didn't want to look, but the impulse was overwhelming. Features formed in the crimson glass, the battered and torn face of Naomi; the way it had looked after I crawled across that garden and found her on the verge of death. She gave me that same look: one of intense hatred.

'Screw you, Naomi!' I screamed at her, while pointing at Sarah. 'This is your fault! *You* drove me to this, you bitch!'

Naomi screamed back at me in complete and utter loathing.

The window imploded, raining shards of glass down on me. I threw my arms protectively over my head. Chunks of Victorian glass pattered on my arms and shoulders, some jagged splinters digging in. Other shards fell around my feet, reminiscent of the bloody glass scattered on the lawn where Naomi had died. It was a sign, I'm sure, but it didn't matter; I went down the stairs, walking on the crimson glass before the last of the splinters hit the floor. I grabbed Sarah, hauled her semi-conscious form through the bathroom door. Behind us the settling glass was joined by a flurry of snowflakes as the blizzard found ingress to my home.

Sarah was dazed, but her instinct for survival was still strong. She struck out with her elbow, catching me in the throat. I gagged, clawed at my windpipe. I almost collapsed, but Sarah tried to get past me to the open door, and her body held me upright. I yelled at her, gave her a shove with my forearms and she went over the rim of the tub.

Unlike the last time Sarah was in my bath, the tub was empty and she was fully clothed. But apparently I wasn't the only one who'd experienced prophetic visions. When I'd hauled her dripping and covered in suds from the bath - fearful that she'd drowned - she told me that she dreamed I was holding her down by the throat. Maybe that's why I leaned in, sunk my thumbs either side of her windpipe and began to throttle the life out of her. 'You're never going to leave me,' I told her through gritted teeth as I squeezed as hard as I could. 'Never. I want you, I want you...to just die.'

She fought me. But I had the leverage, and she had no purchase. Her heels kicked and battered at the sides of the tub. She squirmed and her nails raked my hands and clawed at my face. Yet second by second her movements grew feebler. Choking someone to death takes time, and it's ugly. Her eyeballs protruded and her tongue was caught between her teeth. Her features were beetroot red.

She couldn't get as much as a breath. I continued squeezing, moaning at the effort. Finally her hands fell away from mine and her feet stopped drumming. She lay inert in the old bathtub.

I thought I should keep squeezing, but a noise caught my attention. The racket Sarah made during her death throes had drowned it out, but now that she was still, I heard the other banging clearly.

Somebody was hammering on my front door.

36

The Hammer and the Crown

'You'd best come in, Mr Muir, there's something you need to see.'

For a second or two I expected my landlord to decline. On the way to answer the door I'd called by the ground floor living room and grabbed a cloth with which I'd wiped the blood off my face and hands, but it was obvious to anyone that I was covered in fresh cuts and grazes.

Muir was poised to unlock the door with his master key when I pulled it open. He still held the key extended like a cowboy with a six-gun, shooting from the hip. Snowflakes had settled on his bald head, and had melted on the lenses of his spectacles. I nodded backwards, to motivate him to follow. 'You were right. It's a good job I came home as soon as I did. Someone had broken in after all. There's a bit of a mess, I'm afraid.'

Concern flitted over Muir's face. My dishevelled state concerned him, but I doubted it was as much as he was worried for his property. Or how much the repair bill was going to be. 'You caught them?'

'No. They were in the back alley as I suspected, and had climbed the wall into the yard. They got onto the roof of the outside toilet and broke their way in through the stained glass window. When I got home a couple of minutes ago I surprised them and they went out the same way. I made the mistake of trying to grab them and cut myself up pretty badly on the broken glass they kicked loose.' I showed him my wounded left hand as evidence. It welled blood. He didn't need to see my hand, not when my face was bloody too.

'We should call the police,' Muir counselled.

'I have; they're coming,' I lied. And walked away.

Behind me, Muir stepped inside the house. The open door and busted window caused a wind tunnel. His clothing was tugged by the strong breeze.

'Close the door,' I warned him. 'I don't want the draught pulling loose any of the large bits of glass left in the window frame. Can you help me?'

Muir followed me to the bottom of the stairs. From that angle we could only make out the left most edge of the broken window. I'd closed the bathroom door. Snow swirled down the stairs. I indicated the sheet of plyboard lying on the hall floor, where Sarah had pulled it earlier. 'Can you help carry that up with me? I'll put it over the busted window until a glazier can come out. The snow's piling in and doing more damage than the bloody broken glass.'

'We should wait until the police get here,' Muir said. 'They'll want to inspect the damage.'

I made a play of thinking his wisdom over. 'You're right. But I could still do with a lift. We could put the board on the landing up there, ready for when the police are finished.'

He thought about it for only a fraction of a second. Then he nodded, and bent to retrieve one end the board. He fed his fingers under the board and lifted his end with a grunt of exertion. He turned his head to regard me, blinking at me in expectation through his glasses. I showed my right hand and the claw hammer I held.

He wasn't quick to catch on.

'You'll need some nails,' he pointed out.

'No. I think this'll do the job.'

Even as I drew back my arm he didn't understand my intention. I did: I'd watched my shadow self raise the hammer when I too had bent to lift the same board earlier. The shadow prophecy had shown me what I must do. The claw hammer was swinging for Muir's head before he could even croak in alarm. He dropped the board, and it scraped down his shins. He tried to dodge the descending hammer, but he was wedged by the board, and only stumbled. The hammerhead struck him behind his right ear. It knocked his glasses awry.

Muir stared back at me in shock.

A viscous drop of blood ran down his neck from behind his earlobe. I watched it. Fascinated.

'Wha-' Muir asked. Then his glasses slipped fully off and clattered on top of the plyboard. He made a stunned grab for them but missed.

I hit him again.

This time the hammer found his crown at the point where a few straggles of hair tufted up. It sounded like the single ringing stamp of a shod hoof on concrete.

Muir went to his knees. His toes were still trapped beneath the board, held there by his weight bearing down on the wood. He trapped himself in place like that while I swung back the hammer for a third strike.

His scalp split, and the bone beneath was forced into his brain. Blood welled in the crater, then Muir slipped forward and went belly down on top of the board. I winced. I bet the edge of the board tore the flesh from his shins before his feet popped free: not that it mattered because my landlord was beyond pain.

I hadn't thought things through.

Now I had two corpses to contend with, and I'd no idea how I could possibly dispose of them. It didn't really matter, because at that moment I felt invincible, unstoppable, so who cared? The monster inside me was exhilarated. Only that cowering portion of me that remained locked at the back of my head was screaming in horror at what had happened, and what the consequences of my actions was going to be. If I'd listened to it, then maybe I would have stopped, but the monster forced me to move: if ever there was such a thing as demonic possession then I was living proof. I laughed at the notion. Ghosts I could accept, even spectral visions of future events, but even in my insanity I couldn't credit anything as ludicrous as a belief in demons.

There was a clot of blood, a few short hairs adhering to the hammerhead. I dropped it on Muir's corpse, turning for the stairs. Things weren't ended yet with Sarah. Not if the shadow man was to be believed.

I trod up the stairs. My footfalls were heavy. A few flakes of snow fluttered round me. Beautiful. I pushed open the bathroom door and looked in on Sarah. She was still in the bath. Her eyes were closed, her mouth open. The tip of her tongue was just showing between her teeth. She'd bit it. I watched for a few seconds longer, then retreated onto the landing and turned for the next landing. My feet crunched over splintered glass. I thumped up the short flight of stairs, then swept aside some of the larger chunks of crimson glass and sat on the top step, perched ready to swoop for when Sarah gave up her act and tried to creep from the bathroom.

She wasn't dead.

How could she be? I'd already seen what would happen next, and I looked forward to the chase.

I waited.

Finally I heard a soft clunk.

Scrapes.

Heavy breathing that Sarah immediately caught and held between her teeth. She was trying to be quiet, but her movements sounded thunderous to me. I smiled at the inanity of it. She was wasting her time. Instead of acting like a timid mouse, she needed to flee like a gazelle.

Picking up a chunk of glass, I lobbed it behind me. It struck the wall near to the room I'd once designated for a storage closet. It broke into pieces and they tinkled down. One bit struck a door making a hollow bang. It wasn't much of a diversion, but it worked.

Sarah poked her head around the jamb. Her hair was tussled. Cute. Her eyes were huge. They were cute too as she peered down the stairs towards the front hall and the promise of freedom. I trusted she'd been awake long enough to hear Peter Muir come inside, and neglect to throw the bolts and snib back on. She leaned forward, gnawing her top lip as she decided if speed outweighed silence in this matter. She checked up the stairs, saw me sitting there grinning like a gargoyle and her mind was made for her. She squawked, and bolted from the bathroom. I was up and after her in a split second.

Our feet made a drumroll on the stairs. Sarah, who'd been scared before, was now stricken by terror. Before she was only frightened of what I might be capable of, but now she had first hand experience. She screamed at the top of her lungs. She should have saved her breath. She made it to the front door, but I was only a pace behind her. She hit the door and it rattled in its frame. I braced my hands either side of her, keeping it shut. She tried to turn, to hit out at me, but I gave her no room. I slipped on the bolts. She ducked under my hands, and I allowed her a second of freedom. Then I grabbed her by her face, two hands enfolding her the way the shadow man had Brianne, and slung her down the hall. She didn't fall this time but kept running. That was until she saw Muir's corpse and the bloody indentations in his baldy skull. Her fingers danced over her face as she moaned in dismay. I paced towards her.

Sarah skirted around the corpse and rushed for the back door, but it was locked. I stood, my toes touching the soles of Muir's boots, blocking her route. There was only one place she could go and Sarah took it. She ducked through the hole beneath the stairs and down into the basement. I didn't bother rushing after her. I knew exactly where she was going to hide.

I took my own good time as I descended into that dark subterranean space.

37

Fox and Hound

But for one lambent slice of light from the coal chute the rest of the basement was pitch black. The snow piling over the hatch I'd screwed into place dulled even that tiny glimmer of light. I didn't need to see where I was going though. I picked my way past the dank adjoining rooms and into the old Victorian kitchen. My shoes scraped grit along the floor as I progressed. I couldn't see the cooking range, the dresser with its stacked dishes, or the huge butcher's block table at the centre of the room. But I could make out two faint shimmering forms conducting their own exploration of the nighted place: if only they'd known then how things would end here. I smiled to myself, stayed to the right and followed the empty floor to the right corner where the door to the old cold pantry stood slightly ajar.

'Come out, come out, wherever you are,' I quipped.

Of course Sarah didn't answer.

The darkness was her friend. Stay quiet, stay concealed and I'd never find her. If she'd listened closely to what I told her I'd witnessed that time in the basement she would have understood she was onto a hiding to nothing. I entered the cold room, and found its name suited it to a tee. My frosted breath almost glowed before my eyes.

'Sah-rah!' I sung softly.

The silence was palpable as Sarah held her breath.

'Oh, Sah-rah! I know that you are in here,' I lisped in the same singsong voice.

My senses were on high alert. If Sarah had managed to get her hands on a weapon she could cold cock me before I was even aware of her presence. Not that I was duly concerned about being bashed over the head. I knew from past experience that when she fled this room I would be hot on her tail. 'Sah-rah! Where are you-hooooh?'

My hip touched the bench shelf I recalled was on the wall. I kept contact with it, sliding my body along, allowing the shelf to lead me to the furthest wedge of the room where it projected under the front street. The atmosphere was icy. And that same strange stench of decay filled my senses. Momentarily repulsed, I held back. But there was nothing for it; I had to flush Sarah out of hiding. I reached out with both hands and found I was deeper in the wedge than I realised when my fingers scraped the wall on both sides. I held back a grunt of satisfaction, then crouched to sweep my hands back and forth in the space before me.

That was when Sarah burst from hiding. Not from in front of me as I'd expected, but from behind. She'd been crouching below the bench shelf even as I scraped past her. She must have found a grain of bravery, because she didn't simply flee while my back was turned. She launched herself against me, driving me face first into the wedge. As I hit the slimy wall, I screwed my eyes and mouth tight, but it wasn't enough. The slick wetness of the mould engulfed my features, and the fetid stench of it was all around. I pushed back, shouting in disgust, and swung an elbow at Sarah to force her off my back. I needn't have, because she had already disengaged and ran for the exit. I blundered after her, wiping the vile muck from my face. When I could finally see beyond the scummy stuff on my eyelashes I was almost face to face with the shimmering, translucent glow from my past. That naïve Jack Newman swiped at me as I wove around him, and his insubstantial hand passed through me. A shock like a static charge went through my body, but I ignored it, heading immediately to the right and around the large table.

Sarah's shimmering past echo led me directly where I knew to go. The cupboard adjacent to the cooking range. The door would be open: it had to be. I pushed directly through the shimmering glow, and went for her present solid form where it crouched in complete darkness. My own past echo would be hot after me, hoping to save Sarah from my malicious intent. How absurd, how wickedly inappropriate now!

The physical Sarah launched herself from under my groping hands, and fled. I turned to go after her even as her echo folded under the lunging hands and excitable – but soundless - screams of mine. I ignored them both and rushed after her, confident about where she'd got to this time. It was an unfair game of fox and hound considering I didn't have to sniff out her trail when I had foreknowledge of where she'd go to ground. I turned immediately to the right and entered the small room in which the dumbwaiter was situated. The poor thing was so desperate that she was actually trying to clamber up into the shaft. I caught Sarah in my arms and pulled her back to the centre of the small room.

'Caught you,' I said, leaning close to whisper in her ear.

'For God's sake, let me go, Jack.' Her strength waned in the surety that the game was indeed at an end.

'After what I've done? How can I?'

'You have to let me go,' she cried with little conviction.

'No. That's the last thing I must do.' I looked upwards, as if I could see through the floorboards to where Peter Muir lay leaking his brains on the plyboard. 'I just killed a man. Murdered him, Sarah.

I can't let you run off and tell anyone that now, can I?'

'I won't tell,' she sobbed.

'Of course you will...given the chance. You're the type that was disgusted that I told a few white lies to get a day off work. You told me you hated lies, remember? I can hardly expect you to keep the knowledge of a murder to yourself. Hmmm? And not only one murder. There's also Naomi, don't forget. Hell, I even tried to strangle you to death just now. No Sarah. You won't tell, but only because I won't let you.'

'No, Jack, you can't. Please...this is not you!'

'Actually, this is me. I see it now. That other Jack Newman, the snivelling weakling you felt sorry for, then thought you could play for an idiot, he was the impostor.' I released her so that I could touch a hand to my heart. 'I am the real Jack Newman. It's time to accept the truth, Sarah.'

'No, no, you're just mixed up. It's your illness that's making you...'

I pushed her away from me. 'I'm not ill. Those pills you are all so keen for me to take? They were poisoning *me*, smothering *me*, keeping me down, fucking burying *me*. But I'm free now. And poor little Sarah, I'm going to stay that way.'

I bunched my fist. She couldn't have seen me, but she wailed, expecting the inevitable blow. I allowed my hand to fall.

'Maybe I should thank you,' I said.

She cried, didn't respond to my one small kindness. It didn't matter.

'I should thank you because you helped me open my eyes to the truth. I'd lost my way, you see, clouded under the fog of drugs. I'd lost my belief that there were powerful forces at work in this world. I didn't believe in ghosts any more, and you showed me how wrong I was. You even warned me that Naomi's was a vengeful ghost. Hell, she wasn't only vengeful; she was there all along trying to warn you that it wasn't safe here. She wasn't haunting me, Sarah; she was the angel on your shoulder. But do you know something: I have to thank her too. Because if I hadn't grown to accept her lingering spirit, then I wouldn't have grown to accept the other spectres appearing to me. Those shadow figures, I know what they are now. They're us. They're the consequences of our actions, a foreshadowing of events.' I glanced past her to the dumbwaiter shaft, 'Which reminds me.'

I cuffed her round the head, knocking her down.

'Wait there and don't dare move.'

I stepped quickly to the shaft and peered up. The dumbwaiter platform blocked most of the view up to the top floor, but if I squinted I could make out the faintest shimmer of my past echo, that weak spineless version of Jack Newman, as he peered down, cocking his ear to what he thought might be the voices of trespassers in his basement. Fucking idiot. I grabbed the pulley rope and yanked it with all my might. The dumbwaiter platform responded by falling out of control down the shaft. I stepped back as it first became wedged in the shaft, causing a billow of dust and cobwebs to cover me. I spat grit from my teeth, then returned to the shaft, not yet finished with weakling Jack. I grasped the pulley rope and gave it another angry tug. The platform fell and hit bottom with a loud crash. I leaned into the shaft, saw the shimmering head and shoulders and screamed at the top of my voice, and laughed as it jerked back in terror.

'How totally absurd,' I said as I turned back to my cowering prisoner. 'There he was crying over a grazed palm, if only poor weak Jack knew what was in store for him. I killed him, buried him instead. He's the fucking ghost now.'

I stood over Sarah.

My vision had grown accustomed to the darkness, but still all I could make out were the whites of her wet eyes, a faint glimmer off her pearlescent teeth.

'Ghosts no longer frighten me,' I told her. 'Naomi's vengeful spirit is as pitiful as Jack's. That window she used as her portal in and out of here? The stupid bitch shattered it, thought she could protect you by throwing a few splinters of glass at me. Well, all she did in the end was close the only door she had in and out of here. She can't help you now, Sarah. No one can.'

Alas, Sarah wasn't one to take my word for it. Having terrorised her for so long, forced her to run and scream like a little girl, I'd neglected to remember that she was a tough, resilient woman who wasn't about to take her death lying down.

I also forgot that she knew exactly my weakest spot.

From her position on the floor, she stamped out with her heel and drove it into my injured knee.

The sensation of your patella forcefully misaligning, the supporting tendons and ligaments popping and twanging, ripping free from the adjoining muscles isn't easily described. Trust me, the word "agony" doesn't even come close. All I'll say is that the brain doesn't form descriptions of it, preferring instead to smother everything under an explosion of magnesium white with the intensity of a nuclear detonation. In the next second everything goes pitch black. And if you're even spared unconsciousness it gets worse. Scarlet fills your senses – all of them - and you don't even hear the sound of your own pitiful howls. You know nothing else.

When some lucidity returned I was on the floor, cradling my knee, sobbing like a bitch. It was probably only a few seconds since Sarah forced my knee to bend in a direction it was never designed to, but it was enough time for her to gain her feet and run for the stairs.

Shit! Why hadn't I seen this coming? Why hadn't I had a prophetic vision of the shadow man squirming in the dirt tending to his torn knee and, even if I couldn't stop it happening, I would have at least been prepared for the blinding pain doomed to torment me now.

Righteous fury was strong motivation. It got me up. I yelped with every ponderous step, but made it to the exit and into the short hall to the stairs. I went up them on one foot and my palms, holding out my inured leg like a dog taking a leak. Each time I fought gravity, tried to control the bouncing weight of my leg, the pain shot from my knee to my hip and it was almost enough to make me collapse on the stairs. I raged against the pain though, the monster inside fuelling me onwards, upwards. I had to stop Sarah or the monster would be stopped.

At the head of the stairs light from the hallway flooded in.

I was relieved to see something other than the flashes of agony pulsing through my mind.

Then the light was blocked.

The shadow man was back.

He halted my exit, one arm raised.

But then I knew.

It wasn't the shadow man at all.

It was Sarah's backlit silhouette filling the aperture. Behind her was Naomi's ghost, guiding her hand. Sarah peered over her shoulder at the ghost, unafraid of the apparition, who for once didn't present bloodied or torn up. Naomi nodded once, and Sarah nodded in agreement.

It hadn't been a good idea leaving the claw hammer lying on top of Muir's corpse so close to hand.

With a ghostly hand steadying hers, Sarah swung hard for my head, and I barely had time to close my eyes before the monster died.

Epilogue

After

Take it from one who knows.

Ghosts do exist.

So do the shadow people.

They're not shades of the past but future echoes.

If I'd paid closer attention, I would have understood earlier that those shadows were the consequences of my actions yet to come, and I still had a chance to turn away from them.

All I had to do was take my damn pills on time.

But I hadn't, and look where it had got me.

Back in the Cayton.

After my tumble down the stairs my repressed memories had been awakened in me. Before that I'd mostly held my dark side in check, now it gave strength to the beast that had lurked in some nighted corner of my mind, released it to orchestrate the madness and violence that would follow. When Sarah – supported by Naomi - smacked me round the head with the hammer, it had felled the monster in me well and good. But Jack Newman had proven more resilient than his beastly alter ego would have given him credit for. I survived, but life came with a caveat: I had to pay the price for the crimes committed in my name. The police had arrived even before Sarah could call them, following up on the criminal damage complaint from Catriona and Mark, because it was obvious to all whom'd bust up his car. I was coming round by then and had fought them, professing my innocence, but it was a hopeless battle. Because I was deemed as nutty as fruit loaf, I escaped prison, but not incarceration. I was sectioned and don't expect to be released from this secure mental unit anytime soon, if ever.

I have to pay penance, though the notion will only be fleeting.

I've admitted to my part in Naomi's death.

I've also owned up to doing in Peter Muir, and then trying my hardest to murder Sarah.

My honesty hasn't gained me much pity, and no reduction in my penalty, although the extenuating circumstances of my mental illness mean I haven't been totally reviled.

Catriona paid me a visit, and though we were now fully divorced she was sad about how things turned out between us. She said she was glad I was finally getting the care I needed. She didn't mention the kids and I didn't ask: she didn't want them to know what kind of creature I'd been. Best they had only happy memories of their dad to cling to. What she really meant was it was best that they forgot all about me.

It surprised me to find that Sarah didn't hate me. She visited me once and told me that she had forgiven me. I told her that I'd let her smack of the hammer to my head go as well, but she didn't find it funny. Recalling the moment she'd whacked me on the skull, she paused, grew reflective.

'Was she real, Jack?' she finally asked.

'Yes.'

'I saw her. She held my hand. Guided me.'

'Just like Naomi, she always hoped to bash some sense into me,' I said, but again I didn't elicit a laugh.

'It was her who manipulated our phones, wasn't it? She was leaving messages trying to warn me of what was going to happen. "I WANT YOU". That phrase was pertinent, wasn't it? To what happened to her?'

I didn't reply, but she could tell by my silence that the words did indeed hold relevance.

'The EVPs, the banging in the cupboard, the slamming doors, the screaming your neighbours heard, even when I almost drowned in the bath: she was trying to warn me,' she went on.

She was warning us all,' I admitted. 'When she showed herself to me, she was trying to jog my memory, so that I'd recognise what I was capable of. So that I'd stop.'

'It's a shame neither of us paid her the attention she was due.'

'Yeah, it's also a shame I didn't recognised the shadow figures as the harbingers of future events. Otherwise I could've stopped things before it was too late.'

'I wish you had.' Tears shone in her eyes.

'We're all wise in hindsight,' I said.

She brightened marginally. 'You know I once said you should reach for the unattainable? Well I did it. I took the plunge. I've left BathCo and started my own graphic design business.'

'Good. I'm happy for you.'

'Do you really mean that, Jack?'

'You were too good to be stuck in that dead end job. I hope the contracts come rolling in.'

'They've already started, I'm designing the graphics on a new website for -' she stopped, the words catching in her throat.

'Your Facebook friends,' I finished for her. I sat back and folded my hands in my lap. I'd have thought Steve Walker's nose would have been knocked out of joint with jealousy, seeing as Sarah was now far more experienced at this paranormal stuff than him. 'How is Smarmy Steve, these days?'

Sarah understood it was time for her to leave. A thick plexi-glass window separated us, and when she touched her fingers to it in goodbye I didn't bother touching mine to the other side. What was the point? Sarah smiled sadly, and then she was gone. One thing that gave me satisfaction was that she wouldn't be as vengeful as my first girlfriend has proved.

Naomi Woodall's ghost still troubles me. You'd think she wouldn't have to. She'd done what she set out to do: saved Sarah King, and received the justice she deserved for her murder. Her spirit no longer lingers on our plain; she can pass on to wherever spirits at peace are supposed to go, but she can come back whenever she wants. Apparently the stained glass window hadn't been the sole portal in and out of the other side.

My psychiatrists have tried to convince me that I'm deluded, and once the cocktail of lithium, benzodiazepines and antipsychotic drugs kick in and I can manage my "mixed affective episodes" once more, then I'll again be my old sceptical self. Ghosts don't exist, they promise. Dead means dead.

They should try telling that to Naomi.

Ghosts can visit at will, and the locked doors of a secure psychiatric unit won't stop them. She's proved that nightly since I arrived here. She doesn't do much, just glares at me from the corner of the room, mouthing silent threats. Peter Muir is there alongside her, staring through the cracked lenses of his broken glasses. Blood constantly pulses from the indentations I put in his skull with the hammer. I know he wants to hurt me in return, but is biding his time. He wants me to suffer his ire first. He's angry, and I can't really blame him. He's a vengeful

432

ghost for sure. He also mouths silent words at me. Maybe if I had a digital recorder handy I'd hear their words, but I don't. It doesn't matter. I can do without hearing their bitching. I don't expect forgiveness from either of them, but neither do I care and that's what pisses them off the most.

There's a reason they're here: they know I'm not taking my meds. As soon as my nurse's back is turned, I stick a finger down my throat and bring up my pills, flushing them down the toilet with the vomit. Who needs them when I understand what they subdue?

I've seen my shadow self. Before this I was always a puppet to his will, but this time his actions are fully orchestrated by me.

He runs through the halls of the Cayton, laying about him with what looks to be a shadow axe. Other shadows try to stop him – the future shadows of my doctors, nurses and orderlies - but they all fall under the axe's sharp edge. He disappears after smashing his way through an exit door. He escapes.

Naomi and Muir don't try to warn my doctors, it's pointless. Even if they're seen or their whispering voices are heard, who is going to believe their senses? Not one of the medical staff, for fear they'd end up on the other side of a locked door. Even if someone did pay attention to them, those spirits would be wasting their time: my freedom is ordained, it's only a matter of time. From observing the precognitive actions of my shadow self I've learned that a fire axe hangs in the administration block. My shadow has shown me the way, and what must be done to ensure my escape. All I need do is find a way to that axe and cut my way out of here. Once it's done, and those doctors and nurses stupid enough to try to stop me have fallen beneath the axe, I suppose a few more vengeful ghosts will haunt me. But that's a penance I am prepared to pay.

***

Acknowledgements and Thanks.

During the writing of this novel I have used quotes from "Antigonish" by (William) Hughes Mearns (1875-1965).

Thanks to the teams from 'Ghost North-East' and 'Near Dark Paranormal Investigations' for allowing me to join them in their ghost hunting and paranormal investigations while I was researching this novel.

Thanks to Nicola Birrell-Smith for her exemplary work in designing the cover. Thanks also to Tracey Shaw, Eleanor Cawood Jones, Claire Lawler, Jonathan Davison, Kestrel Carroll, Lisa Elphick, Lynn Doyle, Lois Wacey, Bex Bagot, Dominic Adler, David Foster and Warwick Kay for being enthusiastic readers and putting in their tuppence worth on this story. Huge thanks as ever to Luigi and Alison of Luigi Bonomi Associates (literary agents) who also made this book a much better read.

This novel is based on true events, and actual paranormal investigative practices and findings, but names, locations and dates have been changed, and some incidents added or exaggerated for extra drama.

THE SHADOWS CALL

About the Author

Matt Hilton quit his career as a police officer to pursue his love of writing tight, cinematic American-style thrillers. He is the author of the high-octane Joe Hunter thriller series, including his most recent novel **'The Lawless Kind'** – Joe Hunter 9 - published in January 2014 by Hodder and Stoughton. His first book, **'Dead Men's Dust'**, was shortlisted for the International Thriller Writers' Debut Book of 2009 Award, and was a Sunday Times bestseller, also being named as a 'thriller of the year 2009' by The Daily Telegraph. **Dead Men's Dust** was also a top ten Kindle bestseller in 2013. The Joe Hunter series is widely published by Hodder and Stoughton in UK territories, and by William Morrow and Company in the USA, and have been translated into German, Italian, Romanian and Bulgarian. As well as the Joe Hunter series, Matt has been published in a number of anthologies and collections, and has published three previous novels in the supernatural/horror genre, namely **'Preternatural'**, **'Dominion'**, and **'Darkest Hour'**.

www.matthiltonbooks.com

Other Books by Matt Hilton

Joe Hunter Books:

Dead Men's Dust
Judgement and Wrath
Slash and Burn
Cut and Run
Blood and Ashes
Dead Men's Harvest
No Going Back
Rules of Honour
The Lawless Kind
The Devil's Anvil (Summer 2015)

Joe Hunter E-book short stories:

Six of the Best
Dead Fall
Red Stripes
Instant Justice and other Action-packed Tales

Horror:

Dominion
Darkest Hour
Preternatural
The Shadows Call
Booze and Ooze (Short Story)

One Twisted Voice (Collection of short stories)

Young Adult:

Mark Darrow and the Stealer of Souls

Collections:

Holiday of the Dead (writing as Vallon Jackson)
Even More Tonto Short Stories
The Mammoth Book of Best British Crime Volume 9
Death Toll 2
Uncommon Assassins
True Brit Grit
Grand Central Noir
Blood Bath
Off the Record 2 – At the Movies
Dirk Ramm: Suited and Booted
Action: Pulse Pounding Tales Vol 1
Action: Pulse Pounding Tales Vol 2

THE SHADOWS CALL

80	69	
70	59	48
60	49	38
50	39	
40		

CPSIA information can be obtained at www.ICGtesting.com
Printed in the USA
LVOW07s1458120215

426795LV00005B/470/P

CPSIA information can be obtained at www.ICGtesting.com
Printed in the USA
LVOW07s1458120215

426795LV00005B/470/P